THE SHADOWED PATH

A FANTASY THRILLER

CECILIA DOMINIC

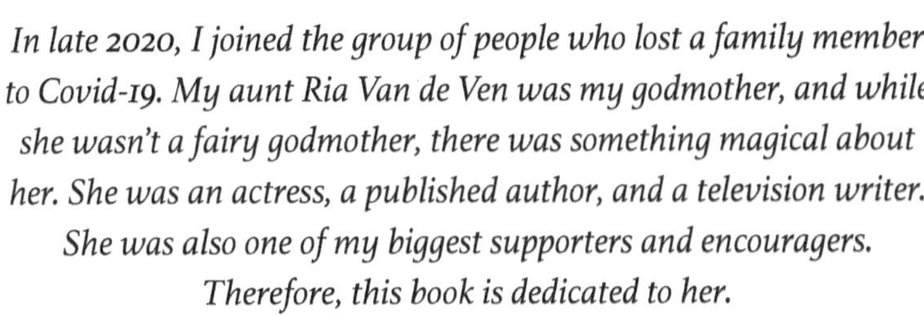

In late 2020, I joined the group of people who lost a family member to Covid-19. My aunt Ria Van de Ven was my godmother, and while she wasn't a fairy godmother, there was something magical about her. She was an actress, a published author, and a television writer. She was also one of my biggest supporters and encouragers. Therefore, this book is dedicated to her.

Editing services by Evil Eye Editing

Cover by Best Page Forward

Ebook ISBN: 978-1-945074-61-5

Paperback ISBN: 978-1-945074-66-0

❀ Created with Vellum

LOOK FOR THESE TITLES BY CECILIA DOMINIC:

Urban Fantasy Series:

The Lycanthropy Files
The Wolf's Shadow
Long Shadows
Blood's Shadow
A Million Shadows

The Fae Files
The Shadow Project
Shadows of the Heart
The Shadowed Path
Shadows of the Sky
Rising Shadows (fall 2022)
Shadows of the Past (early 2023)

Dream Weavers & Truth Seekers
Perchance to Dream
Truth Seeker
Tangled Dreams

Web of Truth

Steampunk Series:

The Aether Psychics
Noble Secrets
Eros Element
Clockwork Phantom
Aether Spirit
Aether Rising

The Inspector Davidson Mysteries
The Art of Piracy
Mission: Nutcracker

PROLOGUE

Aria

A knock at the door of the shop made me look up from the order screen. The charms I'd made for Fae-Con had depleted my stock, and I needed to re-up them for the inevitable rush of parents and teens looking for bags of *Remember* and *Summer Love*, as exams and then summer break would be around the corner. I wasn't expecting anyone, and all I wanted to do was finish the order, take a long, hot shower, and go to bed. There might have been some ice cream in my plans as well. The lure of Ben & Jerry's dairy-free Chocolate Fudge Brownie almost made me ignore the visitor, but my intuition told me I should at least see who it was.

The person who stood at the door wasn't a person, but a Fae. Princess Reine gave me a smile that appeared to take some effort, and her perfect green eyes sported red rims and puffiness. Had she been crying? The predominance of blue and gray in her normally colorful aura confirmed her grief and tiredness.

Ah, Doctor Lawrence Gordon, gargoyle and handsome scientist, must have found out the secret she'd kept from him—that her brother had killed the gargoyle's father in a case of mistaken identity. I imagined that hadn't gone well. But that wasn't any of my business, and I had other things to ask about.

I'd barely gotten the locks open and door cracked before my curiosity made the questions escape. "Did you get the soul-eater? Did the charms help?"

Her pet, a gray cat named Sir Raleigh, slipped through the door and set about sniffing around the shop. She gave him an indulgent smile, then said, "We got it. It's now sealed in a vampire's menagerie, although gods know what she'll do with it. Not sure of the point of an invisible pet."

"And the charms?" I couldn't keep the eagerness from my voice.

"They helped keep enough people safe from the monster's influence. Thank you. I'm here to pay you for them, and for something else."

"That's not necessary, to pay me, and I am happy to give you whatever help you may need." I stepped back and allowed her to enter.

She took a few steps inside, then frowned. "That's odd. Normally the stones greet me."

I hated to tell her, but I had to. "They know of the hurt you caused the gargoyle, and they're not pleased."

She took a deep breath, then nodded. "I'm truly sorry for any pain he feels that I am responsible for, and I am saddened for the rest."

My jaw wanted to drop—a Fae apologizing?—but I kept it in place. "I'm not the one who needs to hear the words, Princess."

She shrugged. "I tried. It didn't do any good except to help me throw off the soul-eater." Her lips twisted into an ironic grin. "It didn't like the taste of shame and vulnerability."

"Fae don't feel shame," I said before I could stop myself. Then, because I did regret my words and I didn't want her to curse or otherwise send bad energy my way, "I apologize, Princess. That was out of line."

"It's all right. Most of the time we don't. I suppose I've learned some things from humans during my time here. As for paying you, please. I've learned you're attached to activities like paying rent and eating."

I laughed. "That's not it. Doctor Gordon already paid for the charms."

She winced at his name, and I bit my tongue on another apology.

"My other piece of business—I need a journal for Kestrel, and I need you to help me put a spell on it so that only she and I can read it."

"Isn't a spell like that within your ability?"

"It should be, but in my current state of exhaustion, I don't trust my powers. I'd rather not accidentally curse it or make it so that she and I are the ones who can't read it."

I led her to the bookshelf, which held several blank notebooks and journals. She selected one with a red and gold diamond pattern and a dark blue one with white swirls and silver sparkles around the image of a full moon. She frowned.

"I feel drawn to both of these."

"Then you must be meant to have both."

She took a deep breath. "I'm too tired to argue with fate or whoever is guiding me at the moment. Which should we bespell for Kestrel?"

"Let's do both." An idea had formed in the back of my mind when she'd apologized for hurting Doctor Gordon. "Is this so she can better keep track of her power surges?"

"Yes."

I waited for a beat for the rest of the answer. "But that's not all."

"No, that's not all. I can't tell you more."

Fear for my friend clutched my throat with icy fingers. "Is she in danger?"

"She could be." Reine rubbed her eyes. "Fine, I'll tell you this much. We're going on a journey. She'll need to record her impressions and reactions in order to give us information for the end."

"All right."

She frowned. "That's it? 'All right?'"

"Look, I want to know what you're getting her into, especially now with her being so vulnerable, but this all feels like it's part of some larger pattern." My vision went gray, and glowing white lines appeared around and through her. I had to tell her what my sixth sense showed me. "Please, though, be careful. I see a spider web, and one misstep could make it tighten until it chokes you and all you care about." I blinked, and the colors returned to the room.

She didn't appear to be concerned. In fact, her mouth puckered into a resigned smile. "That's pretty much Fae life."

We performed the spell on both the journals, and as I wrapped both in plain brown paper as per her instruction, I had another thought that demanded to be voiced.

"Perhaps the other journal is for you. You didn't say what you were hoping to find on this journey for yourself."

She chewed on her bottom lip—a surprisingly human gesture—before replying, "I'm hoping to regain something I lost a long, long time ago." She gave me her credit card, and I rang up her purchases.

I nodded and handed her the packages and her card. "Good luck, Princess. It may be that the other journal is for you. What is a journey for, if not to discover something important about one's self?"

She laughed. "Indeed. Farewell, Aria. May the gods smile on you for all the good you do."

"And you as well."

She and the cat exited the store and faded into the darkness. I returned to my order but found myself unable to concentrate. Concern for Kestrel kept pushing at the edges of my attention. Her mother had just died, and now she was going to Faerie. The least I could do was check on her. I pulled my phone out and texted her.

Hey! What's up? You hanging in there?

She didn't respond. Ten minutes later, I tried again.

Hey, please don't go wherever you're going without saying goodbye. I'm worried about you.

This time she responded.

Hey, sorry, packing. Not sure how long I'll be gone. Bye and thanks! Wish me luck.

Good luck.

If she wanted to tell me more, she would. I pondered warning her—it was never a good idea to get involved with a Fae, but she knew that. I only hoped she would remember when it was important to do so.

1

REINE

"This is going to be a disaster," Ellerin muttered. He and I waited for John and Kestrel in the yard of the Graves' house. Light barely tinged the sky, and we stood in the shadows just outside the reach of the outdoor spotlight. An early cricket chirped good morning. I shifted my weight from foot to foot, ready to get going. As per usual, the humans held us back.

Ellerin had rented a car, and we were packed. He wore his Stetson and had his ubiquitous suitcase, and I'd stuffed a backpack with everything I could fit. Selene, the psychologist who had accompanied me to Atlanta, was holding the rest of my stuff for safekeeping, and if I didn't return, she'd donate it.

Did I want to return? The question had bumped through my brain at inconvenient times over the past two days, mostly when I tried to focus on other things. Important things. But the persistent query never disturbed me when I remembered Lawrence's rejection and how it had stung, but also saved me.

I caught myself rubbing the twin pinhead scars on my neck, left by a vampire who'd promised to heal me. Apparently to vampires that meant stopping blood flow, not preventing scarring. Bitch.

Kestrel walked out of the garage, her backpack dangling from her left hand, and her father's voice floated out after her, "Did you remember pajamas? You can't sleep naked there." Kestrel rolled her eyes and mouthed, "I'll be right back."

"Think she forgot pajamas?" Ellerin asked once she'd disappeared. "Or is John trying to delay?"

"Only the gods know. Thank you for your humor about this, by the way. And for not charging me a ridiculous amount to bring them along."

He arched an eyebrow and cast a sideways glance at me. "I'm starting to question that. You should've let just her come."

"I thought that checking with him first would keep her from accompanying us. I wasn't eager to have to babysit a teenager through Faerie."

"You could've just said no."

I closed my eyes, and my cheeks heated. "I know. I'm not great at that." Hence how I'd ended up in exile in the first place.

Ellerin shook his head. "Maeve doesn't teach her daughters to say no. If she did, they may say it to her."

I opened my eyes at the mention of my mother's name. "Feeling feisty, are we? No one calls her by her name."

He shrugged. "Someone needs to take her down a peg."

I almost asked if that's why he and my grandmother, the queen of Faerie, were conspiring, but that wasn't Ellerin's style. He preferred to drop bits of knowledge in an offhand way and refused to answer direct queries. Typical Fae.

Finally, Kestrel emerged, followed by her father. In the four days since his wife's death, John Graves had shrunk in, then stretched outward again into a parody of himself—thin and brittle. Now his concern centered on his daughter, and the hard line of her mouth told me she barely held her redheaded temper in check.

"Are you ready?" Ellerin asked. "Truly ready? I'm not going to turn this car around."

I almost laughed at the stereotypical dad tone and statement.

"Yes, we are." John punched a code into a keypad beside the open garage door, and it closed with the grumbling of a teenager disturbed too early in the morning. "I made sure we didn't leave anything important behind."

I imagined his pack stuffed with all sorts of random, "just in case" crap.

Kestrel, who had at least a little bit of a clue due to her training for the PBI—Paranormal Bureau of Investigation— had likely packed smarter than her father had. I supposed we would see once we got to Faerie. Some of his "just in case" crap might prove to be useful in a land where the typical rules didn't apply. When they'd asked Ellerin for guidance, he'd merely told them to bring enough provisions for two days and an extra change of clothes, and beyond that, to trust their instincts and John's experience as a field scientist.

I called Sir Raleigh out of the strip of trees between the Graves' house and their neighbor's. His dark gray coat kept him hidden until he trotted into a circle of light, and he looked up at me with slightly glowing green eyes. I wondered what he had been chasing, or perhaps he'd been exploring. Sometimes it was easy to forget he wasn't an ordinary cat.

We got into the car, the men in front. Ellerin started the engine, and John started his mouth.

"Is this a place you've been to often?"

"Not in a long time." Ellerin's tone revealed his reluctance to engage in the conversation.

"Oh." John sat back and pulled out his phone. "Do you need me to punch in some coordinates or something? For directions."

"No."

"But if this is an unfamiliar location for you, how do you know how to get there? This city changes constantly. I thought you said time is of the essence, and it's only open at sunrise."

Ellerin's face, reflected in the rearview mirror, turned pink, and he gunned it when we reached the interstate entrance. "Thanks for the reminder. Hopefully, your delays won't make us miss it."

John sat back, and now his mouth hardened into a similar line to the one Kestrel's had been in earlier.

She gazed at the horizon, which had gone from navy to dark royal blue. "We still have plenty of time. I can feel it."

I closed my mouth. I'd been about to say the same thing. Would this be our journey—Kestrel and me keeping John and Ellerin from killing each other? Maybe I should've just said no.

But...

"How's your magic?" I asked Kestrel. "Is anything flaring right now?"

"Nothing major." She looked out of the window. "I can feel life energy around me and the waxing power of the sun."

"Just like an earth witch," John added. "Maybe you're finally settling into something."

Kestrel shook her head. "No, I still feel it separate from me."

If it was possible for someone to go still while driving, Ellerin had. "Right, that's why you're coming with us. So the physician in the Light Court can help you figure out your powers."

Had he forgotten? We'd talked about this. But he'd been studying Kestrel like he'd never seen her before the entire morning.

Kestrel, seemingly oblivious to Ellerin's odd reaction, said, "Yes, hopefully."

I leaned over and caught John's gaze in the rearview mirror. "And what about you, John? What are you hoping for?"

He turned away. For the first time, John didn't say anything.

Maybe he didn't know.

WE SPENT the next hour in blessed silence. John looked out of the window or checked his watch. Ellerin drove. At times, the car floated and touched down so gently I doubted the humans could feel it. I suspected Ellerin avoided speed monitoring cables and other devices that would alert the authorities to his very fast driving. He pulled into a gravel parking lot on the side of a mountain at half an hour until sunrise. Here, away from the light pollution in the city, we had barely enough light to see by.

The silence when he cut the engine pressed in on my pointed ears.

He frowned at the sky. "Hurry, we're almost there."

Each of us grabbed our respective backpacks, and I gave mine an extra squeeze to make sure the present I'd bought for Kestrel was still in there. Not that I expected it to be gone, but when one dealt with Fae, one could never be sure. We had a different definition of gifts. They all had strings, which made me wonder about what I had been gifted when I'd gotten Kestrel's.

Our footsteps crunched along a path that turned from gravel to dirt and muffled our passage. About half a mile in, Ellerin led us off the path onto a small trail hidden by brush. No one spoke, which gladdened me because I could hear the birds and the forest creatures. Morning had its own rhythm, and the trees added their greetings as harmony to the brushes, snaps, and songs of the animals' waking and preparing for their days. Sir Raleigh trotted along beside me and looked around with wide, yellow eyes. The hoot of an owl momentarily silenced everything else, and Ellerin grinned and hooted back.

"What is it saying?" Kestrel whispered.

"Hello, and we're almost there."

Indeed, we walked into a clearing that looked like a campsite ringed with boulders. A pile of wood sat in a stone circle, and Ellerin rubbed his hands together like he was cold, then held them toward the wood such that his palms faced the stack. He murmured something, and it burst into green flame.

"What? How did you do that?" John asked.

"Magic, Dad." Kestrel bounced on her toes, her delight apparent in her grin. "Can you teach me to do that, Mister Ellerin?"

Ellerin chuckled. "Hush, and watch."

Rather than illuminating the boulders right away, the green glow crept through the air and along the ground. When it passed over me, it tingled like I'd been doused with fizzy soda. The boulders around the campsite reflected the light like mirrors, then grew taller until they took on familiar shapes—standing stones.

"What is this place?" John sounded more afraid than awed.

"A passageway. It will take us to the Shadowed Path." Ellerin paused for a second before adding, "It's not one of my usual entrance points, so be alert."

I'd never heard him sound anything but confident, and Kestrel and I exchanged worried glances.

"Wait." John paced back and forth in front of the fire. "I thought you were a guide, that's all. Not that you would put us in danger. There's enough of that as it is."

Ellerin chuckled, not in a friendly way. "All Fae are more than they appear, Doctor Graves. You and I have more in common than you think. And there is always danger along the Shadowed Path, especially for those who aren't sure about following it. There's no room for doubt in Faerie."

"Look!" Kestrel pointed toward the east, where the pink glow of morning sunbeams tracked through the trees. When the light reached our circle, it concentrated itself into a rectangle under the one pair of stones that held a plinth on top of them, forming a doorway. The glow prevented me from seeing what was inside.

Kestrel started toward the doorway, and John grabbed her arm. "What are you doing? This is ridiculous. I've changed my mind. We're going home. Ellerin, give me the car keys. I'll make sure it's returned."

"Dad, come on. We talked about this."

He turned her and held onto her upper arms. "Kestrel, sweetie, there's a difference between danger in theory and practice. We don't have any skills that could be helpful here."

"Dad, I'm a Paranormal Bureau of Investigations agent."

"You're a rookie who's still in training."

"Still, I have skills." She shrugged, but he held tight.

Ellerin walked over to them. "Stop it, you're hurting her." He gently pushed John away from Kestrel until John let go. "Only those with true commitment to their course can walk the Shadowed Path. She's an adult and can make her choice. The question is, what will you do?"

John looked at the ground, his expression stricken. "You don't understand. I've lost her mother. I can't lose her, too."

"You can't wrap her in tissue paper and keep her on a shelf."

John raised his head and nodded. "You're right. But I can keep her from doing something rash, stupid, and dangerous." He lunged toward Kestrel, and she darted away and through the portal.

"Kestrel!" John yelled.

"She's made her choice. May blessings be on her and the path favor her." Then Ellerin rushed through after her.

I arched an eyebrow at John. "Your call. How committed are you to your daughter?"

"How dare you question me?" he growled. Then Kestrel's scream split the air. He didn't hesitate—he sprinted through, and I followed.

2

REINE

No matter where you're from, home has its own smell. The first thing I did when I stepped into the cave that served as an entrance into Faerie was take a deep breath. In spite of the cold atmosphere, the delicate perfume of moonflower and something indefinable—like electricity and the petrichor odor of leaves after rain—tinted the air. I doubted the humans could smell it, but it enveloped me like an olfactory hug. The humans stood to one side, marveling at the smooth, sparkling walls. Ellerin squinted into the watery light of a winter sky that shone in through the entrance.

The second thing I did was swat at the creature that left a stinging welt across my cheek. Sir Raleigh, in full bat-winged panther form, growled and lashed his tail. Glowing purple lights appeared and streaked across my vision, darting to and fro.

"Duck!" Ellerin called out.

I grabbed John and Kestrel and pulled them to the ground with me. John, his glasses askew, moaned and rubbed the side of his neck. Kestrel looked up with wide eyes...that glowed firefly gold.

"Ow!" Whatever it was stung my ankle. A buzzing noise and streak of glowing lilac alerted me that the thing was coming for another bite of my face. When I swatted at it, I added Fae repel energy, and it disappeared in a puff of violet sparks. But not before it showed me what it was—a creature resembling an Earth lightning bug, but twice as large and with a tail that glowed light purple rather than yellow.

John asked with an edge of panic, "What are they?"

I searched my memories for Faerie creatures and found one that fit. "Black lightning bugs. They can hurt, and enough bites can kill a human."

He whimpered.

Luckily, being back in Faerie meant I had access to all my powers. When I reached into the core of my spirit, blue light and bliss flooded through me, and I closed my eyes in ecstasy and stretched out my hands. I didn't need to see the black lightning bugs to take care of them—I felt them. Little jerks. They buzzed around, seeking exposed skin, weaving among us so as to confuse.

Ellerin called out, "Princess...?"

With a mental push—a mere nudge, really—I dispelled them all back to wherever they had come from. I opened my eyes to see the showers of sparks as my will-spell expanded outward and caught them. I did enjoy a good show, after all.

"Thank you, Princess." Ellerin's face under his gray fedora had a sheen of sweat and a couple of welts. I touched my ankle, then stood and put a hand to my cheek, fixing my own injuries. Then I healed John's neck. He looked at me wide-eyed, and I asked, "Are you all right?"

He took a shaky breath and nodded. "What...just happened?"

I helped hoist Kestrel to her feet but—as per usual—didn't sense anything odd about her. The golden aura had faded when I'd banished our attackers. Sir Raleigh prowled around the perimeter of the cave, his eyes glowing green.

"Yes, Ellerin," I said, glaring at him. "What was that? I thought no one knew we were going to be here. What's with the welcoming party?"

"I don't know." He closed his eyes and sighed. "I truly don't. This isn't my usual entrance, so perhaps the black lightning bugs were here to attack someone else."

"Uh huh." My intuition told me otherwise, that they had been meant for us, or me in particular, but I couldn't tease apart whether he lied or he didn't know. "Were you testing me?"

"No, I know better."

I crossed my arms. "How?"

"One of Maeve's daughters could take care of those pests easily. No, Princess, I suspect they were here for a different reason."

"What did you do to them?" Kestrel asked. "Did you kill them?"

Ah, right, human girls liked their pretty things, even if deadly. I grinned. "No, they didn't deserve to die for being what they were. I sent them back to whoever had decided we needed a welcoming party."

Ellerin chuckled. "As much as I appreciate the thought of someone getting black lightning payback, we should get moving. They may come to investigate."

"Good point." I motioned for him to lead the way.

We emerged from the cave into woods crisp with winter air and bare branches that clawed at a heavy leaden sky. Dry brown leaves and grass crunched under our feet.

Home. I was home. The air tingled along my skin in a wash of welcome. That didn't mean I'd let my guard down. Dark vines twined through and over the naked hardwoods, and a thick mist wound among the trees like a living creature, giving the illusion of movement.

Apparently, it felt cold to the humans, who glanced at the mist and then back at us with wide eyes. Kestrel zipped her jacket, and John dug a navy-blue fleece from his backpack and put it on.

"Where are we?" John asked in a hushed tone. He took in the scene with a bewildered expression. "Is it always like this? It's not what I was expecting."

Kestrel giggled, almost giddily. "What were you expecting, Dad?"

"I don't know. More green?"

Ellerin cocked his head to the left, where a path wound into the trees. "This way. And this is the realm of the dark Fae. Faerie is divided into three realms. Well, two, really. Light and dark, and the Gray Zone in the middle, where chaos and light over-lap. While many feel that the dark realm is the most hazardous, the true danger is found in the gray space between, where things are less predictable."

"As predictable as they are in Faerie," I added. I shivered at the memory of my recent visit to the Gray Zone, where I'd over-heard Ellerin talking to my grandmother. What role did she play in all of this?

"So, this is where the evil Fae live?" Kestrel squinted into the trees like she searched for goblins.

Ellerin snorted. "No, at least not technically. I can give you a full history lesson later. Now we should be quiet and keep our ears open for other trouble. Whatever you do, stay on the path. Princess, take the rear." He moved forward, and the light gray mist parted in front of him. What sort of Fae could command the mists?

"All right, let's go so we don't get separated." In the dark Fae lands, obfuscation ruled, and I had no doubt that if we lost sight of Ellerin, we'd be in trouble.

In truth, Sir Raleigh ended up being last in line. He let out a startled, "Mrrowr?" just before the sound of my shirt ripping and pressure, like someone pushed my shoulders, alerted me to drop my pack. A sudden weight on my back made me stumble and land on all fours.

"What now?" John asked. "Are we being attacked again?"

"No," I ground out. "I forgot one very important thing. It's been so long since I was here."

Then the sensation of someone pulling my shoulder blades from my back and stretching them made me bite my lip so I wouldn't scream.

"Wings," Kestrel breathed. "You have wings. They're beautiful, Reine!"

The pain disappeared, leaving relief and lightness in its wake. I stood and almost fell backward before regaining my equilibrium. Note to self—balance would be different from now on. I pulled a mirror from my pack and used it to look behind me. I saw not my usual blue and gold butterfly wings— royal Fae issue, Rhys and I used to joke—but ones of rainbow hue with dark red starting at my shoulders and moving through the spectrum to end with dark purple tips at the points of the wings.

"Huh, that's different." I forced myself to not touch my neck where the vampire had bitten me. She'd told me something I hadn't believed about my origins, that I had light and dark Fae blood. And Rhys had then revealed my aura had all colors as well. No Fae I knew had multicolored wings like this. My scientific curiosity borne of centuries of being a healer in the Earth realm kicked in—could our wing characteristics be determined by what we knew or believed about ourselves? That would be an interesting window into Fae psychology.

Ellerin, who had walked ahead a ways, returned, and he raised his eyebrows. When we left the cave, his normal gray suit had morphed into attire that resembled traveling clothes from a different Earth century but kept their neutral colors. Now he wore a cloak over a tunic and soft leather pants and boots. His briefcase had turned into a cross-body satchel, and he walked with a crystal-topped staff. A flat cap had replaced his Stetson. Rather than being hinted at, his dangerous nature and power showed through.

"Really?" he asked, and his disapproval stung. "Rainbow? That's not subtle at all. Can you furl them? You've made yourself into a brightly lit target."

I drew myself up to my full height and quoted something I'd heard often from my mother. "A Fae princess doesn't furl her wings. And..." I rolled my shoulders, unaccustomed to the extra weight. "I've, uh, forgotten how."

"You've forgotten..." He shook his head. "Never mind. Here." He approached me, his right hand extended. I took it. He hadn't deliberately touched me before, but I found something familiar in his energy, confirming my suspicion we were related somehow.

Tingles raced up my arm from our joined hands. I looked at him in surprise, and the slight wrinkles at the corners of his green eyes—the same shade as mine—deepened as he grinned. The electric sensation flowed from my shoulder through my torso and into my shoulders, which relaxed as the weight of the wings disappeared.

"Where did they go?" Kestrel asked.

I exhaled with relief. "They're furled." A sensation of pressure along the tops of my shoulder blades told me they were still there and would appear when I wanted them to. I promised myself I'd figure out flying again soon.

Ellerin released my hand, and a pang of remembered loss shot through me along with a brief flash of memory, a child saying, *"I don't want you to go."* I blinked so tears wouldn't emerge, and the crush of grief faded into the realm of strong feelings during dreams—only the echo of it remained.

John frowned. "Doesn't furled mean that they're folded against you, not hidden?"

"Not for Fae," Ellerin explained. "And hers had been furled for so long while in the human realm she's forgotten how to control them."

"We can't use them to fly anywhere but here in Faerie," I added. "As he said, they make us targets." But that didn't explain the color change.

He gestured to my ruined attire. "Best change your shirt so we can move along, Princess. Doctor Graves, if you will accompany me. Miss Graves, can you assist her?"

John and Ellerin walked ahead. Kestrel wrinkled her nose. "What does he mean, assist?"

How to explain to an American girl that we'd come to a place where social hierarchy meant something beyond social media influencers and celebrities? I went for direct honesty. "I'm a princess. You're a young woman accompanying us. He means for you to be my maid."

"What?" She lowered her eyebrows in the exact same way her father had done at me moments earlier. "I'm not a maid."

"Yeah, don't worry about it." I pulled off my now ruined T-shirt and bra. Thankfully I hadn't put my favorite faux leather jacket on. I'd've been pissed if that had been torn. I put the scraps of clothing in my pack and pulled a new set. Again, sorrow pricked at my heart when I put on the bra, which was the one I'd been wearing during my make-out session with Lawrence. Hades, I didn't need to be thinking about that right now. Or his rejection.

I donned a light blue T-shirt as quickly as I could to cover the offending bra and the memories. As for the jacket... I left it off just in case of more wing surprises.

"Hurry, Princess," Ellerin called.

The urgency in his tone made me bite back the sharp retort I wanted to make. "What is it?"

"We need to get going. We're not alone."

"How can you tell? The mist makes it look like lots of things are following us."

"Trust me. I know these lands. Something is back there, and it may not be friendly."

Kestrel and John exchanged worried glances. I needed them to be cautious, not terrified, so I smirked at Kestrel and whispered, "How's that for stereotypical fantasy dialog?"

She giggled, but it sounded forced. "He sounds like my dad in the morning when he used to drive me to school, always rushing."

"Indeed." Yes, Ellerin and I had a lot to talk about. However, with him being a gray Fae, the question was whether he'd give me any straight answers. I looked down at Sir Raleigh, and he gazed back at me, then over his shoulder behind us, as if to confirm what Ellerin had said.

We had more important things to worry about.

None of us spoke as Ellerin led us along the twisting path through the woods. Our silence, only broken by the crunch of our steps on the dead leaf matter along the trail, worked for me. I could be with my thoughts uninterrupted, but they swirled around, caught in a whirlwind of confusion, grief, and regret. Fae didn't do regret, but I did.

If only I had trusted Lawrence to do the right thing and still help me even after he'd found out about Rhys' role in his father's death... but I hadn't. I'd kept the information from him, fearful he would go after Rhys. Not that I'd known Lawrence to do anything so impulsive. He planned out everything he did, and even if he'd gotten caught up in the moment—a certain dance ending with a kiss came to mind—he tied himself up in knots over it after. But we'd only been interacting for a few days, so how could I know with certainty?

Even those few days had been enough time to get a sense of who he was and what he could do.

Ellerin's voice broke through my reverie. "Reine, could I talk to you for a moment?"

I walked to the front of the line, leaving Sir Raleigh to guard the rear. I'd hoped that once we were in Faerie, the grimalkin would start speaking to me via secret conversation—what the humans referred to as telepathy—but no such luck. Or maybe, as he had taken the form of a cat, he'd decide when it was time.

The path broadened so that we could walk beside each other. Good timing or the fluidity of Faerie? There was no telling.

"What do you need?"

"We're about to come to a fork. Going one way will take us around Cruaidh. The other branch will bring us to and through the city."

"Which will keep us on the Shadowed Path? Isn't that the point of this exercise—to walk it so we can remain undetected?"

The crystal atop his staff glowed golden, shot through with pulsing silver sparks. "Indeed, Princess, the Shadowed Path is more metaphysical than physical and can change with each journey. That's why you need a guide."

"So that's part of your magic." I looked away from the mesmerizing light show in the crystal. "Which would you recommend?"

"You're correct in your supposition that staying in the forest will keep us more hidden. However, we are being followed, and so we have a better chance of eluding them in the city."

That decided me. I wasn't entirely convinced that the black lightning bugs had been meant for someone else. "Then we go through the city."

"Good."

We stopped and informed the humans of the decision. As I expected, John didn't take it well.

"But is it safe?" He rubbed the bridge of his nose before replacing his glasses. "I mean, truly safer? There could be dangerous creatures there. Dark Fae."

"Well, it is their main city," I said. "Of course they'll be there."

"And won't they want to eat us?" Kestrel asked. "That's what dark Fae are, right? Goblins and trolls and such."

"As long as you're with me, you'll be safe," Ellerin assured her. "I am the Wanderer. I belong to no land and am mostly welcome in all."

"Mostly?" John sounded skeptical.

"Everyone has enemies, Doctor Graves."

Kestrel and I exchanged another almost-smile. That made for two instances of fantasy movie dialog.

"I think it would be more prudent to stick to the woods," John asserted. "It will be easier to take on one enemy than a whole city."

"Are you sure it's just one? I have allies in the city should we need them. Plus, taking the path around the city will add two days to our journey."

John sighed and opened his mouth, probably with another objection, and Ellerin held up a finger.

"Most importantly, Doctor Graves, this is not your decision to make, and you are wasting precious minutes with your arguments."

John flushed and shook his head, but he didn't say anything.

Ellerin nodded. "Good. Come along, then."

This time the glance Kestrel and I exchanged told of our mutual concern that our little party would splinter before we could get to the Faerie capital of Lorien. Meanwhile, I would also be concerned about what Ellerin had said regarding John. Would the Shadowed Path take its revenge on him for his resistance?

3

LAWRENCE

Everything about the situation made me want to turn the car around and return to the safety of my house and work. Well, of my house. As for work, that was a different matter, although we now knew who had killed Beverly Graves and why. In a sense. I was still mentally sorting through all the details.

Meanwhile, I chauffeured the Fae who had killed my father—the Fae whom I'd spent centuries wanting to take my revenge on. And where were we going? To a place where we could sneak into Faerie before the gateway opened by the Gray Fae—a not entirely trustworthy character—closed. I didn't like being vulnerable to attack, but what could I do? I had to make sure John and Kestrel Graves got home safely. What had they been thinking, deciding to go into Faerie? Right, they wanted an answer to why Kestrel's witch powers wouldn't settle, a problem that had consumed Beverly, Kestrel's mother, and led her to the actions that resulted in her death.

Witches were a stubborn bunch. But then, so were gargoyles, and don't even get me started on the Fae.

"How do you know this is where they're going to enter Faerie?"

Rhys slid me a glance.

I ignored the look. "I mean, this all seemed rather suspicious, don't you think?"

"I have my sources, and that's all I can tell you. It's above the pay grade for a gargoyle."

I almost snapped that he was the one who'd invited me, so he might as well let me in on the secret, but I gritted my teeth over the words. There was no point fighting with him. He was the only connection I could use to rescue my best friend and his daughter, who was like my own child.

"You said Reine has enemies waiting for her. How do you know they won't be waiting for us as well?"

Silence. The suspicion that had been planted in my gut early that morning when he'd accosted me in my driveway finally bloomed into a full-grown thought. "Or are you in league with them?"

"Well, I've made some mistakes. You know that. Just help me protect my sister, all right?"

"And my friends," I had to remind myself to loosen my grip on the steering wheel. It was probably pointless to continue to engage him in conversation, but I couldn't resist. "Do you at least know what kind of enemies we might be up against?"

"You remember the soul eater, right?"

"Yes."

"Think about creatures like that, but worse."

That wasn't comforting. But then, nothing with the Fae ever was.

We pulled into a dirt parking lot that ostensibly led to a hiking trail. Only one other car was parked there. I pulled into a space a few spots over from it.

"This is it." Rhys got out of the car before I could cut the engine. He tapped on the trunk, where our packs were stored.

I counted backward from ten. Forget some nameless, faceless enemy. Rhys was going to kill me with elevated blood pressure.

I took my time turning off the air conditioning, confirming the lights were off, and cutting the radio. Not that I really needed to do any of these things. I just needed to make sure Rhys knew I wasn't going to take his command on everything.

He scowled when I finally joined him by the trunk. "Took you long enough."

I shrugged. "I like to make sure everything is taken care of before I move on to the next step."

Rhys looked up to the sky. "Goddess grant me patience."

I, too, looked up, where big fluffy clouds gathered over a robin's egg blue sky. It was going to be a lovely day, the kind where I would hate being inside an office and would wish I could go to someplace secluded, change into my gargoyle form, and spread my wings and fly. "Me too."

Rhys did not look amused. I unlocked the trunk and stood back so he could pick up his backpack. I grabbed mine as well and closed the trunk. My thumb hovered over the lock button on my key fob. From what he had said, leaving my car unlocked in a deserted place would be the least risky thing I could do. I acknowledged that locking it gave me an illusory feeling of control, so I pushed the lock button twice. The beeps echoed through the woods.

"Feel better?" Rhys sneered.

"Where to now?" I looked around, enjoying the smell of the early spring buds and leaves over the morning-warmed dirt and rocks. No matter what happened to me, the cycle of the seasons would continue.

"This way." Rhys gestured for me to follow him and led me to the path to the trail. About a mile in, he took what looked like a side trail carved by an old stream. This brought us to a clearing, where the air still crackled with magical energy.

"What happened here?" I rubbed the small hairs that stood up on my arms.

Rhys sniffed the air, even though I knew he didn't need to. "Good, they only left an hour ago, at most."

"How do we follow them?"

"The sunrise showed the entrance to the portal, so all we have to do is figure out where it would have been shining." He closed his eyes, and I stepped back. The Fae were more attuned to nature, at least its rhythms, than gargoyles. However, I could still sense the boulders surrounding the campsite were more than just boulders.

One in particular drew my attention. It thrummed like a guitar string that had just been plucked. I walked over to it and placed my hand on it. Instead of stone, my palm met the sensation of cool, sticky air. Before I could say, "I think I found it," it pulled me in. I tumbled to my hands and knees inside a cave. I rolled out of the way just before Rhys tumbled through as well.

We lay panting on the floor, which was covered in fine sand. I stood and brushed off my hands on my pants. Then I held out a hand to help Rhys up. He ignored it and rolled to his knees.

"You could have told me you sensed it."

"I didn't have time. It pulled me through just as I figured it out." I mimed placing my palm against the stone.

"That's lesson one. Don't touch anything unless I tell you to."

I again clenched my jaw. As much as I hated it, I had to concede that he was now the expert.

We walked out of the cave and into a scene of midwinter bare trees and leaden gray sky, but warmer.

"Is Faerie always seventy degrees?"

"Not always. The air here is warmer because of all the magic. It was probably a good fifteen to twenty degrees cooler before we got here."

The degree to which I was sweating didn't make sense for

the air temperature. The smell of the air clogged my nostrils, like strong perfume in an enclosed space. "How often do gargoyles come into Faerie?"

Rhys shrugged. "You're the first in a long time as far as I know, mate. How is it working for you?"

I doubled over, hands on my knees. I knew this feeling, although it had never overtaken me so quickly before. My pack hit the ground, followed quickly by my shoes and shirt as I shed clothing.

"Whoa, whoa, mate, what are you doing?"

I would have laughed at Rhys' distress had I not been putting all my effort into stalling the change so I wouldn't ruin one of my two changes of clothing. I had just pulled on my pair of larger pants, which swallowed me in human form, but...

With a roar, I straightened and flung my arms back. My wings sprouted with ferocious speed, and my gargoyle form overtook me. In what felt like an instant, I exploded from inside. I grew a foot taller, and all my muscles bulged under my skin as my jaw grew squarer and my teeth larger and more pointed. My skin darkened to gargoyle gray. Now the black leather trousers fit perfectly.

Change complete, I again found myself on my hands and knees, panting.

Rhys looked at me with wide eyes. "Are you...all right?"

I glared up at him. "Do I look all right?" I leaned back so I knelt and dug through my pack to find the leather thong I used to pull my now-long black hair back.

"You didn't have to change." He gestured to our surroundings. "No threat that I can sense. Or did you?"

"I don't know." Gods, I hated those words. "It came over me. I couldn't stop it."

"Well, you're just going to be full of surprises, aren't you?"

I gathered the garments I'd shed in my haste and noticed the indentations of footprints in the grass. With my heightened gargoyle senses, I could pick out five distinct ones—the sneakers Kestrel favored, John's sensible hiking boots, Reine's almost as sensible walking boots, another man's boots with flat soles, almost like they were from another era—Ellerin's?—Sir Raleigh's large paw prints, and...

"Hey, Rhys, look at this."

"What? Oh, footprints. Very good. We're in the right spot."

"But what are these?" I pointed to a semicircular indentation. In fact, several of them went around and over the others.

Rhys frowned. "Those are a dark Fae creature. Not sure what kind, but..." He walked to the edge of the clearing, where the trees parted to show a trail. Great. Another path through the woods. What would this one lead us to?

"Best get a move on, mate. Whatever it is, it's following them."

4

REINE

The path turned upward, and I found myself using my wings to give me forward momentum. This of course was interesting, because I couldn't actually see my wings. Yet they were there, supporting and pushing me along. At least something in my life did.

John continued to walk in front of us, and Kestrel caught up to me.

"My dad is sulking, but I know he and I have the same question. What can we expect from the dark Fae city?"

"I don't know. I've never been there."

"But aren't you a princess? Haven't you visited all the parts of your kingdom?"

"The parts belonging to the light Fae, yes. This is like a different country." But her question made me wonder. Who had made the rules that Fae couldn't visit each other's regions? Wouldn't it make more sense? We could learn from each other and perhaps even come to some sort of peace rather than the cold war we'd been in for centuries, possibly millennia.

Or was I thinking like a human still? Or something else? Most people didn't seem to desire peace and mutual learning.

"So, you don't know what we're walking into. How well do you know him?" Kestrel nodded toward Ellerin, who stalked ahead. I could almost feel the tension between him and John. Both men were used to getting their way and having their authority respected.

"Not very, but this was my only way in, at least without my mother knowing."

"Do you trust him?"

Ellerin glanced over his shoulder and put a finger to his lips. My cheeks warmed, and Kestrel's turned pink.

I touched her arm to emphasize the point. "One thing to always remember—Fae have excellent hearing."

No one said anything until we reached the tall obsidian walls of the city. Rather than having a smooth facade, they rose from the landscape in jagged layers that would tempt enemies to try to scale them. Anyone foolish enough to climb them would meet their death on the slippery slopes and shark-tooth edges.

John looked at the walls, and his face betrayed his uncertainty. "There's a gate around here somewhere, right?"

Ellerin chuckled. "Yes, although not everyone knows how to find it."

We followed him through another copse of trees, which felt like we were walking away from the wall, but I could feel illusion thick in the air.

"The Shadowed Path leads here as well as many other places. Only a few have the keys to make it lead where they like."

Kestrel and I exchanged smiles again.

Ellerin paused and held up his hand, and we all stopped. "Everyone be quiet. This is where I summon the gatekeeper."

Kestrel mimed working a video game controller. I snorted and nudged her with my elbow.

Ellerin closed his eyes and held up his staff. The crystal at the end glowed red, like blood, and a chill slithered down my spine.

A small, blue creature appeared and sat on a large toadstool about ten feet away from us. It had humanoid features, pointed ears, and wore a witch's hat, which was not white, thank goodness. I didn't know what I would do if Kestrel started singing the theme to *The Smurfs*. Or was she old enough to remember them?

The creature pulled a checklist and pencil from its cloak, crossed its legs, and squinted up at Ellerin. It challenged him in a squeaky voice, "You're not on my list."

Ellerin spoke with more deference than I had heard him use to this point. "We had to take an unexpected detour, Gatekeeper."

The creature shook his head. At least, I think it was a he. The chaos of the dark Fae lands defied or resisted all attempts at categorization—gender among them. "Ah, yes, the forces of chaos abound, no matter how much one tries to avoid them." They added with a sinister grin, "Especially if one has a debt to it."

Ellerin made a sweeping motion with his hand—*don't talk about that here.*

"I request entrance to the dark Fae city of Cruaidh."

"Hmmm." The gatekeeper tapped its pencil on its list. "Looks like there's four of you, five with the grimalkin. I can get you in next Tuesday."

"Told you we should've gone around," John grumbled and pushed his glasses up his nose.

Ellerin frowned over his shoulder at John, then turned his attention back to the gatekeeper. "This is an urgent matter. We need entry to the city today."

"Fae cities require reservations?" Kestrel asked me.

"Sometimes, yes. Although this is a land of chaos, we try to be careful to make sure the magic is balanced and not concentrated too much in any one place."

"Yes, young lady, and I cannot allow a party of two Fae, one witch, a grimalkin, and one..." This time Kestrel was the object of the blue creature's squint. "What are you, miss?"

Kestrel sighed. "I wish I knew."

Ellerin motioned for us to walk a distance away, and we complied.

John kept looking back at Ellerin. "What is he doing? Is there a problem? Should we just go the other way?"

"No, it's the custom. There needs to be a bribe, haggling over it, and finally a reluctant resolution." I was relieved to find how easily the customs of Faerie came back to me.

"So, there's not a problem with there being too much magic?" Kestrel's body was ninety-nine percent still, but I could see her jaw muscles moving, and I guessed she had a nervous habit, something to do with her tongue.

"Unlikely."

John looked at his daughter, and back at me. "You're sure? What if she has more magic than any of us realize? Even the gatekeeper didn't seem to know what to do about her."

"If anything, the mystery around her will make the gatekeeper more likely to let us in. It was a rookie mistake for them to betray their curiosity."

Ellerin returned. "We're in. Follow me."

The gatekeeper gave us a cheery wave as we walked past, and I noticed their eyes lingered on Kestrel. I wondered if there was something in the bribe Ellerin had given the gatekeeper having to do with her. He wouldn't do something like that without asking me first, would he?

We walked straight toward a particularly jagged-looking piece of the wall. In fact, it appeared as though we were about to voluntarily impale ourselves on a shard. We stopped just short of it.

"The gatekeeper said you have to go first," Ellerin gestured to Kestrel. "Remember, much of the Fae lands are an illusion, especially to humans."

John stepped in front of his daughter. "No! I will not allow it. Are you trying to kill us?"

Kestrel cocked her head and narrowed her eyes at the spike. "It's okay, Dad. It's not real."

"Are you sure?" John asked at the same time Ellerin queried, "What do you see?"

"It's flickering, like a bad hologram."

I turned my Fae sight on it, which I had to remember to do, as I had gotten out of practice using my Fae senses in the human world. I saw what she meant. Rather than glittering black stone, the shard appeared like projected gray glass.

Kestrel moved around John and walked straight toward the spike. John lunged as though to stop her, and I held him back.

"You have to let her go and grow up sometime. That means allowing her to make her own decisions."

"Don't tell me how to parent." He wrenched his arm from my hand with surprising strength. Kestrel disappeared with no blood or screams. John relaxed for an instant, then became antsy again as his overprotective tendencies, highlighted by his wife's recent death, reasserted themselves.

Ellerin frowned again but didn't say anything to John. "You're up next, Reine."

I walked toward the spike and deliberately relaxed as the illusion touched my breastbone. The magic of the dark Fae did not reward fear. Rather, they fed on it, and I was not going to allow them to leech any more of my power than I could help.

As soon as it would have stabbed me fatally, the spike disappeared in a puff of smoke, and I found myself on a sidewalk in a modern-looking city.

Kestrel stood to one side, watching wide-eyed. I joined her, careful to be out of the way of whoever came through the gates next. When I looked back at it, I saw not an intimidating wall, but a large, decorated stone arch, like the Arc de Triomphe in Paris.

"What do you think about your first look at a real Fae city?"

Kestrel rubbed her right temple. "This is going to sound crazy, but it looks familiar."

"Familiar how?"

"Like I've been here before."

I took a deep breath and took in the scene. I'd visited many of the major Earth cities during my time there, but none of them compared to Faerie with its senses of magic and otherness. Part of that came from the jumble of architectural styles, which kept me from feeling a true sense of time or place. Tall buildings of stone—no metal—and glass mixed eras from squat medieval stone, to medium-height Victorian, to towering crystalline structures that defied categorization with their multi-faceted planes. The inhabitants also presented an interesting mix. A wide assortment of dark Fae creatures ambled, strolled, stalked, and otherwise made their way along the concrete sidewalk. While vehicles drove along the street, they were more of the wagon and coach variety, and cobblestones replaced pavement.

In other words, it was like the human world mixed up. The absence of the typical city odors of gasoline and tobacco smoke disoriented me. Instead, the smells of wet dirt and stone hung in the air, like an exposed hillside after a rainstorm, although the surfaces didn't appear to have been rained on recently.

I pulled Kestrel out of the way of a small, brown, wrinkled creature who rode a two-wheeled wooden conveyance powered by nature magic, which explained the smell. The rider of the wooden bike almost ran over another of its kind, who shook its fist.

"Thank you, idiot."

"No, thank *you*." The first one retorted and shook its fist back over its shoulder.

Kestrel watched the one on the bike roll away. "What was that about? Were they being sarcastic?"

"Brownies," I explained. "It's an insult to thank them."

"I'll...keep that in mind."

I suspected she'd forget. She appeared to be awed at the spectacle around us. Truth be told, I, too, found myself a bit overwhelmed. As I'd told her, I hadn't been to Cruaidh, or indeed any of the dark Fae lands, and I didn't know where danger would come from. For the threat was there, a dark shadow just outside of my peripheral vision, both Fae and mundane. I extended my extra Fae senses, and dark alleys became visible between the buildings. They reminded me that no matter where we walked, something could reach out and snatch any of us. Sir Raleigh, again in his less threatening cat form, twined around my ankles.

"Reine, where's my dad?" Kestrel looked back at the gate. "Shouldn't they have come through by now?"

"I suspect Ellerin is taking the opportunity to speak with him outside of our hearing. Plus, here would be the worst place for your father to dig in his heels and argue."

"Yeah, my dad can be kind of overbearing. My mom knew how to handle him."

I didn't know what to say to that. Her mother had been killed in front of her the week before, and I could feel her grief simmering below the surface. "Can you...handle him?"

"Maybe? He seems to think I'm still twelve or something. Honestly, that's when he got super busy with work and basically ignored my existence until I got that internship at the center. Not that it did a lot of good." She sighed. "Do Fae parents act differently?"

"To a point. Once we get to a certain age, we're on our own."

"So, you raised yourselves?"

"Again, not exactly. I did, and I looked after Rhys long after he became an 'adult' at the request of my mother. That led us both to be exiled through his stupid actions. So yeah, Fae are horrible parents."

John came through the gate, his face pale, and he rushed over to Kestrel and enveloped her in a hug.

"Are you okay?" He held her by her shoulders away from him. "Did it hurt you when you came through?"

She batted his hands away. "I'm fine. I told you it would be no big deal. Why don't you listen to me?"

"Watch your tone, young lady. I've had enough browbeating for one day."

"John," Ellerin warned. "Later."

John pressed his lips together and nodded. Poor guy. No one liked to be scolded, especially someone used to being in charge. He turned away, and his mouth softened into an "o" of wonder as he took in the city around him.

I grinned and turned my attention to Ellerin. "Where to? Can we get transportation across the city?"

"This way. As part of my bargain to get us in, I had to promise that you and I would meet with someone. I'm going to stash the humans in a safe place where we can stay the night in case our meeting runs long."

"Stay the night?" I asked. John's face turned purple with his unspoken objections, but he held them in.

"It's highly unlikely." He started walking away from the gate, and we had no choice but to follow him.

Kestrel moved into step beside me. "You Fae like that word, unlikely."

"We technically can't lie, so we speak in non-absolutes. It makes life easier. Now, no more questions, please. I need to remain alert to any threat."

Ellerin led us along a series of gradually narrowing streets until we found ourselves in a neighborhood that wasn't shabby so much as old and dark. The gloom thickened at street level and I sensed eyes watching us from alleys and the shadowed alcoves of doorways. The crowds had thinned such that the nearest inhabitants walked a good ten feet in front of and behind us. Keeping their distance? Or respecting ours? Ellerin certainly looked like he could take on more than one or two dark Fae, either physically or magically. My own powers continued their gradual awakening, and they practically itched to be tested in a fight.

Where did that come from? Light Fae didn't sully themselves with direct conflict. They hired others to do their dirty work for them.

Kestrel walked closer to me. Seeking protection? Her wide-eyed gaze had turned anxious.

"This is more like I pictured. Like in fairy tales."

"Me, too." I had to admit I'd considered the dark Fae to be less civilized and advanced than the light Fae, so the modernity of the rest of the city had taken me by surprise. What did it say about me that I was relieved that my lower expectations were fulfilled? Buildings in a variety of stone colors and textures clustered together in a hard rainbow that curved around the narrow streets. The mismatch felt like a rebellion against the city of the light Fae, where everything glowed in shades of white, cream, and the occasional gold. Away from the magic that powered the vehicles, more odors filled the air, some pleasant and some not so. Kestrel wrinkled her nose as a plume of sulfur smoke came from a residence above us, and the yellow particles drifted down toward us.

"What was that?"

"Some sort of spell, I suppose. This is the type of place travelers come and pay dearly for favors, enchantments, and other ways to make their lives easier, or so they think."

Ellerin glanced over his shoulder. "Almost there. Are you all right?"

"Yes," Kestrel and I answered in unison. John didn't say anything. Ellerin either didn't notice his lack of response or didn't care.

The next bend brought us in sight of a large white building with accents that looked like wrought iron. But that couldn't be —all Fae were intolerant of the stuff. The ground floor housed a restaurant, from which savory smells of tomatoes and spices wafted toward us. My stomach growled and reminded me we hadn't eaten in several hours.

We followed Ellerin straight to the building, and I braced myself against the repelling force of the iron. But as we got closer, I didn't find the resistance I thought I would. I caught up to Ellerin and asked him, "Is the iron an illusion?"

"Mostly. This building exists both here and in New Orleans, and the iron is mostly there. It keeps the riffraff out."

I didn't ask how. Some places had a mystical connection that allowed such things to happen, and rules got bent in Faerie. As much as I wanted to believe in consistency, it didn't mean there was any. That's why I needed to get to my grandmother sooner rather than later—I believed she would take care of me if I could plead my case, but being in Faerie, in this alternate reality, meant that every day longer away from her made for erosion of my memory and favor with her. I hoped she hadn't forgotten about me already.

INSIDE, the hotel continued the New Orleans theme with bright colors in a small but warm lobby with rich red carpeting, ornate wood, and brass accents. A crystal chandelier hovered without a chain and cast rainbows through the space. The two Fae behind the check-in desk, one male and one female, also would have fit right in at a fancy hotel with their dark uniforms and name tags. A quick glance at one name tag revealed that instead of languages spoken, it listed magical talents. As it turned out, the female Fae was named Lorelei, and she specialized in pet behavior and removal of curses from objects.

I had to ask, "What do you mean by pet behavior?"

She smiled at me, her sky-blue eyes striking. "I calm the animals and convince them not to scratch, bite, or engage in insolence toward their human or Fae companions."

"Insolence, huh?" I arched an eyebrow at Sir Raleigh, now in non-threatening cat form at my feet, and he glared back at me.

She leaned over the desk to take a look at him. "Oh, what a cutie! Grimalkins are a bit more challenging. They tend to have the personality of their summoners."

"Thanks for the hint."

She handed me the keys to my and the humans' rooms and gave Ellerin his with an extra broad grin. "Good to see you again, Wanderer. I'm working my usual hours."

Ellerin's face flushed, and I bit back a laugh at his discomfort. Dare I say, that was the first human expression I'd seen him adopt? I resisted the urge to comment until we'd climbed a couple of flights of stairs. The thick, red carpeting muffled our footsteps and would hopefully keep sound from carrying.

Still, I teased him as quietly as possible. "Her usual hours, huh?"

"None of your business, Princess."

John drew in a breath behind me, and I just knew he was going to say something about not letting romantic dalliances interfere with our mission. I had started to turn to tell him to keep his mouth shut when an, "Oof" told me Kestrel had thwacked him.

With gentle tugs, our keys pulled us along to the fourth floor, and we went to the humans' room first. The rooms turned out to be mostly like human hotels with a few exceptions. Each had a tree resembling a Ficus growing in three of the four corners. Their trunks disappeared into the floors, and fairy lights moved among the leaves, but didn't attach to any cords. The canopied beds looked like they'd been purchased from Fairy Tales 'R Us, and vines twined through the bathrooms along the tops of the mirrors and dangled to make up the shower curtains. Instead of a television, antique bureaus held a black obsidian mirror. Thankfully, the towels looked normal.

"This is amazing." Kestrel walked through her and John's room and gasped with delight at each new Fae feature she discovered. "How does housekeeping work?"

Ellerin leaned against the doorframe and watched her with an indulgent smile. "The branches from the tree and the vines in the bathroom will take care of it."

John, meanwhile, stood as far away from the living hotel room features, arms folded. "Are they safe?"

Ellerin sighed. "Yes, for the most part. Just don't touch them."

Kestrel drew her hand back from the tree in the corner to the right of the window. "Why not? What will happen?"

"Probably nothing, but you never know."

Kestrel walked over to the mirror. "Is this the TV? How does it work? What kind of channels do you get?"

"That's for scrying. Please don't... Well, wait until you touch it. It could be informative, but we don't have time now. Princess, are you ready?"

We ordered room service for John and Kestrel and admonished them not to go anywhere. I told Sir Raleigh to stay and watch over them. Then Ellerin accompanied me to my room and waited outside while I put my pack in the hollowed-out boulder that served as a safe. When it came time to choose a code word to seal it, I said the first one that came to mind— Lawrence. I hoped he was managing back at work, where it must still be chaotic.

I walked into the hallway to find Ellerin looking at a menu card for the restaurant below. Some of the food listed made me homesick and even hungrier than I had been, and I couldn't hide the eagerness in my question, "Are we eating downstairs?"

"No, not right now. We have our meeting to get to."

He motioned for me to follow him, and I did. We took the stairs down to the lobby—no elevators in Fae hotels—and I grabbed an apple from the bowl on the front desk on the way out. I ate as we walked.

"Where are we going?" I hoped the meeting would be short. The apple wouldn't keep me satiated for long.

"You'll see."

I shrugged. From what little I'd heard of the gray Fae, they liked to be more inscrutable than even the high light Fae. I again felt sympathy for the humans who had entered into Fae bargains as I had when I accepted my original mission from my mother. Not knowing what to expect was stressful, and here in the capital city of the dark Fae, I anticipated a surprise around every corner.

As far as I could tell, Ellerin led us away from the gate that had brought us into Cruaidh, which I surmised must be near the city center. While I had a decent sense of direction, I'd never had to develop it—high Fae were typically driven everywhere by servants. I managed in the Earth realm by taking my cues from nature. Here, I found myself at a loss, as the streets themselves seemed to have a purpose of confusion for the unwary. A defense against invasion? But who would invade a Fae city? All our enemies had been driven out, and the realm made inhospitable to them. I didn't know how. Something in the air? A Fae-concocted microbe? When I'd left Faerie, I'd been a healer, but I hadn't pondered it that much, just accepted it as part of Fae history and moved on. In other words, I'd focused exclusively on healing Fae, and an unexpected gratitude for my time and experiences in the Earth realm bloomed in my chest.

I reminded myself to pay attention. Why the confusion spell

on the streets? Did the dark Fae expected to be invaded by the light or the gray Fae? The notion made me shiver. Had the treaty eroded, or had something else changed?

Ellerin looked lost in his own thoughts, his mouth set in a determined line, so I cleared my throat to get his attention. He blinked. "Yes?"

"Has there always been an Obfuscation Charm here in Cruaidh?"

He stopped and raised his chin, his nostrils flared. "Ah, right, I feel it now. In this part of the city, yes." He started walking again, this time more quickly, like where we were headed drew him toward it. I found myself almost trotting to keep up with him.

"You couldn't feel it before?"

"As a Wanderer, such spells don't affect me. I'm enemy to no one, so they're not aimed at me."

"Really? You don't have any enemies?"

He chuckled. "I have enemies, but there is no one I wish ill. Well, almost."

"I knew it. Everyone has been wronged by someone, and it's hard to get over. Who's been the bee in your bonnet?"

"Such a human expression, Princess! And my business is my business."

Message received—*not* my business. I thought about a roundabout way to get more information from him, but before I could ask, the street we walked on dead-ended in front of a large, stone wall topped with iron spikes. Unlike at the hotel, these created a sense of friction in the air, a high-pitched whine that made me want to cover my ears and head the other way.

I placed my hands over my ears, not that it did any good. "What is this place?"

"The Fae Asylum. And this is where we're having our meeting."

5

REINE

"I'm afraid to ask how we get in. Do we have to?" Each word became more of an effort as my jaw wanted to clench against the repellent sensation.

"Yes, I'm afraid so, Princess. This is where your Shadowed Path has led. I am only your guide." Ellerin walked along the wall, and I followed him. The building on the other side of the street, a gray brick warehouse of some sort, huddled close enough that it served as more of a second wall. It also put us in a narrow alley that didn't allow me to satisfy my desire to put as much distance between me and the asylum wall as possible. I had been in the Earth realm for much of the period where the care of those who thought and behaved differently changed. They went from being respected to being feared as witches or possessed to being locked away as dangerous or inconvenient. The thought floated through my iron noise-fogged brain—had I been deemed inconvenient? Was Ellerin going to lock me up? But Fae didn't have asylums. Those who didn't want to comply with the edicts of the light Fae went to live with the dark Fae, where they would be absorbed into its lawless and chaotic society.

But what I had seen of the dark Fae city hadn't been lawless or chaotic. It still had its rules, even if not apparent at first. Had that changed? Or had I been taught wrong?

That latter question was coming up way too much for comfort on this journey.

A wall of iron energy, like stinging mist, made me stop, and I lifted my bowed head to see we'd reached a black-barred gate. I stepped backward, and Ellerin grabbed my right forearm.

"No you don't, Princess. I promise, you won't be stuck here. There's something you need to see." He lifted his staff, and the crystal atop it blazed white. The gates vanished, and although I still felt the iron spikes atop the walls, I sagged in relief.

Ellerin tugged on my arm. "They only disappear for a minute. Woe to any Fae who gets caught in them when they reappear."

The thought of being impaled by suddenly materializing iron drove me forward. Should I have turned and run? Perhaps, but then I would have been lost with the obfuscating spell, which I surmised had been placed to confuse those who would try to escape.

If Ellerin had trapped me, I had walked right into it, and so there was no choice but forward.

The gates reappeared, and I stumbled forward with the force of the iron's energy. My wings reappeared to steady me and provided some cushion between me and the gates, which they shouldn't have.

Ellerin raised his eyebrows. "I thought that might happen. It's impossible to hide what one is in here."

I studied him, but he looked just the same—an older middle-aged Fae with gray at his temples and green eyes that matched my own, reinforcing my guess that we were related somehow. If anything, he looked more...him. Was that why his wings didn't appear—they didn't need to?

A broad lawn of blue grass stretched to either side of us,

and our boots crunched along a gravel path leading up to the building. In the Earth realm, it would have looked like some venerable college building with its dark gray brick, light stone accents and many-paned windows. Bars of Fae iron, an alloy with the same strength but without the repellent properties of true iron, hung in front of the windows. The bars and the chiseled gold lettering in the white marble lintel over the door, which read, simply, "Asylum for Fae" gave it a sinister air. As we got closer, I could make out smaller writing painted beneath along the top of the frame: "Welcome to this place of respite for those who can or will not conform to Her Majesty's rule."

"Which Majesty?" I asked, aware that there was my grandmother, Tatiana, and the dark Fae queen Lilith. Both had ruled for over a millennium.

Ellerin turned and dropped his reply into the oppressive silence. "Both."

"But that's not..."

"...what you were told? No, I imagine not. Both queens rule their realms with wands of iron even if it's killing their subjects."

A memory bubbled to the surface of something whispered among the servants in my grandmother's palace. *The gray Fae are rebels. They're the only ones who dare oppose the queens.* That had been my first nurse, Olred. She had left soon after, supposedly because her daughter had had a child and needed her help. Never mind that it was highly unusual for lower Fae to reproduce, and if they did, they often hid the children away from the high Fae, sometimes leaving them with human families to raise and retrieve later. Rather than being changelings, the Fae babies were surprise twins left along with the human infant. I imagined that became more difficult after the advent of ultrasounds, but by that point, human construction involved more iron than most lower Fae could tolerate. I managed in modern cities since the steel support beams were typically wrapped up in enough stone.

Either way, I needed to remember that Ellerin had his own agenda, and I couldn't allow him to drag me into treason.

A voice came through an opening about an inch across to the left of the iron-studded double doors, which could've come straight from a medieval castle. Maybe they had. I couldn't imagine Fae artisans working with the stuff.

The squeaky voice sounded much like that of the creature who guarded the city gates, but more annoyed. "Ellerin, you're late."

"They know you?"

He waved for me to be quiet, which would have gotten his hand chopped off—and him exiled as a result of his mutilation—for his disrespect to a granddaughter of Tatiana in Lorien. I crossed my arms and scowled, but I didn't say anything.

"Your cousin decided to call forth the spike at the gate. The humans balked."

The sound of wheezing laughter came through the door. "Of course they did. He's an ass like that. Come in."

The door on the right opened to reveal another blue, gnome-like creature, this one dressed in saffron yellow. It straightened its stooped shoulders and bowed to Ellerin, who bowed back. I did so as well and wished Ellerin had taken some time on the way to let me know about the protocols of this place.

"Ah, Princess Reine, it is an honor to have you."

"Thank you, um...?"

"I am Healer Wilfrin, and I am glad you're here."

Thankful he didn't follow that up with, *"Your room is right through here,"* I said, "Thank you. To be honest, I'm not sure why I'm here. Not to stay, I hope."

Wilfrin and Ellerin laughed. Wilfrin replied, much too cheerfully, "Probably not. The high Fae get the courtesy of exile, where eager dragon-hunters or mobs will finish you off for witchcraft."

I smiled as a courtesy, recognizing the gallows humor of a healer who's seen too much and was down to their last mental resources before they either quit or went mad themselves. Also, I hoped his *probably* meant *definitely*, considering how Fae spoke.

"Is she ready?" Ellerin asked.

"Yes, you're lucky. She didn't want a nap this afternoon. Of course that makes her scream more, but..." Wilfrin shrugged his thin shoulders under his robe. "It keeps things interesting."

His disregard for a patient's distress reminded me of some of the things I'd heard about in Victorian asylums, and I shivered. At least I was now pretty sure they weren't referring to me.

He led us through a large hall that in a castle would have been the banquet hall, but no long tables or tapestries broke up the expanse of gray stone. I couldn't see, but definitely felt, the iron bands around the windows and between the panes, which would have been admired in the Earth realm for the delicate diamond rainbow pattern the beveled glass created across the plain floor.

A winding staircase brought us to an upper floor, where a long hallway stretched in both directions. Glowing crystals illuminated closed wooden doors, spaced apart like they would be in a hotel. But this wasn't a hotel. A series of thumps rattled one of the doors to my left.

Wilfrin huffed and walked to the door, which he knocked on. "Settle down there, Larry. This visitor isn't for you."

For a second, I feared that Larry was Lawrence, but that couldn't be. Still, I asked, "Do you have creatures in here that aren't Fae?"

Ellerin turned away, but not before I caught the smile on his face. Dammit, he probably knew what I was thinking.

Wilfrin tapped his lower lip with one claw. "What sort of creatures?"

I tried to sound nonchalant. "Oh, you know, former Fae allies, like gargoyles."

Wilfrin's eyes grew wide. "Never those, Princess. They're too strong, and iron only increases their ability to cause damage, whereas it weakens our usual residents. These walls are built to resist magic, not brute force."

"Good to know."

"This way, please."

Wilfrin led us to the right, and I sent some soothing magic toward Larry, whoever or whatever he was. Fae hated being trapped, and wasn't this the worst trap of all—a place where our legendary cleverness and ability to deceive would be conflated, and there would be no release?

"Through here, Princess." He led us down another hallway, which I hadn't noticed. When I looked back the way we came, I saw two corridors, likely due to another confusion spell. It disturbed me how well the magic of the place and area surrounding it worked on me.

I squinted against the sudden presence of natural light, which streamed through a stained-glass window at the end. Once my eyes adjusted, I smiled at the scene portrayed—a beautiful woman with streaming blond hair conveying a blessing on a young knight, who knelt at her feet. My grandmother had always been fond of that type of painting, which was one reason she had been so liberal with me and Rhys going into the human realm. She wanted to know what was going on, both historically and with regard to human arts.

A plush, red couch faced the window. I couldn't tell whether anyone sat on it. I glanced at Ellerin, who didn't appear nearly as charmed as I felt. Another case of me being susceptible to the magic of the place, whereas he wasn't?

Ellerin turned toward me, and his disgust disappeared from his face, but not his voice. "Look familiar?"

"Yes. Tatiana loves those images."

"Ah, so you remember. Yes, this is the hall where those who were special to your grandmother are housed. Their rooms are nicer, and they are sometimes allowed to sit beneath the window."

Wilfrin appeared from one of the rooms. He must have slipped away while I was entranced by the window. "She's ready."

"After you, Princess."

I hesitantly approached the open wooden door. Inside the room, a tall, stately woman turned from the window, where the black bars on the outside obscured the scene below, of a lawn with a pond. Were we at the back of the building? When I tried to figure it out from the twists and turns we'd been through, I couldn't, and I found it impossible to sense the location of the sun, which would have given me a clue. Frustration built in my chest, but it evaporated when the woman's face lit with a delighted expression.

"Oh, Ellerin, is this her?"

Hearing the beloved voice my memory had just evoked made a sob rise through me. I'd forgotten how much I'd cried when Olred left, how much I'd mourned. That had been before I had learned that Fae don't do grief or regret.

But we did. "Ol-Olred?"

"Come here, my little Reine. Not so little now, are we?"

She enveloped me in her embrace, and my aura and hers met in a spiritual hug. But it had thorns, as her multiple shards of grief poked me in the heart. I tried to stop my tears but could only manage a shuddering sniffle before starting again. She still smelled like I remembered, of sunshine and fresh-baked bread, but something sour now joined her familiar scent.

Once my crying stopped, she held me away from her like she had when I'd been a little Fae. "There, all cried out?"

I nodded. "Yes, thank you, Olred."

"Good. You don't want your mother to see you with tears on your face, do you?" She wiped them from my face with her thumbs, another familiar gesture that almost re-started them. "Oh! What's happened to your wings? Look how pretty they are!"

Her words shocked me out of my nostalgic haze, and I looked around. Her room resembled the one she'd had in the palace, with the same humble bed against the wall, the in-room shower and toilet glamoured to look like a chamber pot.

"My mother isn't here, Olred."

"No?" She frowned, and lucidity appeared in her eyes.

Wilfrin started forward with a syringe he must've conjured from his robes, but I erected an invisible wall so fast he bumped into it.

"Bad idea, Princess. That kind of magic isn't tolerated here."

"What did you do to her?" Now my physician mind recognized evidence of the presence of certain substances known to dilute understanding and presence. "How often are those being administered to her?" In a place like this, they could be counted as a mercy, but with grave risk.

Wilfrin rubbed his nose. "Not too often, don't worry." He scowled up at Ellerin, who shrugged.

"I warned you she was a healer here and is a doctor in the Earth realm."

"You didn't tell me about her power."

"She's a granddaughter of Tatiana. What did you expect?"

I decided to leave them to their argument and turned back to Olred, who had released me and now rubbed her hands together.

"How did you end up here?"

She narrowed her eyes at Wilfrin. "I spoke of treason, of the gray Fae. I was warned they didn't exist, but..." She gestured to Ellerin. "I knew what he was. Is. I kept his secret, but it wasn't enough, was it, was it, *Ellerin*?" Ellerin's name turned into a primal scream, and her formerly placid features distorted into a monster parody of her face. I leaped back and pressed a hand to my chest, where my heart pounded. Shock at her change rooted me to the spot.

She lunged at Ellerin, but the invisible wall held, and she staggered back and fell. On the floor, she looked weak and frail, and only the rage that twisted her face kept me from approaching her to see if she was okay.

I did ask, "What is he?"

"He's one of them. He's a gray Fae. And—"

Ellerin held up the hand that wasn't gripping his staff, and Olred put her own gnarled hands to her throat.

"There will be time enough for those secrets to come out later."

Olred staggered to her feet, and I searched her face for any sign of my beloved nurse, but only hatred showed now. Then, when she looked at me, she took a deep breath.

"You can look all high and mighty over there, Maeve, but eventually they'll know what you did. I see it in your wings."

The shock at being called my mother's name made my hold on my magic slip—or maybe the iron around me and lack of practice weakened me so I couldn't hold it as well—and Wilfrin darted through and stabbed her in the thigh with his needle.

"What did you do that for?" I almost incinerated him on the spot, but I kept my anger in check.

"You don't know how dangerous she is, Princess. Especially if she thinks you're Maeve."

Olred swayed, and Ellerin and I rushed to her and guided her to fall on her bed. Her eyelids fluttered, and I took one of her hands between mine. Ellerin moved to the other side of the room.

"Give them some space, won't you, Wilfrin?"

"Yes, she should be sedated now." The little creature left the room. Ellerin stayed. I didn't have the energy to argue with him, and I knew Olred would only have a few more conscious moments.

"I'm sorry, Olred. I'm not Maeve. I'm Reine."

"Reine, the queen." She put her other hand to my cheek. "My beautiful little queen."

She'd call me that when I was a child, and tears burned in my eyes again. "I'm not the queen, Olred. I would never have done this to you."

"I know you wouldn't. That's why you're here." She nodded, and she went limp. I placed her hands along her sides and rose.

Ellerin started forward, his hand outstretched, but then stepped back and clenched it into a fist.

I wish I could say I left her side with reluctance, but I had to keep myself from running from the whole disturbing scene. "Let's go. She's going to sleep for a while after all that excitement and the ambrosia cocktail Wilfrin gave her."

"Yes. You could tell what's in it?"

I crossed the room in two angry strides. "She practically reeks of it. Do they know what that is? What it can do? She may be deprived of her death rest, sent to a final sleep, if they use it too much."

"They claim everything is perfectly calibrated to each guest."

I turned back from the door and allowed the ridge on the handle to bite into my hand. "Guest? Is that what they're calling the poor Fae stuck here?"

"That's what your grandmother calls them." He knocked on the door. "Wilfrin, please let us out now."

The sound of a lock being turned preceded the door being opened. "You locked us in?"

"It's for safety, in case she overpowers you and tries to escape."

I shook my head. "In this place? She wouldn't get very far."

Wilfrin scowled at Ellerin. "You'd be surprised."

He led us out the way we came...I think. I fumed until we'd gotten out past the iron gates and walked up the alley that had led us to the asylum. When I got far enough away that the iron no longer felt like it stung in my bones, I wheeled around and put a hand on Ellerin's chest.

"What was the point of that? Why did you bring me to see her? You've ruined my memories!"

"That *was* the point. Come along, Princess. I'll explain."

6

LAWRENCE

Rhys and I followed the Graves party's footsteps through the woods. It appeared that at some point, Reine had taken a spill. Hope that she was okay flashed through my mind before I could catch it. I didn't wish her ill—I just didn't want to care. Fae were fickle creatures, and whatever happened, she could take care of herself. She'd demonstrated that she would do that above everything else.

At some point, the fifth set of footprints disappeared. Rhys and I searched the ground around the path, but the forest floor wouldn't give up its secrets.

"What could it be?" I scratched around in the pine needles as though they somehow hid the secret to the creature's identity and intent.

"Another Fae, most likely." Rhys looked around, then up. "Not a flier, though. That would've been the easiest way to follow them without being detected, unless they didn't care."

"So which Fae can disappear?" I shivered, although I couldn't tell whether the feeling of someone's gaze on the back of my neck was real or my own imagination. Still, could it be watching us even now? What did it want?

Rhys shrugged. "Many of them. What? Don't have your complete taxonomy filled out?"

I growled before I could stop myself. Yes, I'd prided myself on being an expert on the Fae to my human colleagues. It had greatly annoyed Reine when we'd first met. Apparently, I hadn't been expert enough—she'd still surprised me when she'd made a bargain with a rogue vampire against my expressed wishes and betrayed my trust by keeping a big secret from me.

Rhys grinned. "Better keep a lid on that animal side of yours. It could get you in big trouble here."

My inner gargoyle wanted to rip his head off in order to wipe the condescending smile from his face, and I stifled it. I needed to find John and Kestrel and get them out of here, away from Fae intrigue. We could keep working on Kestrel's unsettled witch powers at home.

Home... It felt like a long way away, although I knew Faerie and Earth paralleled and touched in different places.

We continued to follow the remaining footsteps until we reached a jagged wall made of some sort of reflective dark rock. Not glass, the mineral told me.

I laid a hand on it. "It's obsidian."

Rhys smacked my arm so I lost contact. "What did I tell you about touching things?" He darted aside as I lunged at him out of instinct, and I stumbled, suddenly out of breath from the effort.

The dizziness passed as soon as it had come. "What did you do to me?"

"Nothing, mate. Just shut up."

With a pop of displaced air, a creature about the size of a German Shepherd appeared. It looked like the older, alcoholic cousin of a Smurf.

"Well, well, well." It pushed black wire-rimmed glasses farther up the bridge of its nose. "What have we here?"

"Gatekeeper." Rhys bowed. I did as well, although I didn't know why. It irked me that I had to trust Rhys.

"Ah, the scarred prince. And a gargoyle. Haven't seen one of you in these parts in several hundred years. Maybe a thousand."

Rhys straightened and spoke more deferentially than I thought he was capable of. "Greetings, fair keeper of the Gate of Cruaidh. We seek a party of travelers, one of whom is my sister."

"I know where they are." The creature checked its ledger. "They entered the city not long ago. However, you know you may not."

Rhys didn't react with disappointment. "What bargain may I make you?"

Oh, right, a bribe. That made sense. I thought through what I had brought, but I couldn't think of anything this strange being would want.

"No bargain, Prince. You know the rules. No disfigured Fae in the cities. No gargoyles, period. It's very inconvenient when they die."

"But this is Cruaidh, not Lorien. It's the bastion of chaos."

"And chaos births its own rules. You may not enter."

I stepped forward. "What do you mean, it's inconvenient when we die?"

Rhys glared at the gatekeeper, then spoke with reluctance. "It's part of the old magic coming from the traditional enmity between our people. There are things in Faerie designed to entrap and slay gargoyles."

"It would've been nice of you to mention that before I agreed to come."

"You would've come anyway, for the humans."

"Human," the blue creature corrected. "The male witch is human. The girl, though..."

Could the gatekeeper know the source of Kestrel's strange power issues? I had to ask, "Do you know what she is?"

"No." Rhys made a flat waving motion with his hands. "Even if you do, don't tell us. Not until we settle on terms."

"Alas, I wish I did know, because I can tell the answer is greatly desired by you, gargoyle. No, only that she is something very interesting."

I decided to capitalize on its interest in Kestrel. "If you let us in, I'll find a way to let you know once we figure it out."

It practically doubled over with wheezing laughter. "It is only a matter of academic interest to me, desperation to you, so no. Entrance denied." It winked out, and the air stirred around us to fill the vacuum it left.

"Well, Hades, that's not how I thought that would go." Rhys clenched his fists and turned to me. "You have to let me do the talking. Otherwise, you're going to end us both in a big steaming pile of trouble. You don't know the rules here, and no matter how smart you are, you're going to get caught by them."

"Right, sorry. But I need you to be honest with me as well, like about what danger I'm in, especially since I can't change back." That scared me enough. The longer I remained in gargoyle form, the harder it would be to will myself to return to human, and gargoyles who stayed in true form for too long would turn to stone. I had to find Kestrel and John, and I had to do it soon, for all our sakes.

Rhys seemed to think the same. "You can't stay here for long. Neither can Kestrel. She's attracting too much interest, and here that's never a good thing."

"Right. So now what? Do I attempt to fly over the wall?"

"No, you won't be able to. We'll have to figure out another way in."

"Or wait for them on the other side."

"If we have to go all the way around, we'll end up a day or more behind them, and we'll never catch up."

Something moved in the corner of my peripheral vision, and I turned to see the shadows writhing and coalescing into a man-shaped form. This time I didn't stifle the rumble in my chest and throat. Rhys put a hand on my arm.

"Wait."

The darkness solidified, and then lightened into the form of a blond-haired, dark blue-eyed man with features that belonged on a Hollywood romantic lead. The last thing to appear was a harp in his hand.

"Well met, friends," he said and struck a clear note. The tone made the air around me vibrate at a frequency that almost calmed my inner gargoyle enough for me to change back to human.

Rhys waved a hand through the air, and the sound disappeared. "None of that trickery here, Bard. Who are you? Why have you been following my sister?"

7

REINE

lthough my anger at Ellerin simmered under the surface, I had no choice but to furl my wings and follow him through the long, brick alley and the maze of streets that had led us to the "asylum." I shook my head. The word had quickly lost its meaning in the Earth realm, where such places of refuge had turned into their own prisons and, for some, another form of slavery. At least now I knew what had happened to Olred. My mother's explanation had never sat right with me. Or was my mind trying to cast its own obfuscation spell, one woven of false memory that would buffer me against self-recrimination? I should have questioned, but I had only been a child accustomed to listening to and obeying—and believing—the adults around me.

We emerged from the warren of narrow lanes to the boulevard that led through the center of Cruaidh. Perhaps our visit to the asylum had put me in a Victorian mood to notice the Gothic architecture, or perhaps the dark Fae queen, Lilith, had a thing for it. Ellerin led me to a teahouse, where lettering on the sign outside read, "The Purple Karma."

My grumpiness emerged in a muttered question. "What does that even mean?"

Ellerin, apparently unfazed by my mood, chuckled. "You'll see."

We followed a young male Fae dressed as a human goth through a courtyard and into the building itself, a narrow blood-red brick structure with painted cream-colored windows, the sills of which had been textured to look like the paint had been applied, partially scraped off, and applied again. Black petunias waved at us from Fae iron window-boxes. By the time we reached our table in an alcove off the main dining room half-hidden by thick—what else?—velvet curtains, I found myself hiding my laughter and delight. Whereas I'd seen plenty of humans pretending to be Fae and imitating what they thought we were and how we decorate, this was the first time I'd seen Fae interpret human culture.

"Interesting choice of period." I opened the menu booklet, but the pages showed nothing. "Wait, mine is blank."

"'Tis the concept, fair maiden." Another goth Fae, this one in a tuxedo with a half-mask over one side of his face, flicked the curtains back and snapped his fingers. The dark purple wax candles in the seven-pointed candelabra in the center of the table lighted.

"A restaurant where we can't eat?" I became aware of the gnawing in my stomach that the apple I'd consumed earlier had only delayed, not satisfied.

"No, of course not. The chef will fix the meal he feels you deserve." He whisked the not-menus away, and Ellerin sat back against the black faux-leather banquette with a grin.

"You're enjoying this way too much. What in the world is this? Since when do Fae have restaurants with kooky concepts? Hades, since when do Fae have restaurants?"

"Since they've been going back and forth to the Earth realm more often. They're curious and interested and tired of hiding."

"But if the humans were to find out about us, what we can *do*..." I dared not speak aloud the fears that had been drilled into me since I could understand them.

"They're going to learn eventually."

The curtains parted to reveal the masked Fae with a tray, upon which sat two drinks in tall glasses. He grinned and set down one that was ruby-red and fizzy in front of me. Ellerin got what looked like a glass of iced tea.

I sniffed mine, and the bubbles tickled my nose. "What is it?"

"A concoction our mixologist calls Vampire's Kiss." He winked and disappeared before I could ask... What? How could they know I'd allowed a vampire to feed from me? No, I wouldn't give away that kind of information.

I arched an eyebrow at Ellerin.

"Sometimes secrets aren't so secret, Reine."

I sipped the drink through the straw. It had just the right mix of sweet, sour, and fizz. And definitely the bite of something intoxicating. I placed it on the table far enough away that I'd have to make an effort to reach for it.

"What did you get?"

He held up his. "I believe it's called Wanderer's Punch."

The server set a trio of plates on the table. "Right you are, Wanderer. And these are Traveler's Tapas. Roast beef with Roquefort on toast with balsamic-roasted Vidalia onions, which Chef refers to as a Gargoyle Slider." He paused for us to laugh. Ellerin did. I managed a faint smile, but I couldn't do more around the stab in my heart. And knowing that my pain could only be a faint echo of what I knew I'd put Lawrence through made my cheeks redden.

"Ahem." The server didn't look nearly as jovial now. "That's a Broken Heart Salad, or endive with beet, goat cheese, and sherry vinaigrette. It tastes bittersweet and a little funky." Now he frowned directly at me. "And the third is a Royal Honey

Trap, or Brie baked in phyllo with honey, thyme, lavender, and some sort of fruit. You'll have to guess what got trapped this evening."

After he left, I pressed my hands between my knees to make them stop trembling. "Purple Karma, indeed. Why do people, er, Fae come here?" I felt like I'd gotten a lecture along with my food. Who was the chef?

"Some see it as a sort of confession, where they can get absolution for their mistakes. Others bring their partners hoping that something will be revealed." Ellerin picked up one of the Gargoyle Sliders and took a bite. "Regret never tasted so good. You should have some."

My stomach flipped at the thought of eating, but I picked up the other one and took a bite. Ellerin was right—sharpness, smoothness, and a sweet crunch took some of the edge off my shame. I guessed that was part of the magic of the place. The other dishes proved to be equally as delicious, if guilt-inducing. Good gods, what would dessert be? I'd never been one to turn down sweets, but I might have to make an exception here.

As soon as we were finished and our drinks refilled, Pomegranate Punch for me and Traveler's Tea for Ellerin, the next course came out. The plate the server set in front of me had a puff pastry filled with a creamy chicken-mushroom combination. It smelled heavenly, but I frowned at the young goth Fae.

"Chicken a la Reine? Really? That's a bit on the nose, don't you think?"

He shrugged, but the corner of his mouth twitched as he set down a steak and crisped vegetables in front of Ellerin. "I only bring the food, lady. This is Unsettled Venison with Toasted Roots."

This time it was Ellerin's turn to raise an eyebrow at the server's back.

Relief that I wasn't the only target made me giggle—goodness, what was in those drinks? "Toasted roots, huh? I guess the chef couldn't come up with anything else that referenced burned bridges." Then the recollection of our time in the asylum sent a shiver through me. "Is that what Olred meant?"

He cut and stuck a piece of venison in his mouth instead of answering me, so I turned to my food as well. Even if the dish called me cowardly, the chicken and mushrooms had been cooked perfectly, and the salty, crispy pastry balanced the creamy sauce. I could see why Fae came here. While we technically couldn't lie to others, we did very well with deceiving ourselves. If we were going to look in the figurative mirror and uncover uncomfortable truths about ourselves, we might as well have a good meal while doing it. That still didn't explain why Ellerin had chosen this place for us, so I asked him.

"Because I need you to see who you truly are, what you've become, for your progress on your journey."

"How so?" Perhaps I should have been offended or concerned, but the food and cocktails had settled into my stomach and radiated through my body in a happy, full glow.

"You're not the same Fae you were when you left, and your realm needs you."

I snorted, and then cringed away from the curious looks the sound had brought from other diners. When they returned to their food—and perhaps their own troubles—I said, "Really, Ellerin, you're hilarious with the fantasy movie talk, but I'm tired. It's been a hellish day, and you need to be straight with me."

"I'm trying to. You asked why we visited the asylum. That was the condition of the gatekeeper letting us into the city, to show you that your memories about Faerie aren't accurate, and indeed, what you'd been taught never had been true."

"Great." I put my face in my hands. "I need chocolate to deal with this. Go ahead and tell whatshisname to bring the Bitter Memories Mousse out."

"How did you know?" The server put a beautiful cut glass

dish that turned the candlelight into rainbows along its crystalline sides. Inside, strawberry, chocolate, and vanilla mousse swirled under a small mountain of whipped cream, topped with chocolate shavings. He also placed a small silver pot on the table, from which came a wonderful, earthy aroma.

"What's that?" I asked.

He gave me a strange look. "Coffee, of course."

"No clever name?"

He poured some in each of our cups and winked. "We had a small revolt over that. Coffee, being the elixir that fuels us all, did not deserve to be made light of."

"That makes sense."

Ellerin didn't have dessert. Instead, he poured a clear, amber liquid into his coffee before fixing it. "I told them you're the one with the sweet tooth."

"Thanks." The flavor and texture of the mousse had the same satisfying and magical characteristics of the rest of the meal, and the coffee woke my brain up from the fog that had tried to settle over it. "So why is it important for my memories to have been ruined?"

"Because you're the one the rest of the Fae have pinned their hopes on."

"To do what? I'm just trying to be let in, not rule the realm." I brandished my spoon like a scepter and giggled. Okay, maybe the alcohol hadn't worked out of my system yet.

He rubbed his right hand over his face, and for the first time, he looked old and tired. "That was another reason I brought you here. In the past century, the human realm has exploded with technology. At first, the Fae ignored it, thinking the humans would destroy themselves with nuclear bombs."

"I did, too." I had to put the spoon down in spite of only being half-finished with my dessert at the recollection of the panic I'd felt any time the human governments seemed to be moving in that direction.

"That must have been terrifying."

Something small in my chest, a piece of the wall I tended to put up between my heart and others, loosened at his sympathetic remark. "While other supernatural creatures could retreat to other realms or their prepared bunkers, I knew Rhys and I would be left out to fend for ourselves, and I had no idea what would happen to our powers. Or if we'd be captured and exploited in our weakened state."

"I'm sorry." He sounded like he meant it, too.

"It's not your fault."

But he didn't argue. "Anyway, once technology got to be more useful than destructive—and yes, I know that point could be argued—Fae took more notice. It's not like they're completely isolated here. We still get the occasional human visitor who comes through a circle or portal that hasn't been closed properly. And once a young Fae got to play with a smartphone..."

"I can only imagine. We can't resist addictive things." I resumed the consumption of my dessert. Sugar had always been my weakness. Thank goodness for high Fae metabolisms.

"And as it turns out, Fae are very good at playing Angry Birds. But the queens are stuck in the old days and have been moving from tradition to tyranny."

I looked up. "Watch what you're saying. That's treason."

"We're safe here, at least to a point. You'd be surprised how many Fae feel this way."

"And my mother?" I had to ask.

"She's been struggling to maintain a balance, as has Princess Desdemona here in the dark Fae lands."

"Did she ever have a daughter?" I had wondered since I left if I had a counterpart. Faerie liked its symmetry, and it had been highly unusual for the dark Fae crown princess to have only produced sons until my exile.

"Yes, but she's been missing for many years."

"Interesting... But you still haven't gotten to what you want me to do."

"That's going to require more time."

"What do you— Oh!"

I looked to where Ellerin's gaze had tracked and saw someone in the uniform of the hotel we were staying at whispering to the host, who inclined his head toward us. The young male Fae, whom I recognized from the front desk, came over to us, followed by our server.

The hotel Fae bowed. "I'm sorry to interrupt your dinner, Wanderer, Princess, but there's a problem with the human girl you brought with you. Please come with me."

Our server waved his hand, and the rest of my dessert boxed itself up. "Here you go. Wanderer, the bill is on your tab."

Before I could ask why Ellerin had a tab at the place, we rushed into the purple Faerie twilight.

8

REINE

Sir Raleigh met us at the door of the hotel in his cat form. He let out a low, "Mrrrrowrl" and lashed his tail.

"Yes," Ellerin replied.

"You can understand him?" I followed him and the grimalkin through the lobby and up the stairs.

"You can't?" he shot over his shoulder.

"Well, sometimes, but not like you. He's good at getting his point across."

"Then maybe that's all you need."

Sir Raleigh let out a huff, and I almost echoed it. Did he feel as frustrated with my inability to communicate with him as I did? And why couldn't I if Ellerin could? A unique bond often existed between a Fae who summoned the creature and the creature itself, and Sir Raleigh did seem to be bonded to the older Fae. That brought up yet more questions I thought I knew the answer to, but knowing the answers didn't necessarily mean I knew the reasons behind them.

The cat led us to the room where we'd left Kestrel and John, and we found a distraught John standing in the hallway.

"What's wrong?" I asked.

"It's Kestrel. She's glowing."

"Let me in."

He stepped aside, and Sir Raleigh and I entered the room. A soft golden radiance filled the space, and the source of it sat on the bed reading a book.

I didn't want to interrupt her before I could catalog my own reactions, so I remained silent for a moment. So did Sir Raleigh. It was time for a Fae medical exam.

First, I inhaled to catch the scent of the glow. An assortment of *warm* floated through my nostrils—fresh-baked bread, sun on marble, the sharp tang of tomato stem when you pick the fruit at high summer, humid tropical storm. The latter led me to the feel of it—a roiling turbulence underneath in spite of its steadiness, like the depths of the ocean or wind in a hurricane. It all had the sense of something that had been contained for a long time struggling to be set free.

Kestrel looked up from her book. "Are you coming in or not? You're creeping me out just standing there and staring at me."

"Nice glow." I approached and noticed how the energy seemed to swirl around her the closer I got. I placed a hand on her forehead. "No temperature, though. When did this start?"

"About half an hour ago." She looked down at her book. "I didn't do anything to start it, and I can't make it stop."

"Are you sure you didn't do anything?"

"Well, I may have tried scrying in the mirror. It didn't work, but this happened."

I filed that piece of data away for later.

"Do you remember when we were attacked by the black lightning bugs?"

She nodded.

"Well, your eyes were glowing, but then they stopped. This may be something that happens when you're in physical contact with magical objects or creatures."

"But not Sir Raleigh."

"He's different."

"And not you."

"Maybe it has something to do with engaging with the magic. Or trying to."

"I did feel like I should be able to do something about the bugs, but I couldn't figure out what." She huffed. "And you were going to tell me about my glowing eyes when?"

I sat on the bed beside her and took her hand. The energy of the glow ran beneath the surface of her skin and made my skin tingle where we touched. "When we had a moment. Like now. I didn't want to alarm your father."

She rolled her eyes. "He's constantly alarmed. When I started glowing and couldn't make it stop, he ran downstairs and tried to get some of the hotel employees to help."

"Well, one of them did come and get us." Probably more to shut John up than to help Kestrel. I couldn't imagine that a glowing guest would cause much alarm unless they were about to explode, and Kestrel wasn't.

"Can you make it stop? I mean, it's kind of cool, but it's going to be hard to sleep with the light behind my eyelids, and I'm guessing I'll need my rest."

She put on a brave face, but the quaver in her voice let on how scared she was.

"Give me both your hands." She did, and I sandwiched them between mine. "Good, now close your eyes and tell me what it feels like to you."

She complied and wrinkled her nose. "Ugh, like an electrical current, but alive, like a million electric eels swimming under my skin." She opened her eyes, and this time fear shone through them. "That's not helping."

"Shhh, it's okay. Close your eyes again and see if you can catch hold of one of them."

"How? You have my hands."

"Yes, that's the point. You need to use your internal hands, or if you want to continue the sea creature analogy, one of your spiritual tentacles."

"That's gross." But she relaxed and smiled. "Okay, I'm reaching out, trying to snare one. They don't want to be caught, but... Oof! Now what? It's wiggling?"

"What is its name?" I had a suspicion, but I couldn't manipulate her into giving me the answer I expected.

"Oh... They're changing colors. They all have names. This one is wind."

The air in the room stirred, and she tried to draw her hands back, but I held them fast.

"All right, let wind go. See if you can find one named light."

"There are too many."

I pressed her hands between mine. "You can find it. It's going to be right at the surface. You're an octopus. Swim toward the glow and you'll find it."

"Okay..." Her skepticism came through her voice and her hands, although she complied, her brows close in concentration. "All right, there it is. Argh, it's big and slippery, but I've got it."

"Tell it you see it. Thank it. You'll call upon it when needed."

The room went doubly dark as the glow blinked out to be replaced by its after-image. Now the only light in the room came from the streetlamp outside, which cast flickering orange across the walls and furniture.

Kestrel opened her eyes and slumped back. "I did it."

"Yes, you did." I squeezed her hands again and let go.

"But what does it mean?"

The words, "That you're unusually powerful for a human," tried to cross my tongue, but I wouldn't let them. What did it mean that she had all these abilities simmering below the surface? She couldn't be an ordinary witch. So, then what? She wasn't a high Fae, for whom that level and variety of magic would be normal. Could she be the missing daughter of dark Fae, Princess Desdemona? No, she had human parents, and changelings had been outlawed.

Yeah, and Fae paid attention to laws.

She was a mystery, and I could answer honestly without thinking about a way to twist the words. "I don't know yet."

She looked at her hands. "I'm a freak, aren't I?"

"No, you're interesting and special. Which means you're going to be in danger. You're going to need to stick extra close to me. Don't go anywhere without me, Ellerin, or Sir Raleigh."

She nodded, her eyes wide. "I understand. What kind of danger?"

"I don't know yet," I said again. The answers eluded me, and it frustrated me. I looked down and saw the bag on the floor with my dessert in it. "Have you eaten yet?"

"Yes, but I'm hungry again."

"Not surprising. Hang on, I'm going to slip out and order something for you, and then we can have dessert, and I'll give you a present."

"Okay."

"Sir Raleigh, you stay here."

The cat jumped on the bed and curled up on Kestrel's lap. His purr rumbled through the air, and she rubbed his ears.

I walked into the hallway and found John and Ellerin waiting for me. "Ellerin, wait here. I need to have some words with Doctor Graves."

Ellerin's response was an uncharacteristically meek, "Yes, Princess."

"Doctor Princess right now," I replied with a smile to take the sting from my words. "John, follow me."

~

JOHN TROTTED AFTER ME. "Is she all right?"

"Yes, but I need to ask you some questions." We arrived at my room, and I unlocked the door. Everything was as I'd left it, thankfully. I locked the door and put a Quiet spell on the room so no one would overhear us.

John rubbed his left ear. "What sort of questions?"

"Was there anything interesting or unusual about Kestrel's birth?"

"What? No, she had a normal, healthy birth."

"What about afterward? Did she seem to be one way, and then suddenly shift in behavior or demeanor after you put her down for a nap or left her alone?"

"No, not at all. And honestly, Beverly was so protective of her she brought her everywhere, even into the bathroom. She never left either of our sight and slept in the same room with us until she was almost a year old."

I tapped my lips. I was missing something.

John sank to the bed. "You don't really think she's a changeling, do you? She looks just like Beverly did when she was young."

"No, but I had to ask."

He sat there, gazing at his hands, for a whole minute before saying anything. Then he looked up at me, his forehead lined and the corners of his mouth tense. "You're sure the court physician will help us? That we'll find our answers, and Kestrel will be able to claim her magic?"

I sensed another layer to his questions, so I asked, "What are you really worried about, John?"

"My daughter," he snapped immediately, but his brief look to the side gave away the partial lie.

"That's not all, is it?" I decided to approach him as I would a nervous patient who dreaded getting the results of their labs. I sat beside him, not too close. His fear radiated from him like a whine, and underneath, an old wound thrummed like a plucked bass string. "John, I know this is difficult. If there's something you're not telling me about Kestrel, it could hurt her. And all of us."

"I don't know anything with certainty, so I can't say. She's not the only one this would affect, although..." A sigh lifted and dropped his wiry shoulders under the fleece he still wore. White embroidery outlined the letters C, and underneath it, DC, while the P lay hidden after the first C in navy blue thread, a good reminder that this man, this scientist, wouldn't endorse knowledge without proof and also could keep secrets for a long time.

"Then when you're ready, please tell me first. That way I can figure out what to do."

He shook his head. "I thought Ellerin was in charge of this mission."

"He may be, but I'm a Fae princess, so my authority overrules his."

John chuckled like he didn't believe me, but he said, "I need to remember that. To not underestimate you. Lawrence made that mistake, didn't he?"

The gargoyle's name lanced through me. "I've already eaten my feelings about that tonight. Literally, in fact. I'm not discussing him."

John stood. "I could tell something was up, and I know that you hurt him. It was in his voice when he called to let me know the soul-eater had been defeated. Know this—I don't trust Ellerin, and I don't trust you. I'm here to help Kestrel, and I'm not going to reveal my past secrets and pain so you can use them against me later." He walked out, and the door slammed behind him.

"Was that really necessary?" I asked the tree beside the bedside table. It shook its leaves at me, but I didn't know what it meant. My backpack tumbled to the floor from where I'd set it on the antique bureau, and the two wrapped journals spilled out. "Oh, right. Thanks. That's what I originally came in here for." I closed my eyes, searching. My sense that helped me identify and find other Fae, which I affectionately referred to as my Fae-dar, found Ellerin in the hallway outside Kestrel's room.

"*John's upset,*" I told him via secret conversation. "*Please head him off. I still have important business with Kestrel.*"

"*You ask a lot, Princess.*"

"*I know you've dealt with worse.*"

"*You don't know what you're asking.*"

Of all the times for him to be difficult... "*Just please do it.*"

"*Your wish is my command.*"

That last thought came through with a full dose of male Fae irritation. Well, screw the males. I'd had enough of their attitude, and that included Lawrence. I grabbed the journals and headed up to Kestrel's room.

9

LAWRENCE

Rather than answering Rhys's question, the ridiculously handsome Fae looked us both over with half-lidded eyes. He didn't seem to be concerned about being outnumbered. He moved to pluck another string on his harp, but Rhys snapped his fingers, and a thick leather glove appeared on the other Fae's hand.

"No magic, Bard."

A deep sigh, then a sulky, "Very well." With a shake of his hand, the glove disappeared.

Rhys made an exasperated sound. "I am a prince of Faerie, and I command you to tell us who you are and why you're following us."

"Oho, pulling out the authority now, are we? Must feel good after so long."

Something about the Fae's tone and way of speaking struck a familiar chord—no pun intended. "Keep him talking," I mouthed to Rhys, whose face had turned an unbecoming dark red, his scar a white line against it.

"You must answer my questions under pain of torture."

Another finger snap, and a circle of flames sprung up around the mystery Fae.

"Flames, really? How classic of you. And pedestrian." He moved to stomp the edge of the circle, but drew his foot back with a hissed, "More than I expected." He straightened, lifted his chin, and looked at us like we were the ones trapped in a circle of fire. "Gentlemen, we seem to have come to an impasse."

Rhys crossed his arms. "Not really. You tell us who you are, and I'll think about letting you go."

"That's rich coming from a mutilated former Fae prince."

Rhys went to lunge for him, and I held him back with more effort than it should have cost me in gargoyle form. The Fae prince was stronger than he looked, and Reine had said something about her being the stronger of the two.

That only added to her appeal, dammit. I wondered what she would think of the situation. She'd probably be amused. She'd also know who...

The Fae's manner of speaking and costume clicked together in a satisfying deduction. "Troubadour. You're Troubadour, the dark Fae who was helping Reine."

Rhys stopped wriggling in my grasp, and I let him go. He rubbed his shoulder where I had held him and scowled. "Damn, you're a strong brute."

"Well, strong, anyway. I'm still me, not a brute."

Troubadour had been studying us from inside his fiery prison and nodded. "Ah, you're the gentleman scientist gargoyle." He sniffed with nose wrinkled in disdain. "Not sure what she sees in you." His next gesture—running his hand through his thick blond hair—made me want to punch him.

"Better a gargoyle than a vain Fae. What do you want with us?"

"Well, I suppose you won't let me out of this silly fire thing until I tell you. Very well— Oh! Watch out."

Something solid landed on my back, and I found myself in

a tussle with a creature that seemed made of claws, teeth, and wet fur. The stench of bait bucket that had been left in the sun too long washed over me and made me fight my own gag reflex.

"Water wolves!" Rhys yelled. Flashes of sky-blue light illuminated the clearing as Rhys engaged them.

Troubadour's bored voice cut through the chaos. "I could help you with this, but you'll have to let me go."

I shook the wolf off my back, and it left a stinging, slimy residue across my shoulders. It shook its shaggy head, which resembled a furred eel face, and lunged at me. Its nose met my fist with a satisfying crunch, and it let forth a gurgling howl and ran off.

Another wave of them came, and Rhys snapped his fingers, releasing Troubadour. The Fae bard struck a note on his harp, and the wolves—about a dozen of them—stopped and sniffed the air.

"Don't just stand there," Troubadour ground out from behind his performer's smile. "Take care of them."

I grabbed the two nearest me and growled as their fur stung my hands, but I bashed their heads together. Rhys shot a funnel of his light blue magic at the four in front of him, making them disappear, but then staggered back and supported himself on a tree. One ran for him, and I kicked it, impaling it on a shard of the obsidian wall, against which they'd trapped us. I shook my hands as the remaining five retreated, then circled us. The waning light of the day reflected in their copper-colored eyes.

"What is that stuff?"

Troubadour wrinkled his nose. "Water wolf slime. Toxic to Fae. Not pleasant for you, I imagine."

"Great." I attempted to wipe my hands on the grass, but what little dew remained had been stomped on and didn't provide much relief. The wolves edged closer.

"Allow me, gentlemen." Troubadour lifted his harp.

"I can't banish many more," Rhys panted. "We need to get out of here."

"Can you fly?" Troubadour asked Rhys.

"No. My wings haven't emerged yet."

"Wait, you have wings?" I gave mine a rustle with a side glance at Troubadour. "I could carry the two of you, but probably not far."

The air around Troubadour shimmered, and leathery, bat-like wings appeared. I couldn't help scowling when he grinned at me and said, "Then it's fortunate I know a safe place nearby. Do you trust me?"

I wanted to say, "Hell, no," but a water wolf we couldn't see howled, and the others joined in. There were now a lot more than five, and their hungry growls rumbled through the air, making my own stomach clench in panic.

Rhys and I looked at each other, and Rhys' tone took on an uncharacteristic resignation. "What other choice do we have?"

Troubadour's smile faded as another howl started a chorus. "Touché. But I can't carry you. It will have to be the gargoyle."

"Lawrence, do this." Rhys cupped his hands, blew into them, and water appeared. "You can call upon your elements here."

"Good to know." I mimicked him, and my hands filled from some unseen source with cool liquid. I used it to wash, and with Rhys' help, removed the slime from my back as best I could. He snapped his fingers, and leather gloves appeared on his hands "in case of residue."

"Makes sense." I knelt so he could climb on my back. Again, his weight surprised me. Between him and the two packs I carried, one in each hand, this would be a workout.

I can handle it. My inner gargoyle's voice sounded a lot like mine, but sometimes I didn't want to believe it was me. Other times, like now, I wanted to own its confidence.

Troubadour didn't wear a watch, but he looked at his wrist. "When you're ready, gentlemen?"

"Lead the way."

With a couple of powerful downstrokes, he lifted off. I crouched, then jumped and flew after him. When I looked back, the wedge-like faces of the water wolves stared up at us. One jumped and snapped at the air—a warning they'd be waiting if we fell?

Troubadour led us straight up the wall, which curved inward, instead of over the woods. The higher he flew, the more my lungs burned with the exertion of hauling Rhys and the thinness of the air. One would think that an environment with large, winged creatures would have better oxygenation. I made a mental note to jot that down when I could. I'd brought a notebook to record my impressions so I wouldn't be caught unprepared when I next encountered a Fae in Atlanta. Which I hoped would be never. The last one had left me with a bruised heart...

...and the answer to the question that had plagued me since childhood—who had killed my father. The murderer now rode on my back.

It would be easy to slip him off, let him tumble to the shards below...

I shook my head, eliciting an, "Oy, what's that about?" from behind me. Rhys tightened his grip. Unfortunately, so did my inner gargoyle, which relished having been released for so long. Troubadour turned and headed straight toward the wall.

"What are you doing?" I shouted.

"Trust me!"

He disappeared, and rather than trusting him, I put my faith in my inner gargoyle sense that the rock would welcome me. As for what became of Rhys...

10

REINE

I made a quick call to room service, then returned to Kestrel's room. She stood behind one of the two, large, wingback chairs that faced away from the windows and gazed down to the street below. I squeezed around the other chair, upon which Sir Raleigh had curled up, to join her and followed her gaze. John and Ellerin faced each other on the sidewalk. We were too high up and the window glass too thick and enchanted for me to hear them, but from their gestures and postures, I could tell they argued.

I groaned. "What is it with those two?"

Kestrel shook her head. "Why are they even out there? I thought you were going to be my dad when you came in."

"I, ah, asked Ellerin to keep your dad busy for a few minutes. This wasn't what I meant." Perhaps it had been a bad idea to send Ellerin after John considering John's mood when he'd left my room. If he didn't trust me, he definitely wasn't going to trust Ellerin, not even to grab a drink. Hades, I'd half-hoped they could...what? Bond? At least come to some sort of understanding.

"Why?" Kestrel turned toward me, and the tightness around

her eyes showed her fatigue. "I'm ready for sleep. It's been a weird day." She yawned and rubbed her eyes with her right index finger and thumb. "Weird week."

"Come on." I led her around the chair she'd been standing by and sat in the one opposite. The tree behind each of us brightened its lights, but not overly much.

Sir Raleigh gave her an annoyed look but jumped down before she plopped on the other chair.

Kestrel yawned. "This is comfy. I could sleep right here."

"Not before you do some homework." I placed the wrapped journals side-by-side on the table between us. Sir Raleigh stood on his hind legs and batted at the corner of one. I shooed him away. "Pick one."

She leaned over the side of the chair and looked at them. "What are they?"

"You'll see. Just choose one."

"All right." She picked up the one on the left. "Can I open it?"

"Yes."

She squinted at the brown paper, which I now saw had a watermark. "It's from Aria's shop."

"Yes, she helped me."

Kestrel raised her eyebrows but didn't ask more. I guessed she knew her friend enough not to question the actions of a powerful witch. I still pondered some of the things she'd said to me when I'd gone to buy the journals.

Kestrel didn't tear the paper open, but instead un-taped and unfolded the corners, slowly revealing the red and gold diamond pattern on the journal inside. She folded the paper once she'd removed it. "I know this is silly, but I don't want to let go of something from home."

"I understand." How long had I held on to my wand from Faerie even though it turned out to be weakening me? I doubted the paper would do something so nefarious to her.

"So... A journal. What do you want me to do with it?"

"Record your impressions of Faerie, what stood out most to you. Definitely your magical experiences like with the glow. It will be good information for High Court Physician Caduceus."

"His name is really Caduceus? Like the snakes around the pole medical symbol thingy?"

"Some things cross worlds." I smiled and handed her a pen. "Now start writing. Oh, and dessert is on the way. You can go to bed after you do your homework and eat something. I suspect your father won't be long."

"What's in the other one?"

"Another journal." I stood and picked up the wrapped parcel.

"What's it for? My dad?"

"No..." I looked down at it. "It's for me." I touched the paper and made it disappear, having it reappear folded with Kestrel's on the table. I looked down at the blue journal, the moon and stars embossed in silver on it and reflecting in a lake. When I'd picked it out, the scene had been beautiful, but now the lake appeared to harbor something deadly. With a shiver, I wondered what Rhys was up to. I attempted to halt my brain before it went in the direction of Lawrence's activities at the moment, but without success. I hoped he was at his house with a glass of good wine trying to distract himself from all the weird stuff that had happened. That I had dragged him into.

"It's beautiful."

"Do you like this one better?"

She wrinkled her nose. "No. It's lovely, but it's cold. And there's something about the lake..."

"I feel it, too. Perhaps I'll go downstairs and write in it and see what comes up. By the way, these are bespelled so only you and I can read them. I'll unlock yours for Caduceus when it's time. Even if I'm not there, you can still read it to him if necessary."

"Why wouldn't you be there?"

I looked down at the journal's cover, and it again gave me a sense of foreboding. "I'm not sure, but it's not a bad idea to be prepared for anything, even the worst."

ONCE WE RETURNED to my room, Sir Raleigh wasted no time in choosing the fluffiest bed pillow for himself and curled into a circle of comfy catness. He made it too easy to forget his grimalkin nature. Or did he, like I, feel like he straddled two worlds, with the influence of each fighting for his identity?

I shook my head and turned my attention to the journal. How should I start? I pondered the question, my quill-shaped ballpoint pen poised over the page. *Once upon a time?* No, too trite. *Herein are the words and observations of Princess Reine, daughter of Maeve, granddaughter of Tatiana, queen of the Light Court of Faerie* (with lots of flourishes, of course)? Too pretentious. Plus, it made me feel the weight of my heritage and responsibility, which caused the sensation of being overdressed in my little hotel room. All Fae-ed up and nowhere to go.

Ellerin's secret conversation broke into my thoughts. *"Dear Fae, you* have got *to be finished with Kestrel. I can't take much more of this."*

"We're done." Guilt stabbed through me at forgetting the favor he was doing for me. Luckily, I'd only just returned to my room and decided to practice what I preached with regard to record-keeping.

Instead of a fancy preamble, I wrote a date at the top right corner of the first lined page and started with, *I got up way too early today, hungover from sad dreams and sour regret over the hurt I'd caused someone else. Was that why I decided to allow the humans to accompany me into Faerie at great cost to myself? Not that I couldn't afford it, but why would I want to? Am I going soft? Or have I continued to go human?*

A knock on my door made me look up and close the journal, grateful that my train of thought had been interrupted. Was that why the journal had decided to come with me, that like Kestrel, I needed to figure out who—or what—I was?

No, I thought as I padded to the door. I was a princess of Faerie. Of that I had no doubt.

"Who's out there?" I asked the shard of obsidian mirror nestled into the door at eye level. It showed me that Ellerin had decided to come for a visit. His red-rimmed eyes told the tale of how he'd been trying to deal with being in John's company.

I opened the door. "To what do I owe this honor? And how much moonflower nectar did you drink?"

"Can I come in?"

I stepped back, and he stumbled by me. The subtle, sweet scents of night flowers and alcohol wafted along with him. I closed the door and followed him to the set of chairs in my room, similar to the ones in Kestrel's. He collapsed into one of them. Sir Raleigh looked up, blinked sleepily, yawned, and settled back down. Ellerin looked like he might follow suit.

"You can't sleep here." Bemused, I sat on the other chair. "You'll get a terrible crick in your neck."

He waved one hand. "I'll be all right. I only needed some sane, logical conversation."

"What do you mean? If John Graves has any faults, it's that he's overly sane and logical. He could make do with some crazy, mix it up a little." Then I shivered, remembering that Faerie had an asylum. "But not too much."

"You're not wrong. But I can't stand the man all the same. He asks too many questions, like a child."

His grumpy tone warned me not to argue, but I couldn't help it. "He's a scientist. That's what they do—ask questions.

Study things. This is a completely new experience for him, so why wouldn't he?"

Ellerin squinted up at me with bleary eyes. "Those weren't the kinds of questions he asked."

"Then what were they?"

"He wanted to know about me. How often I came to the Earth realm. What I did when I was there. How often I'd come to the Atlanta area. I felt like a Fae-damned specimen."

Had I not recently had the conversation with John, Ellerin's complaints wouldn't have meant anything, but now an idea wriggled at the back of my brain. "Is this trip the first time you've seen Kestrel?"

"Yes, of course. And if you were hoping I'd get some answers out of him about her affliction, you're wrong."

"I didn't think you would. I already tried. Was this trip the first time you've seen John?"

Ellerin didn't say anything, just stared at the briar rose pattern on the rug.

"Ellerin?"

What had Aria told me she'd seen? A web tightening its threads around me and those I dared to grow close to. Although the room had been set to the preferred ambient temperature for Fae—seventy-two degrees Fahrenheit—my skin prickled with a chill.

"What are you not telling me?"

He snorted. "Many, many things, most of which you're not meant to know."

"And what of the ones I am? What are you holding back?"

"Nothing of *grave* importance. Trust me, I'm giving you the information you need."

"That is not acceptable." I stood. "I'm going to ask you again, and you're going to answer me. What are you holding back about John Graves? How do you know him before, and what's behind the enmity between you?"

He looked up at me and had the audacity to laugh. "You really think that's going to work."

"Don't make me do this..."

"Don't make you do what? You can't force me to tell you, Princess."

A prickly wave of frustration rose in me. First John and now Ellerin withheld information, and I'd had it. "Ah, but you're forgetting. Although I'm not in the light Fae lands, I have access to all my powers." I took a deep breath and pulled power from the living things around me. They gladly gave it, as they knew I wouldn't deplete them dangerously. Why couldn't I have that kind of trust with my companions?

I drew myself up to my full height, and the weight of an invisible crown settled on my head. My skin glowed with light blue and golden energy, and my wings appeared. I couldn't see them, but I suspected my eyes blazed green.

"As a crown princess of Faerie, I command you, Ellerin the Wanderer, to tell me the answers to the questions I asked. Tell me what your history is with John Graves."

The glow arced from me to him, surrounding him in clear, glowing strands of my signature colors. He opened his mouth again, but only to laugh. With a shrug, he snapped my influence bonds. And kept laughing.

My glow diminished, and astonishment and curiosity swallowed my anger. "Who are you that you can resist a compulsion by a royal high Fae? I outrank you."

He stood and bowed with a flourish, then straightened and replaced his hat. "As I said, there are many things you're not meant to know, at least right now. And if you can't handle that, you may as well turn back. I can show you how to get back to the Earth realm."

"Go back? Are you kidding me?"

"Not at all. As you told John, the Shadowed Path exacts its price from all. Can you handle the uncertainty?"

At least he hadn't gone into a "You can't handle the truth" speech. I swallowed the knot of anxiety that had risen in my throat. I'd faced worse, but I'd always felt in control except when dealing with my mother.

Apparently, my decision to trust Ellerin would have to be made more than once.

"I can handle it. Remember who I am."

The corners of his eyes crinkled as he almost smiled. "I can't forget. Good night, Princess."

He let himself out, and the door clicked closed and locked behind him. I looked at the tree to my right.

"What the Fae was that?"

Of course, it only shook its leaves at me.

I moved to the window and attempted to gather my thoughts. I could be angry at John, then Ellerin, for not being cooperative, stupid males, but I'd lived long enough to know not to waste my energy. Plus, emotion would cloud my judgment. That brought me to my next question—should I trust Ellerin? A part of me I couldn't tease into conscious light knew I shouldn't. He'd shown he had his own agenda. But what could I do? Take the humans and strike out on our own? If the path we traveled had been merely physical, that would have been an option, but the Shadowed Path required a guide.

A faint echo of music drew me out of my reverie. My room overlooked the hotel courtyard, and I looked down to see that a string quartet played in the night.

"Window, allow me to hear the music."

The notes floated through the glass. Brahms, I thought. I had just allowed the sound to relax me when another broke through, stealing any peace I'd found—the howl of a water wolf. I prayed it came from outside the city walls. If they swarmed, it would be a rough night indeed for any travelers. Perhaps staying with Ellerin's guidance for now would be the wisest path.

No matter how much education I'd had in Faerie or the Earth realm, I still struggled with the same questions everyone else did... Would it be safer to face the danger I knew, or the one I didn't? Could there be such thing as too much information?

And, finally, although I was on my way to getting what I wanted, would it be worth the risks I took to get there?

I looked down at the journal, which lay on the table, and for a second, the shadow of what looked like a flying gargoyle crossed the moon.

"No!" But when I picked it up and looked more closely, the image had disappeared. Had I imagined it? What was my mind trying to tell me?

That I should write in the damn journal.

I picked up my pen, skipped a few lines, and wrote, *I knew from the beginning that this mission would be trouble.*

11

LAWRENCE

Darkness swallowed us and the noises of the outside world like the gaping maw of a monstrous being. I half-expected to hear a heartbeat as I followed Troubadour, who glowed with purplish light, through a series of increasingly tight twists and turns that made my stomach clench.

The Fae on my back swore and asked, "What is this, the world's worst video game?"

"Yes, but with just one life."

Again, the words, *Do you trust me?* echoed in my head, but from my inner gargoyle, who loved the flying challenge. I let go of control more than I ever had and let him drive. A buoyant sense of elation and a new sense of welcome from the rock around me almost drowned out the rage that had simmered within for centuries.

We can't hurt him, no matter how much we want to, I reminded myselves. *We need him to find John and Kestrel.*

Troubadour came to a stop in front of a stone face that reflected our images like ghosts in a cloudy black mirror.

The bard Fae grinned. "Final twist. You ready?"

I hovered with some effort. "As long as this is almost over."

"Yep. Fold your wings."

"What?"

"Do as I do. Fold your wings. Otherwise, you can't follow me." He did as he'd suggested and dropped like a stone out of view.

Rhys' voice pitched higher with his panic. "You're not going to do that, are you?" I could tell from our reflections that his skin had taken on a green cast.

I grinned, which looked like a grimace on my gargoyle face, but there was no mistaking the gleam in my eyes. "Hang on."

After a split second of nothing, we dropped. It's entirely possible that Rhys' arms around my neck kept my abdominal organs from escaping through my mouth. There was a moment of regret, a whispered, "Sorry," to anyone I'd wronged in my life, before a cushion of air slowed our descent and set us gently on the ground. Rhys tumbled from my back, landed on all fours in the soft black sand, and threw up. It had been hours since we'd eaten, so not much came up. A whisper of laughter echoed around us, and I strained to see who'd made the sound, but Troubadour's black light and Rhys' blue glow didn't dispel the gloom. My gargoyle sense of the minerals around us told me we stood in a large chamber, the only entrance to which lay above us.

I dropped the packs and patted my belly to make sure everything had returned to its position.

Troubadour frowned down at Rhys, then rolled his eyes. "That one doesn't have a strong stomach, does he? It's no wonder his wings haven't appeared."

"About that..." I reached for my pack, then stopped. I could ask those questions later. "Never mind. Where are we?"

"Under the dark Fae capital of Cruaidh. Welcome to the Cavern of Dark Echoes." Troubadour struck his harp, and the note echoed and grew stronger. As its volume increased, the cave illuminated with metal-ensconced torches, the flames from which reflected in a million crystals of all colors. Rhys, who had finally regained his feet, and I looked around, open-mouthed. The torches remained lit as the note faded away.

When I could tear my gaze away from the beauty above us, I found we stood on an island of dark sand. The rest of the cave's floor shone like the mirror we'd flown by and had several seating areas with furniture ranging from tenth century Turkish rugs and cushions to a circle of leather recliners with an ottoman in the middle.

"What is this place?"

Troubadour walked to the nearest area, a table with antique velvet-upholstered chairs arranged around it. His wings disappeared, and he plopped onto one of the chairs and placed his harp on the table.

"A place of rest and refuge for those who know how to find it and don't mind a little drama to get here."

I ended up carrying over an ottoman I could sit on since my wings wouldn't disappear to accommodate a chair. "You seem good at drama."

"It's a Fae thing."

Rhys prowled around the room and poked and prodded at cushions with his index finger. "This is all human furniture."

"That's how it's remained undetected all these centuries."

Rhys joined us, taking the chair furthest away from Troubadour at the table. "So, who else knows about this?"

"Only a few powerful dark Fae who don't trust our leadership." Troubadour shrugged. "You may get to meet one of them if we hang around long enough, but with Princey here, they may opt not to come out."

"I have a name," Rhys growled. "It's Prince Rhys. Don't forget it."

Troubadour answered his complaint with a bored, "Wouldn't dream of it."

"Gentlemen, please." I didn't need to have to referee a Fae fight, which I imagined would be like a cat fight but not nearly as cute. And as a veterinarian, I never thought cat fights were cute.

My heart still pounded in my throat, so I stood and walked among the furniture to get it to slow. When I glanced back, I saw Rhys watching me.

"You all right?"

"Yeah. I need to cool off after all that hard flying. You're not exactly a light passenger."

At least the primitive part of me had stopped actively plotting Rhys' death, although I sensed it hadn't gone too far underground. It wouldn't as long as I felt in danger, which would be this entire trip. Was that why I couldn't change back to human?

I stopped in front of a leather couch that looked like something I would buy and folded my wings as closely as I could. Then I attempted to lie down on it. One of my wing tips punctured the leather, and I looked over to Troubadour to see if he'd noticed. He hadn't—he and Rhys leaned toward each other and engaged in some sort of debate, which didn't look too hostile, so I turned my attention back to the torn sofa. I removed my wing tip and attempted to align the material so it wouldn't show so much. To my relief, it closed on its own.

"Huh, self-healing furniture. That's handy." I resisted the urge to puncture it with one of my claws to see if it would repair itself again.

"What did you do?" Rhys' tone had the singsong cadence of a parent asking after a naughty child.

And like a boy who'd been caught, I replied, "Nothing."

I gave up trying to arrange myself on the sofa, which wouldn't fit my larger frame, and returned to the table. A rumbling came from my abdomen, reminding me it had been several hours since breakfast, and I'd just had a tough workout. My heart rate still felt elevated, but slower than before, so I sat.

"Do you have anything to eat down here?" I hoped the answer would be yes. After all that, the thought of a protein bar or camping meal didn't appeal in its small amount. I wanted meat, preferably roasted, with nice crusty bread to sop up the juices... *Stop that,* I warned my inner gargoyle. *You can't drive me to distraction with food and then take over to kill Rhys.*

I needed to turn back to human. Otherwise, who knew how long I could keep control?

"Sorry, lads, you're on your own, although..." Troubadour struck a chord this time, and Rhys and I both leaned forward. I know I hoped food would appear. Instead, the cramping in my stomach subsided slightly. Still...

"Thanks, but music didn't soothe the savage beast. Nice try, though." As much as I hated to reveal a weakness, if it could be called that, I continued, "Do either of you know a spell or technique for a stuck shift? I would like to return to my human form and rest, if possible."

Troubadour and Rhys exchanged glances, then shrugged and returned their Fae gazes back to me. I sensed they conferred, possibly using what Reine referred to as "secret conversation."

Rhys shrugged. "Sorry, mate, can't help you. Faerie does strange things to gargoyles."

"Yes, you'd mentioned that. Is there anything else I should be aware of?"

Another silent conversation, at least from my perspective, ensued. Finally, Troubadour set his harp on the table, stood, and said with what I was coming to recognize as his typical dramatic flair, "If you don't tell him, I will. I swear, you high Fae hoard information like it's gold."

"Wait," Rhys sighed. "Fine, I'll tell him." He turned to me. "You can't spend too much time here in Faerie. Our physiology isn't compatible, and so you're not using the air as efficiently as we can. If you ate our food, it wouldn't fuel you like it does us."

"What will happen if I don't leave?"

Troubadour didn't appear at all distressed when he informed me, "You'll waste away to nothing and/or suffocate."

"Did you think it would be a good idea to tell me this before I agreed to come?" I asked Rhys.

"Obviously not. And would it have made a difference?"

"No." I slumped, my wings heavy. "No, it wouldn't have. My best friend and his daughter, my goddaughter, are here and in danger. I need to find them so you can send us all home."

But we were in the pit of a cavern waiting out the night, and I had no idea where they were, only that they followed the Shadowed Path, and who knew how far ahead they were? Then a thought chilled me, wings and all. "Could the water wolves have gotten them?"

No help from the two Fae there. They both shrugged.

Troubadour ran his finger along the carving on his harp. "It's unusual for them to gather this time of year, at least like that. Typically, their swarm is a spring event."

"Wait, what season is it here?"

Rhys snorted. "Isn't it obvious? Late autumn."

"So Faerie is in the Southern hemisphere?" This time I did dig my notebook out of my pack and start to take notes. I ignored how comically small my pen looked in my hand.

"It's nowhere." Rhys gestured around us. "Space and time are more fluid here. It's like a parallel or alternate dimension, but not exactly parallel because this world and yours touch at certain points."

I put my pen down and almost became mesmerized by the twinkling of the flames on the crystals. With a shake of my head, I returned my attention to the two Fae, who looked more annoyed than bemused at my questions. Screw them, they could deal with it. "So, it's more of a quantum physics sort of thing?"

Troubadour frowned, and annoyingly few wrinkles appeared. "A quantum what-sics?"

"Human science." Rhys didn't bother to hide his condescension toward human scientists. "They're still figuring things out."

"They're doing a great job of it, considering they don't have the shortcut of magic. And what's the problem with your wings?"

Both Rhys and Troubadour recoiled, and Rhys snapped, "That's personal, mate!"

I made a note of that as well. It was always good to know what your enemy was sensitive about.

Troubadour strummed his harp, the sound both sweet and eerie as it echoed around the space. The torches dimmed. "We should take advantage of the opportunity to rest."

"Yes." Rhys stalked off and picked a pile of cushions on the far end of the cave. I pulled a protein bar from my pack—again, noting how small it looked, but it was better than nothing. I munched as I finished my notes and my account of the day, including my observations of the two male Fae and their behavior. Reine had been irritated by my treating her as an object of study when we first met. As for these two, I didn't care about their opinions. I knew how they felt about me as a gargoyle, which ranked below humans in Fae estimation.

Troubadour played a lullaby on his harp, and the music didn't bother me. It conferred some sort of civilization and order to a situation that had none. As he played, I flipped back through my journal because I knew I needed to ask him something, but it had fled my brain in the intervening dramatic hours. Then, when I found it, I couldn't believe I'd forgotten it considering how tied up it had been in the issues around the CPDC and my and Reine's becoming connected to each other.

"Hey, Troubadour, can I ask you a question?"

"Hey, gargoyle, it depends on what it is."

"When Reine and I encountered you before, you said you'd

helped to summon the soul-eater. Rather, that you helped a light Fae do so. Who was it?"

Troubadour struck a sour note, and the crystals chimed in with their own discord that shook me to my core.

"I can't tell you."

"Can't or won't?"

He sighed, and for the first time, I believed the sad expression on his face. "Can't. They disguised themselves down to clouding their energy. Powerful Fae can do that."

"But you know it was someone from the Light Court."

"Yes, because only a high-ranking light Fae could have cooperated with me to summon the soul-eater." He stood. "Good night, gargoyle. Rest well."

"I'll try."

I found a different pile of cushions to rest on, far away from Rhys. It seemed I had barely closed my eyes before Troubadour was nudging me awake with his foot.

"Get up, gargoyle. It's almost dawn, and we have to leave."

"What, why?" I shook my head to clear the fog.

"Because the owner of the cave is on her way, and she won't be pleased to see me."

An angry female voice chased the rest of the cobwebs from my brain.

"Troubadour, you useless prince. What in Hades are you doing here? And why do you have a *gargoyle*?"

12

REINE

Ellerin roused us all early the next morning, and we had to eat our breakfasts on the go. Luckily the hotel, used to travelers with all kinds of needs and schedules, accommodated us with easy-to-carry vegetable and egg wraps. Still full from the feast the night before—and the dessert I'd finished while I journaled—I stuck mine in my backpack, intending to eat it later.

"Why are we up and going so early?" Kestrel sounded like a grumpy teenager, and she clutched the takeaway coffee cup in her hand like it held the fuel to life itself. I had to remind myself that although she was twenty and adult in appearance, human children had slow development, although not nearly as much as Fae did.

"Because I said so." Ellerin didn't sound super happy, either. I suspected he still felt the effects of the liqueur he'd been drinking while out with John, who, wisely didn't say anything to Ellerin or Kestrel. I guessed he knew his daughter's moods.

Instead, he dropped back to walk beside me. "Penny for your thoughts?"

I looked over at him. "Why?"

"Because you're the one familiar with this world. Has it changed much since you left?"

We walked through quiet city streets. The morning mist lit by the rising sun gave the mixed architecture a ghostly feel.

"As I told Kestrel, I'd not visited Cruaidh before, so I don't know. I suppose so, though." I thought back to the asylum and the goth-themed restaurant. "This may be different in Lorien, but it seems like the Fae have been more influenced by human culture. It's almost like you're the fairy tales, not us."

John chuckled. "That's an odd thought—us the fairy tales. Wasn't the purpose of those to scare children into good behavior?"

"I suppose so. Or give them a distraction."

"What do you think the purpose of the human tales would be, then?"

We'd reached the walls, and Ellerin motioned for us to be quiet. "I need silence so I can make the key to exit."

Kestrel's head snapped straight from her slumped posture. "You mean people, I mean, Fae, are trapped in here?"

"No, the dark Fae can exit as they please. It's harder for everyone else."

Another way to constrain the enemies of the Light Queen. I didn't voice the thought, but it made me ever more eager to escape this place, this trap within a trap. That was another change—the cooperation between the queens. Could Faerie be in danger from something outside of it? I couldn't think of anything else that could possibly make them work together.

Ellerin murmured a spell in the old Fae tongue, "*Key to the heart of stone, unlock that which remains hidden and render safe passage for those who wander unfettered by land or loyalty on the Shadowed Path.*" The crystal atop his staff glowed golden, and a rumbling sound came from within the wall. A dark crack appeared and expanded so it would be just wide enough for the largest of us to pass through.

"Here we are." Ellerin smiled, and the fact he seemed relieved made me question just how much control and power he had in the dark Fae lands. "Follow me."

As per usual, Ellerin led the way, and Sir Raleigh and I brought up the rear. Before I walked into the just-made entrance, I looked down at Sir Raleigh, who gazed back at me with big, green eyes.

"Is he okay?" I asked, inclining my head toward where Ellerin had disappeared.

Sir Raleigh looked to where I pointed, and his ears flattened, then straightened. A cat shrug?

"Well, might as well follow. We don't want them leaving us behind."

Sir Raleigh twitched his tail, then darted into the cave. I took a deep breath as though I was about to dive into water and followed.

The gloom inside the wall swallowed us all, and the sense of the tons of rock around us pressed in on me. I'd never been claustrophobic, but I'd also never walked through a city wall that emanated the desire to crush and devour me. Apparently, Cruaidh had more ways than one to intimidate those who dared breach its defenses.

We emerged into more mist, and I exhaled. The two humans looked around with uncertainty. The only thing we could see clearly was the wall at our backs, now a smooth pane of obsidian with no handholds or cracks to be seen. Otherwise, a thick fog pressed in on us, the trees ghostly shadows.

"Is this where we went in?" John asked, his voice barely above a whisper.

The crystal atop Ellerin's staff glowed golden with the mist a halo around it. "No, this is the other side."

"It's not like things stay consistent here."

I covered a chuckle at John's complaint. It made sense that his scientist sensibilities would be offended at a place where the normal laws didn't apply. Faerie did have its rules, but not ones that couldn't be broken. Hence, many Fae didn't understand the laws of physics that governed the human world. Even there, we could bend them, which made the Earth realm particularly dangerous for us. If anyone found out we could manipulate the very nature of matter...

Kestrel's voice also emerged hushed and anxious. "So we go into the fog?"

"Keep the light of my staff in sight. Don't get separated from me, or you'll be in grave peril."

I winked at Kestrel, and she moved to walk beside me with John in front of us. Sir Raleigh followed us.

"Should I be keeping a list of fantasy movie dialogue in my journal?"

I snickered. "Why not? It may inspire a story for you someday."

"Like all this hasn't already?"

The perceived presence of the wall receded as we walked, and I resisted the urge to go back and move along it. Another spell to make sure those who escaped stayed close? Maybe that's why I'd never visited Cruaidh. I might never have left, at least not without someone like Ellerin to guide me. Now, the trees we passed felt like they watched us without protecting us in the gloom.

The thoughts disturbed me, so I decided to distract myself and asked Kestrel, "What power are you feeling today?"

She wrinkled her nose, showing the freckles along her cheeks. "I'm not sure. There's an uneasiness inside, like a bunch of stuff is trying to come through."

"Is anything stronger than the others?"

"Maybe?" She shook her hands. "My fingers are tingling."

"Interesting. Try this." I held my hands out in front of me, palms up, and had a little flame dance along my fingertips.

"I don't know that I can do that and walk at the same time. That's harder than chewing gum."

I laughed. "Just try making a little flame then. Like this." Keeping my right hand facing up, I pressed my fingertips together, and a flame appeared.

Kestrel mimicked me, and her flame appeared, then shot into the sky with a whistle like a firework. It fizzled with a hiss somewhere in the trees above us.

Ellerin wheeled around. "Ladies! You do *not* know what lurks out here. If you continue the magic lessons, please be more subtle."

I'm sure that Kestrel and my faces had turned the same pink shade, and I murmured, "Sorry."

We had just started moving again when something snatched Sir Raleigh away from me. He yowled, and I wheeled around. "Raleigh!"

His yowl turned into a growl. A high-pitched yelp and gurgle followed.

"Raleigh!" I called again, and only Ellerin's strong hand around my wrist kept me from running toward the horrible noises.

"Wait." He tugged at me, so I turned to him. "Wait. You'll see."

Sir Raleigh emerged from the trees in his bat-winged panther form with blood dripping from his mouth. For a second, I thought he was injured. Then he spat something at our feet, a couple of vertebrae with flesh and gray skin with both fur and...scales?

"Oh, gods." Kestrel turned away, her hand over her mouth.

John rubbed her shoulder as she composed herself. "She's never been good with blood."

Fur and scales. "A water wolf?" I flared my nostrils. "I heard them swarming last night. Please tell me they're all abed now, and that was a straggler."

Ellerin snuffed the light on his crystal. "Let's hope. Now move along quietly. And no more magic in case others are having trouble sleeping."

We followed him without speaking. I'm sure we all strained our eyes to see through the gloom. Sir Raleigh again brought up the rear, and while I felt safer with him behind me in his full grimalkin form, I also knew the water wolves would go after the next weakest-appearing members of the party. That would be the humans. Consequently, we moved along in as tight a cluster as possible.

The path widened, bringing us to the shores of a glassy lake. The mist lay in broken clumps over the water, giving us tantalizing glimpses of the shore beyond.

Kestrel nudged me. "It's like the one on your journal, but without the moon."

"I know." And it still looked as sinister. "Ellerin, can we get around?"

"Unfortunately, we have to go across. Otherwise, we'll lose another day."

I removed my pack, and my wings appeared. Thankfully I'd thought to have the hotel tailor put slits in my T-shirt so I wouldn't ruin another one, and I wore a bra with straps that crossed in the back and hooked to the cups in the front, leaving room for wings and the ability to actually get the thing off if they were unfurled. Now I understood the appeal of overbust corsets.

I glanced at John and Kestrel, who huddled together and watched us. "I haven't flown in years, and I don't know if I can carry anyone."

"Hopefully you won't have to." Ellerin walked to the water's edge and planted his staff in the dark gray mud. This time the crystal glowed green, and a low-slung boat with a curved prow shaped like a wolf glided over the water through the mist. It didn't have anyone rowing or otherwise steering it. I thought I could see dim shapes inside, but every time I looked closely, they disappeared.

"Ellerin, do you see the shades in the boat? Are they a trick of the mist or something more sinister?"

He squinted at the boat. "We're not too far from the border of the Gray Zone. Don't trust your eyes, and stick to the path, at least as much as you can."

The boat bumped against the staff, and Ellerin caught it as it toppled. He frowned and didn't say anything. Did he and the boat have some sort of issue with each other? That's not what I needed right now.

A dark, ghostly whisper floated through the air. *"I can take three of you."*

"That's ridiculous. There's plenty of room."

"Talk to the princess. She saw the shades. I'm almost full."

"Why are you full of shades?"

"There's a convention. I don't know. But only three."

Ellerin sighed and turned back to me. He rolled his eyes. "I'm guessing you heard all that."

"Boaty McWolfface has a sarcastic side. Shade convention my ass. Why won't they get off?"

He snorted. "That's a very good question. And only means we need to hasten our journey. If shades are avoiding the dark Fae capital..." Again, a worried expression flitted over his face, but it passed so quickly I missed the opportunity to ask about it. Or maybe I didn't want to. I needed Ellerin to be the rock, the one in charge. The one responsible.

"That's not very princess-y of you."

Dammit, I forgot that some magical beings could read thoughts. "Shut up, Boaty."

Ellerin handed his pack to me. "Here. You need the flying practice. Take the packs to the other side. The humans and I will get in the boat."

"Wait." John approached us. "You want us to get in that thing? Is it seaworthy?"

"Probably not, but it's lakeworthy, and that's all that needs to be true for that to happen. Hurry."

Kestrel wrinkled her nose and looked at the boat. "But it's full of dead things. Like zombies, but transparent."

"The girl sees more than she lets on."

Ellerin studied Kestrel. "Indeed. Your pack please."

Kestrel started to hand it to him, then hesitated. "Wait. Let me get something out so it won't be as heavy." She pulled the journal out and tucked it in the inside pocket of her jacket, then closed the backpack and gave it to Ellerin, who passed it to me.

John relinquished his pack. Now I held four of them—their two, Ellerin's, and mine.

"Uh, Ellerin, I haven't done this in ages. Give me a hint as to how I get started?"

"Why don't you ask that water slitherfin by your feet?"

"What?" I shot up in the air and hovered, looking down to where I'd been standing. There was no slitherfin, which would be a cross between a snake and a fish. I'd always hated how creepy they looked.

"You tricked me!"

He chuckled. "All's fair in love and Fae."

Kestrel snickered and got in the boat, but stayed close to the edge. John followed her, as did Ellerin. They spread out along the back bench, and the boat pulled out into the lake and turned around. With Sir Raleigh as my flying shadow, I followed its trajectory and tried to keep abreast of its slow pace, but I found myself getting worn out. I flew over to where I thought it would dock and hung the packs in trees, then circled back to find the boat had just reached the middle of the lake.

Bubbles popped along the surface of the water around them, and the water itself tossed the boat in small waves. Kestrel grimaced at something in front of her.

John patted her hand. "What is it, honey?"

"Apparently shades can get seasick."

"Um, Ellerin?" I called.

"What?"

"Can you come up here? Something doesn't look right."

He stood and took his cloak off, and his wings emerged. They were of black, gray, and white feathers—fitting for a traveler through many lands. With a gentle jump, he was airborne and came to hover beside me.

The water now foamed and frothed, and John and Kestrel clasped hands.

"Oh, that's not good."

"What is it?"

"Those shades weren't passengers. At least not in the traditional sense. They're the last people and Fae who rode in the boat."

"What happened to them?"

"Water wolves."

Now dark shapes swirled beneath the boat, and I didn't think they were slitherfish.

"Oh, Hades."

13

LAWRENCE

I propped myself up on my elbow and rubbed the last of the sleep from my eyes. Troubadour stood in front of me, and his legs framed a beautiful, dark-haired Fae with chin-length black hair, ruby-red lips, and large, luminous dark eyes. The crystals hadn't fully illuminated, but their dim light still showed the ivory color of the Fae woman's skin. And the blood red tips to her nails. And the curves of her figure, accented by the tight leather catsuit she wore. Its neckline plunged down to her navel, and I admired her assets.

"Well, hello, gargoyle," she purred. "Why don't you come say hi?"

I found myself on my feet moving toward her. She filled my vision, and I could only take one halting step after another.

"Yes, come on then, handsome. I haven't seen a big, brawny brute like you in ages. All I've had to entertain myself with are these spoiled princes. Don't get me wrong, I've heard that one's talented with his fingers, but we're not that kind of family, and I would tire of competing with a bit of wood and wire anyway."

Something barreled into me and knocked me into a 1950's

dinette set. Luckily it was all plastic and bounced around rather than splintering. I shook my head and found myself looking at Rhys.

"Don't let her bespell you, Lawrence Gordon."

I blinked at him using my actual name rather than calling me "gargoyle," but it did the trick. I rolled to my hands and knees and then straightened and checked myself for injury. If anything, Rhys seemed heavier than previously. Was being in Faerie doing something to him? Or was it affecting me as they'd said?

Troubadour walked toward the woman, his charming smile in place, although the tension around his eyes told a different story of his emotional state. "Dear cousin, what a pleasant surprise!"

"Don't 'dear cousin' me, you ruffian." She crossed her arms and planted her feet. Whatever their relationship, it had involved a lot of conflict. "Why are you in my palace?"

"If you would take your place, you wouldn't need this glorified yard sale."

Fae had yard sales? Wait, Troubadour could come through to the Earth realm by possessing humans. I shuddered at the thought of some sweet old lady playing with her Ouija board and then coming to her senses the following evening having bought a full set of velvet *Magic Mike* posters or something else tacky. Not that Troubadour would like such things, but he would probably enjoy messing with someone's grandma.

Rhys and I edged toward the patch of dark sand where we had landed the night before, both because it felt somehow safe and like the exit, although I didn't know what the Fae would do to me if I tried to fly straight up. Something told me fireballs were not completely out of the question.

"I'm actually happy you've come with your friends, dear cousin. I have some of my own I'd like you to meet." She snapped her fingers—Fae must like the theatrical effect of doing so, I noted to myself—and various large pieces of furniture tumbled aside. Nightmare creatures emerged from underneath. I counted two vampires, a mummy, a sort of swampy sea creature with big fish eyes and green scales, and something that looked like a giant Halloween bat decoration that had been left out too long. Rhys later told me it was a were-bat.

Troubadour wrinkled his nose. "What are these creatures from the land of nightmares doing here?"

"Tatiana decided to cause some trouble and give them a way through to the Earth realm. Sadly, someone interfered with her plans, so they got stuck here. I decided to adopt a few."

The vampires approached, and they had eyes only for Rhys. There was something different about them. All vamps had beauty and grace, but these had a feral edge to their attractiveness, which surpassed that of most humans.

"Des, those aren't true vampires." Rhys backed away from them until his back met the wall. "Those are revenants, risen Fae."

"Oh, Rhys, is that you? I didn't recognize you with that scar on your face. What happened?"

"Gargoyle and Templar. Long story." He made a ring of fire at the vampires' feet. They looked confused, then stepped over it and came on like nothing had happened in spite of their pants legs smoking. "Call them off!"

"Oh, but they haven't had breakfast yet."

Meanwhile, the sea creature had fixed its fishy gaze on me and ambled over. I didn't know what to think or how to react—it was outside the realm of anything I'd experienced. What would a predatory fish do?

It circled me, then bumped me, and I jumped out of the way just before it bit my shoulder. Right, some sharks liked to bump their prey before biting to see what they were. From the looks of its teeth, it could be somehow related to them.

She clapped her hands. "Oh, good, Goldy likes you."

I looked to Troubadour for help, but he had been surrounded by the mummy and were-bat. His normal composure had crumbled. "What do you want, Des? Call off your friends."

"Get out of my caves. Get out of my life—"

He held up his hand before she could say his true name. "Fine. You won't see me again."

"Good." She snapped her fingers again, and the creatures all raised their heads and looked at her. "Come."

They all moved toward her except for one vampire—risen Fae?—who had locked eyes with Rhys and made a sort of crooning sound under his breath.

"Gentlemen, catch!" Troubadour tossed our packs to us. "Uh, cousin, one of your friends isn't moving."

"Ugh, Farri has a thing for princes. It's what got him killed in the first place."

The vampire lunged for Rhys, and Rhys dodged, then drove him back with a hard punch to the gut. "I don't want to hurt you, mate."

"He's too far gone." Troubadour joined us. "What have you been giving him, Des? Fae blood?"

"What kind of fool do you think I am? I take them hunting in the woods outside the city sometimes. They eat what they can scare up." Then she laughed at her own joke.

"Then it's possible. I was wondering what I'd been seeing evidence of."

"Why is it bad for vampires to consume Fae blood?" I asked Rhys and assisted him in blocking the half-crazed vampire against the wall with whatever we could grab. The chair fortress we built wouldn't last for long.

"Because they get addicted to it. Especially if they're risen Fae like that one."

"What's a risen Fae?"

"Too complicated to explain now." He grunted and pushed another chair into the structure we'd made. "We need to get out of here."

"I agree. Ready?"

He nodded and hopped on my back. I took off and found myself pushed back down, albeit gently, by the same cushion of air that had welcomed us the night before.

"What are you doing? Go *up!*"

"I can't." The air smelled vaguely of ozone and stone. That gave me an idea. I placed my palms on the wall in front of me and whispered a request. Unfortunately, Faerie stone did not respond to Earth elementals like Earth minerals did. At home, it would have given me handholds or something to hold on to. Here, my hands slid down until we landed, leaving a pair of sweaty trails behind.

"Well, that's annoying." Rhys hopped down. "Let us go, Des. We're not here to hurt you."

"But now you know my secret. Well, one of them." She smiled, and although she didn't have fangs, her expression sent a spike of fear through me. "You can build all the blanket forts you want. Eventually, my risen Fae will get to you, and I'll enjoy watching the fun. It's been so long since I've had any sort of entertainment."

Her attitude shouldn't have surprised me. Rhys, although he had his moments, wasn't quite the ruthless Fae I'd heard about. Had I grown complacent with him and Reine, who also had her moments but at her heart was kind? Ugh, I didn't need to be thinking like that right now. What had my parents told me when faced with a Fae who toyed with me like a cat did its dinner? Ask what it wanted, but Troubadour had already done that. But I knew what he wanted. He wanted us to take him to Reine. As much as I hated the idea—and I'd have to explore why later—he would be our key to getting out of here.

"Uh, Troubadour, what about that thing you wanted us to do? Can't you figure out a way out of here?"

Des hopped up on a table and looked down at all of us. "Wait, my cousin actually *wants* something? How delightful. What do you want, cousin?"

Troubadour shot us an annoyed look. I returned it with a glare of my own. He hadn't exactly been helpful. Had he decided to let his relative destroy us, and oh well, he'd figure out another way to Reine? It wouldn't surprise me if he pulled a fickle Fae move like that.

Rhys seemed to clue in. "We're going to tell her unless you get us out of here."

Troubadour sighed and walked over to us. "You're starting to annoy me."

I matched his aggressive posture with my own. "You've been annoying me. Now get us out of here, or we spill." I didn't know why he wanted to talk to Reine so badly, but I counted on it.

"Fine." He spoke in secret conversation on a band so tight and focused it hurt. "*When it goes dark, fly straight up.*"

I nodded.

He struck a tone on his harp, and all the torches extinguished in a puff, leaving behind total blackness and a sharp, smoky odor. Rhys jumped on my back, and I again jumped into the air. This time nothing impeded me, and I allowed my sense of the wall to guide me.

"*Follow me.*" Troubadour glowed, although not as brightly as before, and led us out through a different set of twists and turns.

Just before we flew out into the morning, I thought I heard the echo of cackling laughter.

Troubadour took us out over a different set of woods, these with more leaves on the trees, but only a few more and most of them brown. I couldn't see into the forest through the fog that clung to the ground. The sky above us also hung heavy and gray, but at least we were in the open air, such as it was.

I noticed the trees getting closer, and I focused on maintaining my altitude, but I grew weaker with each stroke.

"Troubadour, I need to land soon. I can't carry Rhys for this long."

"Well, if Rhys would find his damn wings..."

"Trying," Rhys gritted out through clenched teeth. "You think I like this?"

Troubadour gave him one of his heavy-lidded side glares. "One never knows with the light Fae males."

Rhys tensed, and I wondered if Rhys had been flying, if he might have punched Troubadour. Or...

"It's better to be flexible than impotent and bored," Rhys shot back. "It's not like the Dark Court is known for its *productive* orgies."

"I didn't think orgies were supposed to be productive," I couldn't resist commenting, although each word came out with effort.

"Look, up ahead!" Rhys' finger emerged in my peripheral vision and pointed to a break in the trees, which as we grew closer, proved to be a lake. I could see shapes in the middle and two hovering over it, but not clearly enough to identify them.

I landed on the shore, and my feet sunk about half a meter into the soft, dark-gray mud. Rhys tumbled off my back, and I drew what strength I could from the land below me. Once my breath calmed and no longer rasped in my ears, I heard voices coming over the water. The first one somewhat familiar.

"Those shades weren't passengers..."

Then, a voice I had both desired and dreaded hearing again. "What happened to them?"

"Water wolves."

"A little help down here!" That was John.

I let go of the packs and launched myself into the sky. Troubadour flew just ahead of me. Without Rhys, I outpaced him and saw Reine. My jaw dropped at the stunning sight of her rainbow wings. Ellerin, the gray Fae, had somewhat drab colors to his, but they were well-shaped and nicely feathered.

Both Reine and Ellerin dropped through the patchy fog that floated over the lake and disappeared from view.

14

REINE

One of the water wolves in its aquatic form—all scales and teeth—leaped over the boat.

Ellerin and I both flinched, and he asked, "Think you can carry Kestrel?"

"Yes." I didn't know if I could. My back and shoulder muscles were already tired from the activity thus far, but I'd try.

"You get her, I'll attempt to grab John. On the count of three. One, two..."

On three, we dove through the clouds and snatched the humans up. John clutched Ellerin's cloak as well. Kestrel, although slender, still weighed more than I expected, and I struggled. One of the water wolves jumped after us, and Kestrel screamed.

Sweat beaded on my brow as I turned toward the shore, which now seemed miles away. I gritted my teeth and forced my wings to beat. Then a shadow blocked the light from above, and strong hands grabbed me by the waist.

"I'll help you. Keep your wings out so you'll glide." The voice —a deep, resonant version of one I thought I'd never hear again

—almost made me want to sob with relief and regret. Almost. A Fae princess didn't show weakness.

Kestrel didn't have any such restrictions on her emotions, and she sounded gleeful. "Uncle Lawrence?"

"Hang on tight, sweetie. We'll get you to land safely."

I glanced over to see another Fae helping Ellerin with John. The newcomer winked at me, and while his appearance didn't spark any memories, his cocky but familiar attitude did. I wanted to study him to figure out how I must know him. All right, I'll admit, his handsome blondness and muscular physique made him nice to look at as well, but I turned my attention back to providing lift where I could.

Lawrence and the mysterious Fae helped us to land on the far shore. We all sat slumped in the light gray sand for a minute or so before struggling to our feet.

Ellerin bowed to each of them. "My thanks." Then he turned to me. I cringed. Would he chastise me for not being strong enough? No, he only inquired, "Where are the packs?"

I pointed up to where they dangled about twenty feet overhead. Those of us with wings looked at each other. Then a voice floated over from across the lake. "Oy, what about me?"

I squinted through the fog. I whispered a plea to the water to carry our voices so we wouldn't have to yell, and it grudgingly acquiesced. The water wolves made it grumpy. "Rhys? Is that you?"

"Yes, sis. I'm stuck, and I'm not getting in that boat." I filled in what he didn't say—he needed help. Ever the Fae prince, he didn't want to admit it.

Lawrence and the other Fae looked at each other.

"Can't," Lawrence panted. "I'm toast for now." In spite of his strong, muscular appearance—holy Fae, I couldn't look away from his pecs and abs—his aura showed that his energy drooped. Something tickled the back of my brain about gargoyles in Faerie, and while I couldn't tease it out, I knew he shouldn't be here.

My wing joints also ached. "Me neither."

Ellerin crossed his arms. "Why doesn't he fly? Where are his wings?"

"Haven't emerged yet." The blond Fae shrugged. "No idea why."

"Still over here!" Rhys' voice had taken on an anxious edge. "And there's a big shadow in the water coming toward me."

"What's keeping your wings from appearing?" I tried not to let my frustration show in my tone.

"I don't know." Now he sounded panicked. "You're the healer —you tell me."

"Our wings are a sign of identity. Have you not embraced your Fae prince side upon returning?"

A long pause, then, so quietly only I could hear, "It's hard with the scar."

"Then you need to do something noble that's hard. Think! Is there a wrong you can right?"

"Not much time for that now, is there?"

Lawrence stumbled, then righted himself. Seeing his clumsiness and how wrong it appeared loosened the knowledge that had eluded me, and my heart dropped to my stomach.

"Did you tell Lawrence about what happens to gargoyles in Faerie?"

At his name, Lawrence's chin lifted, and he straightened. "He said I won't be able to process the food or air here as well."

"Not only that..." I crossed my arms so I wouldn't fling a face-slap spell across the water to my terrible little brother, whom I should probably leave on the far shore, but... "Rhys... You need to tell him the full truth."

The water carried the soft huff of a sigh to my ears, then, "Lawrence, mate, I'm sorry. I needed your help, so I lied. It's not only that you can't breathe as well. The air here is poisonous to you. If you stay here too long, you'll die."

"No!" Both John and Kestrel ran to Lawrence's side like they could protect him from the problem. I squeezed my eyes closed at the overwhelming sorrow the realization gave me.

"How much time does he have?" John stalked over to me. "Tell me."

"I don't know. It's been so long since a gargoyle came into Faerie, we don't have good records or data."

Kestrel put a hand to Lawrence's cheek. She had to reach for it. "Uncle Lawrence, how do you feel?"

"I'm a little tired from that flight and the one before it, but I'm feeling okay. How are you?"

She put her hands on her hips, and the painful expression that flickered across John's face made me wonder if that was a posture she'd learned from her mother. "I'm not the one who's important here. Why did you come? Why are you putting yourself in danger?"

"I came to find you and John. To bring you home."

She dropped her hand and stepped back. "But we're here on a mission. Reine is taking me to the physician to the High Court so he can tell me what's wrong with me, why I can't access my powers."

"And what about you, John?"

"Did you think I was going to allow my daughter to do something this dangerous on her own?"

"I suppose not." Lawrence didn't look convinced, and again, I questioned what John's motives could be beyond protecting his daughter. I mean, that was enough, but the longer we were here, the more something about him made me suspicious. Call it Fae-tuition.

A rhythmic chuffing sound drew our attention to the fog over the water, and Rhys appeared carrying what I assumed were his and Lawrence's bags. His wings had formerly been royal blue and gold—the colors of the higher echelons of the light Fae colors—but now they appeared faded with red streaks through each of them. Another evidence that wings reflected identity. He landed with a less-than-graceful plop.

"I'm out of shape," he gasped.

"Don't get too comfortable." Ellerin pointed with his staff to the water. "You know how water wolves aren't supposed to swarm during the day? Looks like no one told them."

ONE THING that many people can gather about Fae from fairy tales is that we have a certain hierarchy we like to follow. Consequently, in a pinch, we'll look to the highest-ranking one to make the decisions. Unfortunately, that meant that the other Fae looked to me...except Ellerin, who paced along the shoreline and murmured to himself as the lake's waves grew choppier. He drew shapes in the mud at the edge of the water, and I sensed he placed defensive spells.

He could do what he wanted, but there was no telling how long they'd hold. Meanwhile, I had humans, a weakened gargoyle, and two Fae princes to worry about.

"Rhys, grab our packs. Lawrence, you, John, and Kestrel head into the woods and find somewhere to hide, preferably in a cave where you can seal yourselves in."

"What about in the trees?" John pointed up. "Those things can't fly, can they?"

Rhys' scar made his expression grimmer. "No, but they can climb."

"Fuck." Kestrel shot a side glance at her father. "Sorry."

Rhys returned with the packs, and everyone got theirs.

"I can help. I can fight." Lawrence flexed his hands. "I'm not useless yet."

"You need to do what you came to do and protect the humans. Ellerin, can you send them home?"

"The Shadowed Path doesn't work like that, Princess. Once you're on it, you're on it until you get what you came for or die trying."

John crossed his arms. "Somehow that wasn't in the agreement we made."

Ellerin turned to him. "You didn't ask. For an experienced earth witch, you're pretty dumb when it comes to dealing with its elementals. Haven't you ever heard of a Fae bargain?"

Kestrel tugged at John's sleeve. "I'm sorry, Dad. I didn't know."

"Me, neither," I added. "And I am sorry. I would never have allowed you to come had I known."

The blond Fae shook his head and chuckled. "I knew you'd be something else, Princess, but this is too much. Apologizing to humans?"

"And who in Hades are you?"

All traces of mirth vanished from his face, and he smiled. The dim light glinted off his slightly pointed teeth. "What, you don't remember me?" He took a harp from his cloak and struck a note that almost made me weep with its sorrow...and clued me in to his identity.

"You're Troubadour, the dark Fae who helped me."

"And who..." Kestrel trailed off and looked at her father, then shut her mouth. Smart girl. John didn't need to know his daughter had been possessed, albeit briefly. He muttered to himself, and I hoped he hadn't finally gone over the edge. Poor guy had been through a lot, and I knew when the shock of his wife's death wore off, it wouldn't be pretty.

"If you're going to run, then go." Ellerin pointed into the forest. "The border to the Gray Zone is not too far that way. Stay on the path, and you'll get there. The water wolves, being dark Fae creatures, won't be able to follow you."

"What about him?" Lawrence inclined his head to Troubadour. "Isn't he a dark Fae?"

"The rules are different for the high Fae." And I sensed he qualified.

I looked at Lawrence, magnificent in his gargoyle form, and shooed him with my hands. "Go. I'll catch up to you."

"Very well." He and the humans headed into the woods, and the mist soon swallowed them up.

I took Sir Raleigh's head in my hands and said, "Go and help protect them." I could tell he wasn't happy, but I couldn't send them into the wilderness with only a sick gargoyle for protection. Sir Raleigh knew his way to and through the Gray Zone, and I hoped Kestrel could call upon something useful. I'd forgotten her parents were earth witches. Although he might not be able to access his full power here, John might be able to help somewhat.

"And what about us?" Rhys asked.

I opened my mouth to answer, but Ellerin beat me to it. "I've set up some defensive illusion runes in the sand. They should turn back the first wave, but more will come. Troubadour, can you use your music to further confuse them?"

"Yes, but to what end?"

"If we can get them turning back on each other, they may possibly attack the rest of the swarm, not us."

"And us?" I asked.

"Stand ready. Unfortunately, the two of you, being light Fae, can't do much destructively." He sounded doubtful, and his gaze lingered on me like a challenge.

I didn't have time to ask for clarification. The leading edge of the swarm hit the shore, and as promised, turned back and attacked their fellow water wolves. Unfortunately, although Ellerin had drawn the runes high up, the melee soon obscured them, and they lost their effectiveness.

Then Troubadour played a series of notes, which worked

for a few minutes, but the water wolves howled and growled in an effort to drown him out, and we found ourselves in a line backing toward the trees.

"Hades," I muttered. "Why are there so many of them?"

Troubadour rolled his eyes. "Probably because someone is interested in you not making it to Lorien and decided to wake and summon them. That's why they're so grumpy."

"They're not supposed to know I'm here."

"When you entered Faerie, the trees sang their joy in your coming, Princess. Not all could hear it, but enough could. I did."

"Well, that's sweet but damn inconvenient."

The water line moved sluggishly with the pieces of water wolves who had torn each other to bits, and the stench of their slime made me breathe shallowly through my mouth, then nose, alternating since it stung my throat. I blinked tears away in time to see a new wave of water wolves, their eel-like faces in rictus grins, the slime dripping from their teeth. These didn't rush. They knew they had us trapped and wanted to play with us.

But Ellerin wasn't going to give up. "On a count of three, fly. The humans should have had enough time to make it close to the border by now. We only have to hold the wolves off a little longer."

I gaped at him. "You mean, you were stalling for them?"

"Why did you think, Princess? Their fate is tied to yours."

"Wow." More and more surprises.

He counted, and we jumped just before the wolves reached us. We managed to hover out of their reach, and Ellerin used his staff to shoot lightning at any who dashed toward the woods. I'd just started to relax when something else came out of the water. It had the dark coloring and stench of a water wolf, but it also had wings and a lizard face. It shook itself off and roared, leaving us gagging from its rotting fish breath.

"Water wyrm!" Rhys drew on our light Fae ability to create

something out of nothing and made a bow and arrows materialize. His wild shots and wobbly flying revealed he'd not figured out his wing balance well enough.

Ellerin continued to pick off the wolves, leaving me and Troubadour to face the wyrm, which rose slowly from the water, each beat of its massive wings scattering the wolves underneath him.

"Got much experience with dragons, Princess?"

"Not for a long, long time." And typically, they and I would drink mead and make fun of the knights who came to rescue me from them. "You?"

"Same."

"Got any tricks in your harp?"

"Nope."

"All right, then." I knew my light Fae powers wouldn't do much against the massive creature, and I found myself rubbing the vampire scars at my neck. What had Ashlee Wyatt, the vampire club owner, told me? That my parentage wasn't as pure as I'd thought. And I had managed fire before, being a high Fae in command of all five elements. Of all of them, it would be the easiest to turn to destruction, which didn't come naturally to light Fae, and it opposed water.

"Stand, er, hover back!" I stretched out my arms and mentally reached to the sun, which hid behind the thick clouds above me. I whispered a spell to bring its warmth to me and added a plea for an extra boost.

By now, the wyrm had managed to hover over the water and study us each in turn to see who would be the easiest pickings. I waited until it was distracted by Rhys and his not-so-great aim with bow and arrows and launched a fireball at its head. As far as fireballs went, it lacked in size and impact, but it definitely met the annoyance quota.

"Hades." I rubbed my hands to try again.

"Hey, sis, light one of these!" Rhys flew to hover beside me and held out one of his arrows. He changed the tip from stone to a triangle of wood and flammable resin, and I lit it aflame. He notched it, and I sent another fireball—this one bigger, harder, and faster—at the wyrm's head. When the creature opened its mouth to roar, Rhys shot the arrow down its gullet. It shut its mouth, its yellow fish eyes wide, and then burst into flames. The water wolves scattered away from it back into the lake, and it sank from view. We landed and watched the water bubble.

Ellerin mopped his brow with a handkerchief. "Nice work, Prince, Princess."

"Thanks."

"See, sis?" Rhys nudged me. "We make a good team."

"Sometimes." I shoved him, and he stumbled backward. His wings disappeared, and he landed on his ass in the slimy mud.

"What was that for?"

"What were you thinking, bringing Lawrence here? Didn't you know it could kill him?"

"Ohhh." Troubadour put a hand to his mouth, and I could tell he feigned shock. "Has the princess fallen for the gargoyle, then? That's juicy. Talk about star-crossed lovers."

Rhys stumbled to his feet and cupped his hands, allowing water to fill them so he could rinse off. "It's been so long I forgot. I didn't know it would be this bad."

"But you knew it wouldn't be good for him."

"I swear, I was trying to help!"

I itched to send a small fireball his way, but I knew it wouldn't do any good.

Troubadour pointed to the water with his harp. "As lovely as all this family reunion is, we should get going. Who knows what else is in that lake? Has it occurred to anyone else that that was too easy?"

He had a point—the water hadn't stopped bubbling yet. The wyrm could have been a prelude to the main event, and a sense of exhaustion seeped in at the edge of my adrenaline high. How much energy had those fireballs cost me?

We trudged toward the tree line, and I'd just made it into the woods when something hissed across the sand and leaf mulch behind us.

"Ooof!" Ellerin fell face-down and slid backward toward the lake. He turned and aimed his staff at something, sending a beam of light through the thick, black tentacle that had reached out for him. His efforts severed the connection, but five more came out of the lake, waving and searching for prey.

"Go!" He motioned for us to flee. "I'll be right behind you."

All five tentacles paused, then headed straight for him.

I tried to run back to help him even though my magic was beyond depleted. "Ellerin, no!"

But Troubadour grabbed me and dragged me into the trees, and I was too tired to resist.

15

LAWRENCE

With Sir Raleigh in the lead, we ran into the woods. My steps dragged, both because of physical weariness and the tug of the battle behind me. Old memories emerged, of gargoyles around a fire toasting to the heroes of legend...who didn't run away. I again felt my inner gargoyle close to the surface, the animal instincts that wanted to run back and snarl in the face of danger, protecting...

...protecting the Fae who had betrayed and lied to me. Who had put me, my best friend, and my goddaughter in danger for who knew what purpose? I lifted my chin and marched on. These humans were my task now, not the Fae. The legends of how gargoyles had protected them in the past must have been a mix-up or something. Old tales did that—took the kernels of truth and dressed them up until they became practically meaningless fodder for kids' movies. What would this one be called —*Lying Beauty? Blood Is Thicker Than Truth? Gargoyles Be Stupid?*

The farther we went, the more the trees and mist pressed in on us, and we had to slow down so we wouldn't lose the path. Although I had no Fae blood as far as I knew, I had no doubt that if we were to step off the trail, we'd be faced with a mirage of the same rows of trees in all directions, basically like a hall of mirrors without our reflections that would swallow and starve us...or worse.

Kestrel's voice floated through my anxious reverie. "Uncle Lawrence, are you okay? Would you be better if you changed to human?"

"Probably, but I can't. I'm stuck."

John glanced over his shoulder at me. "You're stuck? Has that ever happened to you before?"

"Never." Although Sir Raleigh led us, and I suspected he could report to Reine or Ellerin, there was no point in deception, and I needed them to know the truth. "And the longer I'm in this form, the more likely I am to be stuck here."

Kestrel's eyes widened. "And then what happens?"

"Then I go insane and turn to stone." I shrugged. "Y'know, the fate of magical creatures who tempt the gods."

John, ever the scientist, asked, "Do you have actual evidence for this, or is it legend?"

I chuckled since I'd just been pondering something similar. "Unfortunately, I have evidence. My Uncle Augie, my father's brother, succumbed to his inner gargoyle and stayed there too long. He tried to return to the Aerie—where the gargoyle clans, or what's left of them, now live—but didn't make it before sunrise on his final day. He now guards the entrance to the Aerie in stone form along with all the others who have failed."

John didn't look convinced. "That's a family legend, but a story nonetheless. Have you ever *seen* this stone gargoyle?"

"No, I've never been to the Aerie." I hoped they didn't ask why. I didn't know myself why some gargoyles lived there and some didn't. I suspected those who didn't liked modern human conveniences, whatever *modern* meant at the time. Or maybe there weren't enough resources.

Kestrel tripped over something, then righted herself. I couldn't see what had made her stumble. "You okay?" I asked.

"Yes. Something about this place feels off." She wrinkled her nose. "It's like when you walk into a place where something has died, but a long time ago. Like, you know it happened, and there's a sense of wrongness, but you can't tell why."

"Then we should probably stop talking and pay attention."

Sir Raleigh looked over his shoulder and nodded at me, then bared his teeth. *Yes. Danger.*

I blinked. Had he just spoken to me? He turned back to the direction we traveled in.

The mist grew thicker, although I hadn't thought that was possible. Soon we practically walked on top of each other and held hands so we wouldn't lose anyone. As the rear guard, I felt like something pressed in on me, or at least watched me, from behind. My shoulder blades under my wings twitched with the discomfort of vulnerability and exposure.

John stumbled to a halt and bent, moving his hands from ours to his knees. "I don't know how much longer I can go."

"Dad, what's wrong?" Kestrel placed a hand on his shoulder, then the other to her mouth when she looked up and saw... something. "Oh, gods. Mom."

John stood and put his arms around his daughter. "You see her, too?"

Sir Raleigh sat on the path, his paws pointed forward, for which I was grateful. At least he'd keep us moving in the right direction.

I squinted into the mist. "I don't see anything. It must be the magic of the place."

Sir Raleigh stood and twitched his tail in my face. I hesitated to grab it—what cat likes its tail pulled?—but he flicked its soft end against my nose. I held it, then touched Kestrel. She blinked.

"She's gone. Mom? Mom!"

John straightened. "I don't see her anymore. Beverly!"

"It's something the grimalkin is doing." I smiled down at Sir Raleigh. "You're a creature of the gray Fae, aren't you? That's how you can protect us from its magic."

Sir Raleigh nodded and stepped forward. We moved along with me holding on to him with one hand and to Kestrel with the other, leaving John in the rear. I wanted to ask what they'd seen Beverly doing, but I also sensed that they might sink into sorrow, which wouldn't help any of us get to where we needed to be.

"Are we there yet?" I asked, not expecting an answer but needing to do something to dispel the thick silence around us. All forest sounds had ceased, and although the air moved, it didn't rustle the leaves or give any other indication of its presence. Another illusion?

"Almost. But the Gray Zone demands a price."

"I see."

"What?" Kestrel squeezed my hand. "Is he talking to you?"

I half-smiled. "Reluctantly. He said the Gray Zone demands a price. Whatever happens, don't let go."

The path turned downward, and the shadows of trees around us disappeared. We came to a stream just wide enough that we wouldn't be able to easily step or jump over it.

Sir Raleigh turned to me and gently pulled his tail from my hand. He touched the back of my wrist with his cold nose. *"This is as far as I can help you. Remember your path."* Then he jumped across the stream and disappeared into the mist beyond.

"Wait!" John's voice had gone into full panic pitch. "Wait, don't leave us! What did he say to you?"

"To remember our path." We joined hands in a circle and looked into each other's eyes. "Remember why you're here. That's the moral of most fairy tales, right? Remember who you are and do the right thing. We're in one and have to play the game right."

16

LAWRENCE

"No way but forward, huh?" Kestrel sighed and eyed the stream. I couldn't imagine what she must be feeling. I'd caught her staring at me, which reminded me that she'd never seen me in my gargoyle form. While I didn't know what she and her father had faced before we rescued them from the lake, the encounter with the water wolves had terrified me. And due to my gargoyle form, I had more power and strength...theoretically.

Now Kestrel watched the stream, her expression the carefully neutral one she must have learned to cultivate in her training for the PBI.

John gave his daughter a smile of mingled weariness and pride. "No, I suppose not."

Standing here wouldn't do us any good. "I suppose we should go." I released John, and, holding tight to Kestrel, waded into the stream. My feet found purchase as the burbling water and the smooth stones beneath welcomed me as a water and earth elemental. It tricked me, however. Once we reached the middle of the stream, a rumbling vibration made the water froth and foam, and I looked upstream to see a wall of water rushing toward us.

"Hang on!" I gripped Kestrel's hand so tightly she cried out. The wave narrowed to a wedge and ripped her from us, carrying her away.

Both John and I shouted, and I had to half-fly to grab John before he dove into the stream, which had suddenly deepened, to go after her.

"Kestrel!"

The raw pain in his voice broke my heart, but I didn't let him go.

"Did you see that? The water wanted only her."

"Yes, I saw that." He stopped struggling, and we made our way to the opposite shore. Then, when we tried to go in the direction Kestrel had been taken, an invisible wall blocked us. Both of us kept looking downstream to see if we could spot either the mini-tsunami that had taken her, or her dark red hair bobbing along the surface. Nothing out of the ordinary appeared except for a shadow swooping low over the stream in the far distance. A sliver of relief made the tension in my chest loosen. The grimalkin hadn't abandoned us completely, after all. Had he known something like this would happen?

"I can't tell with certainty, but I think Sir Raleigh is following."

John slumped in partial relief. "Good." Then he sat on the bank and cleaned his glasses with his shirt-tail, which left wet streaks along the lenses. He didn't seem to notice as he put them back on. "I feel so helpless, Lawrence."

"I suspect that's the point." I sat beside him on the grass but kept one foot on the path so we wouldn't lose it. "The Gray Zone has a price, but I can't believe it would be that steep."

He shook his head. "When it comes to the Fae and their institutions and magic, I could believe anything."

We waited for several more minutes. A warm breeze stirred the grass, and the clouds parted overhead to reveal the famed sunshine of Faerie.

"What are you looking at?" John asked. He squinted up.

"There are legends—again, based on who knows what?—that the sunshine in Faerie has magical properties. Like, it can heal those who are injured and worthy."

He snorted. "There's always the worthiness bit, isn't there?"

I turned to him. "Don't let yourself be bitter, John. You've done what you can."

John leaned forward, his elbows on his knees. "Have I? I keep going over and over what happened. Could I have fought harder for Kestrel, for Beverly to let her be a normal girl? Or should I have reassured Kestrel more about her shifting powers?" He shrugged. "At the end of the day, would it have mattered? You know how stubborn Beverly could be."

I recognized what was happening. I'd seen it in my mother after my father's murder at the hands of... No, I wouldn't let my thoughts go in that particular direction. "After my dad was killed, my mom seemed fine for a while. She had to make plans, figure things out quickly because we didn't know if more Fae would come along and finish the job, kill the family. They could be vindictive like that."

"Not helping, Lawrence."

"Sorry, that's not the point. The point is that once we escaped, went elsewhere and had the chance to breathe again, that's when she broke down. Some people call the first stage of grief denial, but for a lot of us, it's more like shock."

"So, you think the shock has worn off, and now I'm starting to really grieve?"

"Yes. I mean, I'm a veterinarian, not a therapist, but I've seen this before."

"You have it wrong, though." John looked down the river

again, and sorrow tugged the corners of his mouth down. "I've been grieving for a long, long time."

Before I could ask about what, the sun fully broke through the clouds above us, and something made us scramble to our feet. A figure in a blue robe with its hood pulled up appeared on the path in front of us.

John and I looked at each other, and I asked, "Who are you, and what do you want?"

"The truth." The voice, pitched too high for a male and too low for a female, spoke with the finality of the wind. "You each have something you're hiding from yourself." It pointed to John with a genderless hand. "You have an old suspicion that you fear voicing as evidence points to its truth." Then it turned its attention to me. "And you, gargoyle, are ignoring more than your animal instincts. If you want the girl returned to you, to move along the Path, you need to admit these things to yourself."

My gut twisted. What could I have been ignoring? That stab of joy when I'd seen Reine? The way it killed me to leave her in danger to protect my friends? The growing glow of understanding and forgiveness that she'd been doing what she needed to protect herself and her brother, and she hadn't intentionally hurt me?

The fact that I had fallen hard for her and wanted to see how things could go between—

My inner gargoyle emerged with a full wing spread and roar, and I had to fight to keep him from fully taking over. As he had just a few days earlier, he wanted to find her and claim her for his—our—own.

Down, dammit. Things don't happen like that anymore. She has a choice.

I closed my eyes and breathed deeply, fighting for control as the memories flooded through me. Gods, I couldn't keep myself from needing her, from wanting to finish what we'd started in the hotel room, to having more intimate candlelight dinners where we spilled our secrets and stripped away the things that kept us apart.

Could I trust her? She was a Fae princess, after all, and returning to Faerie was what she'd been working toward the whole time. The painful truth was that even if I decided I wanted to explore the possibility of a future together, I couldn't stay, and she might not want to leave. Troubadour seemed to be interested in her, and the woman in the caves had called him a prince. Would Reine choose to make an alliance between light and dark Fae? Even if her heart wanted otherwise, it might not matter. If there was anything the past few days had proved, it was her loyalty to her people. And it might break my heart, but that characteristic made me fall for her even more.

"That's it, gargoyle." The being's voice vibrated through the air around me. "The Gray Zone may be a place of deception, but there's no hiding from oneself."

Then the clouds returned, and John and I stood alone once again. We looked at each other, and I suspected that the pain in my eyes mirrored that in his. With the understanding of long friendship, we both nodded, a silent agreement that we'd talk about these things when we were ready.

The air around us vibrated, and Kestrel appeared, eyes closed and mouth open. I caught her just before she tumbled to the ground, and John cupped her face.

"Kestrel, sweetie? Please open your eyes. Please be okay."

Her eyelids fluttered open, and she grinned. "Dad, Uncle Lawrence, guess what I just did?"

"What, sweetie?"

"I just teleported." She wrinkled her nose. "And I lost it, but I caught it for just a second."

We helped her to her feet, and we looked up the path, which had become shrouded in fog.

John pulled the straps of his pack over his shoulders. "Well, I guess we should get going."

I looked behind us once again, hoping to see Reine and the others, but the mist swirled too thickly for me to see more than a few feet beyond the stream, which burbled merrily again.

17

───────

REINE

Rhys, Troubadour, and I furled our wings. We feared they would only be a drag on our retreat should they become entangled in the trees. Thick trunks crowded the trail through the woods and seemed to reach down with gnarled branches to claw at our hair and clothing. Once the path itself became littered with leaf mulch and other debris, we slowed to a trudge so we wouldn't accidentally leave it. Without Ellerin to guide us, we had to be extra careful.

Without Ellerin to guide us, would we make it? What had he been thinking?

He'd been thinking he would distract the kraken, or whatever it had been, and save us. I had to hope he had more tricks up the sleeves of his robe than he'd shown us. Yes, I wanted to go back and save him, but I also couldn't leave Lawrence and the humans to their own devices for too long. Who knew what stunt John might try to pull, or how Kestrel might accidentally manifest some sort of destructive power?

Troubadour's question broke through my rumination. "Penny for your thoughts, Princess?" His soft tones hit my ears like warm saltwater—simultaneously soothing and somewhat irritating in its surprise.

"Trying to figure out what I could have done. What I have to do."

His eyebrows darted up his high forehead in what I surmised was surprise at my honest answer, and he nodded. "Makes sense."

"Well, you have her here," Rhys grumbled from behind us. "You wanted to talk to her so badly. Go ahead and say what you need." He didn't finish the sentence, but its conclusion hung in the air—*and then leave us alone, dark Fae scum.*

Those of us in the Light Court hadn't gotten along well with those in the Dark Court, and the two royal families had given up trying to mingle several hundred years before Rhys or I had been born. Consequently, while we might know of our counterparts, we still missed a lot of details. Like how Troubadour fit in with the high darks. He carried himself like a prince, and I guessed he could be a nephew to Lilith, but I couldn't remember any of the princesses aside from Desdemona, my mother's opposite.

"You wanted to speak with me?" I asked in a gentle, inviting tone and shot Rhys a look to dial back the hostility.

"Yes, but I don't know that this is the proper place or circumstances." Troubadour gestured to the forest around us. "As you well know, these woods can hide nasty surprises."

"But we'll be in the Gray Zone soon, and I don't expect you to accompany us outside of your lands."

The snap of a twig jerked my attention to a curve of the path in front of us, and three figures stepped out of the mist and blocked our way. The greens and browns of their attires had allowed them to blend in with the forest. They all wore similar clothing—short variegated green cloaks with hoods pulled up to hide their hair and faces, which were also masked from the nose down, high boots, fawn-colored pants made from some sort of thick cloth that resembled the microfiber of the Earth realm, and rough-spun gray shirts with tooled dark brown leather vests over them. I couldn't see the designs, but I guessed they had spells etched into them to repel physical and magical attacks. Worse, they held weapons, long knives that glowed ice blue and sang with their own lethal music.

"Fae steel," Rhys murmured behind me. "Fuck."

"Fae princes don't use Earth curse words," Troubadour and I said in unison, and in spite of the sudden direness of the circumstances, we met each other's eyes with smiles. He winked. I turned away with a blush and a laugh.

"What do you want?" I asked the Fae in front of us.

"Your lives," the one in front snarled.

Troubadour stepped forward, but not in front of me. "I believe you have the line wrong, gentlemen. The proper answer is, 'your money or your lives.'" He fingered the strings of his harp but didn't play anything. I suspected he was already planning a spell. Behind me, the warming air told me that Rhys was gathering his strength, although I didn't know what he could do. Would his defensive spells come out as flawed as his wings?

"Think you're so smart, don't you?" The Fae highwayman didn't advance, but he shifted his weight forward.

A line of flames appeared in front of him, and Rhys growled, "No further, peasant. Let us pass, and we may let you live."

I'd had to commend his nice bravado later. Illusions and spells were all I could expect from an already exhausted Fae prince...and myself.

The three would-be assassins disappeared, and Rhys doused the flames.

"Were they actually there?" I whispered to Troubadour. "I thought I could sense them, all of them, magic and everything."

He nodded, his eyes narrowed. "They were there. And they're more than common thieves or murderers."

"I agree."

I searched within to find what strength I had in reserve and shivered at the answer—not much.

Rhys spoke up. "Well, we can't just stay here."

I let out an exasperated sigh. "No, but I don't want to move forward until I know what to expect."

Troubadour snickered, and not kindly. "Isn't that a useful philosophy?"

"Sometimes it can be."

"Here," Rhys said. "I'll go first. Then Reine in the middle, and Troubadour behind."

"Wait," I protested. "I'm not a damsel in distress who needs your protection."

"No, but you're the one of us with the life that's most valuable, at least in terms of, well, who we are." Rhys shrugged, and I admired his intelligence in not saying we were all royalty. Although, it would be easier to survive a kidnapping attempt than an assassination.

Once we'd gotten into position, I told him, "You bring up a good point. Do either of you think they know who we are?"

Troubadour answered. "Maybe. Their blades aren't cheap, and their energy is masked, so it's possible that someone from either capital sent them."

"Brilliant." That meant someone definitely knew I'd returned and meant to cause trouble.

We walked forward in single-file, which we would have had to do anyway since the trail narrowed. I scanned the trees and mist for signs of the strange Fae, but nothing appeared. Rhys set a fast pace, and Troubadour and I marched after him. We almost bumped into him when he bent to retrieve something.

"What are you doing?" I hissed. "What did you just pick up?"

Rhys grinned. "Shhh! I'll tell you later."

We rounded the curve, and I had just drawn a relieved breath when something cold grabbed my wrist and dragged me off the path. I couldn't see who it was, and the world tilted. Wave after wave of fatigue crashed over me, and I struggled less and less effectively against whatever held me as it drained my strength.

A clear, high note vibrated through the air, giving me a burst of energy and dispelling the fog in my head. I pulled with my captured hand and aimed my other elbow outward. It stung as something crunched into it, and the cold vise left my wrist. I stumbled backward into Troubadour's arms. He handed me off to Rhys and played another note, then another, a series I somehow recognized as slowing time. The figure of the leader of the strange Fae trio appeared in flashes, his hood down and his nose streaming blood. One eye already swelled shut with a bruise.

"Good for you and your bony elbows," Troubadour said.

"Thanks." I rubbed the joint in question, thankful I hadn't further injured myself. "I lucked out. He wasn't expecting me to fight back. He has quite the energy-sucking ability. Is that still rare, Troubadour?"

"Yes, quite."

The vision of the strange Fae stabilized. He held his nose and came toward us again. This time Rhys captured him in a cage of fire, and he couldn't break out.

I glanced around for the other two. "Have either of you seen where the others went?"

Rhys pulled something out of his pocket, two stones about the size of pound coins that glowed slightly with the blue sheen of labradorite. "There aren't any others. He used these."

He handed one to me, and I tested its weight in my palm. It tingled against my skin. "Mirror stones. Clever."

Troubadour walked over to the Fae in his cage of fire. The captive poked at the flames and drew his hand back, shaking it. "Let me go."

I joined Troubadour in front of the curved wall of flames.

"Not until you tell us who sent you and how you aren't high Fae and yet have two major powers—time-sped invisibility and energy drain. Someone must have loaned you their ability."

Troubadour continued to study the would-be assassin, his arms crossed and his harp dangling from one hand. "There's something very familiar about this Fae. Something having to do with what I wanted to tell you, Princess, although it won't come as news anymore."

"Which is...?"

"I couldn't detect the identity of the light Fae who approached me to help him with summoning the soul-eater, but I could tell one thing beyond the gender. He'd borrowed abilities from a high Fae, a very high Fae, which means someone in your grandmother's circle. Someone who is invested in you not reaching your goal here."

"This isn't entirely new news, but I thank you."

The captured Fae sneered, and the light from the surrounding flames turned what would have been a handsome face into a grotesque mask of shadows. "You think you're so clever, Princess, but you have enemies. Some of them could be traveling with you."

I drew myself up to my full height and summoned my Fae princess power. "As your princess, I command you to tell me who hired you to eliminate me."

Rhys joined us. "And as your prince, I command you to tell us who loaned you their powers in order to finish us off."

The traitor grinned and opened his mouth, but not to answer our questions. The energy built around him, and he would have to tell us, or he would explode. There was no way he could outrank us, and yet he resisted. He shook from head to toe, and sweat poured from his face. With one trembling hand, he pulled something that looked like a large blueberry from the pouch at his waist and popped it in his mouth.

I grabbed my brother by the wrist. "Rhys, douse the flames, now!"

He did so, but it was too late. The prisoner bit down on the berry, and like a wax candle in a fireplace, he melted from the top down. First his hair fell out, and then his skin poured off of him. I put my hand over my mouth to keep from losing what little I'd eaten that day. Although I was a physician and had seen my share of corpses, the sudden decomposition of one in front of me, leaving nothing but a putrid pile of clothing filled with rotting flesh, invoked a sense of horror from my very core for both that and what he'd just done.

Rhys had gone white. "He...he took a suicide berry."

I put my arm around his waist so he wouldn't topple over. "Thanks for stating the obvious, Rhys."

"That means no coming back, no waking after ten millennia, no new life. He's dead-dead."

"Yes." I bowed my head. "May the gods have mercy."

Rhys pulled away from me. "We don't have gods, Reine. All we have are Fae politics and unreasonable standards. And now we don't even have a path to follow." He gestured around us, and it was true. The path had disappeared, and all I could see were trees in the same view in every direction.

A crunching sound at my feet made me look down, then step back. The forest floor sucked in the remains of the dead Fae. Troubadour reached down and grabbed the leather scabbard holding the Fae-steel knife. The clothing it had been resting against disappeared into the earth.

Troubadour proffered the weapon and its casing. "Princess, for you. It looks like you're going to need to defend yourself."

"Thank you." I hesitated. "What favor will I owe you for this?"

He smiled, showing me the slight points to his teeth, like he had the first time he'd come to me through a medium. "Just remember me. That's all I ask."

"In what sense?"

"You'll see. But at least you're re-learning how to be a Fae."

This time I took the knife and buckled the belt around my waist. It shrank to fit, feeling odd as it slithered against my skin in its adjustments. That only confirmed that the weapon and the belt/scabbard had come from the high Fae craftsmen. Common Fae couldn't afford such luxuries.

"Well, then, shall we find the Path again?" I asked with feigned confidence.

"Lead the way, Princess." Troubadour smiled at me, and this time I felt the warmth coming from him. Underneath his bravado, I sensed the possibility that he might actually be a good Fae, although that would remain to be seen.

18

LAWRENCE

"Mrrowl?" Sir Raleigh plopped in front of me when we started walking away from the stream.

"Hey, there you are." I rubbed him behind his ears, which were slightly damp, strengthening my suspicion that he'd gone to help Kestrel. "I'm glad you're back."

He sat on the path in front of me, and each time I tried to move around him, he blocked me.

"What is it?" I asked. "Are we supposed to wait for the others. We can't see them, remember?"

"We can't just stay here," John argued. "It's going to get dark soon, and it's too exposed out here."

Sir Raleigh gave me a baleful look, then stepped aside. He watched us walk past, then took up the rear behind Kestrel. Message received—we were making our own choices, and he could only help us so far. It would be up to us as to the price we'd pay in the Gray Zone.

We had just walked into the woods when we found ourselves surrounded. Small creatures that resembled the gate-keeper of the dark Fae capital, but grayish green instead of blue, melted out of the trees and encircled us, pointing nasty-looking wooden weapons.

"You come with us," the tallest of them, which came to my knee, commanded.

"Says who?" John asked. "Lawrence, surely you can handle a bunch of gnomes with toothpicks."

One of the gnomes jabbed John in the calf with said toothpick, and he buckled backward. They swarmed him, and in five seconds, they had him trussed and strung on a pole that two of them carried between them. At least they'd bandaged the wound on his leg.

The leader nodded, apparently satisfied, and turned to me. "As you see, we mean you no harm."

"What do you mean?" Kestrel demanded. "Your guy stabbed my father!"

"That was Chirzig. He gets carried away sometimes."

I glanced up, but the branches hung too close together for me to be able to fly and get help from... Well, I didn't know where. For all I knew, Rhys and the other Fae were still battling the creatures of the lake. Sir Raleigh and I exchanged despairing looks. He didn't speak to me, but he cocked his head, and I caught his meaning—*We're outnumbered and trapped.*

"It's fine. I'll take care of them."

The grimalkin cocked his head, and I sensed his doubt.

"What, it's not like you can do much. They have us trapped."

In fact, they kept trying to throw ropes over Sir Raleigh, which he batted away. Finally, one of them looped a rope around his tail, and with a hiss, he disappeared.

We followed the gnomes down the path and then onto a smaller path to the left, which I would never have seen had they not shown it to me. We finally came to a clearing very much like the one in the woods in the Earth realm, ringed with standing stones. A large fire burned in the middle, and a slightly larger creature—greener than the rest, but still wrinkled and gnome-like—sat on a throne. It wore a black shirt and breeches, and over them, a gray-feathered cloak. A silver crown perched on its bald head. It studied us with glittering, black eyes for a few minutes, then turned to the leader of the expedition.

"The human. It resisted?"

"Yes, Your Highness."

"It hurt?"

"Yes, Your Highness."

"Chirzig?" He scowled, and the gnome who had stabbed John bowed his head, his ears going forward in shame.

"No need to say yes." The king of the gnomes snorted. "And the grimalkin?"

"Allowed to escape. Can disappear."

Another snort. "Fae queen will be angry we have her friends. Good bargaining."

Recognizing that somehow we'd been trapped, I decided I needed to act, especially since the humans had no point of reference. I might, but it was shrouded in the mists of time. I stepped forward and bowed, figuring that any king would appreciate the gesture. All the gnomes raised their heads to me, and I found myself the object of a hundred flinty, black, but curious, gazes.

"Good evening, and well-met, Your Highness." I reached back into my memory for the etiquette lessons my mother had drilled into me so many hundreds of years ago "just in case" we were ever to go to the Aerie and meet the Gargoyle Regent. "I and my friends thank you for your hospitality."

The king looked up at me, his eyes going wide, and then he laughed, showing pointed, yellow teeth. He turned to his general. "You didn't mention the funny gargoyle."

"I didn't know gargoyles could be funny, Majesty."

The head gnome looked me up and down, then turned his attention to Kestrel. "This isn't her?"

"No, Majesty. The Fae Queen has lighter hair and has better powers."

Kestrel opened her mouth, possibly to ask what powers they sensed in her, and I shook my head. I raised an eyebrow slightly, and she nodded. I hoped she got the message—figure out something to channel, if she could. We could use a secret weapon.

"Um, a little help here?" John called. "You're not going to cook me for dinner, are you?"

"You're not going to cause more trouble, are you?" the gnome king asked, and his tone mimicked John's.

Listening to him talk made me suspect that they were picking up on our language as we spoke. How fascinating. I itched to take out my notebook and record my observations, but I didn't dare call attention to my backpack. I didn't want it to be confiscated like John's.

"No, sir. I will not. Please release me."

I held up a hand, and if I wriggled my fingertips to emphasize the sharpness of my claws, I couldn't help it. "John, remember where you are. Your Highness, please release my friend with no penalty or lien."

The king grinned again. "Gargoyle knows the rules of the game. Well met, indeed. Cut the human down—no debt."

"Thank you," Kestrel sighed, then put hands over her mouth. "I'm sorry—is that okay to say here?"

The gnomes around us snickered, and the general said, "We see you've been to the dark Fae capital. We're Woodies, not Brownies."

"Excuse me?" Her cheeks turned pink, and I could only imagine the internal snickering a twenty-year-old would be doing at creatures identifying themselves as Woodies.

"Wood gnomes, not house elves," I explained. "I think?" Now

I imagined the big-eyed servants from the *Harry Potter* movies. Would I need to bargain with my socks?

The king waved his hand. "Close enough. We are the Court of the Winter Gnomes." He bowed slightly, and Kestrel returned the gesture, but more deeply to show respect. Good girl. What had her PBI training taught her? Or was she channeling something innate, something from that secret identity that came forward in flashes?

As we talked, the gnomes cut John down from the pole, and he rubbed his hands together, presumably to return feeling to his fingers. Kestrel knelt beside him and massaged his ankles. He grimaced.

"Pins and needles?" she asked.

"Yes, and how."

She closed her eyes, and everyone in the clearing stilled and watched her.

"Catch the eel," she whispered. "Like Reine told me, catch the fishy—aha! There you are, you slippery thing."

She opened her eyes, which had turned more green than blue, and blew on her fingertips. She took John's hands in hers, and his shoulders relaxed with relief. Then she placed her hands over his feet, and he closed his eyes. Finally, she touched his calf where he'd been stabbed. He slumped to the ground, asleep. She stood, her brows drawn together and rubbed her hands over her upper arms like she'd lost a lot of heat.

"I think I healed him, but what happened? He should be okay."

A wizened female gnome emerged from the crowd and patted Kestrel on the leg. "It's okay, dearie. It happens. He's fine. You'll get more finesse with practice."

"Thank you." Kestrel smiled down at the gnome. "I'm new to this."

The gnome healer cracked a sharp-toothed grin back at Kestrel. "It's okay. Tricky, you are."

The Winter Gnome king cleared his throat, and the healer bowed her head and melted back into the shadows that gathered at the edge of the clearing as dusk fell.

"Stay with us," he said. "We will feed you and keep you safe. Danger lurks in the dark."

I crossed my arms and tried to look intimidating, but they had me outmatched in number if not size. "Are we your guests, or your prisoners?"

"That, Sir Gargoyle, is not for you to decide. It will be her decision."

"Whose?"

"The new queen's."

19

REINE

We wandered around for a while, and by a while, I mean for about an hour. Fae aren't known for their patience. Finally, when it felt like we came back to the same set of trees and rocks, Rhys plopped down on one of them.

"We're lost."

"Again, thanks for stating the obvious, dear brother." I sat beside him, and Troubadour remained standing, scanning our surroundings.

I scowled at him. "You're the dark Fae, and these are your lands. Don't you have some sort of trick or guidance for us?"

"Yeah," Rhys agreed. "That chick in the cave called you a prince, and you've got the vibe. You should have some sort of command of the forest or something else Fae-ish going on."

I directed a silent question to Rhys. *What chick in what cave?*

I think it was Desdemona, but I'm not sure. They're cousins. Tell you the rest later.

Troubadour arched an eyebrow and ran one hand through his hair. The dark blond strands seemed to relish being out of their controlled coif, giving him a rakish air. I looked away, my cheeks heating. What was wrong with me? I mean, yes, I was attracted to him, but I had gotten way too old for silly schoolgirl reactions. Or had I secretly been fascinated with him since he'd appeared through Aria at her shop? He certainly didn't act like a Fae prince.

He plucked at his harp, and the notes sounded hushed, like they, too, had gotten trapped in whatever space-time loop Faerie had built here. The melody tugged at my heartstrings with its sadness.

"Ish is about right for me." He continued to play, the song bittersweet, and inclined his head toward Rhys. "A Fae prince doesn't have to be scarred to be exiled from his court."

Rhys put a hand to his marred cheek. "Harsh, mate."

Troubadour had the grace to appear somewhat abashed, although I doubted the genuineness of the expression. "I do apologize, but surely you've become accustomed to it by now."

"There's no getting used to something that keeps you trapped away from your home."

"That, Light Prince, is very true." Troubadour sighed and sank to a cross-legged posture on the ground. I think we all held our breath in case we needed to rescue him from the forest floor sucking him in, but nothing happened. Maybe it waited until the Fae or other creature died or at least succumbed to exhaustion and starvation. My stomach growled.

"Oh!" I dug in my pack. "I still have a breakfast wrap from this morning. Who wants some?"

The looks on their faces resembled something feral, so I divided the wrap as best I could and handed it around. A golden glow flowed between our hands as I did so, and I smiled. Even in a temporal trap in the dark Fae lands, the magic of breaking bread (and eggs and cheese) held. Thankfully Fae food didn't spoil.

Eating made me recognize the despair that had crept in

underneath my tiredness, and I stood to shake it off. "Let's go again. We have to find our way out—"

Troubadour finished for me, "Before dark, lest the water wolves swarm again."

I shuddered. "You don't think we dealt them enough of a blow?"

"There are always more predatory creatures, Princess. If not the wolves, then something else. There's a reason the walls of the city are so high and impenetrable."

"I thought they were to repel invading Fae armies."

"That's a nice side benefit, although if the invaders were as beautiful and charming as you, I wouldn't mind."

I laughed. "That was a clumsy flirt. Come on, you can do better than that."

Rhys rolled his eyes, then frowned and looked up. "Stop it, the two of you. Wait, I have an idea." His wings appeared, and he flew upward. Not willing to be separated vertically or horizontally, I followed him, and Troubadour came close behind me. Rhys reached the tops of the trees, and we turned and searched for any sort of landmark.

Troubadour sighed. "We should be able to see the lake and possibly the city from up here, but there's nothing. Just waves of unbroken trees."

"Wait." I squinted into the distance. "Over there. Do you see it? There's a gray smudge."

They turned toward where I pointed.

"I do believe you're right, Princess. That could be the border of the Gray Zone. I've heard its magic is powerful enough to overcome most spells, including defensive ones."

"That's why we have to stay to the path once we get there. But let's go."

"How do you know it's not an illusion?" my ever-so-skeptical brother asked.

I paused and closed my eyes, reaching into the well of

memory. I found the signature of the Gray Zone's energy, a certain vibration and feel in the air. The echo of the same drew me forward. "Because I can actually feel it." I flew onward, the guys flanking me.

Troubadour turned to me with a frown. "No one can feel the Gray Zone except the gray Fae."

"Perhaps I've picked up some tricks during my time in the Earth realm. Or maybe I've always been good with places."

"She has always had an uncanny sense of direction," Rhys agreed. "That's why my mother insisted she come with me when I forayed out into the Earth realm."

I glanced at him, my brows raised with surprise. He didn't often talk about our life before our exile. Both of us found it too painful. He grinned and shrugged.

We crossed something, an invisible resistance in the air, that made my body twang like one of Troubadour's harp strings. I paused and flew back, testing it. The two princes circled back.

Rhys asked, "What is it?"

"Something shocked me. Didn't you feel it?"

"No, but look." Troubadour pointed downward, and now that I floated in the energy that tingled with welcome, I could see a break in the trees that formed a line.

"It's the Shadowed Path." I descended, and when my feet met the hard-packed dirt, relief flooded through me. "Thank the gods."

The others landed beside me, and Rhys swiped the back of his hand across his brow. "Phew. I'd forgotten how hard flying could be after not doing it for so long. Good thing you had the food."

My stomach twinged again, and now that we'd come out of the perpetual afternoon of the forest trap, I could see the sun had progressed on its descent. The shadows had grown longer, and the light more golden.

"Yes, and we should hurry, lest we become food for something else."

Troubadour fell in behind me. "Do you know what Ellerin had planned for you in the Gray Zone?"

"No, but I hope I'll be able to figure it out once we get there."

"With your strange affinity?" Rhys sounded skeptical and a little disapproving. Oh, well, he could feel what he wanted.

"Probably from having been there before, although Sir Raleigh guided me." The tightness of the forest spacing loosened with more room between the trunks and grass appearing in patches here and there. The blades had started their autumn fade from green to brown, and all around me the land emanated the waning vibration of the cooling season. A pang of homesickness for my little cottage in Scotland, which would be surrounded by leaves of red, yellow, and orange, darted through my chest. That was odd—this was my home, even if I hadn't quite reached Lorien yet. Why would I feel nostalgic for a place I'd longed to escape?

The forest gave way entirely to grassland, and we walked down a gentle slope to a stream. I stopped, sensing the border.

Rhys and Troubadour flanked me again, and we all looked at the water.

Rhys spoke first. "That's not a normal stream."

"No," Troubadour agreed, "it's not. That's the border of the Gray Zone, so it's a transition feature. We'll need to be careful crossing it."

"So, you're coming with us?" I asked, my heart giving an unexpected skip. "You don't have to. You gave me the information you intended, and now you can find your way back."

He shook his head. "I'm in it for the long haul, Princess. Besides, I have business in Lorien I've been putting off, so I may as well come with you. It seems like you could use the help."

I looked at Rhys, who scowled but didn't say anything for a few seconds, then, "Your call, Reine. He has been helpful."

"That's fine with me, then. Shall we cross and see what awaits us on the other side?"

WHEN WE CROSSED THE STREAM, which took only a brief appearance of wings, I had the sense we'd taken a step that couldn't be un-taken, like if we'd crossed back, we'd only be back on the same side of the stream. Faerie could be tricky like that. While Fae were known for reversals and deceptions, our land had a determined will of its own, sometimes manifested in something like the Shadowed Path.

Once we landed, we found footsteps showing that Lawrence, Sir Raleigh, and the humans had made it that far, too. I glanced over my shoulder to check the position of the sun and found it difficult to locate. As before, the thick clouds of the Gray Zone obscured its light such that it appeared as a faint moonglow, which hovered over the trees on the other side of the river.

"I hope they're not too far ahead of us. We need to find someplace safe for the night."

"Can you call the grimalkin?" Rhys asked. "It's attuned to you."

"It's a he, not it, and good idea." I closed my eyes and reached out mentally to find Sir Raleigh's energy. I couldn't imagine him as his Faerie creature self, though. I brought to mind the way he purred as he curled up in a ball in the crook of my neck when we went to sleep, his tail tickling my pointed ear. That's how we communicated, not in words but in touches, like many owners and their pets, although he'd turned out to be much more. Underneath my concern for the humans had been a fear that Sir Raleigh would be hurt or worse, or that he would decide to stay in the Gray Zone since he was a creature of the gray Fae.

"Mrrrowr?" The sound came from the tree line ahead, and I started forward.

"Sir Raleigh? Where's my kitty?"

Rhys frowned at me. "Really? You're referring to that thing as a kitty?"

"He's my sweet kitty, even if he can look scary. He wouldn't hurt me. Maybe you should get a pet. Then you'd figure it out."

When I reached the trees, I looked around, but I couldn't see him. Then I heard a rustling to the left and had almost stepped off the path into the thick fog that wound through the trees—did it never burn off outside of the light Fae lands?—when Troubadour caught my arm.

"Remember where you are. It could be a trick."

"That's true." I sighed and willed the irritation at being kept from my goal to subside. He had a good point. "Thank you for reminding me."

We trudged through the woods until a flickering up ahead made us stop to get our bearings. We switched to secret conversation so no one would overhear us.

"Is that a fire?" Troubadour's voice felt like honey to my brain, and I had to not succumb to its charm. I doubted he was intentionally trying to bespell me—most times, Fae couldn't control how their secret voice sounded to others.

I wondered how mine sounded to him when I replied, *"It looks like it, but who would be stupid enough to build a fire on the path?"*

"Unless it's another illusion." Rhys made a little flame dance over his fingertips, much like I had done with Kestrel earlier. It made me more worried for the humans and others.

We crept forward until we could see a wall of flames across the path. The trees knit their branches just above the top of the fire, so we wouldn't be able to fly over it.

"What now?" Rhys asked, and I could tell he wanted me to answer.

Being in direct line for a throne, I was highest-ranking Fae, although the two Fae with me had proved their initiative to this point. In fact, Troubadour answered before I could.

"This is the Gray Zone. We need to figure out whether it's real, and if it's a gateway."

It did look like it could be a gate to a different part of Faerie, a different realm, or even a dimension. The Gray Zone did have the interdimensional quicksand, after all. And razor grass. And large things that sounded frightening and probably looked worse, although I hadn't stuck around long enough on my previous visit to actually visually confirm anything.

"How can you tell what it is?" I asked Troubadour.

He pulled his harp from under his cloak and strummed it. The barrier across our path didn't do anything, but a dark figure appeared in the middle of the flames. It wore a cloak of black, and I couldn't see what lay beneath the hood, which covered its face.

"Does everyone in this place have to wear a hood and mask?" I didn't bother to hide my exasperation.

Perhaps I'd thought a little too loudly because the newcomer raised its head and said in a sibilant voice, "Perhaps you should recall who you are, Princess."

I put my hands on my hips. "Who are you to tell me who I am?"

It mimicked my posture. "And who are you to forget it?"

That did it. I was sore, tired, getting hungry again, and I needed to see my cat and human friends and...well, whatever Lawrence was to me. We could figure that out later. I managed to stand as straight as I could, ignoring the twinges along my spine from wing support muscles that hadn't been used in several hundred years.

Thunder rolled around me, and the words of an old spell came back to me. "I come like a storm in the night." Electrical energy tingled along my spine, then through my shoulder blades and fingertips. "Give way for your princess, douser of flames and bringer of true light." I held my hands about a foot apart and generated a ball of shimmering blue light, shot through with storm energy. A new verse came to my mind, then, and I tried to clamp my lips over it, but the words tumbled out. "Make way for your queen of shadow and light, water and flame, wind and stone!" Then I held the energy ball above my head and lobbed it at the gate. When the two collided, the flames turned blue and disappeared. The hooded Fae bowed low, then also winked out of sight, and the trees straightened.

I glanced to either side of me to see Rhys and Troubadour looking at me with mingled respect and fear. Then both of them bowed.

"Oh, Hades. I so did not mean to do that."

A dark furry shape bowled into me, and a delightful, "Mrrrowl?" reached my ears just before I landed on my ass.

Although Sir Raleigh most resembled a cat and purred his happiness, he also licked me in a wide, wet swath across my cheek with a large sandpaper tongue. I didn't mind. I hugged him to me, careful not to crush his wings.

"There you are! Where have you been, silly boy?"

He stepped back and cocked his head in a clear signal for me to follow. I staggered to my feet, suspecting I'd end up healing some bruises in some uncomfortable spots from that tumble.

Troubadour cleared his throat from behind me. I noticed he stayed well clear of the grimalkin.

"Begging your pardon, Princess, but you keep strange company. Why do you have the grimalkin with you still?"

I felt the wrinkles form between my eyes as I scowled at him. "Why wouldn't I? He's my..." I almost said *pet*, but Fae creatures weren't pets. "He's my protector, and my friend."

Sir Raleigh licked his chops with a smug look, which I

supposed was as close as he would get to sticking his tongue out at someone.

Troubadour looked between me and Sir Raleigh. "'Tis true that such creatures can be sent as protectors, but once their function is over, they traditionally return to the one who summoned them. If he was your protector while in the Earth realm—and I sensed him to be as such—why is he still here?"

I rubbed the top of Sir Raleigh's soft head. "Why, indeed? Is it possible he decided to stay with me? His summoner gave him the form of a cat, after all. They do have minds of their own." A whisper of memory teased me—Ellerin saying something similar. I had known with my gut sense that Ellerin had summoned Sir Raleigh, and I also knew with that certainty that the grimalkin's mission wasn't finished yet, that he was more than a protector. Perhaps mediator would be the best term, and I turned to him.

"You're here to bring me to my next challenge, aren't you?"

Rhys pointed to the darkening sky. "Don't get too ambitious, sis. We need to find somewhere to shelter. The Gray Zone is no place to be exposed after sunset."

I turned to Troubadour. "So, it's either go with the grimalkin or wait to see what happens here in the woods. What do you think?"

Troubadour sighed and said, "Lead the way, cat."

20

REINE

S ir Raleigh brought us off the path, and I made notice of how the intersection of branch and path felt so that I would be able to find it back if needed. I'm not sure what happened at the fiery gate, only that something had shifted within me, and I had access to more Fae power than I ever had previously.

Rhys might have noticed the differences well. He kept looking at me strangely, and finally I asked, "What? Do I have something on my face?"

He shook his head. "No, what you said back there... I'm not sure what to make of it. It sounded like you were saying a spell, but it's not one I'm familiar with."

I lowered my voice, hoping Troubadour wouldn't hear me. "I don't know either. The words just seemed to come out."

Troubadour might or might not have heard me, and his words made me wonder. "I have heard legend of when a Fae queen is dying, her heir may start showing signs before the queen even knows herself."

"I'm not the heir, my mother is."

Troubadour only smiled. I sensed he knew more than he was letting on, but then, that's what we Fae did.

Sir Raleigh led us into a clearing, in which a gray-green gnome sat on a throne. A fire illuminated the center of the area, leaving the edges in shadow. The eyes of other gnomes sparkled in the reflection of the firelight, like a sea of fallen stars. I couldn't even begin to count them because my attention was immediately drawn to the two humans and gargoyle who stood to the left of the throne.

"Kestrel, John, Lawrence, I'm so glad to see you." The two humans smiled, and Lawrence looked surprised. But I had spoken the truth, I was happy to see him. Even though we had a lot of history between us, I hoped we could work something out. Even if it was only him forgiving me.

I gave the Winter Goblin King—for this is who I surmised sat on the throne—my most brilliant Fae princess smile.

"Thank you for your hospitality, Your Majesty." I felt silly curtseying while wearing pants, so I bowed, and Rhys and Troubadour did as well. When I straightened, I met the king's eyes, hoping he would return the expression, but he sat and drummed his fingers on the arm of his throne.

"You do realize your presence here could cause grave trouble for us, Princess."

"I'm afraid I have been away for quite some time, so I am not familiar with the current state of Fae politics. Is there a reason why you are now housed in the Gray Zone rather than in the lands of the dark Fae?"

I wished Ellerin were there. He would have probably given us the scoop before arriving in the court of the Winter Goblin King. Anxiety and grief unfurled in my chest. Was he okay? If he had managed to defeat the lake creature, wouldn't he have joined us by now? I suspected that he knew what had been going on in my absence, and I regretted not taking the opportunity to sit down with him and really get a good sense of the state of Faerie.

Since he wasn't there, I would have to keep my wits about me. I suspected that the humans and Lawrence hadn't ended up in the clearing by accident. That meant the Winter Goblin King had captured them, and he wanted something from me.

"I have been trying to speak with somebody from either of your courts for some time." He nodded to me, then to Rhys, then to Troubadour. "Having all three of you here is a true blessing from the goddesses. However, I was not expecting to have representatives from both courts in my humble home. Please, rest yourselves, eat, drink, and we will speak of this matter in the morning."

I knew not to accept anything from him without knowing what he would want in return. That was Fae 101. "I thank you for your generous offer, and I would not dare impose on you unless I knew what I could do for you in return."

He nodded, like he was hoping I would know how to play by the rules. "Very well, Princess. I offer you the hospitality of my people for the night in exchange for you remembering me and my petition, which I will give you in the morning, when you reach your throne."

"I feel compelled to be honest with you, Your Highness. I am not here to take the throne. I am here in order to petition for my and my brother's return."

"I am aware of your exile. However, as you said, you are not entirely aware of the situation here in Faerie. I would offer to enlighten you, but that is not my place. The cost would be too high."

I noticed he didn't specify whether the cost would be to him or to me, but I respected his caution and his consideration. "I hope you'll forgive me for asking one more question of you this evening, but I do want to make sure that our bargain encompasses hospitality for we three Fae as well as the two humans, the gargoyle, and the grimalkin."

This time he smiled, showing a full range of yellow, pointed teeth. He really did belong in the dark Fae lands, and he had definitely piqued my curiosity as to why he and his court had taken up in the Gray Zone. "Yes, Princess. You and your entire party are welcome to our hospitality." He looked at each of us, and his gaze lingered longest on Kestrel. Then he winked at me.

Heat flooded to my cheeks. I had just made a rookie mistake —letting on that I didn't actually know what Kestrel was, and he had let me off by mentioning my entire party rather than limiting it to just me and what I had specified, specifically the two humans. Did I appear weak? Hades, I was tired. I didn't resist when one of the gnomes came over carrying a lei of autumn leaves and motioned putting it around my neck. I bent over and allowed her to do so, except I found it wasn't a lei, it was a crown.

"Thank you, but in my lands, only queens can wear crowns."

She winked—the gnomes liked doing that—and bowed, and I noticed her belt with several pouches on it.

"I am many centuries older than you are," she said, her voice cracking as one would expect for someone over a millennium old. "As the humans would say, I call them as I see them."

She led me to a side of the clearing, where my companions had all taken seats on the ground, sitting cross-legged or kneeling, and other gnomes brought plates of food. For a while, we all ate, because we were so hungry.

The first one to fall asleep was Kestrel, whose eyes drooped while she leaned against her father's shoulder. He sat with his back against the tree, and soon his head dropped forward. Rhys and Troubadour followed suit, Rhys with his head on his pack, and the dark Fae Prince curled up under his cloak. I suspected he had spent many a night under the stars, although how many nights had he spent surrounded by them? The gnomes might look ugly to some, but I found their craggy faces to be beautiful, especially their dark, sparkling eyes.

"What are you thinking?" Lawrence's voice poured like warm chocolate into my ears. Had it only been a few days since we had connected on a fundamental level, and then I had broken his heart?

I dared not move lest I broke the spell and cause him to disappear, or, more likely, to turn away, his eyes and expression hardened. "Their circumstances are humble, but look at how they take care of each other. Even the king is considerate of the lowliest of his subjects."

Indeed, the Winter Goblin King smiled fondly down at a gnome child, with whom he shared a piece of bread. A relative? Who knew? Most kings—and, in my experience, queens— would foist the child off on its mother, even if it belonged to him.

"That's how things are in the Aerie, at least from what I've heard."

I turned to him, and for a moment, I searched for his human features before I remembered he was in gargoyle form. Ellerin had told me that in Faerie, at least at the asylum, we would be revealed for who we truly were. Was it not the case for him? Or was it part of the fairy curse on gargoyles?

He smiled awkwardly. "Do you find me repulsive?"

"No, I find you fascinating." I turned my head away. That was a bit more honest than I had meant to be. I had to ask, "And do you find me repulsive?"

He paused for a while, and with each second that passed, my heart sank lower toward my stomach. "I suppose that, as a doomed man, I shouldn't hold anything back."

Tears stung the corners of my eyes, and I braced myself. The memory of his last rejection still played vividly in my mind. Even if it had helped me to defeat the creature that had been trying to take me over, it still hurt. A lot. "You're not doomed. We'll figure out a way to get you through this." But the question still hung in the air between us—would he trust me to?

He didn't answer it. "Fascinating is a good word. You're strong and powerful, but you value truth and beauty, and you are very loyal to your kind."

I wanted to confront him on his non-answer, or maybe it was not the answer I wanted him to give. I didn't trust myself to say anything, though. It seemed like the more strength and power I gained, the more confusion came along with it.

Sir Raleigh came and plopped beside me, forcing me closer to Lawrence.

Lawrence peeked around me and grinned at Sir Raleigh. "It's funny how he's so cat-like."

"I know. Does he have a sense of how big he is?"

Sir Raleigh yawned, showing his intimidating set of teeth, then looked at us as if to say, "I'm right here."

Lawrence and I exchanged a smile. Sitting there with him, our arms touching, our knees pressed together, everything feeling comfortable and familiar in spite of our weird circumstances... I shook my head to dispel the fog of desire, both physical and emotional. Even if he was willing, it wouldn't be a good idea or possible. No, I reminded myself, I wanted to stay here, and he would have to leave. In fact, his being here put him in danger, both of becoming stuck and turning to stone, and of dying outright. And of being hurt by me again. That I couldn't forget, and he knew it, too. Why else would he have pointed out how loyal I was to the Fae?

So, what did I want? The memories of our kisses, our romantic encounters edged out the rejection recollection. Would he be willing to have a Fae with benefits?

I ran my hand over the strong muscles in his forearm. "You might be a very stony earth elemental, but you're surprisingly warm."

He chuckled, and the sound rumbled through me. "Gargoyles don't get cold. We store up the warmth of the sun, even if we don't see it for most of the day."

I leaned against him, then. He put an arm around me, and we sat there in silence. I had so much I wanted to say, so much I was afraid to say. The words tangled in each other and blocked each other from coming out. A Fae princess didn't say she was sorry, and I already had once. And he had rejected me.

He gave me a quick squeeze, then moved away, leaving me cold where we had been touching. "You should get some sleep, Reine. You need to be at your best tomorrow. It sounds like you're going to have a lot of bargaining to do."

I nodded. Sir Raleigh shifted so he could curl up around, instead of against, me, and I snuggled up to him. He covered me with one of his wings, and the last thing I was aware of before I drifted into sleep was the ache in my heart and a chime in my ears like the one from the bell my grandmother had used to summon her servants—and her daughters and granddaughters—in the castle.

21

LAWRENCE

I walked to the edge of the clearing and tried to ignore the baleful look Sir Raleigh gave me. "Coward," he seemed to say. My skin held on to the memory of Reine's feel and weight against me, and I relished the way her soft hair had brushed over my biceps and chest.

The sense of restlessness burned through me, a push-pull of desire and caution. My inner gargoyle seemed to be confused about the whole situation. Why didn't I just claim her? He wanted to know. I wanted her, she seemed to want me, and wasn't it time I took a mate? Sometimes my inner gargoyle seemed to channel my mother and her various guilt trips.

The moon had risen overhead, paving the way in silvery light that poured through me as well, a calming benediction for a creature of stone and earth. I had never felt the moon as I did here, and I debated going back and retrieving my backpack in order to note the sensations. However, something drew me forward, tugging at my protective instincts. The sense of the ground, the dirt and stone beneath me, also felt more vivid than in my home realm, lending confirmation to what I'd been taught—that gargoyles had once lived in fairy and been the guardians of the high Fae. What had happened to make the atmosphere so toxic for us? Or had that been a result of the break between gargoyle and Fae, since this was a realm where it was impossible to hide the truth? An interesting irony, that, considering how deceptive the Fae could be in spite of their inability to lie.

I drew on the power of the minerals beneath me, and they gladly gave it up for an earth elemental. In spite of my size, I managed to cloak myself so I appeared to be just one of the shadows. I gave into the impulse to follow the narrow dirt trail in front of me and soon heard voices.

The path opened onto another clearing, this one also ringed with standing stones, and with a large reflective pane of obsidian—the preferred surface here, I noticed—at the far end. The healer gnome stood in front of it, and she was flanked by two others, whom I sensed were younger. One of them wore a robe of light gray, and I could only see the back of her head and tips of her ears over it. The other one wore black, and the only way I knew she was female was from her voice.

"When do the dreams start, mother?"

The words came through somewhat distorted, and I frowned, then had the sense of an old piece of magic clicking into place.

"The old bond between gargoyle and the Fae creatures," something explained to me. *"In order to protect the high Fae, they allowed your kind to be able to understand the languages of the others as long as you could channel the power of the moon, which lightens and also hides."*

I bowed my head in thanks and wriggled my fingers to dispel the compulsion to find something to write on. The situation not only piqued my scientist's curiosity, but also a sense of my heritage and how I could potentially fill in the gaps in gargoyle history.

"Later, my son. Pay attention now so you can protect."

Gah! More questions, but I obeyed and turned my attention back to the gnomes.

"Patience, daughter. It takes time for brains to reach dream sleep. They need to go through other stages first."

I wish I could ask if she knew this from her own studies here, or if they had some way to know about the human science of sleep medicine and what it had found. I chose to remain hidden. Something told me that things were about to get very interesting.

The gnome in black spoke again. "Maybe you should have increased the dose of dream wort you put in the food."

Interesting and disturbing. So why hadn't I succumbed like the others? Right, because I didn't absorb food and air as efficiently in this realm. I wished I could set up a lab, take blood, and do some analyses to see how and where I fell short, what enzyme or whatever else I lacked. Did the healer gnome know? Probably not, or she would have managed to figure out something to compensate for it.

While we were both in the business of healing others, she apparently had other, sinister intent. Or perhaps she and the king had agreed for her to spy on us so she could report to him what was going on in our subconsciouses. I could see how that would be interesting, although I didn't know how useful it would be.

Images flickered across the obsidian, and the three gnomes clasped hands and began a murmuring chant so quiet I couldn't make out the words to it. Multiple foggy fragments of dreams played out, and they appeared and disappeared so quickly I couldn't tell which belonged to whom. Well, except for the one featuring some sort of large rodent. I guessed that belonged to Sir Raleigh.

The main healer gnome, whom I decided to refer to as Mother, as the others had, raised her hands, palms facing the stone.

"Great goddess of the night, revealer of hopes and dreams, thank you for your blessings. Please heed our cry to you for help knowing the strangers in our midst."

The fragments stabilized, and they played out in quadrants, although they still looked hazy, like we watched through fog or some weird camera filter.

The gnome in black shook her hood back, revealing a head full of luminous, blond hair. "Which one belongs to the girl?"

Mother, whose hands still faced the stone, spread them, enlarging the movie playing out in the lower left quadrant and covering the others. The three of them leaned forward to see some sort of detail I couldn't make out from where I was. In fact, I couldn't tear my eyes away from the scene that played out in spite of my desire to allow my adopted godchild her privacy.

The scene took place from Kestrel's point of view, and so it tracked what she saw and chose to look at. It was back in the main CPDC laboratory, and it bounced back and forth between Lucius Cimex waving a gun and her mother during their final argument. I placed a hand over my heart as the ache of loss, and the knowledge that what I experienced could only be a shade of the grief she experienced, split my chest. Poor kid. This had been an adventure for her, but there would still be sorrow and adjustment when she returned to the Earth realm.

Although I knew how the scene ended, I wanted it to be different, desperately desired for Lucius to miss, for Beverly to duck, something... I tensed, knowing the final conclusion would occur any moment.

A golden glow filled the scene, and instead of shooting, Lucius lowered the gun, and Corey tackled him, knocking it away. Beverly stood, shaking, and Kestrel rushed to her. The three gnomes bowed their heads, as did I, in sympathy at what Kestrel must be experiencing and how she would wake from the joy and relief to find out it was all a dream, and she could very well be in a different kind of living nightmare.

The gnome in gray broke the silence. "Go back a few seconds. There was something..."

Mother rotated her hands in a backward wheel motion. Well, I supposed that's what they had to do without remotes, and I admired the control. The scene rewound to just before the golden glow had taken it from a memory to a fantasy, and all three of them leaned forward again.

"There it is, see?" The one in black pointed to something at the lower left corner. "Like at the beginning."

The silver-cloaked gnome cocked her head. "Are you sure it's not a piece of her hair in the periphery of her vision? It's the same color. What do you think, Mother?"

"It could be either. The vagueness shows that she isn't aware of it."

I strained to see what they talked about, but I was too far away. Mother zoomed it out, and it appeared to be a blur of orange-red, sort of in the shape of an animal, but like a photo had been taken while it moved. It was streaked with gold, though, so it could have been her hair.

The blonde gnome huffed. "Was it really there? Can't you make it clearer?"

Mother turned and gave her a warning look. "I've done what I can. I cannot extrapolate more than what the dreamer sees."

The other dream watcher, who seemed to be the mediator between the other two, asked, "Should we go back into her dream, then? See if she loops through again?"

I almost sighed as the tension between Mother and the black-cloaked gnome dissipated. I suspected the two younger ones were sisters, even if they were not the actual daughters of Mother. They had a certain connection, and the way the atmosphere felt with the three of them told me that this type of conflict and distraction-resolution happened frequently.

Mother brought her hands together, then popped them apart, fingers spread. The image they'd been studying disappeared, to be replaced by a close-up of Corey's face. His golden eyes sparkled as he leaned over Kestrel, and I caught the curve of his naked shoulder as he brought a hand forward to caress her cheek.

I almost shouted, "Whoa, stop!" but caught myself. Luckily Mother brought her hands together, and the four foggy images reappeared with more fog over whatever Kestrel was dreaming.

"Awwww!" the two younger gnomes chorused, their disappointment evident.

Mother scowled at one, then the other. "Remember your dream ethics, Daughters. The girl deserves her privacy."

"But he's so nice-looking. A shifter, couldn't you tell?"

"Yes, Daughter, I could. The girl has her own set of complications. Alas, I don't know that we can give our king any more information than what he already suspects. Our evidence was not conclusive, as is often the case with that sort of thing."

I wanted to ask, "What? What does he suspect?" but I held my tongue. Mother dismissed the other two, who left the clearing by a different path than the one I crouched beside. Perhaps they'd go on to have their own dreams of handsome shifters in compromising situations, hopefully without the complications. Kestrel's relationship with Corey wasn't nearly as secret as the two of them wanted to believe, but I had never gotten up the courage to ask her about it, to see if she wanted to confide in me because her parents and I were such good friends. Had she and Beverly ever talked about Kestrel and Corey? I didn't know, and now I couldn't ask Beverly.

Mother turned back to the screen. "And now for some treason," she muttered. She turned to the top right quadrant and zoomed it out, again with her hands.

This one must have been Reine's. I could tell because of the wisps of white-blonde hair that blew across her vision. She climbed a rocky path, and while lightning split the sky around her, no rain fell. Again, there was no sound.

An older Fae, whose age only showed in the depth of her eyes, appeared at the top. She wore a sparkling platinum crown, and I could see the resemblance between her and Reine. This must be her grandmother.

"Yessssss," Mother hissed. "I will be well-rewarded for this."

Reine bowed, showing her focus shifting to the ground in front of the other Fae's feet, and then back up. I crept closer, willing to do something to distract the older gnome from spying on Reine, whom I suspected was not having a dream. However, the older Fae—Tatiana, I believe—looked up and seemed to be gazing out of the crystal.

"Be still, Reine. We are not alone."

Reine looked around, her frown showing she could only see the blackness of the storm clouds around her. She returned her gaze to her grandmother, who looked through Reine and out to us.

"You need your rest, gargoyle. And as for you, healer gnome, you are not welcome here."

Tatiana moved her right hand like she flung something, and the obsidian screen shattered into a glittering cloud of black shards.

Mother emerged from under her cloak, which had saved her from injury, and turned toward me. I froze.

"Well, don't just stand there, gargoyle. You're an earth elemental. Help me clean this up, and we'll talk about what you saw."

22

REINE

I felt something whiz by my head, but I couldn't tell what my grandmother had thrown, or if it had been some sort of spell. A shattering sound, like that of glass, heralded a change in the air. It felt less like the crisp chill in the heart of the forest in the Gray Zone and more like the soft humidity of the lands of the light Fae.

My grandmother smiled in a way I had forgotten—with malice. "Now that we have our privacy, we can discuss important matters."

In spite of the warm air, chill bumps raised on my skin, and I resisted the urge to rub my hands over my arms. Tatiana, Queen of the Light Fae, could have that effect on people. Being in her presence always felt like standing too close to a place where lightning had just struck—electric and potentially deadly.

And not a place where one could show weakness. Now that I had shown my respect by bowing to her, I raised my chin so I could look her in her ice blue eyes. "I am glad you summoned me, Grandmother. I have traveled to Faerie to petition you."

"And you know as well as I that petitions must be made in

person with witnesses to attest to the agreement of both parties, not in dreams, Granddaughter."

"Yes, but I was hoping..." For what? The softness of rules and laws that humans relied on? A loophole? I shook my head —this wasn't about me. "Why did you summon me, Grandmother?"

"I told you in our last visit that there is danger, and I thought it was in my inner circle." She sighed, and the impression of wrinkles flitted over her face before her skin smoothed to its usual youthful texture. "Whereas that may be true, I am facing something more troubling."

"What? Are you ill?" I immediately thought about all the things I could do for her, could try. Human medicine had advanced tremendously since I had been banished, and I suspected I could use my skills in Faerie.

"It's worse, Granddaughter... I'm dying." She bowed her head in uncharacteristic surrender.

I gasped. "That's not possible!"

She raised her head and again smiled, this time with wistfulness. "How old do you think I am, Reine?"

"I don't know. A thousand years?"

"And you're taking off half a millennium to be polite, aren't you?" She held out her hands, palms down, and I saw veins under thin skin—signs of an old woman underneath the surface. "I'm thankful Fae don't get liver spots. No, Granddaughter, I am two-thousand-years-old plus a few hundred years. I have been alive long enough to see the rise and fall of the Roman Empire, the Dark Ages, the Great Rebirth, and now the Darker Age of a humanity so drunk on its power and technology it cannot see the destruction it brings to itself and the planet. Or the repercussions here."

Considering how time didn't pass the same in Faerie and Earth, that made her more than the math she had given me, but it didn't matter. Old was old, no matter how one put it, and no living creature lived forever, not even the most powerful of the Fae.

"What can I do, for you and for Earth and Faerie?"

"I mourned your exile, my little Reine, but I allowed it to happen."

Now the ache of betrayal flooded through me. "Why?"

She leaned forward and placed a hand on my head. Love and regret flowed through her hand to me. "Because I foresaw what was coming, and I knew the next Queen of Faerie needed to have a wider perspective. I could have sent you to study in the Earth realm, but you needed to struggle and learn from a place of needing to survive, not of privilege."

That honest Fae impulse compelled me to say, "But Faerie did support me, at least mostly."

"It supported you for my ends—to have you continue your journey as a healer, to meet many others, both humans and other creatures, to give you just enough but still leave room for you to sink or swim depending on how you allocated your resources."

"Suddenly my almost four centuries in the Earth realm feels like a big test, not an exile."

"And that's what it was, mostly. You still failed to protect your brother, leaving him maimed. And now you put me in a difficult position, bringing him here."

"I didn't bring him. He followed me, although I'm not sure why."

She cocked her head at me. "There are still dark forces at work in my court, ones that will see the light Fae infiltrated and destroyed. I was serious when I said that the actions and ambitions of humanity have had their effects here. Some Fae have taken the example of human power too seriously and have decided to model themselves after it."

"That's...not good."

"No, and alas, they are still hidden, which means they have the blessing and backing of someone very powerful."

"What does this have to do with Rhys?" But pieces were slotting into place in my mental game of Fae Tetris, and I continued before she could answer. "My mother sent him to me. He delayed the vampire team from reaching me as I battled the soul-eater. He brought Lawrence here, for what? To distract me?" I pressed the heels of my hands to my eyes. "Gods, how could I have missed all that?"

"Because after all these years, all these troubles, you still love your little brother. And that's something else that's been lacking in the Court, that I cannot bring myself to do—to show mercy and allow someone the chance for redemption."

I removed my hands from my eyes, but the dizziness of the revelations remained. "And what about my mother, the Crown Princess? I don't think she'll be too happy if I try to hop over her to be queen." The words left behind a stifling sensation. "And what if I don't want to be queen, at least not yet?"

"What is it the humans say, 'duty calls?'" She sighed. "Maeve is most definitely a creature of Faerie, and I have neglected my duty in training her to be a good queen because she and I have and lack the same qualities. That's why I let her choose an unconventional way to have you—I hoped you'd be different, and you are."

"What do you mean, an unconventional way?" My head spun. "I thought my father was one of the male consorts in your court."

She smiled. "That's a secret for you to find out in its own time."

"Great, so I'm the result of a breeding project plus a four-hundred-year behavioral experiment." My identity and reality had already been shifted enough, but I had to ask, "Is there anything else?"

She placed a hand on my cheek and raised my head so I looked at her. "I know about the vampire's bite." She placed a hand over the spot. "Now it is hidden so that no other Fae will sense it. Hurry, Granddaughter. If I die and your mother becomes queen before you arrive and petition me in person, you know what will happen."

"She'll kick me out again, or worse. She won't let me go somewhere I could plot against her. The asylum..."

She nodded. "One of my biggest regrets. Again, the mistakes of humanity infecting us without our realization until it was too late."

I would also petition for Olred's release, but I didn't say so. While my grandmother seemed to be in an expansive mood, she was still Fae, and therefore would be hiding many things from me. I took a deep breath. "I will hurry to you as best I can. I have lost my guide."

Now she moved her hand to my chest. "At the risk of sounding too much like a Faerie godmother in a fantasy tale, have faith in yourself and follow your heart."

The scene faded around me, and I woke to find myself surrounded by the angry faces of several of the winter gnomes. Behind them, the silvery light of dawn illuminated the trees.

Something told me today would be a very interesting one.

I SCRAMBLED TO MY FEET, as did Sir Raleigh, and I put my hand on his head to stop him from lunging at any of our hosts. A deep growl rumbled through him, and they disappeared. And not just the ones who had been surrounding us, but the rest of them, leaving the Winter Gnome King standing on a mound of dirt where his throne had been. I coughed, and turquoise-colored smoke emerged from my mouth.

"What the...?"

The others in my party woke, and Rhys rolled to his feet

with movements as lithe as a panther. Troubadour propped himself on his elbow, rubbed his eyes, and got up less gracefully, but still in a charmingly rumpled way. The humans stood together, clutching their packs. Upon standing, all of them coughed the strange smoke. As for Lawrence...

Where was Lawrence? I first searched for his human form, then recalled he had garged out, but no strange piles of stone had appeared, so at least I knew he hadn't turned permanently.

"Sleep well?" The Winter Gnome King's eyes glittered, as those of his kind did, but not happily, and he drew his small mouth into a line like a schoolmarm waiting for a recalcitrant student to make a confession.

I put my hands on my hips and matched his sternness with my own expression, or tried to. "Yes, thank you. Where is my gargoyle?" Okay, he wasn't *my* gargoyle per se, but he was still part of my squad.

"Where is my healer?"

I threw my hands up. "How should I know?" Then the memory of something crashing behind me at the start of the dream conversation with my grandmother popped into my head. "She's more than a healer, isn't she?"

Troubadour came to stand beside me. "There are rumors that the Winter gnomes are dream watchers."

"That would explain the smoke." I narrowed my eyes at the king. "You fed us dream wort, didn't you? So you could gather information from our subconscious images."

Lawrence's deep voice made my worry for him un-knot, at least the immediate concern part of it. "Yes." He came into the clearing with the healer, who wouldn't meet my eyes. Lawrence carried a basket of what looked like shards of black glass. Or an obsidian mirror.

The king turned his scowl on the healer, who bowed to him. "The gargoyle didn't respond to the dream wort, Your Majesty. He caught us in our watching."

He put a hand on her head, and she disappeared, as did the basket from Lawrence's arms. I wanted to ask where she went, but I knew we were in for a game of word chess. The fact he hadn't followed his people to wherever they hid—elsewhere in the Gray Zone or in a neighboring realm?—meant that he wanted something badly enough he would try to bargain for it in spite of being at a disadvantage.

I decided to send the first volley—an accusation. "She was spying on me. My grandmother could tell, and she kicked her out." I didn't mention about the broken mirror. That would be my grandmother's debt to negotiate, if there even was one.

"Yes, Princess. She was. You see, I need to know where things stand in the high Fae courts because we lower Fae have been petitioning for autonomy."

My Fae-dar, now more sensitive, told me that he'd given me one piece of information while hiding another. Granted, what he'd told me had its own interest and grave repercussions. I decided to go with that line of questioning and see what else I could glean from him.

"What kind of autonomy? I want to make sure I under-stand." I didn't add, *in case I am the next queen* because I didn't want to entertain the fact. That was a whole different box of complications with my mother.

"We no longer want to have to pledge allegiance to the light or dark courts. We want to move freely between lands."

"That's why you're here in the Gray Zone." How many other lower Fae courts and tribes had settled here? Was that why it seemed to grow—the population was forcing it to expand outward?

"Yes, Princess. So, in exchange for our hospitality, I only ask that you remember my petition."

There was that phrase—the request for me to remember. I glanced at Troubadour, who had first made the petition and who now wouldn't meet my gaze.

"What do you mean, remember?"

Lawrence stood beside me on the other side of Sir Raleigh. "It's old courtly language," he explained, his professorial mode coming out even though he was in gargoyle form. "The full phrase is, 'remember with favor,' and it means you'll be willing to plead their case when the time comes."

I turned toward Troubadour and arched an eyebrow. "Is that so?"

"You already agreed," the bard Fae said. "Twice."

I sighed. "We're going to have a full chat later, you and I." Then I turned back toward the king. "Why should I remember you with favor? You drugged us and spied on us."

"Surely you cannot blame a fellow ruler for doing what's best for his people."

Lawrence coughed. No blue smoke from him, I noticed, but of course he might not have absorbed the dream wort's active alkalines with his gargoyle physiology. "That wasn't all, Reine. They were interested in Kestrel's dreams."

"Mine?" Kestrel squeaked. "Why mine?"

I didn't miss the pink that came to her cheeks, and I stifled the urge to tease her. "Why, indeed?" I asked the king. "What can a human girl's dreams have that are of interest to the Winter gnomes?"

"Mere curiosity, Princess."

Lawrence looked distinctly uncomfortable.

"What is it?" I asked him.

He looked over his shoulder and tightly furled his wings so he could look at Kestrel. "Do you remember what you dreamed last night?"

Now her face had gone full redhead blush, and she nodded.

"Can I tell them? It may help figure out the puzzle you're here to solve."

She nodded again.

Lawrence faced the king. "You had your healer and her two

daughters searching Kestrel's dreams for clues as to what she is. I won't say what they saw—or thought they saw—because that's her business and her privacy." Pain flickered through his expression, and I suspected Kestrel had been having night-mares about her mother's death, which we all had witnessed. So, what had made her blush?

That would be yet another conversation for later. I seriously needed an office I could call people into and speak privately with them.

Meanwhile, I had to call on my Fae princess authority again. "That's an invasion of privacy and identity. What have you to say for yourself, Winter Gnome King?"

He bowed his head, and the way his ears drooped would have been cute had I not been so angry.

I stifled the things I wanted to scream and instead told him in my calmest voice possible, "You can make all the obeisance you want, but how can I even think of granting you autonomy if you're going to break the law we should all be following, that of respect for another's dreams and visions? No, I will not remember you with favor."

His head jerked up, and he held up a hand, palm-out. I mirrored his gesture before the spell he shot at me could get to me, and it shimmered when it hit my magical shield.

"You dare attack me?" My hands warmed as I called upon the light of the sun to grant me the gift of fire again.

He folded his hands together and bowed. "Forgive me, Princess. I am desperate for my people. I ask the one thing I can of you—we kept you and your party safe from those who hunt you, and I will show you the way back to the Shadowed Path if you spare me and my people."

I thought for a moment and mentally picked through his words looking for traps. "Very well, I will spare you, and I will not take retribution on your people for your acts of treason against a high Fae who requested hospitality and whom you attempted to deceive. For as much as you desire autonomy, you have acted as a dark Fae creature would."

"Thank you, Princess. And so there are no hard feelings, I leave you with the Path and a gift." He bowed again, and in his place stood Ellerin, dripping wet and looking confused. The ground shifted underneath my feet, and I found I stood again on the Shadowed Path.

Ellerin laughed. "Nicely done, Princess, although I thought you were going to send him to his room to think about what he did."

Relieved laughter bubbled up in me, and I ran to hug him, even if his clothing soaked me. He folded me into his arms and whispered a spell, drying himself and me.

"I thought you had died." The last word cracked, and I bit my lip so the tears I'd been holding back wouldn't escape.

"No, once the kraken realized who I was, it invited me to its lair, and we had a little chat about how it shouldn't welcome water wolves to its lake. In fact, it had all kinds of interesting information for me. Let's walk, and I'll tell you. I'd like to make it to the lands of the light Fae before dark."

Ellerin and I walked ahead of the others. I still couldn't believe he had made it out of that harrowing situation alive. How powerful he must be, the Wanderer, the gray Fae! How did the other Fae not fear him?

Or perhaps they did.

"What did you find out?" I asked. "And how did you convince the Kraken not to hurt you?"

He chuckled. "So many questions! You were always..." He stopped, then shook his head. I sensed he felt relieved to see me, too. "It felt my power when I defeated the first few tentacles and came up for a closer look." He held one hand out, palm-up, and showed me an image of the kraken with its giant yellow eyes, shiny black skin, and sharp beak.

"Who are you?" I turned to look at him, *really* look at him, again, and saw what I always had—a nondescript Fae gentleman with graying temples and wrinkles at the corners of his eyes, which would make him really old. If my grandmother's age was starting to show at her two-plus millennia, Ellerin must have been even older. Or perhaps he had lived harder or in other realms, where time passed and we aged differently. Hence why my hair was white rather than blonde, as it would have been had I been allowed to stay in Faerie.

"I am Ellerin," he replied with a shrug. "I'm sure you'll figure it all out eventually, Reine. You sometimes still don't know how to see what's in front of you."

"Ouch." I wasn't kidding—for a healer, missing the obvious was an insult. "What am I missing?"

"The kraken told me something interesting. The water wolves weren't native to his lake. They'd been sent there, and he couldn't get rid of them with his dark Fae creature power because they'd had the blessing of someone in the light Fae court. Someone very high up."

"Meaning they'd likely been sent to come after us."

He nodded. "Now you're getting it. Someone really doesn't want you coming home."

"That's too bad because I have to. Tatiana is dying."

He sighed. "I knew that, or at least I suspected. I can confirm that she wants you to return." He paused like he waited for me to put something together, and indeed, the suspicion that had started back in the cave in Scotland and had grown, no matter how much I battled it, bloomed into despair.

"You know how you told me that Maeve trains her daughters not to say no?"

"Yes..."

I looked ahead, where the trees broke, and the fog dissolved into finger-like wisps that seemed to point rather than grasp.

"She also taught us not to question her. However, I'm starting to." I couldn't bring myself to voice my thoughts, not yet, and not to this strange being who obviously had his own secrets and connection to my mother and my past.

"That's good, Princess. Very good."

We emerged from the trees to find another stream that, improbably, flowed uphill and over the crest. A small, golden bridge crossed it, and beyond, trees of another forest waved leaves of an eternal spring green. Even here, I could smell the perfume of a thousand moonflowers. The warm and cool air chased each other around me in playful eddies, and giggles tinkled in my ears along with cries of, "Home, she's almost home!"

"What is it?" Kestrel held out her hands and grinned. "Something's tickling me."

"Air sprites. They're welcoming me home."

Home...the land of eternal spring, unless the queen deemed it to be winter. The question was, what season would it be for me?

23

———

LAWRENCE

"Do we need to be aware of any tricks?" I asked, surprised that John hadn't beat me to it. He'd been uncharacteristically quiet since that morning. What had he dreamed under the influence of the dream wort? I understood the herb to work somewhat like Melatonin, notorious for prompting vivid dreaming in the Earth realm.

"I don't know." Ellerin held his staff up, and the crystal glowed white. "Let me check."

He wandered along the stream, and the rest of us plopped onto the cool, soft grass.

"Are you okay, sweetie?" John rubbed Kestrel's back. She sat with slumped shoulders, her elbows on her knees.

"I'm fine, just hungry."

Right, no one had eaten since the night before. I'd become accustomed to the gnawing feeling in my stomach—the unsatisfactory way the food of Faerie left me feeling.

I poked Rhys on his shoulder. "Can't you make something to eat appear?"

The three Fae exchanged grim looks. Reine answered. "Troubadour is a dark Fae, and Rhys and I are light. Our power is limited here in the lands of the gray Fae. Once we cross, we should be able to find something. That's why we told you all to bring food with you."

"I'm all out," Kestrel complained.

"Check again," Reine encouraged her.

John, Kestrel, and I all dug through our packs. I was pretty sure I'd eaten my last protein bar, but there, hiding in a place where the lining had torn, I found another one.

My gaze met Reine's, and she wriggled her fingers and winked. What did this mean?

"Found something!" Kestrel pulled a granola bar from her pack, and John brought forth a candy bar.

"Huh, I don't remember packing this."

"Things were a bit rushed the morning we left," Reine pointed out. "Maybe you stuck it in and forgot."

We ate our snacks, but the Fae refused our offers to share.

Reine again spoke for the group. "We're close enough to home, we can wait."

Kestrel giggled. "Oh, for a second I thought y'all could make nutrients via photosynthesis."

Reine laughed, and the sound melted the stone around my heart, like it always had. She turned her face up to the sun, which shone on us again after what felt like years.

"It does feel glorious, but no, we don't engage in photosynthesis, as useful as that would be."

"It's too bad," John said. "Being able to turn sunlight into food would be a neat trick."

"Yes, it would be."

Rhys and Troubadour shot her alarmed looks like she was in danger of revealing too much. She smiled at them and gave a slight shake of her head. And just like that, the feeling that she held something back from me, some tasty morsel of knowledge about the Fae, re-hardened my feelings and reminded me not to trust her.

Ellerin returned from his walk along the up-flowing waters. What sort of place was this where gravity could be suspended? I shouldn't be surprised, but Faerie kept startling me with its topsy-turvy rules.

"It's safe as far as I can tell. Those of you with water element powers should be able to cross fine. Those of you without, meaning John..." He frowned. "And Kestrel, I suppose, need to be holding on to a Fae or gargoyle."

"Why 'you suppose?'" John rolled to his feet. "She's as normal and human as I am. Well, mostly."

"Dad, it's okay." Kestrel stood and brushed off her pants. "Let's just play it safe and figure stuff out later."

Why would Kestrel have water element powers? I didn't ask. The tension stood like a third being between John and Ellerin. I wished I could ask Kestrel or Reine what had happened in Cruaidh.

Even though Ellerin said it would be safe, we all stood and looked at the bridge for a few minutes. It appeared benign. When I reached out with my water elemental senses, I couldn't detect anything amiss about the stream itself, but the last one had tricked me and carried Kestrel away.

Ellerin shook his head. "Fine, I'll go first." He did, and when he reached the other side, he turned and waved. He mouthed, "See? It's fine," but no sound carried across the water.

"I'm ready to be home." Reine held a hand out to John. "Shall we?"

He hesitated, then clasped hands with her. "Let's do it."

They crossed without incident. Then Kestrel grabbed my hand. "Let's go, Uncle Lawrence. You're a water and stone elemental right?"

"Yep." We ascended the stairs at the end of the bridge, and it felt like it barely held my weight. We crossed slowly, and I kept one eye on the stream for surprise waves. Nothing happened, and we reached the other side without incident.

Rhys crossed, leaving Troubadour. However, when the Fae bard reached the center of the bridge, he seemed to bump up against an invisible barrier.

He straightened with a haughty look. "I demand passage."

The stream whispered back, *"No creature of the dark Fae may enter the lands of light without permission from the queen."*

"Since when?"

"Since the Eleventh Edict of Maeve, twelfth era, fourteenth day, seventh hour, ninth minute, fifteenth second."

"You're very precise with your law timing," John said to Reine.

She didn't answer him, only frowned at the stream. "Since when is Maeve issuing edicts?"

The stream didn't reply, but its burbling increased. Reine looked at each of us in turn, then turned and walked to the water. She knelt by the stream and dipped her hand in. I tensed, alert for a wave that would take her from us, but Rhys put a hand on my shoulder.

"Let her do her thing, mate. She knows what she's about."

Instead of his customary cynical expression, something like awe made him look younger and almost vulnerable, almost like he was seeing his sister for the first time.

"What happened back there, with the lake creatures? Did she do something?"

"What? No." He lowered his voice. "Not there, anyway. It's too long a story to tell here. Just know that things have changed drastically, but we don't know what it all means yet, except she can't let Troubadour get split off from our party. He knows and has seen too much."

That was more information than I'd gotten from Rhys, well, ever. "What happened? What did he see? Look, I can't do much here, but I can at least fulfill my ancient mission to protect her."

"Fae business."

I deflated. "I should have known."

He patted my shoulder, then moved his hand. "You know more than you realize. Reach inside to that instinct, and it may tell you what's happened."

My inner gargoyle had been quiet. Or maybe his thoughts had become mine. I returned to scanning the stream for signs of danger.

24

REINE

"*Don't let anyone near. I don't want them to hear this,*" I told Rhys in secret conversation before walking to the stream. I looked down at its burbling surface, and it welcomed me with its watery giggle. Even the stones on this side of the stream sparkled with tiny crystals, giving the water a magical appearance. When I knelt, the grass and dirt cradled rather than pushed against my knees.

I dipped a hand in the stream, and the face of the dryad who lived in it appeared.

"Melisane, I thought I recognized you."

She grinned up at me. "It has been too long, Princess. My sister at the other side of the Gray Zone said you'd come."

"And how much mischief did she cause?"

More laughter, which sounded like an increase in the water's movement over the rounded pebbles. "Enough. You have an interesting crew with you. I suspect you'll have more surprises ahead of you than you expect."

"Well, that's the point of surprises, isn't it?" Talking to her loosened something in me. Had I been afraid that my own land wouldn't want me back, would enforce the terms of my exile?

Her face turned serious. "You have trouble ahead of you. I cannot tell you more than that, for only rumors reach me here." A shadowy hand appeared under the water and touched my fingertips, which to me felt like warm water swirled around them. "Oh! You've already had a big surprise, haven't you?"

I sighed. "I couldn't help it. The spell came out of me. I suspect something or someone set me up so it would. But it's a secret." I didn't know what good it would do to ask a stream to keep something hidden, for the very nature of water was to uncover and clarify, but I could at least try.

"Yes, Your Majesty." Her head bobbed like she bowed. "I am honored that you trust me to help you."

Okay, that didn't make me feel guilty at all after my prejudiced thoughts. "Now, knowing what you do, will you allow the dark Fae to pass? He is an important part of my party." I dropped the volume of my voice even further. "And he knows. He was there."

Her eyes widened. "Oh, yes, of course!"

On the bridge Troubadour stumbled forward and sent me a curious glance as he walked across and alighted on the path. The grass to either side bent away from him slightly.

"Thank you."

The water around my hand warmed like she gave me a squeeze. "Any time, Your Highness. Just be sure to remember this humble stream when you take your throne."

"If I accept the throne, I will." I didn't mind promising her. I'd long thought the border waters needed more protecting and encouragement, as they were our first lines of defense. Even though there hadn't been a war in centuries. But was that coming? All the more reason to cement the alliance with Troubadour.

I stood and rubbed my eyes with my cold, wet hand to stop my thoughts. I couldn't think like a queen, not yet.

Troubadour stepped off the path, and the smile he gave me

prompted some very roll-in-the-hay peasant thoughts. His secret conversation seemed to caress my brain. *"Thank you."*

I pressed the cool hand to one cheek, which I was not surprised to find had heated. *"You're welcome. I appreciate your discretion."*

"Of course, Princess." He winked when he thought my title at me. I appreciated how not-serious he was, although I reminded myself that he was a dark Fae, and therefore could not stay long-term in my territory.

We turned back to the others to see the humans looking confused, Ellerin suspicious, Rhys amused, and Lawrence... Uh, oh. He glowered at us, his expression even more fierce on his gargoyle face. Now guilt uncurled in my stomach, and I reminded myself it didn't need to. He and I didn't have any kind of understanding. In fact, he'd made it quite clear that he didn't want to pursue anything with me. And yet, he was here, and that bit of female intuition that tells you when a guy is into you vibrated with the awareness he still had interest in me.

As did Troubadour. Oh, Hades, this could get complicated. But a Fae queen could have more than one consort. And Lawrence couldn't stay in Faerie.

The thoughts buzzed through my brain like black lightning bugs, and I mentally swatted them away.

Ellerin's tone echoed the suspicion on his face. "You convinced the stream?"

"We're old friends." I put my hands in my pockets and shrugged.

He regarded me skeptically, but he didn't argue. He stepped back onto the path, which still apparently included all our Shadowed Path, and we followed him. As we walked, I breathed in the smells of nature and of home, and I held my hands out so I could feel the warm-cool of the dappled sunlight moving over them. The trees rustled their green leaves in welcome, and I grinned up at them, then turned to John.

"Is this more like you imagined?"

"Yes, thank you."

Hmmm, that was a surprisingly subdued response for him. I wanted to ask what was wrong, but then Kestrel fell into step beside me. "You're happy to be home."

"Yes. I'd forgotten how warm it is here, how soft the air is." I'd gotten some whiffs of the magic in the air when I spoke to my mother through her portal, and I relished the feel of it all over me. It had felt thinner, attenuated in the lands of the dark and gray Fae, as had my abilities, although they'd been stronger than in the Earth realm. Here I knew I could draw on all my powers fully and defend myself and my friends.

Ellerin stopped and held up his hand. "Wait. We're being watched."

We moved into a knot with the humans in the middle and the Fae and gargoyle ringing them. On some signal we couldn't see or hear, armed soldiers melted out of the trees. They wore dark green clothing, which along with concealment spells, had made them invisible.

Ellerin spoke before I could. "What do you want with us? We are passing through with no ill intent."

One of the soldiers stepped forward and bowed in my direction. "We are here on behalf of the Lady of the Forest. She would like a word with the princess."

I eyed the crossbows that were being leveled at us. "This is one hell of a way to issue an invitation, gentlemen. Why not just ask us?"

"Because we were told not to take no for an answer. She said to tell you that it has significance for your mission."

Ellerin and I exchanged glances.

"Is this part of my path?" I asked him.

"I can't tell. It feels both expected and not expected."

"Great."

"What does your sense tell you?"

"I can't harm them, or at least I shouldn't. But I hate being forced into something, especially since I don't know where it will end up."

"Your call, Princess."

I felt the trap. If I fought back and hurt or killed some of these Fae soldiers, it could come back to bite me when I petitioned my grandmother for clemency and suspension of my and Rhys' exile. But if I let them take us, we'd be wasting valuable time.

In the end, I chose not to hurt anyone needlessly. I had become a healer because I believed in helping, not harming, and I didn't sense any lethal intent.

"Very well, take us to your leader."

Kestrel snorted.

I linked my arm with hers. "What? No one said I couldn't play, too."

"Wrong genre."

The soldiers fell in around us, and while half of them seemed to disappear, I knew they were there as we followed their commander down a side path.

I LOOKED out over the forest from a throne room in a high parapet. The other side gave me a view of Lorien, my home, but I couldn't bear to look. It drew me so much I practically salivated when I saw it, and drooling just wasn't princess-like.

My crew had been taken into a banquet hall, where food had been laid out for them. I trusted Ellerin to determine whether it was safe.

The head soldier, apparently deciding I didn't pose any kind of threat to him, had brought me and Sir Raleigh up several flights of spiral stairs and left me alone with the admonishment, "You'd best tell your pet to behave."

Once he walked out, I rubbed Sir Raleigh behind his ears.

"Better be your sweet kitty self, Raleigh, at least until we know who we're dealing with." The air around him shimmered, and the bat-winged panther turned into the gray cat with one white paw. I picked him up and kissed him on top of his head. "That's more like it."

He gave me an insulted look before wriggling out of my arms and dropping to the floor, where he licked his white paw, then, nose twitching, wandered around the room.

"Good idea." I, too, investigated our surroundings.

The throne itself stood on a dais against the north side of the room, giving whoever sat there an almost three-hundred-and-sixty-degree view of the lands around it with the farming region straight ahead of it, Lorien to the left/East and the forest and Gray Zone to the right/West. The trees themselves disappeared under a blanket of fog after about half a mile into the Gray Zone.

"You're not choosing the best view, Princess." The husky voice belonged to a lovely raven-haired woman wearing red robes and a golden circlet on her forehead. She hadn't walked in, but rather had appeared on the throne. "I thought you'd be facing the capital city."

Sir Raleigh growled from beside me, where he'd teleported to from the other side of the room. His fur stood in a line down his spine and his tail in a bottle-brush poof, but at least he was waiting to reveal his true self. Not wanting to give the woman the satisfaction of surprising me, I took my time turning to face her. When I approached the throne, she stood and dipped into a deep curtsy. Her face, when she lifted it to me again, betrayed her with a blush.

"Forgive me, Your Majesty. I... I didn't realize it was you. Thank you for sparing my soldiers and myself for my rude welcome." But as she said the words, it was with a satisfied smile.

"This...isn't a surprise." I crossed my arms. "Who are you,

really? And what do you want? Don't say to remember you—I'm all out of rememberings for the day."

She laughed, and I appreciated that it was the deep, throaty laugh of a confident woman. I'd had enough of simpering and self-effacement with some of the women I'd worked with in the Earth realm. That's why I had become a doctor—to be with others who weren't afraid to show their intelligence and abilities, both doctors and nurses.

"Oh, Reine," she sighed. Then she did something unexpected—she held out her hands. "Trust me. I have something to show you."

I looked down at Sir Raleigh, who nodded. "Well, this day is full of surprises." I took her hands, and her robes turned brown, then green, and her hair lightened to a lovely dark red shade. The circlet on her forehead shimmered and turned to platinum with an emerald in the center. Her eyes, now green to match her dress rather than the cool blue of her brunette appearance, twinkled, and her features turned more elfin and angular. I found myself looking into the face of a long-lost...friend? Did Fae have friends?

"Now will you remember me?" she teased, her voice softer.

"Aoine!" We clasped in a hug, and then I held her away from me. "That was some powerful magic. You've improved since Spell School."

She waved a hand, and a comfortable red velvet couch appeared by the window overlooking the fields. We plopped down on it, and Sir Raleigh jumped up in between us. She held out a hand for him to sniff, which he did, and then he rubbed his head under it.

She smiled at me, but instead of teasing, admonished, "And you need to be more careful, Reine. As adorable as your grimalkin friend is here, he may not be enough to protect you. Remember what Headmaster Leafmore taught us..."

We spoke the rhyme in unison as we imitated the stuffy tone and accent of our old teacher:

A careless Fae loses more

Than her right to her virginity.

In fact, her reputation lost,

She'll be mocked for all eternity.

I laughed. "I'd forgotten how misogynistic our education was, especially since the consorts have more to worry about than we do with regard to sexual rights. You seem to have done well, though. I don't see any male Fae vying for your hand or other things."

"Ah, yes, our poor headmaster. I think he taught us those rhymes out of some hidden desires of his own."

"Whatever happened to him?"

Her face went pale. Well, paler. "He disappeared soon after your travels."

"You mean my exile."

"Well, yes. He stuck up for you, although none of us were supposed to know. I believe he went and appealed in the Light Court for you to be allowed to return. Not that you'd ever come back without your brother. Is he here?"

I didn't miss the eagerness in her tone. Aoine had always had a thing for the bad boy Fae type.

"Yes, and you'll love how he looks now. All shaggy and scarred."

"Scarred?" She put a hand to her mouth, but the sparkle in her eyes told me she feigned her shocked expression. "How scandalous! That's why you were exiled?"

"Yes." I decided to heed her warning and not say too much. "What did the rumors say happened to Headmaster Leafmore?"

She squeezed my hand. "You always did have a little crush on good ol' Larry Leafmore, didn't you? No one knows. No one ever saw him leave the court. Inquiries were made by the school, but of course no one would stand up to your mother or grandmother for him. They didn't want to end up in the same place, wherever that was."

She tacked on the, "wherever that was" too quickly, and I filed the observation away. Something else tickled the back of my brain, and I teased it forward... Healer Wilfrin at the asylum in Cruaidh knocking on a door and saying, *"Settle down there, Larry. This visitor isn't for you."*

"Oh gods." That must have been Headmaster Leafmore. He would have recognized the signature of my magic, which he had helped train, and known it was me. Had he hoped I'd come to rescue him? Although there was no way I could have known or done anything, guilt passed like a shadow over my heart. He'd been nothing but kind, if a bit tough...and he'd stood up for me.

"What is it?"

"Nothing." I patted her hand. "I should warn you I came with quite a party. Why did you have your guards arrest us, by the way? We didn't have any kind of threatening intentions."

She paused for a long few moments, and I could almost see the mental game of chess going on under her red curls. Whatever she was about to tell me, it would be mostly true, as the rest of it had been.

"The Queen Spell set off a vibration through the forest," she explained. "The lore tells us that when that happens, there will be unrest. I told my men to detain anyone coming from the border. They didn't hurt you, did they?"

"No, not at all. I just didn't appreciate their attitude."

She clapped her hands, her delight plain. "I didn't hire them to be nice, Reine. I hired them to do a job. Now think, if you'd been a group of vagabonds, you'd be detained, maybe tortured a little, and then released with dire warnings, maybe with one of you staying behind as a hostage I'd eventually have to decide whether to keep feeding or sacrifice to my moat monster, who gets hungry every couple of months or so."

"I'm guessing I'd be resentful for holding one of my party and seek revenge."

She laughed again. "Yes, but you're high Fae. The lower sorts don't think like that. They'd run with their figurative tails between their legs, and I wouldn't have to worry about them coming back."

I smiled so she wouldn't see how horrified, if unsurprised, I was by her ruthlessness. That's what Fae did, after all. "Ah, high Fae. We're a privileged bunch."

"Yes, and I would also consult with you about what a good Fae bargain would be in order to give them hope, have them secretly further my agenda, and then destroy themselves in the process of trying to meet it. You and your mother were always the best at those."

Her words hit me like a splash of icy water down my spine, and I suppressed a shudder. Was that what I'd been doing for my mother—furthering her agenda and destroying myself in the process? That was the classic formula, after all. So, what did that make Aoine? Friend who would help me through it, or a secret foe?

I stood. "Thank you for your hospitality. My party was low on food, and I'll be sure to remember you since we were school-mates, but I must get going."

"Why? You just got here."

I wasn't going to tell her my grandmother was dying. "I have an urgent matter to attend to at the capital."

"Surely it can wait a couple of days? Or even an evening? It's been too long, and I am hosting a party tonight to celebrate the full moon."

I had to ask, "Do you host a party every twenty-eight days?"

"Only when my best friend comes back from exile." She stood and clasped her hands. "Please? It will be a good chance for you to meet some of your current court members outside the stuffy confines of the court.

"*And outside of the view of your mother,*" she added in secret conversation. Her eyes still stood wide, and I thought I saw a calculating glitter among the Fae sparkle there. I searched for the Path and thought I sensed it outside, waiting, but not tugging at me. Could this be part of my journey, a re-introduction to my court and my Fae princess life?

"Very well, one evening. My group and I need to make plans for how to approach the light Fae court, anyway."

"Ooh, yes, do fill me in! You have Rhys and who else?" She linked arms with me and steered me away from the window toward the stairs. Sir Raleigh padded after us.

"Well, there's a gargoyle, Lawrence."

She turned to me, her mouth a perfect O of astonishment. "A gargoyle! And he's doing okay?"

"That's part of my urgency. He needs to finish his path so he can go home."

She gave me a long, pitying look, but only nodded and asked, "Who else?"

"A dark Fae named Troubadour and a gray Fae named Ellerin." She had always believed in the gray, so I felt comfortable telling her. She'd figure it out soon, anyway.

The shock returned to her face, and when she spoke, it was tinged with awe. "The Wanderer."

"Yes, you know him?"

"Only that he's rumored to be the most powerful male Fae ever to live, almost equal to your family. And Troubadour... I've heard of him as well. He's a talented bard, but a tricky one. Some say a Fae prince who refuses to do his duty by his court."

"I should've figured you'd know them. You were always the Fae version of *People* magazine." Seriously, had we been in the Earth realm, she would have been one of the few people to keep all the royal families straight.

"Is that all? Look at you traveling with all the boyz." She nudged me, and I raised my eyebrows.

"Boyz? Have you been peeking in at the Earth realm to learn some of its slang?"

She shrugged, her white shoulders pale in her green gown. "Maybe a little. Perhaps I've even read a few copies of *People* magazine. And who else?"

Huh, she'd asked twice. "A couple of humans, father and daughter. They're journeying to work through the loss of their wife and mom to a killer who had been possessed by a soul-eater." There, that would give her enough to chew on. And, I hoped, keep her from looking too closely at Kestrel.

"How sad." She wrinkled her nose. Fae found human grief disgusting. We had a different view of death, and our afterlife would come theoretically at the same time as most of our friends' and families', so we didn't bother with grief. Typically. The sorrow at losing my grandmother still pricked my heart when I thought of her, and I almost insisted that we leave. But when we reached the dining hall and I saw how exhausted everyone looked, I knew we needed to take the night to rest. Otherwise, none of us would survive the challenges that could still lay between us and Lorien.

I clapped my hands, and they turned to me. "Everyone, this is Aoine." I made introductions, and thankfully Aoine's gaze passed over Kestrel and John with the barest acknowledgment. However, she and Troubadour stared at each other for a moment longer than necessary.

"Welcome to my home, all," she said. "I am pleased to have you, and I hope you have enjoyed your lunch. Now go rest up because we have a celebration tonight."

"Reine, a word?" Ellerin asked.

AOINE'S SERVANTS showed everyone to separate rooms except for John and Kestrel, whom she put together.

Ellerin and I decided to walk outside on the castle grounds, which included vast gardens that seemed to be untouched by the change of seasons elsewhere in Faerie.

We had walked in silence for several minutes when I asked, "You wanted to speak with me?"

Ellerin looked over his shoulder and murmured something. I resisted the impulse to ask if he could only cast spells at low volume, or if he was powerful enough that if he actually enunciated, he might blow a hole in the space-time continuum, whatever that meant here. The sounds around us hushed, and I again viewed the world as though I was inside a soap bubble.

His question, although phrased in a perfectly neutral and harmless tone, irked me. "How well do you know Aoine?"

"Well enough. We were in school together. Got into some scrapes as young Fae do. I admit I didn't keep up with her as well as I should after we graduated, but I had princess things to do, and she needed to return here to her family's land."

"Are you aware that she's the new Lady of the Forest as of about twenty years ago?"

Only a Fae would consider twenty years recent enough to specify a change as *new*, but I didn't comment on that. "I thought as much. She has some impressive powers. She was able to sneak up on me and Sir Raleigh." The grimalkin in question was currently hanging out with the humans. I didn't dare leave them alone, both because I didn't want someone getting too curious about Kestrel without me knowing and because I didn't trust John to not do something stupid.

"You're smart to want her as an ally, but don't forget—things here are always more complicated than they seem."

"I'm aware of that, thanks." I crossed my arms and turned to face him fully. "Is there anything else you want to tell me, o Bearer of Great Secrets? Because I know you're holding out on me, and I'd like to have all the knowledge I can before we head into Lorien."

"Nothing that I *want* to tell you, Princess."

I didn't miss his emphasis, meaning I'd asked in the wrong way, or my title. He wasn't addressing me as though I was queen. It was a good reminder that I needed to not try on the regal authority, particularly as I didn't want it. The Queen Spell only proposed an option, after all.

A dark shadow in the corner of my vision caught my attention, and I turned to see Lawrence walking along on a nearby path. Every so often, he'd spread his wings, take off, and fly for a short distance before landing. Ellerin and I watched him for a while.

I couldn't tell what he was doing, but I could guess—testing his current strength. He'd want to know how quickly he weakened. "Those landings are getting rougher." I reached into my pocket for my stethoscope before remembering it wasn't there, it was in my pack in my room. I didn't want to run and get it, so I snapped my fingers and brought it to hand.

"Reine, wait." Ellerin put a hand on my arm and looked into my eyes. "You've been a healer for so long, you have these instincts. But remember, a ruler can't take care of everyone equally. They have to choose, even if it breaks their hearts to do so."

I glanced at Lawrence again and winced at how hard he was breathing. In the Earth realm, his activity would have barely made his heart rate rise. How much longer did he have before his systems gave out in what amounted to a poisonous atmosphere?

"He says he's here for the humans, but I don't know..." I couldn't bring myself to speculate he'd come to help me, to protect me, because I didn't want to be disappointed again. Plus, I'd feel guilty at him taking such a big risk.

"Human. Just one, John. Do you have any idea what Kestrel might turn out to be?" The corner of Ellerin's mouth twitched —he was teasing me.

"You know, don't you?"

"I may. Like you, I have speculations and many questions about the girl's history."

"Which questions in particular?"

He chuckled. "Nice try. Go to your gargoyle. He could use your help."

Indeed, I looked over to where Lawrence had been and didn't see him. The bubble around me and Ellerin popped with the sound of wind chimes when I left it.

Wait, had he just said *my* gargoyle? When I looked back to ask him, Ellerin had disappeared.

25

LAWRENCE

I lay on my back and looked at the Fae sun, now heading toward the horizon of an impossibly blue sky. There weren't even any clouds to find shapes in, and irrational resentment curled up in my chest like a satisfied cat. Indeed, there was a grave sense of, "I told you so" pinging around the back of my brain. The longer I stayed in Faerie, the more I felt in touch with my gargoyle heritage and history. I had started writing things down, but I didn't know if my notes would make any sense to me when I got home.

If I got home. The thudding of my heart and the shallowness of my breath no matter how hard I tried to suck in the air made me doubt it. At least I could appreciate the irony of a gargoyle dying doing something noble in Faerie.

"Don't move."

Reine's soft voice made me open my eyes. Huh, I hadn't realized the black dots swimming in the periphery of my vision had melted together into me closing my eyelids. That was disturbing. When I focused on her, or tried to, I saw two of her. Her soft hair brushed over my abs as she leaned over me, and she held the cold end of a stethoscope against my chest.

"Take a deep breath."

I tried, but I ended up coughing and rolled to my side toward her. She scooted back but didn't get up.

"Thanks." She reached around me and put the infernal thing on my back between my wing blade and spine. Her brows drew together. "There's a murmur. Did you know about that?"

"If there is one, it's new. Perhaps being here is breaking down my heart muscle."

"Don't joke about that." She sat back on her heels and turned the full force of her frown on me. "I don't want..."

"Don't want what?"

"For you to come to any harm." While the sentiment was sweet, the word choice placed a cool wall between us.

I propped myself up on my elbow, and she helped me to sit. My wingtips gouged lines into the turf behind me, and I drew some strength from the naked dirt.

"Maybe you should put me in the ground like a plant," I suggested. "Gargoyle flower—it might bloom where you want it, and it might not."

She smiled. "If I thought that would help you, I would. Can you stand?" She did so and held out her hands. Her stethoscope hung around her neck, reminding me of meeting her as Doctor Renee River. She hadn't been wielding any medical implements then, just a wicked case of Fae jet lag and an understandable amount of irritation for a know-it-all gargoyle.

I allowed her to pull me to my feet. "Ooof, you're strong."

She arched an eyebrow. "For a girl?"

"If you say so." I tried not to lean on her because I stood at least a foot taller than she, and I didn't want to throw off her balance. We started making our slow way back to the dark gray stone castle, which rose against the backdrop of the woods like a fairy-tale setting, both beautiful and ominous at the same time.

She shot me a sideways glance. "When you were sitting

there looking at me, what were you thinking? You had an interesting expression on your face."

"About when I met you. How you were so beautiful and intimidating...and it scared the hell out of me."

"Why?"

Now, being in Faerie, I understood. "My mother had told me stories of the Fae from the time I was a wee lad, and after my father was killed by—"

"By my brother."

"I was going to say by a Fae, but right, by your brother *in a case of mistaken identity*, I now know, none of them were good. So, when I saw you and your pointed ears and your haughty Fae attitude, I knew I had to defend myself. And, as irrational as it seems, my place on the team at the CPDC."

She laughed. "You were intimidated by me? I was weak and heartbroken from having to leave Sir Raleigh, and I do not do well on planes."

"Yet you were and still are the most beautiful creature I've ever seen."

She stopped and turned so we faced each other. Crossing her arms, she challenged, "'Creature?'"

I didn't need my inner gargoyle to tell me I'd just made a mistake. He didn't seem to be paying attention, though. In fact, the nearness of our bodies made him hyper-aware of the curve of her neck and the points of her ears, which, as I recalled, had some intriguingly erotically sensitive nerve endings. "Well, you're not human. And you're not animal, vegetable, or mineral, so..." I shrugged. "Whatever you are, you're still quite lovely."

She cocked her head. "Am I, though? Lovely?"

I traced a finger down her cheek. "Don't you believe you are?"

She looked down, and I raised her face with one finger under her slightly pointed chin. Instead of weak and elfin, the feature gave her face a delicate strength, like a cat's. Then, reluctant to lose contact with her, I tucked a stray lock of hair behind her ear and rested my hand lightly on her shoulder.

She didn't seem to object. "I don't know if it matters, honestly."

"No? Isn't it an issue that Rhys doesn't have a perfectly symmetrical face?"

Guilt flashed through her eyes. "Not for me, but yes, for others. It's something I want to change. It's not fair, and fear of something like that keeps us from truly living." She placed her hand over mine, but also so she touched the side of her neck. Neither of us said it, but we both remembered the vampire and how she'd scarred Reine, albeit with two raised pinpoints of white flesh.

I moved Reine's hand out of the way with one hand and curled my arm around her waist with the other. She didn't resist as I pulled her to me, and I leaned down and kissed her neck where the vampire had bitten her.

"You could never be less beautiful to me, even if..."

"Even if what?" Now her challenge came in words puffed against my ear.

"Even if you weren't perfect. Perfect is boring, anyway."

She pulled back and grinned. "Is it?"

I put my other arm around her waist and held her loosely so she could continue to pull back but tightly so she'd know what I wanted. "Yes. You always know what to expect. And I never know what to expect from you."

"Is that so? Does that mean I'm not your usual selfish Fae, motivated only by her own interests?"

As much as I didn't want to let go of her lovely ass, I couldn't resist the urge to tuck another stray curl behind her ear. "No, you've definitely changed my mind about Fae. You're unselfish to a fault. Otherwise, why would you have agreed to bring Kestrel and John? They must be dragging you down."

"It's been interesting. I won't argue that." She put her hands on my chest, two warm spots, and didn't push away, so I pulled her closer. She tilted her face up toward mine, and I leaned forward to capture her lips.

Her mouth met mine with eagerness, and I had just tangled my fingers in her hair when a male voice interrupted us like a bucket of snow dumped on our heads. "Really, Princess, he's a handsome brute, but is that absolutely necessary?"

26

REINE

e broke apart like teenagers who had been caught snogging behind a parent's couch, and my cheeks burned, but in anger, not shame.

Troubadour stood a few feet away, his arms crossed, and a smug grin on his face. "I don't mean to interrupt you, Princess, but I have something to discuss with you, and I appreciate that we may not have any more opportunities for undisturbed discourse."

I bit my lip over calling his bullshit about not meaning to interrupt us and confronting him for making 'undisturbed discourse' sound like something dirty. But he did have a point. We'd be heading into Lorien the next day, and I still needed to talk to Ellerin and the others about how we'd approach it—directly or with stealth. Either way, I wouldn't have time alone with anyone where we could discuss things freely. Or, I thought as I squeezed Lawrence's hand, which had found mine, do other things without anyone watching.

I turned to Lawrence. "I'm sorry, I truly am, but I need to attend to this bit of business."

Somehow wistfulness managed to steal over his stern

gargoyle features. "I understand. You're a Fae princess. You have to do what's best for your realm." He let go of my hand and trudged toward the castle, his wings drooping. Poor guy—he needed to go home, and soon.

"What do you want?" The question came out more harshly than I intended.

"He's the one who helped you with the soul-eater, isn't he?" Troubadour held out an elbow, and I took his arm.

We walked away from the castle toward the tree line, which had paths through it, at least as far as Aoine's lands went. In spite of my wearing my stethoscope and modern Earth clothing, it felt like we were a couple of noble Fae out for a stroll on a lovely sunny day. Or a couple, full stop. That didn't help me feel better about how I'd left things with Lawrence. But he couldn't stay, and I had more responsibilities here than I'd anticipated. Perhaps it would be better for us to nip temptation in the bud and not carry things forward.

That would be easy if it hadn't been for the history between us.

"Princess?"

I glanced up at Troubadour's handsome face, and he smiled. I recognized I was doing the flirty female sideways look thing and returned my attention to the path in front of us.

"I'm..." Nope, couldn't say sorry. Fae princesses didn't apologize. "I have a lot on my mind. Yes, he's the gargoyle who helped me with the soul-eater."

"I thought he looked familiar, although I only saw him in human form. He gargs out nicely."

"Yes." I didn't accept his invitation to elaborate.

We entered the variegated canopy of the trees, and the temperature dropped by a few degrees. I welcomed the cool air on my face, arms, and hands. It would help me to think straight.

We reached a lovely little clearing with a small pond in the middle of it. From the other side, a startled deer gave us an annoyed look and bounded off. Brightly colored birds flitted through the branches, and a pair of dragonflies buzzed over the water. I relaxed just a smidge—this was the magical Faerie I remembered.

"What are you thinking?" Troubadour surveyed the scene with a satisfied smirk, and I suspected he'd scoped it out before coming to find me. He would know what a princess, or any high Fae female, liked.

"It's beautiful. I didn't know just how much the misty silence of the dark and gray Fae woods bothered me."

"I thought you might like it. Come, there's a bench over here."

He led me to a moss-spotted gray stone bench, and I let go of his arm so we could sit. The two dragonflies continued to chase each other, and I leaned back and looked up through the branches overhead to the sky. A red bird chirped hello at me, and I laughed.

Troubadour casually draped an arm behind me. With his pose and expression, he could have played a young human male in a movie—*the quarterback makes his move.* "Good, I thought you might need to relax."

"Oh?" I arched an eyebrow. "Please enlighten me, fair Prince. What is all this in service of?"

"What do you mean?" He put his other hand to his broad chest in mock dismay. "I can't bring a lovely Fae to a clearing in the woods to get her away from the prying eyes of the castle and the pressures to fit a certain role?"

He had a point. Although we'd only met through a medium the previous week, I had felt a connection to him that made me perhaps more comfortable in his company than was wise. Still...

"You have some balls pulling me away from a kiss to bring me here, you know that?"

"A kiss that everyone could see from the castle. I saw where that was going and I got there as soon as I could. Please don't think harshly of me for saying this, but remember yourself, Princess. You're not in the Earth realm anymore."

Ouch. "Touché. You're right, I need to act the Fae princess if I have any hope of getting back into my grandmother's court."

He raised both eyebrows at me. "That's impressive humility for—" He shut his mouth, and the words he held inside made his cheeks bulge for a second.

I laughed. "For a Fae crown princess? I suppose the Earth realm wasn't all bad for me even if I did lose the blonde in my hair."

"I don't mind. The white makes you look ethereal, wise."

"Not beautiful?" I teased.

"You'd be beautiful even if you were bald."

I preferred ethereal and wise. "You have a honeyed tongue, Sir Prince."

"And you have a discerning mind, most of the time." He smirked. "And apparently a passionate streak. How often do others get to see that?"

I thought back to my time in the Earth realm. "Not very, admittedly. I had to be careful there about who I got close to. They'd just as often turn against me once I couldn't give them what they wanted."

He made a noise that would have sounded rude and harsh had it come from anyone but him. "Like here."

"Yes, but without the level of games and complication." And no one had tried to put me in an asylum.

A breeze tickled my skin and set the shadows dancing. My inner sense told me that the sun had accelerated its course down to the horizon. "While it's beautiful and peaceful here— thank you for bringing me—I shouldn't linger too much longer. I have a party to get ready for, after all." And my stomach growled. I put a hand to it, embarrassed. "Excuse me. Apparently, I'm hungrier than I thought."

"If I had thought ahead sufficiently, I would have brought a picnic to entice you to stay. However..." He reached into a pocket in his cloak and brought out a chocolate chip-studded cookie. "I grabbed this from the buffet earlier and had thought to save this for a midnight snack, but I'm sure I can get another one."

"Okay, but only if you share it with me."

"Are you inviting me to break bread with you, Princess?"

If it would get him to spit out what he really wanted, I'd kiss him. All right, that wouldn't be too much of a stretch, although I wanted to kiss Lawrence more. "I suppose I am."

He held out the cookie, and we bent it until it broke into two perfect halves.

"A good omen," we said in unison, then laughed.

I nibbled one sharp edge of the crescent. The outside of the cookie crunched beautifully with notes of brown butter and sugar, and the inside had just the right amount of softness. "Oh my goodness, I'll have to compliment Aoine's pastry chef."

"Same here." He finished off his half. Why did males always eat so quickly? Once he swallowed, he said, "I do have something I need to tell you. And another thing to ask you."

Finally. "Yes?"

"I apologize for all the preamble, but I wanted to show you I know how to treat a Fae princess well, even if I'm a dark Fae."

"Okay..." I stilled, suspecting where this might be going but not altogether wanting it to.

"You've now seen my lands, the Gray Zone, and some of yours. I'm sure you can tell there's grave unrest throughout the realm, from the lowest of the Fae even to the highest."

I nodded, although I didn't volunteer anything Aoine had said.

"Some of that started when you were banished. You may not have realized it, but you are beloved here."

"Now you're making things up."

"No, it's true. We Fae like to pretend we're harsh and unyielding, but there was something about a mother rejecting two of her children, when they're not easy to have, that sent a shock through the realm. Even if you hadn't been the darling crown princess, it would have been a wake-up call that the old ways are dying."

"But it wasn't my mother..." Unless it was. His pitying look told me I needed to stop denying the fact. "What are you proposing?"

"I have had a plan for many years, even centuries—we need to unite Faerie. The lower orders don't want to choose between light and dark anymore, and we all need to be on the same page. Creatures from the other dimensions have been coming through."

"What sort of creatures?" See? That's why I hated being called a creature—we Fae used the word as a term for *other*.

"Nightmare realm ones, for starters. Your grandmother allowed them to come through for a while as a way to reach the Earth realm after the barriers between it and the Collective Unconscious had been shored up."

"Really? They'd been crumbling for years."

"And a powerful being accelerated the process. So you see, there are others who are stirring, and we need for Faerie to be strong and progressive. Plus, there are whispers that the nightmare invasion could have prompted the start of a Great Rising."

I shuddered at the thought of thousands of Fae ending their ten-thousand-year sleep. "There's not supposed to be one of those for at least another thousand years."

"No, but please believe me when I say I have seen revenants, more than ever before."

I sat back and looked at the surface of the water, hoping for a glimpse of what had happened, but it remained still and only reflected the sky above. "Interesting. What does this have to do with you? And me?"

"Many of my court are as hidebound as those of yours because they haven't traveled out of their palaces and abodes. My calling as a bard has taken me through the lands, well, except the light ones since I couldn't cross the stream, as you saw. So I couldn't approach any light Fae for an alliance."

"Because we don't travel." Kestrel's question and surprise at my never having visited the other capital city came back to me.

"Exactly." He turned toward me fully and took my hand. "Princess Reine, I know what happened in the woods with the Queen Spell, and I almost wish it hadn't because it makes things much more complicated. You and I have the chance to unite Faerie. You don't have to give me your answer now, but please consider it... I would like for us to broker a traditional marriage deal."

I opened my mouth to protest, but he put a finger over my lips. I resisted my first impulse, which was to bite it—hard— and instead smacked his hand away from my face. "How dare you? Don't ever tell me not to speak. And my court doesn't do marriage."

"I apologize." He did look properly chastened, so I let him continue. "I know your queens take consorts so as not to put the realm in danger of too much influence from outside the family line, but times are different. And I would still allow you to have your consorts, even if one was a gargoyle who came to visit occasionally."

I didn't think Lawrence would go for that, but I kept that thought to myself.

"Think about it," he urged. "Times are changing. We need to change with them. You've seen the beauty of our lands—all of them. Others have as well, and if Faerie is divided, it will be easier to conquer. Do you really want vampires to set up shop in your castle?"

Well, there was one sexy vampire I wouldn't mind, but she had obligations elsewhere. Plus, I had a bone to pick with her for scarring me even if she had helped with the soul-eater.

He didn't need to know any of that. "I see your point. I need to think about it. I haven't even seen my home in centuries, so it's not possible for me to make any decisions until I do."

"Then let me leave you with a preview of what may come." He leaned in, and I tilted my face to his. I couldn't deny I was attracted to him, and if what he said was true... I hadn't detected any deception in his words. The most confusing thing about them was a dark Fae caring about the entirety of Faerie, but perhaps that was my own prejudice getting in the way. Or, could the rumors of an early Great Rising be true?

His lips met mine in a gentle, restrained kiss. Another surprise. I'd always heard the dark Fae were a lusty bunch. Then he pulled back and smiled.

"That wasn't so bad, was it?"

"Nope." It wasn't great, either, but I'd spare his ego. I stood. "Thank you. You've given me a lot to think about, and I promise you I will."

He regained his feet in a lithe gesture that reminded me of Rhys, which did not bode well for Troubadour as a potential mate. "I was completely honest with you, Princess. Don't let it get out that I was. It'll ruin my reputation."

"Don't worry, I won't." Especially since what he'd told me amounted to treason, speaking against both courts. I wondered —did he know about the asylum?

27

LAWRENCE

After I left Reine with the dark Fae prince in the garden, I made my way back to the castle and to my room, where I lay on my side and faced away from the window so I wouldn't accidentally see them doing...what? Fae stuff? Reine was a princess, I reminded myself. Troubadour was a prince. They'd have a lot to catch up on, or he would catch her up on the situation. I imagined that if I were to return to the Aerie, it would be the same. Whoever accompanied me, if they did, would be excluded from certain conversations about gargoyle business.

Still, I couldn't get comfortable and rest, so I wandered up to Kestrel and John's room. I opened the door to find them in an argument.

"I just want to go take a walk," Kestrel was saying as she stepped back from opening the door for me. "I'll take Sir Raleigh with me."

John looked at the cat in question, who bathed himself in the middle of a sunbeam on one of the beds. He paused mid-lick and glared at Kestrel, daring her to make him move. "See?

He agrees. You walked all morning. And all day yesterday. And the day before that. You need to stay here. It's safer."

"What harm could come to me? It's a fairy tale castle, and I don't sense any ill intent from Lady Aoine."

"She's a Fae. There's always ill intent, or at least the desire to deceive, right, Lawrence?"

John and Kestrel turned to me, and I almost left, not wanting to referee their disagreement. It figured that Kestrel would chafe at being limited to their room—when had she ever had the chance to be in a fairy castle? The question was how many trolls it hid.

"I can't say anything about Lady Aoine's intent, but they're definitely tricky."

Kestrel sighed with a huff, and John seemed to appreciate my reluctant agreement with his point.

"How about Kestrel and I walk?" I suggested and refrained from adding, "to give each of you a break from the other." How much time had they spent together before all this happened? From what I had observed, Kestrel was pretty much her own person, and she'd mostly turn to her mother for support. Yes, these two would have a lot to sort out when they—we—returned to the Earth realm.

"That sounds like a wonderful idea, Uncle Lawrence!"

John hesitated, so I told him, "I'll take care of her. I've already been exploring and know what areas are safe."

He took so long to agree that I prepared arguments for Kestrel's and my walk in my head, but finally he nodded with a reluctant, "Be careful."

Kestrel grabbed her fleece. "We will. Bye, Dad!"

We headed outside so I could show her the gardens. We had just stepped on one of the gravel paths in the rose garden, which had been planted on the terrace level closest to the castle, when she said, "I'm glad we got this time to talk."

She sounded so much like Beverly I almost stumbled. Luckily, I didn't. "Me, too. What's on your mind?" I could guess, and I mentally prepared myself to be the godfather and friend her parents had asked me to be two decades beforehand. She and I had had a few frank conversations, but none in such strange circumstances.

She stopped me with a hand on my forearm. "Wait." Ellerin and Rhys appeared at the top of the staircase that led down to the next level. They appeared to be in serious discussion and stopped and regarded us with wariness.

Rhys nodded, his eyes hooded. "Lovely day."

I returned the nod with a, "Quite."

He and Ellerin headed off to the side, and Kestrel and I descended the stairs to a garden of flowering bushes I didn't know the names of. Their bright red, blue, and yellow flowers perfumed the air with a scent similar to honeysuckle, but without being invasive and weed-like.

"How did you know they were coming? They had their voices masked."

"I could feel the magic." She rubbed the tops of her arms even though the air temperature hovered around seventy degrees, she wore a fleece, and we walked in the sun. "It's been growing ever since we got here, this sense of others."

"Can you discriminate the types of magic?"

"Maybe? I don't know. I have to observe some more. But what I really wanted to ask you was what you saw in my dreams, when the Winter gnomes were watching them." The glance she slid my way looked half-fearful, half-hopeful.

"Do you remember what you dreamed last night?" I didn't want to volunteer the scene of her mother's death so as not to hurt her. And I definitely didn't want to discuss the Corey dream.

She sighed. "It's the same nightmare I've had since that night in the lab. It plays over and over in my head. Sometimes I can change it, but that's almost worse, you know? Because then

I wake up and have to remember how it all really ended, and that Mom's gone." She wiped her cheeks, where tears streaked her pale, freckled skin. "Sorry, I thought I was okay, but it's getting harder and harder not to cry."

"That's normal. Now that the shock is wearing off, you're feeling your feelings." I had seen the same with my mother and with others who had lost loved ones through my life. And in myself. When the shock of Reine keeping the knowledge of who killed my father from me had worn off, I'd gone through some anger, mostly aimed toward Rhys. Now I could see why she had done it, especially after experiencing some of the context she'd come from. How much influence had the human world had on her? Could it have possibly softened her?

"Thanks, Uncle Lawrence. There is something strange, though. I keep catching something out of the corner of my eye in the dreams..."

"Is it reddish, like your hair?"

"Well, yes, but it's more solid. Did the gnomes see anything like that?"

"As a matter of fact, they did. They rewound and paused your dream, then zoomed in, but it was a blur for them, too."

"Interesting..." Now she sounded like her father, and I stifled a laugh. "What did you think it was? You have the most experience with animals of all of us. You must have looked at lots of blurry pictures to figure out what things were."

She had a point. I stopped and closed my eyes, bringing the memories of the images in the crystal to mind. "If I had to guess, I'd say it was a fox."

Kestrel grabbed my arm, and I opened my eyes. She pointed to the edge of the garden, where a red fox watched us. The thing seemed to grin, then disappeared.

"Like that one?"

"Yes, very much so."

She let go of me and rubbed her upper arms again. "Do you

ever feel like you're so close to something you can taste it, but it's just out of reach?" She shook her head. "Now I'm doing it."

"Doing what?"

"Fantasy movie dialog. Reine and I have a running joke about it."

Of course they did, but I didn't feel left out. No, I suspected Reine had started it so Kestrel would have something to help her find humor during her dark times and in this odd situation. The flimsy wall I'd built to keep Reine away from my heart crumbled further. "Sometimes familiar is good, even if it's worn. But to answer your question, yes."

"Is it Reine?" she asked with a sly grin.

"Now you're getting personal."

She laughed. "Then we'd be even. If you saw my dreams last night, then you probably also saw one about Corey." Her face flushed a dark pink. "I hope you didn't see too much."

"Thankfully, they moved onto Reine's dream when they saw where that one was going. Are you two that serious?"

A frustrated sigh emerged from her lips. "I don't know. I want to be. He's cautious because of, well, you know..."

I tried to catch the adult impulse, but my concerns, the ones I'm sure she'd heard ad nauseum from her parents, tumbled out. "The fact he's almost ten years older than you and above you in your organization, which could lead him to be vulnerable to accusations of sexual harassment should things not work out between the two of you?"

She raised one eyebrow. "Been holding that in for a while, haven't you?"

"Yeah, sorry. But it's true. You've got to take the long view with these things."

"I'm trying, but everything is taking so long, and it's hard with my powers not settling. Like, is my newfound ability to sense magical talent another temporary one? Will it wriggle away in a day or so? And what will take its place?"

"What does that have to do with Corey?"

"If I knew what I was, I'd know where I'd fit, and he may not be in the chain of command above me anymore."

"Is that why he keeps sniffing around rather than breaking it off?"

Another sigh. "Maybe? I don't know. He's super friendly and seems open, but when it comes to his emotions, he's a typical male shifter—not letting anyone in. No offense."

Was I like that? "None taken. If we're talking shifter psychology, he seems to have decided to claim you as his mate and is holding himself back."

"And what about you? Is that how you feel about Reine?"

"I don't know," I told her at the same time as my inner gargoyle said, *Yes.* I could never be sure whether he was more interested in mating or the act of mating. Freud would have a field day with me—rational, cautious scientist with literal inner beast.

She stopped me again, and we looked over the wall to the pathway below, where Reine and Troubadour walked toward the castle. They seemed to have an easy air between the two of them. I didn't want to, but a growl rumbled through me, courtesy of my possessive inner self.

Kestrel snickered. "I think we have our answer. Were you invited to the party tonight?"

"No, were you?"

"No, but you should crash it."

I put my hand to my face in mock horror. "But I haven't a thing to wear!"

She looked me up and down. "You probably don't have to wear anything different, Uncle Lawrence. Your pecs and abs would put those Fae boys to shame."

Now my cheeks heated. "This hasn't turned weird and uncomfortable at all."

We discussed party crashing strategy until we walked into

the shadow of the castle. She went back to her room, and I mine. When I got there, I found formal attire, which appeared nineteenth-century, laid out for me. The older Fae woman who had led me to my room turned from the wash stand, where she'd laid out a comb and other grooming implements. Unlike the other servants, she didn't have wing stubs.

"It's been so long since we've had a gargoyle here. The mistress didn't say you were going to the party tonight, but she didn't say you weren't, either." She winked at me. "And I have a sense a certain Fae princess would like for her gargoyle guard to be there."

"Thank you. I hope you're right."

She patted me on the arm before she left. "Don't worry, I'm rarely wrong." She walked into the hall and closed the door. I opened it again, wanting to ask her what she had been wrong about, but she had disappeared.

THE OLDER FAE servant appeared again after I had gotten ready. Had she somehow magically known my measurements? Everything fit perfectly. Luckily, I remembered how to tie a cravat, even though it had been a century and a half since the last time I'd had to do so.

Although I still wore my gargoyle face and body, I appeared to be a civilized gentleman in the clothing and with my hair settled after being mussed from all the flying I'd done. My wings still stood out behind me, but more as accessories or signs that I could snatch a Fae princess out of danger if necessary. Not that she couldn't defend herself...

The servant looked me up and down and nodded. "You're quite the handsome gargoyle. This way."

She led me through the hallway and down some back stairs to a different corridor, this one plusher with red carpet and cream damask wallpaper. It had the requisite family portraits, each of a woman who looked related to Aoine. A set of double doors dominated one end, framed with a lintel carved with ornate symbols, some alchemical, but many appearing to resemble vines or tree branches. My fingertips and the end of my nose tingled as we approached.

"What is that?"

The servant cackled. "The Doors of Truth. The only ones who may pass must have their hopes, dreams, and mission firmly in mind."

"Otherwise, what happens?"

She spread her hands in a sudden motion. "Boom!"

"Oh." What did I hope and dream? I'd found out who killed my father, and why. The question that had dominated my life answered, I hadn't taken the time to ask what followed.

Finally find a mate and settle down, my inner gargoyle suggested. Or was that my inner voice? I couldn't tell the difference anymore.

"What do you hope, dream, and strive for, gargoyle? Think carefully on your answer."

I closed my eyes, and immediately the abandoned glee on Reine's face when she'd danced with me in the vampire club came to mind.

"Yes, that's it. Keep thinking. Dig into your heart—what do you truly want? What gives you meaning?"

Did her voice sound younger? I thought of John and Beverly as a couple and my long acquaintance with them, the thousands of small moments I'd seen them share in partnership, both as scientists and in their romantic relationship. My heart ached for John. If I felt lost, what must he be experiencing? "I hope for another dance. I dream of a life where I'm not alone, but rather have the love, respect, and companionship of someone equal to me in scientific curiosity and the desire to help others, my mission."

"Very good."

I opened my eyes to see not an old woman, but a distinguished middle-aged Fae with blond streaks through her red hair.

"Go get her." She blew me a kiss and disappeared. The portrait behind where she'd been standing caught my eye. There was no plate on it to tell me who it was, but I could see it was the oldest one in the hallway, and in the most ornate frame. The same woman looked out at me, a sly smile on her lips.

Well, it was a Faerie castle, after all.

Now very sure of what I wanted, I pushed through the doors.

28

REINE

I looked at myself in the mirror, and I couldn't help but contrast my current appearance with that of myself before the party at the Fae con convention. Whereas there I had had a fake crown and wings, now I wore a crown—well, a tiara of platinum and diamond—and my wings stood out in resplendent rainbow display. Aoine had lent me a gown of shimmering light blue, although none of her shoes fit me. I felt odd bespelling another Fae's footwear, so I wore my sneakers and hoped that they wouldn't show beneath the long hem. I'd adjust them if necessary, but I'd stay as comfy as I could for as long as possible.

A knock on my door told me that it was time for me to present myself to the assembled. I opened it to find a servant, who bowed low, his clipped wings showing as stubby on his back. I had never liked the practice, and now it seemed particularly offensive. A Fae servant would never leave his family of employ unless something terrible had happened, and their clipped wings made their lack of options particularly poignant. He straightened, and I followed him, trying not to stare at the poor, mutilated appendages.

"There you go, Princess. Just go down the stairs." He gestured to the closed double doors in front of me. Their frames lacked the decoration I'd noticed throughout the palace —had they recently been replaced?

"Thank you."

He appeared startled, then smiled and bowed again. Another servant joined him, and together they opened the doors.

Aoine's ballroom kept the same color motif as the rest of the castle, namely shades of forest, although it did not devolve into human hunting lodge. The walls were painted a lovely dark green, and the window trim and fixtures evoked the dark gold of late afternoon. The large chandelier overhead shimmered with thousands of crystals, and the way it sparkled against the dark blue ceiling reminded me of nighttime.

The guests also sparkled and shimmered in a thousand bright shades—well, maybe a hundred. In spite of the size of the room, or perhaps because of it, the clumps of people talking appeared to be fewer in number. I stepped forward, and as if choreographed, all conversation ceased and all heads turned toward me.

The humans had not been invited, so I looked for Troubadour and Lawrence. I found the dark Fae prince easily, but the gargoyle was nowhere in sight. Ellerin and Rhys were also missing, and the spike of fear at the absence of Ellerin's steady presence surprised me.

Well, I'd have to handle things on my own. That's what I did, after all. I descended the stairs slowly, trying to relish the attention. For someone who had been used to hiding, the curious gazes of those from below felt intrusive. But I was a Fae princess, and this was my debut coming home. I couldn't let the survival instincts that I had honed in the Earth realm interfere with my born role.

The men, including Troubadour, mostly looked at me

hungrily. How many proposals to be consorts would I receive this evening? I made a private bet with myself—at least ten. And of course Troubadour's marriage proposal sat awkwardly between us.

When I reached the bottom of the stairs, Aoine walked over to me and curtsied, then turned to everyone, who still watched silently.

"Thank you all for coming. I am delighted to welcome my dear friend and school compatriot, the Princess Reine, back to the light lands of Faerie. She has been long in exile, so I know she must be thrilled to be home. Please do not overwhelm her, however, as she has not yet been to the capital to see the lay of the land. Reine, would you like to say a few words?"

The first words that came to my mind were not of a princess, but of a healer. I hadn't been around a lot of Fae in a long time, but the conditions and illnesses that we had—and that most tried to keep quiet—returned to the catalog in my brain. I couldn't however, tell the gentleman to my left that he was in danger of cardiac arrest if he had one more canapé, the florid nature of his skin telling me that he had been indulging too much in the things we Fae found delicious. Nor could I warn the woman to my right, whose dress hung off her bony frame and whose wings appeared faded, that she needed to get help for her ambrosia addiction. No, I was a princess, and I had to have a bigger focus.

"Thank you all for your warm welcome. I am indeed delighted to be home, and I am most grateful to our lovely hostess for assembling this gathering so that I may ease myself back into high Fae society." A polite chuckle flowed through the assembled. Had any of them ever left and come back? I doubted it. Whereas I would have to connect to them, they might not be able to relate to me, and the thought made me cringe.

Aoine handed me a glass of sparkling wine, and the introduction marathon began. She first brought me to a Fae who was tall by our standards, and dark-skinned. It seemed natural for him to look down his nose at everyone, including me, and it took effort to not bristle under his seemingly condescending gaze. Aoine seemed to not be affected by it, so I followed her lead.

"Reine, this is Duke Henry Alderbranch. He has been the court historian for years."

He bowed slightly, and his tight lips spread. Would his face break if he smiled completely? "I am honored to meet you, Princess." At least he spoke with a pleasant tenor voice. Perhaps he was more comfortable around books and documents than he was around other Fae.

"And I you, Duke Alderbranch. Thank you for the service you do for our court."

"It is an honor to serve, Princess. I was hoping to get some time with you during your visit here to discuss the new methods of record-keeping that have been developed in the Earth realm."

Visit? That was an interesting way to put it. Fae historians often had a special connection to the flow of time, and sometimes they said things without realizing they portended the future.

"What sort of methods are you using currently?" I supposed it would help to see where things stood here.

He sighed and ran a hand through his thinning black curls. Fae men didn't go bald, so it must have been a common gesture for him. "Honestly, thick books, scrolls, and memory."

No wonder he looked frustrated. He didn't even have a card catalog.

"I am definitely happy to discuss how to modernize the records. Besides, I want to make sure the ones that involve me are accurate."

He did crack a true smile at that. "I would be happy to assist you with that. You have been a most fascinating subject of study and observation, although I suspect we don't know the whole story."

Aoine tugged at my arm. "You were always the bookworm, weren't you? It didn't surprise me at all when I learned you had become a full-fledged healer with all of the school it requires in the Earth realm."

The duke's eyes lit with interest at this, but Aoine was already tugging me on to the next Fae, two women who resembled each other, down to the complementary bright blue and green colors of their dresses and the exact same shade of yellow-blonde hair. Each had one blue eye and one brown eye.

"Sorry about that, he can be a bit of a bore." Aoine told me before saying out loud, "Princess, these are Ladies Elder Flower and Scupper Nog."

They curtsied, and I returned the gesture, but not as low as they did.

"We are the landscaping and planting consultants for the capital," one of them, I had already forgotten which, said.

The other one added, "And we would love to know what you have learned in the Earth realm about fertilizing organically and pest control."

"Whereas we used to be able to control everything by magic, we are finding things to be more unruly, and it would be nice to figure out how to conserve our energy."

They stopped speaking in tandem and folded their hands in front of them, waiting for my reply. I looked at Aoine, and her shoulders lifted in a slight shrug.

"That's not really my area, but I am happy to tell you what little I do know. Perhaps later?"

They curtsied again, and Aoine led me away. Instead of stopping by a new group, she led me to the punch table. The other Fae, presumably being polite, left us alone. That was one good thing about the Fae versus the Earth realm—other Fae generally respected one's need for privacy and to have a break.

"I'm sensing a theme here," I told Aoine. "Is everyone here curious about the Earth realm?"

"I figured it wouldn't take you long to catch on. Yes, these Fae have been waiting for you to return for a long time. They want you to help modernize Faerie."

I slid a glance toward Troubadour, who raised his glass to me. Could he and Aoine be in collusion? There had seemed to be some sort of familiarity between them. But he had not been able to come into the light Fae lands, and I was pretty sure she had not traveled into the dark.

But I had been gone for a while...

"How do they expect me to change thousands of years of tradition? I did see some evidence of modernization in the dark Fae lands, but I doubt it would catch on here."

"It would with the right leader." She tilted her glass toward me. "They are aware that the Queen Spell has been spoken, and they are hoping it was by you."

So, she could tell, but the others couldn't. Did she really know what she was asking for? I guessed she wouldn't appreciate it if my process of modernization included ceasing the practice of clipping servants' wings.

Before we could say anything further, a murmur rippled through the room. Ellerin had entered through the doors leading out to the balcony.

Different Fae spoke the words, "the gray Fae" in different tones from wonder to fear to frank disdain. Ellerin strode toward me, his crystal alight, his cloak billowing behind him. Rhys followed him, seemingly enjoying the shock on the other Fae's faces. Good for him. The sheltered capital residents would not have seen a maimed Fae in their long lifetimes.

Aoine's expression went from dismayed to conciliatory.

"Wanderer, thank you for coming. I didn't think you'd received my invitation."

"That's because I didn't." He gave her a stern look. "Don't think I don't know what you're trying to do."

"And what is that?" She crossed her arms, but she swallowed, and her luna moth-patterned wings fluttered slightly.

"Drag the princess into something treasonous."

A gasp went through the crowd, but I could hear the insincerity in it. My cheeks burned with shame—I had sensed something going on, but I had ignored it in favor of dealing with the attention.

Aoine laughed, but uncomfortably. "Treason? That's quite the accusation, Wanderer. What are you basing this on?"

He leaned over and murmured something in her ear. I couldn't catch it, but she blanched.

He stepped back. "I didn't want to say it any louder so Reine wouldn't feel conflicted between her family loyalty and her affection for you. Although with friends like you, she doesn't need enemies."

I looked around for Kestrel to grin at her for the clichéd dialogue, then remembered she was upstairs in a room with her father. And I stood in a situation that became more precarious by the minute.

Troubadour joined our little group. "Whatever Lady Aoine was trying to do, I'm sure she has the princess' best interests at heart. A queen needs to pay heed to all the desires of her subjects, not just the ones she agrees with."

Ellerin gave him a long, measuring glare, and Troubadour's wings drooped. Ellerin nodded with satisfaction. "Come, Princess. We can find somewhere else to stay the night. It's too dangerous for you here."

I finally recognized the emotion that had bloomed in my gut when he'd appeared—the shame of a teenager being chastised in front of her friends.

"No."

Aoine placed a hand over her mouth, but I saw her delighted grin.

Ellerin turned his withering look to me. "What was that?"

"No. These Fae are allowed to ask me and Rhys and the rest of my party about the Earth realm as long as no one says anything directly against the queen or queens." I placed my hands on my hips and gave him a haughty royal look of my own. "Or have the rules changed?" I deliberately did not look at Troubadour. A private conversation between two royal Fae wouldn't count against me...I hoped.

Still, he nudged my mind with private conversation, and I almost preened under the pride in his voice. *"Now you're acting like a royal Fae."*

Ellerin gave me a long, measured look. "You are correct in your understanding of the rules." Now he turned in a full circle and glared at everyone assembled. "I would warn you, however, that there will be Hades to pay should anyone conspire to drag the princess into treasonous conversations or activities." The crystal atop his torch blazed so brightly I squinted, and with another swirl of his cloak, he was gone, leaving Rhys looking sheepish. He stepped closer, making a fourth in the group with me, Aoine, and Troubadour.

"Nicely done, sis."

Aoine took a deep breath and gave me a shaky smile. "Yes, thank you."

"You and I will talk later," I promised. But would we? I could walk away from all this now and negate any risk I'd been in. But I needed to know the desires of my people, as Troubadour had said, no matter what my grandmother thought of them. Or my mother. What would a gathering she arranged look like? I suspected I would find out soon enough.

Aoine nodded to the chamber group in the corner of the room, who watched everything wide-eyed. With a hasty throat-clearing, the conductor waved his baton, and they started playing a waltz.

Troubadour and I found ourselves bobbing our heads in time to the music after a few bars, and he held out a hand. "Would you like to dance with me, Princess?"

"I would love to."

With expert moves, he steered me out to the dance floor, and we fell into step like we'd been waltzing together our entire lives. My mind drifted back to an entirely different dance, one wilder and more fraught with sexual tension, with Lawrence, and I sighed.

A hurt expression puffed Troubadour's lower lip into a pout. "Is my footwork not to your liking, Princess?"

"No, it's fine." I smiled up at him. "I'm just overwhelmed by all of this. I knew it would be different, and there would be drama, but I never expected it to be like it has been."

"Are you happy to be home?"

"I'm not home, though. And I don't know if I will be once I get there. It seems like I'm destined to make people unhappy no matter what I do."

He twirled me, drawing surprised gasps and laughs from the Fae dancing around us, and a giggle escaped from me at his audacious move. Perhaps if I had someone beside me to keep me from taking myself too seriously, it wouldn't be that bad.

"If someone isn't unhappy with you at least part of the time, then you're not being a good leader. As you've seen, others will disagree with you no matter what you do. The question is, how do you handle it?"

How had my grandmother responded when others disagreed with her? The asylum came to mind. Had she banished enough enemies that she'd created resentment among the rest of her people? I hadn't thought of her being someone who ruled through fear, but then, I hadn't questioned her.

Maeve didn't teach her daughters to say no... Well, I just had, but not to her. Still, it felt like a step in the right direction.

As for the Fae prince I danced with... Everything felt right except for one thing. He wasn't a certain gargoyle.

Another gasp—goodness, these Fae hadn't had much excitement, had they?—drew my attention to the top of the stairs, where Lawrence stood, still in gargoyle form, but wearing formal wear that emphasized the broadness of his shoulders and the narrowness of his waist.

"Hot damn," one of the women near me murmured. "I'd forgotten how powerful they were."

"I haven't." Without realizing it, I pulled away from Troubadour. Lawrence descended the stairs, giving those assembled time to admire him, and took my hand.

29

LAWRENCE

When I reached the bottom of the stairs and took Reine's hand, something electric passed between the two of us. Great, now I channeled novel tropes and lines, but it was true.

To say she looked beautiful didn't even approach the truth. She wore a close-fitting gown of light blue that sparkled like the surface of the ocean at dawn. The skirt flared over her hips and the neckline dipped, giving hints of the sensual being beneath. Someone had tried to tame her wild curls, but they already escaped from the updo, making ringlets around her face.

"You're radiant. Like a goddess."

Pink highlighted her cheekbones, and she smiled. "And you clean up well. Who knew gargoyles could be so striking?"

A quick check around the room told me the Fae gathered there had differing opinions of how I looked and whether my presence was appropriate or justified. I spotted Aoine, a rictus of a smile on her face, and Troubadour stood beside her and murmured into her ear.

"Shocking may be the better word. Shall we dance?"

"Sure. Do you know how to waltz or do anything else from the nineteenth century?"

Gods help me... "Hmmm, are you sure we have to?"

We made our way to the musician stand, and the mischievous grin that I'd found typically heralded something good for me, or at least fun, appeared on her face. "Let me see what I can do." She murmured in the ear of the conductor, and whereas he'd previously looked bored with what they were doing, his expression of ennui cleared, and he nodded eagerly. He held out a hand, and she took it. A golden light illuminated their joined hands. Then she returned to me.

"What did you request?"

"You'll see. Something to marry old and new since they're so curious about the Earth realm. Let's see if you can keep up."

We walked to the edge of the dance floor and waited for the minuet or whatever it was to end. Then, in a silence that stretched several beats too long, she brought me to the center of the floor, the room, and the rest of the Fae's attention.

A nervous wave shimmied through me—what would the consequences of our actions be? A burning sensation hit my left ear, and I turned to see Troubadour's stony-faced glare. I grinned. Too late to turn back now, and I'd show him which one of us really knew Reine.

The cello struck the opening notes of the Bach Toccata and Fugue in D minor, an ominous beginning. I dipped Reine, and she tilted her head back sensually as I bent forward, my head almost to her cleavage. The scent of her perfume, nothing that she'd applied, but her own scent, a heady mix of wildflowers, forest rain, and ocean breeze, hit my nostrils, prompting a growl of satisfaction.

Her laugh rumbled through her body into my hands. "Down, boy."

Then at the next phrase, picked up by the viola, I snapped

her to standing, and she made a slow twirl on the tip of her...

tennis shoe?

Now I laughed. "Nice shoes."

"All the better to not step on your toes with. But..." She reached out a foot, and the sneaker shimmered to be replaced by a dancing heel that matched her dress. "Better?"

"I don't care. Your feet are sexy no matter what."

The strings continued to play the melodies of the toccata part, and we moved to each one, following the flow of the music in a sensual manner, a cross between ballet and slow tango. Then, after the introduction, the cello started a throbbing bass beat, and Reine moved around me, her skirt gathered in one hand, her hips undulating to the music. She came back to me, and I clasped her. We moved in unison, the beat throbbing between us like auditory lovemaking. I suspected we wove a spell between us and over the assembled, but I had no chance to peek at them to see. Reine led, which I didn't mind at all, and she telegraphed her next move, her emerging desires, so quickly I had to concentrate on her completely.

We moved through twentieth century dances I knew but didn't know the names of, and by the end of the piece, I had her dipped again, her hand on her forehead and my head bowed over her again. My breath moved the fabric of her dress beneath me. Again, I shouldn't have been so winded, but damn, if that was it for me, what a way to go.

The notes faded, and we stood and faced the largest part of the crowd, hands held. She lifted her chin in defiance of the shocked expressions that met us. Not all of them. The older-looking Fae appeared dismayed. The younger ones giggled and whispered to each other behind fans and hands raised to cover mouths. Rhys started clapping, slowly, and soon the others followed suit. Then cheers erupted from the younger Fae, and Reine and I took bows in all four directions.

Reine held up a hand, and the noise subsided. "Many of you

expressed curiosity about what life was like in the Earth realm. I hope you've enjoyed the sample."

"Sign me up!" one young wag yelled, and the blushing lady Fae beside him whacked him with her fan. The others laughed.

Reine and I bowed to each other, and we walked to the edge of the dance floor. The Maestro's shoulders lifted and slumped with an exaggerated sigh as he lifted his baton, and his musicians began a subdued, more traditionally arranged piece.

Aoine glided over to us, her smile less strained. "That was lovely. And so..." She fluttered her hands. "Different! This party will be the talk of the court for centuries."

Reine inclined her head, but not before I caught the flash of anxiety in her eyes. "Lawrence, would you get me some punch?"

"Your wish is my command, Princess."

The crowd between me and the punch bowl parted as I walked through it. I tried not to squirm internally at being the center of attention. Gargoyles didn't squirm, but scientists sometimes did. This had been our hottest dance yet, and while moving together in that manner satisfied something, it whetted other appetites, and I feared the Fae could feel the hunger for her that burned in my... Gods, I almost said loins. But that's where I felt the desire, in my loins. I almost put a hand to my face, not in shame, but with the desire to keep my emotions private. Who knew what these Fae could feel coming off me? The flush in the cheeks of the women who directed long, curious looks at me and the frowns on the men they stood with gave me a pretty good hint.

Blessedly the punch bowl materialized at the end of my gauntlet. Unfortunately, so did Troubadour. He leaned with his hip against the table and his harp tucked under one elbow of his crossed arms.

"Well, well, I didn't know you had that in you, gargoyle."

I looked at him from under hooded eyelids as I scooped

punch into two cut crystal glasses that looked like ridiculously delicate teacups. "You may address me as Dr. Lawrence."

"Ah, right, because you help critters in your own realm."

"Yes, I'm a veterinarian. Excuse me, Reine is thirsty."

I turned, and with Fae-swift swivel-step, he blocked my path. "I can take that to the princess."

"No, thank you. I've got her."

"So you think." He cocked his head, and he assumed what I thought was meant to be a pleasant expression, but his desire to get me out of the way still emanated from him. Interesting— I hadn't felt anything from the other Fae.

It's the protective instinct, my inner gargoyle, again sounding very much like myself, informed me. *If he wants me out of the way, it may because he wants to hurt the one you're sworn to shield.*

I didn't think I'd sworn to do anything, but maybe I had. Perhaps our dances and making out had tied her to me without either of us realizing.

He plucked a string on his harp, and the noise of the crowd and music around us dimmed.

"May I speak frankly?" He didn't wait for an answer. "I see what you're trying to do. It's not going to work. You're a gargoyle. She's a Fae. We don't mix."

"Look, Troubadour, I don't mean you any harm. I'm only trying to bring Princess Reine a drink." If my explanation came out sounding condescending to match his tone, so be it.

"And then a drink turns into dinner, and dinner becomes a night spent together... I know how you gargoyles work. It's how you were able to infiltrate Faerie so long ago."

The image of the servants' wing stubs flashed through my mind, and a couple of pieces slotted into place in the "What happened between gargoyles and Fae?" puzzle, but not enough to make out the whole picture...yet.

"You're reading too much into it." I tried to move around him, but he blocked me again.

"I don't think I am. I see how she looks at you. How she danced with you." He clenched one fist. "I'm trying to look out for her. You can't stay here forever. You may think that no one can see you're still slightly out of breath or that she was leading and taking most of the athletic moves, but I can. And what happens when you have to leave?"

"We'll part like two consenting adults who had a good time and understand that sometimes things don't work out." I swallowed against the lump that had risen to my throat when I said the words, but they weren't untrue. He was right—we didn't have much of a chance we'd be able to stay together.

Troubadour seemed less convinced than I felt. "Riiiiiiight. As much as I hate to admit it, she'll be heartbroken. I'm a bard, I know love and what happens when it ends. Why do you think there are so many songs about it?"

"Why?"

"Because it's such a painful experience, and that's one thing all of us creatures with emotions share—heartbreak. And Fae don't go to therapy, so we sing to deal with our feelings, purge our pain."

"And you think you know Reine well enough to predict what will happen." I almost laughed, but I wanted to hear what he would say.

"She's a Fae princess. Trust me, they're cut from the same cloth—seemingly independent, but when they attach, they attach hard, and it can cloud their judgment. That's why the Light Court traditionally encourages the queen to have consorts, never a husband she's truly bonded with."

"They don't bond with consorts?"

He shrugged. "They claim they don't."

I snorted and poked the air behind me with one wing bone. The discretion spell around us dissipated with a sensation similar to that of eardrums popping during a flight descent.

"You claim you know Reine, but you don't. If you did, you'd

trust her to make her own decision...and know how angry she would be if you didn't."

"We'll see, gargoyle. Game on." He bowed and allowed me to pass, but I knew this wasn't over. What other tricks did he have up his ornate sleeves?

30

REINE

I followed Lawrence with my gaze as he walked through the crowd. It wasn't hard—he was at least a few inches taller than even the tallest of the Fae males in attendance. What must this realm have looked like when gargoyles could be here without suffering for it? And what had happened to change it?

Aoine cleared her throat, and I returned my attention to her. She smiled with her lips, but her eyes had returned to glittering with suppressed emotion. Should I apologize? No, Fae princesses didn't do that, and while it might be appropriate with Lawrence, I couldn't show weakness with my own kind.

"Well, he's a handsome brute." She inclined her head in the direction he'd gone. "Are you trying to reinstate the old tradition?"

"No, not at all. He came along to protect the humans."

"Yet he's not with them. That's why I didn't invite him, although I would have been willing to if you'd asked."

"Ah, so he crashed." I suppressed a laugh. Cheeky gargoyle! And here I was thinking he'd been weakening, but he still managed to be clever. Although... "How did he crash? The doors to the room allowed him in."

"That's what I'm wondering." She tapped her pink lips with an index finger. "There have been rumors of a previous Lady of the Forest having emerged from her chrysalis, but I've not seen any evidence of it so far."

"It's time for the Old Ones to come back?"

She sighed. "They always say it's time for them to return, don't they? But it hasn't been ten millennia since they went to sleep. Plus, no one has been able to find where they are to watch, and we have problems in our current time."

Her frustration simmered below her polite veneer.

"I sense you're not happy with Ellerin or with Lawrence. What were you planning for this evening, Aoine?"

"Oh, I can't say too much. Treason, you know. But there's a handsome Fae prince here who was hoping for a dance, and now that gargoyle has ruined it for him."

"I can still dance another waltz with Troubadour, if that's what you mean."

"Can you?" She looked at my feet, upon which my sneakers had reappeared, but at least they matched the dress in color now. "Your feet seem to be saying they're done and would like to run away."

I couldn't complain about the sparkly blue sneakers. "If they are, it's because I've been traveling for two days without the help of the usual conveyances I use in the Earth realm."

She didn't seem to buy my explanation. In truth, if Troubadour's kiss earlier hadn't been so, well, boring, I could have been convinced to try another dance with him. But how could I explain that without him losing face, especially since he and Aoine seemed to be in league?

"I am eager to hear all about these vehicles, but we do have a problem." She folded her arms and tilted her head, a familiar gesture from our schooldays. Typically, that happened when I'd gotten us into some sort of trouble and it was my responsibility to get us out of it. But this time I'd done nothing wrong, and I wouldn't take her Fae-tude anymore. I was a fucking princess, dammit. With an Earth language mind, apparently.

"And what would that problem be, Aoine?" I pulled upon one of my tricks from our previous acquaintance—the sweeter I sounded, the more trouble she knew she was in. It worked, too. She unfolded her arms and allowed her hands to rest by her side, a posture of openness but also readiness to sling spells.

Or words. "You are a princess newly returned to your realm. Your mother, if she knows, is biding her time and drawing you into her web. I am trying to help you, give you allies, and yet you snub the Fae prince who could be your key to a history-altering alliance for a gargoyle, a creature who cannot even survive here, much less serve any useful function."

I winced. "I get it. And I trust Ellerin. I can't play for all sides, Aoine, so I play for one—my own. And my friends'."

"Your friends?" She put a hand to her heart. "And what does that make me? Chopped pixie wings?"

"If you want to see it that way. By the way, I'm horrified that Fae still mutilate their servants."

"I inherited them. *I'm* horrified you'd think such a thing."

Although I'd thought we spoke quietly, it wasn't subdued enough. We had a ring of curious onlookers and overhearers around us. Aoine plastered her polite smile on her face again and turned in a circle. "Perhaps it is time for dinner. Please, everyone, go to the dining room, and we'll feast in honor of our princess returning!"

The promise of free food had the same effect in Faerie as it did in the Earth realm—the room emptied, leaving me, Troubadour, Lawrence, and Aoine. Even the musicians fled.

I gestured between Troubadour and Aoine. "How do you

two know each other? And don't say you only met today. I can sense my way around Fae partial truths."

Troubadour spoke, reluctantly. "This plan has been in place for a couple of centuries. We thought you'd come back sooner. What Fae princess accepts an exile?"

Aoine added, "You betrayed your house and your people by staying away for so long."

"I..." Their challenging gazes held enough righteousness it made me question my own perceptions. "I had no choice. My mother held the key to my return, and I had to wait for another way in, which was the Wanderer guiding me along the Shadowed Path." I didn't add that my powers had been greatly attenuated in the Earth realm. I wouldn't admit to weakness unless I had to.

"Your mother." Aoine lifted her chin in Troubadour's direction. "Told you." She turned back to me. "Maeve's been clearing out her rivals for years. It makes sense you'd be one of them."

"Why? She's ahead in line for the throne."

"Because your grandmother always liked you better." Troubadour grinned as he looked me up and down. "I can see why."

A laugh escaped me. "I doubt you and she share the same perspective"

Lawrence rumbled, but he caught himself before it turned into a full-out growl.

I continued to argue, "But it doesn't make sense. She's next in line. That's that, no matter what my grandmother thinks."

"But if she had evidence that your mother had something in her past that made her unworthy..." Aoine raised an eyebrow. "Even if there was a whisper of something."

"What are you saying? My mother is untouchable. Or has something come to light since we left?" Again, those four-hundred or so years of Fae history, which could be plus or minus another hundred depending on how the time stream flowed here versus in the Earth realm, evaded me with maddening mystery. Perhaps I should find Duke Aster-hole or whatever his name was and get him to give me a crash course on what I'd missed.

Troubadour chuckled. "No one is untouchable, Princess Reine. Not Maeve. Not you. And besides, the real test of a leader, or potential leader, comes down to how they handled their past mistakes."

I shot Lawrence a guilty look. "Indeed."

Aoine clapped her hands. "That's enough talk. Let's go on to dinner, and we can continue this discussion later."

"I agree." Another look at Lawrence, who seemed to be as eager to face a room full of curious Fae as I did. I asked as gently as I could, "Aoine, would you mind making sure the humans and grimalkin are fed?"

"Of course." Was that another cunning gleam in Aoine's eyes? "They're important to you, aren't they?"

Again, admit to nothing... "They're on the Shadowed Path with me. Therefore, they're my responsibility."

"There is something about the girl..." Troubadour's perfect eyebrows drew together in a way that was likely supposed to make him look erudite and charming, and perversely, I wished wrinkles to appear sooner on his symmetrical face.

"How so?" I asked, maybe too brightly.

"Something I can't quite tease out." He rubbed his index and thumb fingertips together. "But definitely intriguing. Ah, well. Shall we, Princess?" He crooked an elbow, and I took his arm since it would be overly rude to refuse.

"Lead the way, Prince...?"

"Nope, sorry Princess. I'll tell you my name when it's appropriate." And the look he gave me told me that "appropriate" may involve a situation where either clothing was off or a marriage contract had been signed. I dared not look to Lawrence to see his reaction, but another low grumble reached my ears before he caught himself. Or had I imagined the sound?

It didn't matter. I played a larger game. As we walked to dinner, I couldn't help but wonder... Had Ellerin been right? Was this all an elaborate trap?

I MANAGED to make it through dinner, which was a multi-course meal of Fae delicacies that I had missed, but which didn't agree with me anymore. I begged off due to exhaustion before dessert, which I hated to miss, but I—and my stomach—couldn't take it anymore. Troubadour acted like we'd already made some sort of agreement, and Lawrence glowered through the whole affair even though he'd ended up seated between two Fae maids who cooed over his physique and strong appearance. I won't lie—I might have had to suppress a couple of growls myself.

I changed into my nightgown, which had transformed itself from a T-shirt and sleep shorts to a sheer, white lace, knee-length nightie and satin robe.

"What in Hades is this?" I asked the older female servant and held up my clothing.

She cackled, showing a fair number of missing teeth and her ancient age, perhaps old enough to have escaped whatever change had meant servants had their wings clipped, and eventually, mostly removed. "It looks like the castle has picked up on you expecting a romantic rendezvous. You'll be lovely in that, Princess. And here's a crown for you." She opened a drawer and pulled out a tiara even more ornate than the one I'd worn to the party. Platinum in a snowflake pattern held a sparkling array of diamonds and light blue sapphires.

I snorted. "No thanks. I'm not feeling very Elsa-ish today."

She nodded, seemingly understanding the reference even though she shouldn't have access to Earth realm media. She cupped the tiara in her hands, blew on it, and the pattern changed to one of flames, although with the same stones. "How's this?"

Oooookay.... This was a powerful Fae, then. How in the world did Aoine keep her as a servant? Or was she? Whatever the truth, I needed to get rid of her before any mischief came to me. I knew how stories about ungrateful women went.

"Lovely, thank you."

I allowed her to place the tiara on me, and she turned me to the mirror. I looked like a freaking Fae bride, but I wasn't going to object.

"There, now you're ready for your prince." She grinned again and patted my arm. "Don't be nervous, duckie. You've had enough experience you should be able to handle whatever's coming for you."

Her words sounded ominous enough I didn't take offense. Besides, I hadn't had that much experience, just the occasional lover when things got boring or a certain Earth male caught my eye. I always left them before they could get overly attached to me, although a few probably had pined away for me. Such was the price of falling for a Fae princess. I had warned them, but Earth realm men always thought they were stronger than their feelings, and I'd never trapped them with any sort of commit-ment. Thank Fae we could only conceive with intention.

"What about gargoyles?" she asked like she could read my thoughts.

"What about them?" I blinked, seemingly confused.

"Your and his fates are twined together, Princess. Be careful —destroying him will only come back on you in the end. But if you were to have a little fun..." She shrugged.

"Thanks for the advice. What about the Fae prince Troubadour?"

"Ah, Prince Basil." She pronounced it like a name, not an herb. "He's a tricky one, definitely dark Fae. Be careful with him. You know what they say about friends and enemies."

I made a mental note of that...and that he'd likely not want to be compared to the herb, which would help me remember. "But what if I don't want to keep him closer than my friends?"

"You'd be a smart girl." She patted me on the shoulder in a more maternal gesture than my mother had ever shown. "His part is not over yet, either."

I turned to her, and she grinned again, but I saw past her "clueless old lady" glamour to a hint of smooth skin and forest green eyes. "Who are you, really?"

"Someone who is concerned for our realm, nothing more. Now go out on to your balcony and look at the moon and stars. You haven't really done that since you've returned, have you?"

She had a point. "Thank you. For the tiara, warnings, and everything. I know you're more than you're showing me, and I am honored you desire to protect me."

"I want what's best for the realm, as do others of my ilk. Remember that, do that, and all will be well." Then she disappeared in a puff of dark green smoke with the smell of fresh pine.

"Huh, that was interesting." I wished Sir Raleigh had been there, but he was still upstairs guarding the humans. Hopefully Aoine had sent something to eat for them. I suspected she would—Fae followed the rules of hospitality because we had written them, and we dared not violate them because then the consequences would come back on us. We'd invented that, too —punishing humans who acted selfishly or unkindly to us, like the prince in the *Beauty and the Beast* tale. Now that had been some good Fae-work.

I walked out to the balcony and leaned on the waist-height wall that surrounded it. The robe was thin enough I could feel the roughness of the stone beneath my elbows, and I sighed into the night. The Faerie moon, goddess and guardian of the land, hung full and heavy above me, both delicate like a pearl and solid-feeling like a sphere of marble.

I could imagine holding her in my hand, although I wouldn't dare.

A low voice came from below me. "Legend in my land has it that she looks down upon us all but is sad that she's so far away she cannot help us, only illuminate when we need to see beyond what's in front of us and hide when we need to conceal our own secrets."

I leaned over farther to see Lawrence, who held a bowl with a plate over it with both hands.

"Well, hi there, stranger. What are you doing?"

"Trying to bring you dessert, but for some reason, I can't find your chamber from the inside, and I didn't want to knock on the wrong Fae's door." He'd unknotted his cravat, and the edges hung like a scarf around his neck and down over his chest and dark jacket. With his face tilted up to me, I could admire the strong lines of his jaw and the muscle in his neck. Yes, he was a magnificent beast, and he'd brought me...

"Dessert?" he asked and held the dishes up in front of him. "I'm aware of how much you like your sweets."

"Come on up." Then I remembered his attempts to fly earlier, and I was a good twenty feet above the ground. "Can you?"

"I can do anything for you, Princess."

He leaped and flapped his wings, and if I sent a little extra puff of air to propel him to the balcony and safely land, well, I was only making sure he didn't waste all his energy on flying. When he landed, he did so on one knee with the covered bowl held in front of him, an offering. I was pretty sure I wasn't the only one who saw the resemblance to a proposal, and his eyes widened when he lifted his head and saw me fully.

"I, ah, didn't realize you were already dressed for bed." His cheeks darkened.

"Gargoyles can blush?" I took the cool dish from him, the stoneware heavy in my hands. "What is it?"

"Something called Dirty Fae Secrets. It's chocolate."

I gasped and lifted the lid. The chocolate and vanilla cake, three kinds of mousse, and pretty much every shiny red fruit made me salivate. "Oooh, thank you!"

"You're welcome. Um, I guess I'll be going now." He hadn't stopped looking at me. He rose to his feet.

"Did you have any?"

"No, I saved mine for you."

"Then we should share it."

When we entered the room, I found a small table set up by the bed with two napkins and two spoons on it. If it was going to be a magic castle, at least it would enable my sweet tooth.

"Thank you," I whispered. We sat on the bed, and I set the bowl on the table with the plate beneath it. Then I turned toward Lawrence, which made my robe loosen and fall slightly open across my cleavage.

"Custom dictates that I should feed the Dirty Fae Secrets to you."

"Uh, okay." Apparently, the sight of the tops of my breasts distracted him more than it had previously. It wasn't like he hadn't seen them before. The memories of our previous times together, which had been highlighted with annoyance and frustration at the ends when we'd had to stop, came to mind. But maybe this time...

No, I couldn't take advantage of him, no matter what an elderly Fae—a resurrected?—had told me.

I took a spoonful of the dessert and held it up to his mouth. His eyes followed it, then focused on mine. He turned the spoon toward me and fed it to me. The flavors exploded like an orgasm, which echoed through my body in shivers of almost-pleasure. I closed my eyes in bliss...and frustration.

We sat so close together that his chuckle vibrated through me. "Well, that explains what was happening downstairs."

I opened my eyes to find his face inches from mine. "What was that?"

"Things were getting...romantic. I think your friend Aoine and Troubadour may be having a moment."

I put my hand to my mouth and laughed, but my stomach twisted at the same time. Had I stayed for dessert, would I have ended up tumbling into bed with Troubadour? And what would have happened to Lawrence?

He would have had to watch the whole thing, likely only slightly buzzed from the magic in the dessert. But could it have enough of an effect on him to...

I scooped up another spoonful. "Here, have some. It may not affect you as much, but you'll see what happens."

He pushed my hand down. "I would rather not. Things are too complicated between the two of us, and I don't want to do something I'd regret."

"Oh, I'd make sure you wouldn't regret it." The words escaped from me before I could catch them, and I took a deep breath to rein myself in. "No, you're right. We shouldn't do anything hasty. Besides, tomorrow, I'll be in Lorien, and you'll be heading back to the Earth realm, and I don't know if we'll see each other again."

His dark gaze met mine, and I could almost feel the thought hitting our brains at the same time—if not now, then would we ever? Should we take this opportunity?

He picked up the other spoon. "Well, when you put it like that..." He took a bite and nodded. "This is pretty good. And it may be the last taste of Faerie I really get."

I could tell it didn't affect him like it did me, but I didn't mind. "It would suck for us to go our separate ways, wondering..."

He fed me another bite, and it hit me with even more rich-ness—and desire—than before. "Yes," I almost gasped. "Wondering what it would have been like. I could never be with anyone else because I'd always be comparing them to the hypo-thetical you, what sex with you could have been."

His pupils enlarged to take over his irises, and when he spoke, it was with a resonance that I'd only heard from him a few times before. "Is that a challenge, Princess?"

I fed him the last bite, and he took the spoon with fierce-ness. His throat muscles moved as he swallowed, and then when he took my mouth, he tasted of chocolate and lust. "Is this what you had in mind?"

I sensed that the creature who held me and devoured me with licks and nips and touches encompassed both Lawrence and not-Lawrence, his rational self and his inner beast. The contrast between the rules, control, and hidden motives of Faerie with his directness and the unambiguity of his desire made me recognize something I hadn't wanted to acknowledge —when all was said and done, would Faerie be enough for me?

He pulled back, almost panting, and my breath came quickly to match. His gaze dropped to my breasts, from which the robe had fallen, showing the pink aureoles and nipples through the sheer, white lace. He cupped one with one large hand—larger than previously, when he'd been human—and thumbed my nipple, and my back arched as need shot through me.

I ripped his shirt open, buttons flying everywhere, and straddled him.

31

GARGOYLE LAWRENCE

The princess ripped my shirt off and ran her hands up my chest. Her skin slid so softly against my rough hide. Her mouth, wet and pink, tasted of sweetness and light, and yet I could sense the need to do things good princesses didn't do beneath. I pushed her robe off her shoulders. Yes, I could have ripped it to shreds with my claws, that and the silly thing she wore underneath, both clothing and not-clothing—what was the point?

Obviously, its purpose was to drive me wild, giving me glimpses of her pale, peaches and cream skin between threads, which taunted me with what they hid. When she straddled me, the gown rode up, and I ran my hand up her leg to her bottom. Having her so near engorged my cock, which stood harder and more ready than ever before. I'd never had sex in gargoyle form before—would I hurt her? She didn't seem to care. She scooted back and stood, motioning for me to as well. Words had fled. Now there were only feelings and hand motions and undulating hips when I touched her.

She snapped her fingers, and my pants fell to my ankles. Her mouth went into an—I hoped—impressed O. I wore nothing underneath, and I kicked aside the trousers. I snapped my fingers, but nothing happened to her nightie. She laughed, and the sound taunted and tempted me. I ran one claw down the front of the infuriating lace thing, leaving a neat tear, and it snapped back as her breasts fell out of it, warm and heavy. She shrugged out of the ruined garment, and I knelt, taking one of her nipples in my mouth. She arched against me, and I captured her and brought her to the bed, where the feeling of skin on skin made me want to claim her right then. But I had learned, being one with my rational side, that we needed to wait. She had to make the decision to be claimed, which would give us a relationship as equals.

"I'm the princess," she gasped. At least one of us had words.

"So?" I growled against her nipple, and she trembled beneath me, but she didn't sound afraid when she spoke again.

A rap on the top of my head made me look up at her, and her green eyes glowed with desire and glittered imperiously, which turned me on even more, if that was possible.

"I get to be on top." Then she whispered, "It'll be less likely to hurt that way."

"As you wish." I rolled onto my back, and for an eternal moment, she looked at me, and doubt crept in under my desire. Was I too big? Should I have waited until I was in my other form?

Then she nodded. "I can handle it."

And she did. She slid onto me, achingly slowly. I held myself still, but barely. Then I moved when she told me, stopped when she commanded. I had more physical power, but she had complete control. When we both came, her with a full body shudder and me with a release like nothing I'd ever known, the air around us glowed gold, and a sound like the click of a seatbelt echoed through the room. I had no time to question what it was before she collapsed on top of me, and I was distracted again by the feel of her warmth against my cold, her soft against my hard...the perfect complement.

The glow faded, and I extracted myself from her and held her to me. She nestled her head on my shoulder, and I caressed her hair.

"Are you all right?" I asked.

"Mmm hmm."

"I didn't hurt you, did I?" My voice had lightened. Non-gargoyle Lawrence reasserted himself.

"Nope. That was great."

"Um, we didn't use any protection," I pointed out. "Can Fae and gargoyles mate?"

"Yes, but we don't get pregnant unless we want to, and there are no STDs here."

I'd have to make a note of that, although I doubted I'd forget. A knock on the door prevented us from making any more conversation.

Reine spoke with a fierceness I'd yet to hear from her. "I don't care who that is, I'll fucking kill them."

I laughed. "Probably a servant. Just ignore them."

"Reine?" Rhys' voice came through the door. "It's me! It's important."

She lifted her head and scowled toward her brother's voice. "I don't care. Go away, Rhys!"

As if that wasn't bad enough, Sir Raleigh appeared in a blast of cold air in the middle of the bed in his cat form, yowling at us to get up.

32

***

REINE

"Rhys, by all the gods—" I bolted upright and away from the sex-sated gargoyle and the promise of the first good night's sleep I'd had since coming to Faerie. Before I could come up with something suitable to threaten my brother with, a yowling, spitting ball of fur materialized in the middle of the bed, prompting both me and Lawrence to tuck our legs up at the same time Rhys burst through the door.

I can only imagine the tableau if someone had come in and snapped a picture—a shocked Fae with a scarred cheek, his mouth open in shock and already melting into a delighted grin as his face reddened, one hand on the door. Two lovers squished against the headboard, his wings at awkward angles (mine were furled) with the end of one spoke tangled in my hair. A very distressed gray cat with one white paw.

Considering he'd been guarding the humans, he got the priority of my attention. I pulled the sheet up to cover as much as I could and reached a hand to him, grabbing him by the scruff and forcing him to look at me.

"What is it, Sir Raleigh?"

I let go when his words came through. He'd never talked to me before. "*Humans. Trouble. Guards. Noise.*"

In a blink, I had my clothes on. Should've probably done that when Rhys busted in, but I hadn't been thinking clearly. I rushed past him, Lawrence behind me, using his wings for balance as he hopped into his pants. Rhys stepped back to allow us to pass, then fell into step behind us.

"What about you?" I shot over my shoulder at him. "Why were you so rudely interrupting us?"

"Ellerin's gone again."

Shit. "You mean he left without saying goodbye?"

"His staff glowed red—haven't seen it do that before—and he mumbled something about urgent business. Then he grabbed his bag and popped out."

Crap, crap, crap... This was the worst time to lose our guide, now when we were so close.

"And that was all he said?"

"The only other thing was to get your arse moving and get us out of here. Aoine has something up her dangly sleeves."

"You could've led with that."

Although my wings were furled, I practically flew up the flight upstairs to the non-VIP wing and down the hall to John and Kestrel's room, which I had made sure to know the location of. Two of Aoine's guards, whom I recognized from earlier when they'd "invited" us to the castle, lay in a heap in front of the door. Lawrence picked them up and tossed them aside gently. Well, as gently as a gargoyle could toss anything. It relieved me to see that they still breathed. So not dead then. I should've probably checked that before Lawrence moved them.

I knocked on the door. Something inside buzzed, a repellent sound that made me want to back away. Had that knocked the guards out? What effect was it having on the humans?

"Kestrel, John, it's me, Reine!"

"And me," Lawrence added. Good. If they were panicked, hearing his familiar voice might calm them.

"Reine? Uncle Lawrence?" Thank goodness, Kestrel was alive.

"Is John in there?" Lawrence asked.

"Yes, but something's wrong with him."

"Can we come in?" I pushed against the buzzing force, and it receded enough for me to open the door. Then I saw what it was—a clear glowing green dome over Kestrel and John, who both sat cross-legged on the bed. Kestrel held out her hands, which fed energy into the sphere. John stared straight ahead with mouth open in shock.

Four more guards lay slumped on the floor, thankfully breathing. Kestrel might kill with her powers someday, but at least she hadn't yet.

Lawrence moved to approach the bed, but I held him back. He immediately snapped into scientist mode. "What is it? Can you get past it? How is she doing that?"

Rhys pushed into the room with us, and Sir Raleigh twined around my legs.

Rhys shook his head in wonder. "Nicely done, girl. Very nicely done. That's some advanced magic."

I took a deep breath to clear my head and mentally nudged the dome. It didn't repel my energetic push. Instead, my psychic touch slipped off, like water on a nonstick pan.

"Ohhhh." Rhys and I grinned at each other.

"Well?" Lawrence tapped his large bare gargoyle foot.

I tried my best to translate Fae knowledge to Earth-speak. "To answer your questions, it's a temporal sphere. She's basically frozen time in and around it, which makes Fae pass out and would kill any other creature. It doesn't affect her because she made it, but poor John there is stuck in a moment of shock. I can't get past it. She'll have to figure out how she's doing it if she's going to undo it."

Kestrel spoke through tears. "The guards came in, and I grabbed at the nearest eel, Reine. And this happened."

"Now the fishy has bitten you. You need to shake it off and let it go."

"Fish?" Lawrence arched an eyebrow.

"A way to explain multiple potential powers, as fish in a stream, but slippery like eels. And metaphors."

Rhys' eyes went round. "So that means she's—"

I cut him off with a chopping motion. "This is not the time for that conversation, and I have more testing to do."

"You would." He crossed his arms and leaned back against the wall, his typical arrogant posture. "Whatever you need to do, make it quick. If Aoine's expecting this bunch to bring them to her, she's going to either send more, which means we'll be outnumbered, or come herself with Troubadour, in which case we may be outgunned."

I shuddered at him comparing our powers to weapons. I still preferred to think of myself as a Fae who created, not destroyed, although I now had ample evidence to the contrary.

"Kestrel, look at your hand that's producing the power stream. Do you see anything?"

She did as I suggested and squinted into the light. "Yes, something is wriggling."

"Open your fingers and shake your hand, focus on the desire of letting go."

She uncurled her fingers, and the stream widened, then vanished as she shook both hands. Clumsy, but effective because the dome disappeared.

John blinked and closed his mouth. Kestrel handed him the glass of water from the bedside table, and he took a long gulp.

Sir Raleigh jumped on the bed and pushed under her other hand, demanding reassurance, or maybe forgiveness for not defending her better. Why hadn't he gone full grimalkin?

He turned and blinked at me. "*The castle wouldn't let me. Not my place here.*"

If the castle was turning against us, it was definitely time to go.

"Can you guys move, preferably quickly? We need to go."

"But it's nighttime." Apparently, John hadn't been too shocked to keep him from arguing.

"It's more dangerous here."

Thankfully, they were already dressed and only had to put shoes on. Rhys already had his pack, and I summoned Lawrence's and mine. We had just walked into the hallway when the clomp of boots, about twelve pair, echoed from one end. We ran the other way, and I felt the signature of Aoine's energy coming from the other side. They'd intended to trap us.

I looked backward—no place to hide. Lawrence frowned at something only he could see, then motioned toward a door to my right.

"That's a stairwell."

"How do you know?" Rhys asked.

"I just do."

I opened the door and found it as he said. It looked to be a servants' stair, which would make it less likely for us to find or use it. Perfect.

We descended as quickly and quietly as we could and emerged in the basement of the palace.

I looked at Lawrence. "Now which way?"

He closed his eyes and took a deep breath, allowing the naked stone to speak to him. He did well with naked...

Stop that, I warned myself. I could process what had happened later, when we were out of danger.

Aoine's secret conversation voice came to me. "*Reine... Reine... Where did you go? You shouldn't run. You need to understand we are your friends, not your mother, grandmother, or anyone at the capital. Do you really think they'll let you just waltz in and claim your place?"*

They might not, but what I'd learned from Aoine's little gathering was that plenty of other Fae wanted me to do just that and basically stage a coup. I didn't answer her directly, though. That would give away our location.

"Follow me." Lawrence took off toward the left, and we fell into step behind him. Whereas the hallways above stretched at least ten feet wide, more than enough for a full adult Fae wingspan, down here, they had a width of five feet, max. Was that why high Fae clipped their servants' wings? Because old castles had narrow corridors, and high Fae had grown from the olden days when we'd been more pixie-sized?

We went down for quite a while, and I almost questioned Lawrence, but then the floor sloped upward again. We hadn't seen any doors or storage alcoves in a while, so I surmised we'd found some sort of old escape passage. Indeed, we came to a large, pitted, wooden door, and Lawrence cracked it open. A whiff of fresh leaf-scented air told us we'd found an exit that stretched beyond the castle and into the woods.

I reached for Lawrence's hand and squeezed it. "Nice work."

"Thanks. But what is that shining over there? Is it a body of water?"

"No." My heart dropped as I recognized where Troubadour had had our supposed secret tryst and discussed what could amount to treason. Could someone have heard us? "It's a pond."

Rhys came to join us. "Whatever it is, we need to get off Aoine's land and find the path. And I have something to tell you, Reine. Something important."

"Okay, give me a second. Let me see if I can sense the path." I closed my eyes, and the only way I can describe what I did is that I reached out from a place at the base of my skull, outward, seeking the threads of the web that led us back to our path. That's how I saw our journey now—as traversing toward the center of a web, sometimes hopping from one spoke to the next, but always moving toward the center. I sought that center now, the thing that drew me, the end of my path—the capital city of Lorien and my fate, for good or for ill.

The sensation of a guitar string vibrating in my gut told me I'd found it, and I followed that thread, walking forward with my eyes closed. Although I heard the others behind me, I gave my full attention to the goal at hand. Unfortunately, they continued to distract me.

First John's voice. "Should we be running? Isn't it dangerous to be out here at night?"

Then Kestrel. "Dad, hush! She knows what she's doing. Don't forget who she is."

"Who is she, Kestrel? Do we really know? And what happened to Ellerin? I knew he wasn't to be trusted."

I wasn't worried about Ellerin. He would be able to find the Shadowed Path without nearly as much effort. It was as much a part of him as my desire to heal others was of me. He'd chosen his path, and I had mine, which intersected his for this short while. The question nudged itself into consciousness from the back of my mind, where it had been shoved—*We have the same green eyes. We must be related. But how? Gray and light Fae don't mix.*

Or did they? My rainbow wings hinted at something, or they could have been showing my joy in returning to Faerie.

When I stepped on the Path, the ground shifted to meet my feet, and I would have fallen if Lawrence hadn't caught me and held me steady. I opened my eyes to meet his concerned dark ones.

"Are you all right?"

"Yes, I found it. It's like stepping onto one of those moving sidewalk things at the airport—it'll get you if you're not prepared."

"Right." He let go, slowly, and I moved away as reluctantly. One encounter to get it out of our systems, right? The Fae dessert hadn't hurt. And now I saw Aoine's plan—distract me and Lawrence with each other while she nabbed the humans, or at least Kestrel. Thankfully Sir Raleigh had been on guard.

The cat joined me, now in his grimalkin form, and looked up at me with his glowing green eyes. I scratched him behind one ear—big cats were still big cats, after all—and he purred. The sound calmed some of the anxiety that quivered in my chest at the task of stepping into Ellerin's larger shoes and leading our crew along the path. Hopefully we wouldn't be captured, or *invited*, by any creatures of questionable motivation.

I turned and held up a hand. The murmuring quieted.

"John, to answer your question, yes, it is dangerous out here at night. Although we are in the lands of the light Fae, there are still threats and traps between here and Lorien. We have the advantage of being on a sacred path, but that doesn't mean there won't be surprises. So, everyone, stay alert, stay quiet, and for Fae's sake, don't lose sight of each other. Rhys, you're in rear. Kestrel, behind me, then John. Lawrence, you watch the humans. Sir Raleigh will move among us and use his grimalkin senses. If he indicates danger, cluster up. Is that clear?"

Everyone nodded, including Rhys, who gave me the same look he had after I'd uttered the Queen Spell—surprise, grudging respect, and a little bit of... I didn't know what. What did he have to tell me? I suspected I wouldn't enjoy the conversation.

We moved through the woods, blessedly free from the mist that had obscured the surroundings in the lands of the dark Fae and in the Gray Zone. Now lush foliage and thick vines hanging from the trees collaborated with the dark to keep us from seeing more than five or so feet into the woods on either side of the path. However, they didn't keep us from hearing rustling, the hooting of the gwenhwyfvar owl, or other night sounds that would have been quite pleasant had I been listening to them from a secure castle, nestled in the arms of my lover.

Sir Raleigh trotted to catch up with me and nudged me with his head, which came level with my hip. I placed my hand atop it to reassure him and thank him for helping us, and his voice came through, startling me again.

"Princess fold path?"

"What do you mean?" I whispered.

"Ellerin folded path. Princess can?"

Ah, yes, the Wanderer had his ways of moving from one place to another more quickly than regular Fae. If Sir Raleigh had seen him folding the Path, or basically using a Fae application of quantum physics with its curved dimensions, that meant he'd traveled with Ellerin before.

"Sorry, but I don't think I can."

"Then tragedy ahead." He sounded so matter-of-fact about it, but then he was a Fae creature. *"The gwenhwyfvar hunts."*

I stopped and again motioned for everyone to pay attention to me. "Sir Raleigh has told me that the white phantoms hunt tonight. We need to find cover or..." I swallowed. "I need to try something that could be really risky."

33

REINE

John raised his hand. Of course.

"Yes?" I tried not to snap, but I'm pretty sure I did.

He flinched, but he went on, anyway. "What is a white phantom? Is there anything I, as an earth witch, can do to help?"

Well, that was an improvement. "To answer your second question, no. To answer the first... It's complicated and gets to the heart of Fae death and rebirth."

"How so?" Lawrence's curiosity about all things Fae had apparently been piqued again, but he, too, offered, "If we know, maybe we can assist."

Rhys and I sighed in tandem like we'd practiced the move.

"Top secret stuff there, mate. And I thought it was just a legend."

Sir Raleigh snorted, and I didn't need him to talk to me in secret conversation to get his meaning—*Dumbass.*

Rhys glared at the grimalkin, then pulled me aside. "I know it's not just a tale. I saw revenants, Reine."

A full-body shiver almost convulsed me. That was the

second time someone had mentioned the foul creatures in as many days. "What? Where?"

"In Cruaidh. Under it, rather."

My stomach twisted. "So, the rumors that things may be happening more quickly than the tales foretold are true. We need to give our crew the basics so they'll know what we're up against."

He nodded, but still sounded reluctant. "All right, but keep it vague."

"I'm a Fae, dear brother. That's what we do." I turned to the rest of our party. "All right, quickly—I can't tell you everything, but you know how matter can't be made or unmade, right?" They all nodded. "Well, the same goes for spirit and the connections it forges with flesh. There are parts of the Fae reincarnation process that can be dangerous for those around if they get too close, too early."

I've seen revenants, Reine. If that were the case, there would be a lot of spirits hungering for flesh, looking to steal it so they wouldn't have to grow their own. Or, if it was before their time, they could have grown flesh but hadn't fully redeveloped their intellect, which made them act like vampires. Some rose with reason intact and often elected to stay on as friendly ghosts until they could grow their bodies. I suspected the old woman at the castle was one such spirit-flesh hybrid being.

Kestrel swallowed, like she became nauseated at the thought of flesh-devouring spirits. "Is it like the actions of a soul-eater?"

"Worse. The revenants would consume the flesh and soul for its energy, and you'd become part of them, eternal passengers to horror."

We continued moving down the path, Fae, grimalkin, and gargoyle in a diamond shape around the humans, who remained most vulnerable. Too soon—and too far from any shelter—bright spots lit up the forest around us and disappeared before anyone could get a good look at them. White glowing owls—the gwenhwyfvar, or guides for those who had risen—swooped overhead. I, too, had once thought their role in Fae reincarnation to be just that—a story to explain their color and luminescence. But no, it wasn't, and more and more of them seemed to stalk us.

Sir Raleigh pushed his head under my hand again. *"You need to do it."*

"I can't." I didn't want to waste energy on secret conversation if I didn't have to, especially with what the cat was asking me to do.

"You must. They surround us."

I glanced over my shoulder at Kestrel and motioned for her to walk between me and Sir Raleigh. "Can you make another time bubble if I ask you? One big enough to hold all of us? That fish should be close to the surface and easy to catch."

"I think so." Her eyes had grown wide, and her gaze darted to and fro, following the flashes of white that got closer and faster. "Is it because of the phantoms?"

"Yes, I'm going to have to do something risky, and I'll need time and focus. Plus, your temporal holding space should keep them away from us for a little while. It wouldn't hold them permanently, but there's a chance..." A small one, but I didn't say that.

"What can I do?" John asked. I almost said nothing, but then it occurred to me that his earth witch abilities could be useful in augmenting what I needed to do—connect with the path, and quickly.

"Are you ready to bend some rules of physics?" I grinned at his startled look.

"How?"

"We're going to take advantage of the fact that the Shadowed Path has its own momentum, which keeps it from being entirely fixed in this dimension. Since it's mostly made of dirt, I need you to help me connect to it."

"And me?" Lawrence asked. "What do you need my help with?"

I succumbed to the impulse to place a hand flat against his chest. "Watch over us."

He covered my hand with one of his. "Always."

We all turned and looked at Rhys, who hadn't volunteered his help. He cleared his throat and said, "All right, then. I'll watch, make sure she's got it under control."

It didn't escape me that this was the second time in about a week that he'd stayed back and let me do something dangerous. I walked over to him and grabbed him by the throat, pinning him against a tree.

"I'm not fucking around this time, Rhys. Tell me what you have to say. You almost screwed me back in the Earth realm, and you're not going to get in my way here, *capisce*?" I'm not sure where the mobster threat came from, but I figured I'd own it. Kestrel took a few deep breaths in preparation for her spell and to connect with the power that allowed her to make it. If anything came from this journey, she'd at least found out how to have more control over her powers. Hopefully she'd make it back to the Earth realm to...what? I don't know that she would find it easier, especially if she was what I suspected, a label I couldn't allow myself to think.

Rhys and I stepped to the side, and, conscious of the white flashes around us, some of which had started to have faces and forms—hungry faces and grasping forms—I told him, "What do you have to say? Make it quick."

He ran a finger along his scar, an old gesture of distress, and I willed myself not to smack his hand away from his face with a, *"Stop it, you'll make it worse."*

Gads, my baby brother, always getting me into trouble. What was it this time?

He sighed and folded his arms. "I've messed up, Reine, in a big way. I—I tried to fix it, but I think I may have made things worse."

No matter how many times I'd heard such things from him, the words still had the same effect—my heart dropped into my abdomen, and fear wrapped icy claws around my throat. "What did you do?"

"You know how Mother sent me to help you with the soul-eater? That wasn't all."

"I suspected as much." Not that the confirmation helped me feel better. I'd rather be able to trust him than to be right.

"She told me to work against you, to slow you down, that it would be important to Faerie."

Again, vindicating but not helpful. "How would me not defeating the creature be important to what goes on here?"

"She didn't say." He and I both shook our heads in resignation. "Of course she didn't. But I think I know."

"And what did she offer you in exchange?"

"That I could come back and have a more powerful position at court, that the physician would heal me and make my face normal again." He covered his face with his hands. "I'm sorry. I was desperate. I knew that even if you got us back in, I may not be allowed to stay because I'm disfigured and hideous."

"The Earth girls didn't think so."

He peeked out over his hands. "And what's better about them?"

I shrugged. "If you wanted more than a relationship of consorts..."

"Do you?"

Almost involuntarily, my gaze flicked to Lawrence, who, with Sir Raleigh, prowled the edge of our little area around John and Kestrel. Seeing him so seriously at work being a gargoyle guardian, even if it wasn't of me at the moment, made me smile. "I may."

He dropped his hands and held them out, pleading. "But Reine, you have to listen. Our mother doesn't want you back here. I think she's the one who cooperated with Troubadour to send the soul-eater."

"That's treason, Rhys. No high Fae would act against a crown princess like that, even another one. There are rules!"

"Think about it, Reine."

The problem was that I had. I'd thought a lot about it, sometimes without being aware of it. The soul-eater had been targeting me. My mother had given me an impossible task. But it had to be more than a power grab—for her to act so desperately meant that she feared something, and I aimed to find out what, not just for myself.

My grandmother had warned me that some in her court conspired against her. I needed to figure out what was going on or else Faerie itself would be in big trouble, and none of us, from the lowest servant in the court of the Winter Gnome King to the queens themselves, would have a home.

"Thank you for telling me. How have you been helping?"

"She's been trying to get me to tell her where we are— where you are—but I've been giving her vague locations and half-truths so she wouldn't know. But she figured enough out."

"The water wolves. And Aoine." Although I still didn't know what to make of my former friend.

"Yes. If you go into Lorien, you'll be walking straight into Mother's trap."

I put a hand on his arm, and our eyes locked. "Thank you for telling me. And I know what it is to be desperate and do things you regret later, so I forgive you."

He nodded. "Thank you. I'll lend you whatever strength I can. What are you going to do?"

I shivered and rubbed my upper arms. "I'm going to try to fold the Path, get us inside the city gates. From there, I can find allies and hopefully get to our grandmother quickly."

"But the wards..."

"Shouldn't be a problem for the crown princess...hopefully."

ONCE KESTREL HAD MANAGED to make a time halt bubble big enough for all of us, we stepped inside, and none too late. The phantoms swirled and shrieked around it and knocked into it. With each blow, Kestrel gritted her teeth.

"Hurry," John said. "We're not that strong."

"You're strong enough," I told him with a smile that hopefully showed more reassurance than I felt. I knelt on the path and put my hands flat against the dirt, seeking the flow of energy directing us to the Fae capital. I knew my path ended at the palace, and I suspected the others' did as well. Otherwise, we would have kept Ellerin and Troubadour with us. It troubled me that Ellerin had bailed on us, but I couldn't worry about that now.

I closed my eyes, and my palms tingled against the cool dirt. Or maybe the dirt was charged with electric magic. The sensation of being tugged forward made me lean back against it, but I couldn't open my eyes to make sure I hadn't moved, or that if I had, I'd brought the others with me. I had to trust my Fae senses. Or... I recalled something I hadn't yet tried in Faerie because it had its own risks, so I'd only done it a couple of times before. But this seemed an appropriate situation.

Spirit separated from body, allowing me some perception with my Fae eyes. I looked down to see myself kneeling, the others clustered in a circle around me, holding hands and lending me strength. Lawrence and Kestrel each held one of Sir Raleigh's wing tips, and he gazed up at my astral self with his big green eyes, which shone with adoration. *Find someone who looks at you like my cat looks at me.* Warmth spread through my chest—when had anyone ever done something like that for me? Or when had I allowed them to? Fae didn't do cooperation, at least not willingly at first, and we definitely didn't ask for help.

Beyond our circle and Kestrel's time warp bubble, the white phantoms circled around us, watching. I didn't want to talk to them, but one of them reached out to me.

"We mean you no harm, Princess."

"Bullshit."

A chuckle met my inner ears like icy pellets. *"Why would we take you now when you can set things up for us to take over later?"*

"I am doing no such thing."

Another laugh, and the familiar frustration that I didn't have the whole picture made me grit my literal and spirit teeth. They could be lying—the few hours after rising was the one time Fae could—and if I gave us up now, it would make an easy meal for them. But I felt with my Fae-dar that they spoke truly.

All right, I'd figure it out later. I had a team now, after all, even though most of them wouldn't be staying once we reached the end of our paths...

Speaking of which, it was time to get going. I picked up the end of the remainder of the Path, which looked like a long, narrow, brown rug and focused on the end.

The phantoms howled, which startled me. I'd intended to fold the Path to bring us to just inside the city gates, but my jump sent a wave down it, making the end rear up and head toward us. I held out the part I'd grabbed so the Path's ending edge wouldn't smack me in the face, and when the two sides met, everything went dark for a second. Then the colors around me lengthened and swirled into a tunnel, and I fell forward, sucked through a giant time-space straw.

...And landed in a heap with my companions in the otherwise empty throne room of the Palace of Lorien.

34

LAWRENCE

I n spite of Kestrel's time shield, the chill breath of the phantoms came through, making my hairs stand up on my body—a strong effect to have on a gargoyle, even in my weakened state. Sir Raleigh shivered as well, and the wing tip in my right hand quivered. He looked up at something and gave a little "prrrowl," which sounded like encouragement. What was Reine doing? She'd been kneeling there for what felt like hours, but which had only been minutes. Time passed differently in Faerie, I'd heard, and I suspected the space Kestrel had made for us augmented that effect.

Something knocked me over, and I lost hold of John and Sir Raleigh. The golden bubble around us, which had looked fragile but had held, popped, and the phantoms pounced. A claw passed by my ear, leaving a trail of chill bumps—again, weird for me in gargoyle form—but I fell through the earth away from it into a bottomless pit.

No, the bottom met me with a gentler bump than I'd braced for. I closed my eyes, relishing the sense of stone beneath and around me. Not just any stone—the ancestral part of my memory told me it was Fae-stone, and gargoyle masons had shaped it into its current form in...

"Oh, fuck." I opened my eyes to see we were in a throne room.

"Did you just curse?" Reine's eyes sparkled with amusement. "You never curse. Well, hardly ever."

"I know where we are."

Rhys rolled over to his back and blinked his eyes open. "Ah, home sweet home. After closing time, though. I always thought this place was creepy after dark."

"Is that why you always sneaked out?" Reine teased. In spite of us being in an objectively dangerous situation, she appeared happier than I'd ever seen her. While I felt her joy at finally being home, truly home, a sliver of sadness at the reminder that we'd soon be separated kept me from joining her in it as a lover should. But we weren't going to continue as lovers, were we?

And a deeper sadness throbbed at the bottom of my heart —had I ever known a true sense of home since my father had been murdered, and my mother and I fled?

I forced a smile at Reine, who grinned at me and said, "We did it!"

"You did it. Whatever that was."

"She folded the Shadowed Path." Rhys spoke with awe. "I'd heard some could do that, but I didn't know it could happen with multiple people."

"See?" a familiar voice said. "I told you she could do it."

Ellerin appeared beside the empty throne, and a beautiful woman materialized on it. The relation between her and Reine was apparent. Whereas Reine seemed to be in her twenties, this woman looked late thirties/early forties, and from how Fae aged, I guessed that made her Reine's mother. Plus, I had seen her grandmother, who'd looked a decade older than Maeve, in Reine's dream.

Whereas Ellerin seemed to be bursting with pride to the point that rainbow sparks chased each other through his crystal, Reine's mother appeared less than amused. She snapped her fingers—I'd made a note that Fae liked to do that to add drama to their spells—and the shadows around the edges of the room coalesced into guards wearing light leather and a metal that appeared golden, but which I guessed would be harder and magically charged. They each wore a sword in a scabbard at a belt at their waist and, in a movement that appeared choreographed, drew their weapons and advanced on our little group.

"Good to see you, too, Mum." Reine folded her arms and tilted her chin up, her favorite *are you kidding me?* posture. "Why the welcoming party? And Ellerin, where have you been?"

Ellerin shot a confused look at Maeve. "Why the hostility? Aren't you glad to see your children?"

Maeve shrugged, and her rueful expression only looked half-convincing. "You know the rules. They're exiled, and therefore their efforts to invade our land, even to the palace, constitute an act of hostility, if not treason."

"I demand to speak to the queen." Reine stepped forward and nudged a blade out of her way with a fingertip. Then she winked at the guard, who blushed. "Good to see you again, Darien."

"And you, Princess." He raised his sword so it pointed at the ceiling, not at her. "Lower your weapons, gentlemen."

"What? What are you doing?" Maeve stood. "I command you, as the crown princess, to arrest them."

"They're not under your authority, daughter." Now another presence misted into view in front of the throne. Ah, there was the queen.

Maeve scuttled off the throne with a sneer. "And you should be in bed."

"Where you would keep me away from my granddaughter and grandson I haven't seen in hundreds of years? Nonsense!"

Reine rushed into her grandmother's arms, and tears trickled down her cheeks. "I've missed you."

"And I, you. Rhys, come here."

Reine moved back, and Rhys approached his grandmother more cautiously. She put a hand to his scarred cheek. "Handsome as ever. And a troublemaker. What am I going to do with you?"

When she removed her hand, I half-expected to see unscarred skin left behind, but that didn't happen. Rhys winced, and I guessed he'd hoped the same.

"Let me and Reine back into Faerie," he said.

"Yes," Reine added. "I formally petition for my exile to be ended and to be admitted back to my home and place in the court."

Everyone seemed to hold their breath as Tatiana sat on the throne and considered. What was taking so long?

"Unfortunately, it's not that simple, Granddaughter. I can pardon you as queen, but it will require the convening of the council to remove the conditions of your exile and allow Rhys to remain here in his...state." She sounded doubtful, and she and Maeve exchanged glances. Reine's mouth tightened into a displeased line, but she nodded.

"Very well. I will await your decision. Until then, I ask for hospitality for myself, Rhys, and our friends. We'll leave after if that is your wish."

Maeve shot me a haughty glare. "Your pet gargoyle may need to go sooner."

Confirmed—she did not like me being there. Well, the feeling was mutual. Perhaps it was a good thing she'd never be my mother-in-law.

Tatiana ignored her. "Your desire for hospitality has been granted. You know where your rooms are? Your friends can share your suites, men and women each in their own. Well, maybe not the gargoyle..." She looked perplexed, like she couldn't believe I was standing there. Her expression changing into one of cunning warned me to brace myself.

She snapped her fingers, and the room spun around me. When the dizziness cleared, I found myself kneeling, holding the waist of my pants together. She'd changed me back to human. A yowl made me look over to Sir Raleigh, who had changed back into cat form.

"There, that's better." With a wave of her hand, she dismissed us. John and Rhys had to help me out of the throne room.

"What was that for?" John asked.

"It was symbolic," Rhys explained. "She took away the powers of Reine's guardians, signaling that she is on her own. You all right, mate?"

"I don't know." I hated those words, that answer, but I didn't. I'd never changed that fast, for one thing. My body didn't feel quite right, but was that because of the forced, rushed transformation or a different reason?

"Let's hope you find the end of your path here soon, then. Your gargoyle form may have kept the effects of Faerie from damaging you as quickly."

As much as I hated to leave, especially with Reine in a vulnerable position, he was likely right. But my path couldn't have ended, could it? I was still there.

Or was my destiny to die in Faerie?

35

—————

REINE

I wanted to go to Lawrence, but Rhys and John had him, and I couldn't let my mother and grandmother see how much he meant to me. If they had a sense of the physical connection we'd made, hopefully they'd think I'd been exploring my sexuality. That was one good thing about returning home as an adult—your elders likely expected you to be the same childish person you were when you left. I hadn't been as wild as Rhys, but I'd had my dalliances.

My grandmother's smile told me how pleased she was with herself, and the fact her eyes kept their cunning sparkle indicated she recognized the blow she'd just dealt me. "That's better. Sleep well, Granddaughter."

Kestrel and I bowed, and I led her out of the throne room. In spite of not having been in the castle in several centuries, my feet seemed to know the way to the East Tower and my suite of rooms there. Rhys stayed in the West Tower at the opposite side of the castle, and I felt the separation between myself and Lawrence more than I expected. What had happened?

Once we were out of earshot of the throne room, I murmured to Kestrel, who'd walked along in silence, leaving me to my thoughts, "So, what do you think about your first encounter with Fae royalty in their natural habitat?"

Her smile could be described as polite, at most, and it faded quickly. "Terrifying. Is Uncle Lawrence going to be okay?"

I looked away from the fear in her eyes that likely matched my own. "I don't know. It's not good for him to be here, and he's more vulnerable in his human form." Which was quite nice, and I had to keep myself from falling into an internal debate as to which was sexier—him as a gargoyle or as a very fit human male.

"When can we go home? I know we came here for a reason, but I don't care anymore. I think I have a better handle on my abilities, so what does it matter what I am?"

"We need to know so we can protect you if necessary." That gave me an idea. "Let's go unlock your journal and find Doctor Caduceus. As I recall, he's an early riser."

As my grandmother promised, my suite was just as I'd left it. The magic of the palace had kept it clean, and the windows in the large circular space stood open on the three sides that the tower protruded from the castle. The east-facing window showed a pinkish light tingeing the horizon.

"It's almost dawn," Kestrel said with a yawn. "We pulled an all-nighter."

Seeing her exhaustion activated my own. "You're right. We can find the Fae physician later. Go ahead and do your journaling for the day and night, and don't leave anything out about what you did and how."

"Are you sure? Can't I wait until after I sleep?"

"Nope. You may forget something important."

"Fine, then you have to journal, too."

"Fair enough." I pulled out my journal and recorded the events of the night, including my folding of the Path. Was that something all high Fae could do? It's not something that had ever been discussed, and the nature of magic in Faerie did evolve to meet the challenges of the new era. And then there were the phantoms and the gwynhwyfar owls... Could we be on the cusp of a Great Rising, as the rumors said? That would make things messy for whoever was on the throne.

And what if that person on the throne turned out to be my mother? Or myself? What would be best for Faerie? Neither scenario appealed, but for different reasons.

Suddenly I didn't feel sleepy anymore.

Kestrel closed her journal with a yawn. "There. Now can I sleep?"

"Yes, go ahead and take the bed. I'm going to read for a while."

I curled up on the couch in the corner of the room, remembering Olred's chamber in the asylum. No matter what I wanted to think of my grandmother, she had coordinated with the dark Fae to have a place to banish her enemies, which made her a ruthless leader. I turned back to my thoughts at the start of the journal and read through my impressions of our journey. The more I read, the more and more similarities I found between what I could do, my new abilities I'd discovered, and Ellerin. I'd asked if we were related, and I'd thought maybe he was a distant relative of the consort my mother had dallied with to conceive me. But strong talents didn't generally hide and then pop up by surprise in Fae families. Normally they were passed down from parent to child.

But Ellerin couldn't be my father. He was gray Fae, but what did that really mean? They weren't a different species, per se. They were the high Fae who refused to give allegiance to either dark or light Fae, which made them wild cards...and forbidden. What if they passed their rebellious streak on to their children? Yet Ellerin and my mother apparently had some understanding.

"I need to talk to him." I don't know why I said that out loud, except to hint to Sir Raleigh that he needed to lead me to

Ellerin, who had summoned him. A glance at the bed told me Kestrel slept hard. Good for her, she'd earned it. As for me...

"Come on, Sir Raleigh. Let's go find your summoner."

The grimalkin stretched and showed me the pink inside of his mouth with a yawn, then jumped down from the table in front of the window and blinked with annoyance.

"I'm sorry to disturb you from your sunny spot, but this is important."

He walked to the door and waited for me to open it before slipping through. I followed and closed it behind me, whispering a security spell so no one would disturb Kestrel. Thankfully, my mother and grandmother had essentially ignored her. Hopefully, that would continue to be the case.

Sir Raleigh led me down to the terrace that overlooked the gardens, but we didn't head out into the lush greenery, which dawn had painted with dew. No, we turned and headed toward a large obelisk. Sir Raleigh looked down at the slab of marble in front of it.

"No, that's the way to the catacombs. I'm not going down there."

The grimalkin put his paw on it, and it slid aside without a sound. At the very least it should have some sort of creaking noise, shouldn't it? Or maybe I'd watched too many human-made movies and television shows, where if there was an entrance to someplace creepy, it would have the requisite noise.

"Ellerin?" I called using secret conversation. *"Are you in the catacombs?"*

A resigned, *"Yes,"* came back to me. I took a deep breath and descended the stairs, Sir Raleigh padding silently behind me.

When the door to the staircase slid back into place and shut out the sun, I shivered but kept going. I made a Faerie flame dance on my palm, but it didn't do much to dispel the gloom around me. It did enlighten the words on the arch at the end of the small chamber at the bottom of the stairs: Memento Mori—remember, you will die. Fae didn't like the reminder. We preferred to think our long lives made us immortal, and so we put off thinking about death as long as possible. A ten-thousand-year sleep before reincarnation felt the same as death, for we wouldn't necessarily remember who we'd been. The old lady in Aoine's castle was an exception, which made her powerful.

But that still didn't answer my question—what was Ellerin doing down here?

I'd been to the catacombs once, when I was a girl. Typically, they only admitted Fae when a high Fae had died, and in this case, it was one of my grandmother's elderly courtiers, who had also been a long-ago consort. We had walked in solemn procession, and my grandmother's consort at the time, who also happened to be the High Hierophant at the Temple of the Goddess, intoned prayers. They'd echoed through the space for too long and sounded like the whispers of the dead. Rhys had tickled the back of my neck and made me cry out, which had earned me a scolding from my embarrassed mother.

The corridors held honeycomb-looking stone walls waiting for the next Fae to pass on to their ten-thousand-year sleep. As I walked through them, I hunched my shoulders against any icy fingers that might reach out and startle me. Sir Raleigh led me through what felt like a labyrinth, which eventually contained walls of inhabited tombs, indicated by their bricked-up openings, until we reached a large chamber that felt older than the rest and didn't hold any graves. It was a box about twenty feet long and fifteen feet wide, and its ceiling disappeared in the flickering gloom above. A pool of water with three-foot-high gray walls took up most of the center of the room, and suspended above its middle was a blue flame. The light and shadows danced in the obsidian mirror walls, which had clouded with age, but still reflected blurry images. Ellerin stood at the back side of the pool, and the flame made his eyes sparkle as well. Now he looked like a hierophant, and I felt like a lowly supplicant.

No, I refused to succumb to the image. I had questions, and where better to seek their answers than at the mythical Pool of Knowledge? I'd heard of it, but like many magical places, it could only be found sometimes, by those who desired the truth enough to face their fears.

What fears had Ellerin faced to come here?

Sir Raleigh didn't seem to feel the heaviness of the place. He licked his white paw, then jumped up on the edge of the pool and cat-walked along its edge until he reached Ellerin, who scratched him behind his ears. The chamber amplified his purr and drove the rumbling sound into my chest, relaxing me.

"So, it's time, is it?" Ellerin asked the grimalkin. He still sounded resigned, and he motioned for me to join him.

I did so, keeping an eye on the water in the pool for any sign of disruption. Not that I expected water wolves, but one never knew what surprises Fae bodies of water held, especially ones in places of power. "What are you doing down here?"

My question echoed through the room, and Ellerin nodded to the flame. Had it communicated with him?

"This is a time and space for honesty, so I'll answer your questions, Princess." Rather than a formal title, 'Princess' sounded like a term of endearment, and it gave me courage.

With a sigh, he gestured to the arch I'd walked through. "A son of mine recently went into his long sleep. Elric. Do you remember him?"

The image of a tall, strong, dark-haired Fae came to mind. He'd always been arrogant, and he'd enjoyed toying with Earth witches a bit much, but I couldn't imagine him dying early. "Yes, he was one of my grandmother's favorites. What happened?"

"He was killed as part of an ill-considered plot to allow nightmare creatures into the Earth realm through Faerie." He shook his head, and I sensed what he didn't tell me—he'd questioned my grandmother's wisdom, and he suspected she'd been slipping mentally for some time. "A were-bat tore out his throat." He put one hand to his face and rubbed his eyes. Would he cry?

I resisted the urge to put an arm around him. "I'm so sorry. That's a horrible way to die. Vile creatures."

He nodded and with a deep breath, composed himself. "Yes, thank you for your sympathy." He shrugged off my attempt to comfort him, and I tried not to take it personally. It bordered on miraculous that he'd been vulnerable in front of me. "I came in here to meditate on what I should do. I don't want any more of my children to die prematurely."

Those last words had a weight of prophecy, and I shivered again. "Any more of your children? How many do you have?"

He turned to face me, then, and the light from the flame flickered in eyes the same bright green as mine. "Three. I was Maeve's favorite consort for a century long ago."

"But you're a gray Fae. That's not allowed."

"I wasn't gray the whole time. I began as a light Fae, and my closeness to the throne gave me a unique perspective, one I couldn't reconcile with my principles. So, I left. That act of rejection of the light Fae transformed me into a gray Fae and I became the Wanderer."

I picked through his words. "You said, 'not the whole time.' So that means you still had relations with Maeve, but after."

"Yes, I would come back to court briefly to satisfy your grandmother's curiosity about happenings beyond her realm. Sometimes your mother and I would..." He let me finish the thought.

Olred had said Ellerin knew...what? So many questions piled into my head, but I had to ask the one I'd come down here for. "Ellerin, are you my father? And was I conceived...after?"

He took my hand. "Yes, princess. Your mother attributed your conception to one of her regular consorts, but I always knew." He shook his head. "And I'm sorry I wasn't there more when you were a child."

"Why did you leave? Not when I was little—" Although now the memories tumbled in, of him kissing me goodbye and disappearing on a gray horse at dusk. I shoved them back. "From the Forest Castle."

"Like any parent, I had to let you go on your own. Plus, it was an experiment. I didn't become the Wanderer until after I left the court, and I didn't know if the abilities I developed were adaptive or if they had embedded in my genetic material. Now I know."

Relief flooded through me. "Oh, good. That means I can't be the queen."

"Not necessarily. I was light Fae at one time, so there is wiggle room."

Damn. My irritation returned. "So, you put me and my friends' lives in danger to figure out something about your powers. How...Fae."

He frowned. "What do you mean? There shouldn't have been any true danger, and I didn't think you'd need to fold the Path. What happened?"

I told him about the gwenhwyfvar owls and the revenants. During my telling, his brows drew closer together, and his jaw harder.

"We're closer to the next Great Rising than I thought, then. I'd hoped the Lady of the Forest—not Aoine, the one haunting her—was an anomaly."

"How could you not know when the Great Rising is going to happen? It's part of our history."

"You met the record-keeper. The longer knowledge is kept and passed down orally, the vaguer it gets. Consequently, the record of time isn't exact. This makes your role more important than before."

"How so?" I didn't want to deal with a Great Rising. There were no precedents as there were for everything else in Faerie.

"These are the victims of the last Great War between the light and dark Fae. They will rise hungry and confused, and all of Faerie will need to cooperate in order to make sure they don't destroy it in a wave. You are the one to unite the realm, especially since you do have some characteristics of the gray Fae, which will help get the others on board. And you have a dark Fae prince who is willing to help."

"You mean Basil the Troubadour?" I shook my head. "He's as shallow and fickle as the next one."

"Yes, and be careful not to underestimate him. Plus, you have your brother. He's not one of my progeny, but he's on his way to redemption. He warned me of your mother's plot, which is another reason I left—I came to see if I could pave the way for you." He chuckled. "You didn't give me much of a chance before you plopped yourself and your friends—nicely done, by the way—right into the middle of the court room."

"Oh." Could I count on Rhys? "Are there any other siblings I should take into account?"

He smiled. "You suspect one other, but I'm going to let you figure it out."

All the pieces fell into place, then—Ellerin staring at Kestrel that first morning, him being overly harsh when John grabbed Kestrel at the Earth side of the portal, the sense of them being in conflict, John's growing sullenness... "You mean Kestrel. John's not really her father."

"Bingo, as the humans say."

"Which makes her..."

"Half-Fae and half-earth witch. A trickster. The first to be born in a thousand years." He checked his pocket watch. "And she'll be waking, so you should make sure that old goat Caduceus keeps his mouth shut after he examines her. There's no telling what your mother will do if she finds out."

"She'll freak and not let her leave. And, oh gods, John... Is that why you two didn't get along?"

"That and he's a human ass, but he took good care of her, so I cannot fault him."

"One more question..." I took another deep breath. "Why did you let them come along? If you knew all this, that she'd be in more danger than I thought, why didn't *you* say no?"

He shrugged and gave a typical gray Fae answer. "Because it was their—and your—path to follow."

Problem upon problem piled up in my brain, and like Kestrel with her powers, I barely took hold of one before it wriggled away and another took its place. I turned to go, but he put a hand on my arm.

"Remember what I told you before we left. Maeve didn't teach her daughters to say no, but you're going to have to learn, and quickly."

WHEN I EMERGED from the catacombs, an unpleasant surprise waited for me.

Troubadour stood at the edge of the patio overlooking the gardens. He had his harp tucked against his side, and the wind made his blue cloak billow. If I hadn't had a taste of his arrogance and prejudice at Forest Castle, I would've thought him handsome and dashing in the pose—the effect he no doubt wanted to have.

He seemed lost in thought, and I pondered slipping away, but my conversation with Ellerin had reminded me I needed to act like a crown princess, not a coward. Sometimes that would mean keeping my enemies close, or at least finding out what they wanted.

I thought about waiting for him to turn around, but I needed to get back up to Kestrel and couldn't afford the delay a cat-and-mouse waiting game would cause. Sir Raleigh sat and twitched his tail, so I could tell he felt the same. He seemed to like Kestrel, or feel somewhat responsible for her, which made sense considering her connection to Ellerin.

I took a deep breath and asked, "Looking for something?"

Troubadour turned, and for a second, the sunlight made a halo out of his golden hair. I mentally rolled my eyes.

"You know I was."

"How did you get here? I thought dark Fae weren't allowed in the castle."

"Someone folded the Path, and the resulting energy disturbance allowed me to mask my own."

Great, my actions had allowed a traditional enemy into the heart of Lorien.

He cocked his head and gave me a smile full of charm and wormwood, meant to addle the brain, but not always in a pleasant way. "Aren't you going to ask me what I want?"

"I think I know."

The way he looked me over made me cringe internally, but I didn't change my posture. "Allow me to get you a camera phone. That way you can make me your home screen, and you can look whenever you want."

Hmmm, I'd been trying to say, "Take a picture, it will last longer," in a non-cliché way and had ended up flirting. Dammit.

"I was hoping to negotiate a different arrangement. Come walk with me."

I glanced back at the castle, and the tug of responsibility to Kestrel and a certain growing loyalty and connection to Lawrence nearly held me back, but Sir Raleigh chose the moment to catch my attention by looking straight into my eyes and speaking to me. "*Hear him out. It will prove useful.*"

"Whose side are you on?" I asked him, but he didn't answer. "All right," I said to Troubadour. "It will have to be a short walk. I have obligations."

"As you should if you're taking on your role as crown princess. That's what I wanted to talk to you about." He bent his arm that didn't hold the harp, and with reluctance, I took it. We descended the wide stairs to the gardens, which had more plants of bigger and better quality than Forest Castle, but lacked the sense of wildness.

"Are you happy to be home?" Troubadour asked.

I understood he was making small talk until we were out of Fae earshot. "Yes, it's lovely here." And too perfect, I added without saying it aloud. Not a stray leaf lay on the ground, and the grass and other living things had had all the stray bends manicured and bespelled out of them. It was almost like walking through a poorly done movie set.

We emerged from the shadow of the castle, and the air felt clearer. I sensed that even if someone watched us, they wouldn't be able to hear what we said. Even so, I copied what I'd seen and felt Ellerin do with his privacy bubble.

Troubadour nodded with approval. "It never hurts to be too cautious, and that's why I wanted to find you, to talk to you. You're in grave danger here."

"Yes, I know." My frustration emerged with more than I'd intended to say. "Rhys told me about our mother and her schemes, but I don't know how I'm going to bring anything out. She has me at a disadvantage."

"That's what I wanted to speak with you about. You remember the Fae who attacked us in the forest of the Gray Zone?"

"Yes..."

"He was a proxy, and now that I've been here and have seen

your mother, I recognized her energy. She's the one who teamed up with me to summon the soul-eater."

More pieces clicking into place... "Are you sure? That's a big accusation." One that I finally had proof for...maybe.

"Yes, very. And I know you have reason to doubt me, to dislike me, but I cannot condone a Fae turning against their own family like that."

The fierceness of his expression made me suspect something like that had been done to him. Perhaps that was why he had chosen a life as a bard rather than taking his place as a Fae prince. Or had he been forced into it?

"That still doesn't help me unless you're willing to go public and you have proof."

"I have a letter her proxy sent me. It still reeks of her energy."

"Let me see."

But Sir Raleigh interjected with, "*I sense it on him. He speaks the truth.*" Well, of course he did. Fae couldn't lie, and yet I still sifted through his words for the deception.

He shook his head. "No, Princess, not now. It's too dangerous with too many people watching. Plus, no Fae gives anything away for free. I have a proposition for you."

I didn't suppress my sigh. "Of course you do."

"Your grandmother is dying, and when a Fae queen passes, it's the end of an era. You could allow your mother to take the throne with the shadow of intended infanticide over her, or you could challenge her and take it yourself, especially since the Queen Spell found you. What do you think would be best for Faerie?"

"You know what I'm going to say. Her sins would cause the destruction of the realm, and so much else threatens it." I thought back to the revelations in Forest Castle and the other things I'd learned. What sort of damage had the presence of the asylum—which I would immediately shut down when I took the throne—caused? And that the nightmare creatures had been let in? Could all these circumstances have hastened the next Great Rising?

"Then promise to marry me, to make a true partnership between our realms, and I will help you."

He swung me around and went down on one knee in front of me.

"What are you doing?"

"Proposing to you. You know we're being watched. There will be witnesses."

Sir Raleigh arched his back with a low growl at the castle. *"Danger for Kestrel!"*

"I'm sorry, I have to go."

He grabbed my wrist. "Think about it. If you call upon me to present evidence against your mother, I'll oblige, but know that you'll be promising to be my betrothed."

SIR RALEIGH and I landed in my bedroom, but Kestrel was nowhere to be found.

"Reine, help!" Kestrel's mental voice blasted into my head, and I winced.

"Kestrel? Where are you?"

"Caduceus' office. Hurry! The Fae guard are here for me. They think I'm a trickster."

"Hades, I'd hoped to put off that conversation..." I knelt in front of Sir Raleigh. "Can you be your grimalkin self?"

He looked me straight in the eyes. *"If you will it. You are the daughter of my summoner. You are the crown princess."*

"And I need to act like a princess and say no to both my mother and my grandmother, don't I?" I placed my right index finger against the soft, short fur in the middle of his forehead. "Guardian, come back to me."

I stepped back, and the air stirred as his larger form appeared. Then he blinked out of sight, and I followed his energy. It was easy to do since we were linked.

He brought me to the corridor outside Caduceus' office, which I recognized from the old book and chemical smells emanating from it. A knot of guards stood in the doorway, but they parted when I pushed through.

I glared at everyone except Kestrel, who must have been shaken, but who stood straight with her chin up. Good girl. With the haughtiest, iciest Fae princess tone I could muster, I demanded, "What is the meaning of this?"

Darien replied, "The girl is a trickster."

I narrowed my eyes. "And how do you come upon this knowledge?"

Darien cocked his head toward Caduceus. "He informed me a few minutes ago. You know the rules. They are not to be allowed to move freely among us. They're too dangerous."

And here I saw another parallel between Faerie and the human world—an attempt to restrict one deemed as threatening because she was different. "She doesn't know what she is, what she can do. This is a golden opportunity to observe and train one for our own uses."

"Not what I was going for," Kestrel pointed out using the mental channel still open between us.

"Trust me."

"I do." But she leaned back against the windowsill like she pondered a desperate move if things turned uglier.

More guards came through the door. A younger Fae in a sky-blue, velvet, medieval costume, complete with fancy puffed sleeves and tights pushed through them and looked us over haughtily.

"Your presence is requested in the throne room, Princess. The Council has reached their decision regarding your exile."

36

LAWRENCE

A page came and fetched Rhys from his rooms, where he'd been reading, John had been pacing, and I'd... I'd been half-lying on the couch by the window feeling like every breath took more effort than I could afford. Every so often, John would come check on me, but he quickly came to the same conclusion I had—my ability to survive in Faerie waned by the hour. How long would it take for them to find the ends of their paths so I could reach mine and go home?

And where was Reine? Was she all right and keeping ahead of her mother's schemes?

"Your presence is requested in the throne room," the page intoned as though he read from a scroll. "All of you." If I'd not felt so badly, I would have looked to exchange amused glances with John at the page's golden velvet outfit. Poor kid—I hoped he had comfortable clothes for after-hours.

John and Rhys helped me down to the throne room, where Kestrel and Reine waited. Reine paled when she saw me. Did I feel badly that she hadn't checked on me? No, I understood how courts and royalty worked. My mother had drilled the knowledge into me, as silly as it seemed to study such things in our little cottage by the river. Reine was a princess. I was one of their traditional enemies...

The justifications wore me out mentally, leaving me with the ache of disappointment in my heart. Okay, maybe I did resent her lack of attention.

Kestrel gave John a long, questioning look, and he paled and muttered, "Oh, no."

"What is it?" I asked.

"Nothing." But it obviously wasn't.

Trumpets echoed through the space and set my ears ringing. I swayed on my feet, and Rhys grabbed my arm so I wouldn't fall. Reine and John traded places so she stood by me, and he by Kestrel.

"You look terrible," she said and put a hand on my forehead. "And you've got a fever. We need to get you back to the Earth realm." She dropped her hand when her mother appeared followed by twelve Fae, male and female and a few of indeterminate gender. Each wore robes of a different shade of blue or purple and looked like some sort of very tall performance choir. I almost giggled at the thought that we'd entered a musical.

Right, I was getting delirious. *Just hurry up with it already.*

Reine squeezed my hand. *All in good Fae time, and try not to broadcast your thoughts.* Somehow, she sent strength through the connection we had, more than where we touched, although I drew my hand back.

Don't do that. You need your powers for you.

Don't be stubborn.

Her mother moved to the throne, then stopped before actually taking it. Instead, she stood in front of it, and I could tell she acted as the representative for the queen.

"I am here to announce the decision of the council regarding the exiles of my beloved children, Reine and Rhys."

Her voice caught at the end, and she gazed at the Fae children in question with eyes that shimmered with almost-tears.

I didn't buy it for a second, and even in my weakened state, I had the desire to step in front of Reine and protect her. At least Sir Raleigh had assumed his more intimidating form, and the lashing of his tail expressed his consternation. Reine regarded her mother with aloofness, as befitting a Fae princess. Did she also feel the desire to roll her eyes or otherwise express her skepticism at her mother's description of her as beloved? There was no telling.

One of the Fae in blue robes and of indeterminate gender stepped forward. Their medium-length brown hair had streaks of gray in it, so they must be one of the senior Fae. They pulled a scroll from their robes, unfurled it, and took a breath before saying, "The Council of the High Fae, privileged to meet in the year of Ouros in the century of Pomme in the era of..."

I tuned out for a second. Someone needed to teach the Fae system for designating time. A quick glance around the room confirmed that others felt the same, as their attention seemed to wander with murmurings and shifting back and forth. Their human-like fidgeting comforted me.

"...has come to the following determination based on evidence presented by Crown Princess Maeve and her former consort the Wanderer..."

That got my attention. Ellerin and Maeve had been a thing at one time? Or, more accurately, he'd been one of her things? Interesting...

"That Prince Rhys may remain in the Faerie lands provided he seek treatment for that which disfigures him from the court physician and any other means necessary."

Rhys visibly relaxed and nodded. Maeve gave him a fond smile, the first genuine-seeming expression she'd had. Others around him congratulated him except Reine, who'd crossed her arms and tapped one foot.

"You don't seem encouraged," I murmured to her.

"I've seen enough of these judgments given to know that what comes next is typically not good." She uncrossed her arms and allowed me to take her hand.

"I'm here for you. I wish I could offer more, but I'm not much of a warrior right now."

Her smile, tight as it was, sent warmth through me. "That's enough for now."

"As for Princess Reine..." The Fae gave Reine a stern look over the scroll. "Her case is more complicated. During her time in the Earth realm, she advanced her knowledge of healing, although with some important gaps. She also engaged in dangerous activities with vampires, although that was in the service of defeating a creature unleashed from this realm, so that can be forgiven provided she pursues the same treatment for her disfigurement as her brother does. However, she has also engaged in potentially treasonous activity upon return to this realm that warrants further investigation. Consequently, the council has deemed that she may stay, but provisionally as her case is pursued further, and she may not live in the capital."

He rolled up the scroll. "Thus, saith the Fae Council. I will bring this to Queen Tatiana for her signature on the morrow."

Reine had gone still, and the guard advanced toward her. All trace of friendliness had fled from them, and one of them even mouthed, "Vampire consort scum."

Now Reine did roll her eyes. "Oh, please. You're just jealous. She's hot." She held up a hand, palm out, and caught her mother in a lightning bolt-lasso. "Why don't you tell them the full story, Mother, and we can see who's been treasonous?"

37

REINE

My energy cord caught my mother by surprise, but as she still outranked me, she shrugged it off. Still, I'd had a satisfying moment of seeing her startled expression.

"Nice try, daughter, but I don't know what you mean."

I saw how this would play out, and I wouldn't be in any position to help Lawrence if I was trapped in a probation situation. I knew this would entail losing him forever, but I couldn't allow him to perish. And there was also the issue of Kestrel. "Let's cut the crap, as they say in the Earth realm. You don't want me anywhere near the throne—or you—because I know your secret."

"And what secret is that, Daughter?"

"That you've been working with the dark Fae all along. You made a guard your proxy in order to cooperate with Troubadour to unleash the soul-eater to stalk and kill your own daughter. Prince Troubadour?"

He stepped forward from the edge of the court, where he'd hidden. The crowd gasped as he pulled the hood back from his face.

My mother's expression twisted into horror. "What is he doing here? We don't allow dark Fae into the court! It's contrary to the treaty we have with them."

"I'm here because you and I have had business, which allows me to cross the barriers."

Ah, that made sense. He'd only told me the partial truth when he'd mentioned my folding of the path allowing him to enter Lorien.

I almost did my usual, "Fae, what are you gonna do?" shrug, but I couldn't. Maybe it was the lack of sleep. Maybe it was the repeated disappointments and realizations about my past and how history wasn't as I remembered it, but I couldn't take it anymore. I couldn't attach myself to someone whom I'd always have to question, to wonder if there was more he wasn't telling me.

"Stop," I told Troubadour in secret conversation. *"I can't promise to marry you."*

"Are you sure? This is your chance..."

"Yes, I can't do this. I need someone who respects me enough to tell me the truth, the whole truth..."

I felt his mental grin. *"...and nothing but the truth? How very human of you."*

"Maybe that's who I am now."

My mother cleared her throat and looked back and forth between the two of us. "Would you like to share with the rest of us?"

"Ball's in your court, Prince Basil."

"Oooh, sportsing now. I love a girl who can bandy around a good cliché. And that's not really my name."

He thought for a long moment, fingering his harp, although no sound came forth from it. Then he nodded to himself and took a deep breath. "I am here because Princess Reine allowed me to cross the border stream between the Gray Lands and here. And because you and I have business. The princess speaks the truth—I recognize your magical signature now, although you sent a proxy to do your dirty work."

I grinned at him, and Maeve—I couldn't call her my mother anymore, not even in my mind, since she'd tried to kill me—scowled. Then she went for the classic Fae redirection/misdirection.

"And what about the accusations of treason you're under, Reine? Consorting with a dark Fae prince won't help your chance. Neither will the fact that you've traveled with and even trained, from what I understand, a trickster."

A collective gasp of horror blew through my ears, and everyone turned and looked at Kestrel and John.

To her credit, Kestrel didn't shrink from the scrutiny. Like a Fae, she lifted her chin, regarded Maeve for a long moment, and then turned to the man she'd grown up knowing as her father. "Is it true, Dad? Or is it John?"

"Please stop," John begged Maeve. "Please don't do this. Don't take my daughter away from me. I've lost too much already." He covered his face and wept into his hands. Lawrence walked over to him and put a supportive hand on his shoulder.

My heart broke for John. What would he do now?

"But did you know?" Kestrel asked. "And was Mom really my mom?"

John nodded. He spoke into his hands, and his words came out muffled, but I could hear them. "We hit a rough patch and separated for a little while. No one knew. We'd agreed not to see other people, but she said she went out one night, met a handsome stranger, some guy who was traveling through, and decided to blow off some steam with him." He lowered his hands and glared at Ellerin. "I put it together. There are things I noticed while we traveled. Things that are too similar between Reine and Kestrel to be coincidence, and there was always the thing about Kestrel's powers."

Lawrence lifted his head and frowned. "And the sad irony is

that Beverly didn't need to try to solve Kestrel's power problem by harvesting paranormal DNA."

"No, she didn't. That's why I tried to stop her, but she had convinced herself that Kestrel was ours. Maybe she couldn't handle the guilt."

Kestrel stood straight, but I could see her trembling. "So that means my real dad is..."

Ellerin stepped forward and bowed, then straightened and said, "I suspected as well. I'm sorry for not telling you."

John rushed forward, fist cocked, and took a swing at Ellerin, who stepped back. John stumbled, bent over like he'd lost his balance, and then pulled a silver knife from a hidden sheath at his ankle. Dammit, I knew he'd surprise us eventually. He lunged at Ellerin, who parried with his staff and knocked John backward. Lawrence moved forward to grab John, but John sidestepped him and went in again, his knife aimed straight for Ellerin's heart. Ellerin swung his staff forward and bashed John on the side of his head. The crack resounded through the hall, and John fell forward and lay still. Thick blood pooled beneath him.

"No!" Kestrel knelt beside him and rolled him over. The knife stuck out from his chest, and his breath gurgled. Lawrence knelt on his other side.

"Hang on, old friend."

I joined them by John's head and took it in my hands, but I could feel his life fading. His glasses had been knocked askew, and his pupils were of different sizes, giving him a deranged look.

"I'm...sorry..." he gasped. "I...tried..."

Kestrel took his other hand in both of hers. "Hold on, please hold on." She looked at me, tears streaming down her face. "Please, can't you do something?"

I looked up at Ellerin, who shook his head. We could both feel John's life force leaving him and an extra finality.

"The Shadowed Path has taken its price from he who would not commit fully to it," Ellerin intoned. Then he said something Fae rarely do. "And I'm truly sorry, Kestrel. I didn't mean to hit him so hard."

"I was afraid this might happen," John whispered. "That you might find out I'm not really your father."

Kestrel bowed her head to look him straight in the eyes and said with conviction, "You have always been my father."

I could feel her reaching for the one eel she might be able to use to save him, and I blocked her.

She turned to me, her expression one of full Fae fury. "What are you doing?"

"If you use that power, if you bring him back, you'll doom yourself to be a necromancer, and it will be a much harder road."

"But I can't be alone."

"You won't be. You and I are sisters."

John took one last rattling breath. Kestrel screamed and forced herself beyond my block to grab the necromancy fish, but she was too late. It swam around John as a black blob of smoke and then returned to Kestrel. She sobbed, and I held her until her crying quieted. Then she and John's body disappeared, presumably back to the Earth realm.

"Where did they go?" Lawrence asked. He stood and swayed on his feet. "Please, I have to go to them. Kestrel can't be alone right now."

I activated my Fae sense and saw my mother holding an energy lasso, keeping him in Faerie.

"Let him go," I said. "He doesn't have anything else to do here."

"His path has ended," Ellerin agreed. "And he's not going to last much longer."

Maeve jerked the lasso, which tightened as a noose around Lawrence's neck. He fell to his knees, clawing at it.

"Well, isn't this an interesting predicament? What will you do to save your lover, Reine? I can see the bond between the two of you. How classic, but you know what it means, don't you?"

"We cannot be together. I know this. Let him go."

"No, I'd rather watch you watch him perish." She tugged again, and Lawrence's face turned purple.

Ellerin held up his staff. "Maeve, enough."

"No, why would you take her side?"

"Because she's my daughter, and I stood aside for too long, including with that stupid exile. I see your game, Maeve. Here!" He tossed his staff to me, and I aimed it at her. I didn't know exactly what to do with it, only that it would react to my desire. And what did I want most?

To get Lawrence out of Faerie.

A golden beam of light shot from the crystal atop the staff, and I barely held on to it as the world shifted around me and disappeared in a blur.

WE LANDED in a Faerie circle of standing stones. I recognized it as the one in Scotland where my mother had originally given me the directive to go to Atlanta and figure out who had sold out an industrial secret to the pharmaceutical industry. With it being a liminal space between Faerie and the Earth realm, her energy lasso disappeared, and Lawrence lay on the ground gasping. I ran to him and stood in front of him to block him before Maeve could do anything else.

"Well-played, Reine, but what are you going to do now?" She advanced on me, and her hands glowed light blue, the color of the high light Fae. "I still outrank you and can compel you."

She spoke the truth...or did she? She spoke it as far as she knew it, but I had more weapons at my disposal. And in truth, I outranked her, but I didn't want to invoke the Queen Spell, not now when I had to take care of Kestrel and Lawrence.

A warm breeze blew through the circle, indicating we'd been in Faerie long enough for the season to approach late spring. The trees would be leafed out, and soon the Beltane bonfires would be lit...

Fire. Whereas high Fae magic involved growing and cooling, that of the dark Fae meant destruction. And as a half-gray Fae, I could command them all.

She sent a blast of icy air toward me, meant to catch me and paralyze me, and I called upon my internal flames and blocked her. Where the two walls of energy met, a crystal barrier formed, like a plexiglass shield, but stronger.

"Nice try, but I can still do this." She sent another energy lasso through and attempted to catch me, but I shielded with a blast of gray obfuscation energy...and another weapon.

"Does Grandmother know you conceived a child with a gray Fae? And that you didn't say anything even when she chose me as the crown princess?"

That's what Olred had meant, that she knew about Ellerin being my father and that my mother had hidden the fact. There was no going back now, and Maeve knew it. Drawing from her storm powers for when crops needed rain, and quickly, she sent a lightning bolt through the crystal shield, which shattered. I focused on the feeling of the walls around the dark Fae capital and blocked the energy and the shards, then trapped her within an obsidian cage.

Her hands glowed again, this time bright white, and I barely had time to throw up a shield before the cage shattered, sending shards of black mineral toward me and Lawrence like so many bullets.

This left me with a quandary. She'd keep the attacks coming, and I was running out of time and possibly energy.

I decided to negotiate, or try to. "I don't want to attack you. What did I ever do to you?"

"That's a very human question. Don't you think I haven't noticed how your grandmother always favored you? Now she's fading, and yet the Queen Spell hasn't come to me. Where else could it have landed?"

She sent a lightning bolt toward me from each hand, and I blocked the one heading for me, but the other one was sneaky and arced around my shield to zap Lawrence, who groaned. I dared not look back at him, but the strength he'd gained from being partially out of Faerie ebbed, and he gasped for breath.

"Stop hurting him!"

"The Queen Spell is missing... You have a classic bond with a gargoyle... The Fae love you and have been rejoicing about their lost princess returning. Who do you think is better positioned to be queen of Faerie?"

"But I don't want to be the queen." The weight of the words hung between us.

"You act like you have a choice," Maeve spat. She gathered what must have been the rest of her magical reserves with a wave of wind energy. The shards of crystal and obsidian rose and whirled toward me and Lawrence in a mini-cyclone. She still outranked me, and I couldn't do much against that power...

Or...I could defeat her by pulling rank, uttering the Queen Spell.

A new verse came to me, then, and the implications for what it meant for the land and the forthcoming era of Fae resurrection sent terror through me, but I couldn't stop it. "I am the finality, the darkness beneath and between. I am the queen of all of Faerie and the grave beyond!"

I held out Ellerin's staff and parried with the still, dark energy of the catacombs and the bottomless pool underneath them. I saw another cavern, its walls of crystal, and drew on that silent power as well. The shimmering wall of water met her tornado, and water exploded everywhere, but especially back toward her in a small tsunami that lifted her, then dropped her.

Her energy signature disappeared—had I killed her?

The stone shards hit the ground with a mass tinkle, and the rest of the water fell as snow and quickly blanketed the ground. I kept Lawrence and myself in a heat bubble, but I didn't know what to do, having just taken out the crown princess of Faerie.

The air went still, and I leaned over, hands on my knees, to catch my breath. Large snowflakes flurried around me.

My grandmother appeared, then, as she would have looked when she first took the throne, and I knew she was on the cusp of death.

"You have a choice, Reine," she said and cupped my cheek with a hand already growing cool. "You can take the throne and guide your people through this forthcoming challenge. Or you can stay here with your lover and your sister and their problems."

"What happens if I take the throne?"

An obsidian mirror appeared, and I saw Kestrel standing at a grave, her head bowed. She gathered the necromancy energy in her hands and said, "I can't lose you, too, Uncle Lawrence." Shadows flocked around her, waiting to pounce and devour her, turning her to their own purposes. And then Lawrence... I couldn't bear to see what he'd become.

I had to think like a queen and acknowledge my responsibility. "Kestrel and John would never have come to Faerie had I not let them. Unfortunately, my mother was right about one thing—I can't leave any loose ends before I return permanently. But I cannot leave Faerie un-led."

The obsidian mirror's picture changed to reflect the inspiration that had just come to mind, and it gave me a solution.

"What about this?" I asked.

She crossed her arms and tapped her lips with an index

finger. "It is unconventional, to say the least, but it could work. You know it doesn't get you off the hook forever, though. You will have to return. The Old Ones are rising, and Faerie needs its queen."

"I know. Oh, and by the way, I'm closing the asylum."

She bowed her head. "One of my biggest mistakes. You will be wiser than I. You already are." She kissed me on the forehead and disappeared, leaving me with a very sick gargoyle in the cold rain, which now fell from the sky.

I walked to where my mother's body should have lain, but it had disappeared. Apparently, I hadn't heard the last from her, either.

38

LAWRENCE

I opened my eyes to an unfamiliar white plaster ceiling in a room with gray stone walls that spoke of long-ago human construction. Not Fae, thank gods. Bright morning light trickled through the diamond-paned window.

My body—still in human form—felt like I'd been worked over with a mallet, but at least I could draw a deep breath. Then, as when I'd wake from a deep sleep, my hearing returned, and I could make out the rhythmic beeping of a heart monitor. I tried to rub my nose and found an oxygen tube, which explained the tickle on my upper lip and the cold in my nostrils. There was another tube as well, which I could feel in the back of my throat. A feeding tube? How long had I been out?

Although it took effort, I turned my head from side to side and found I lay in a hospital room-type place with stone walls and furniture that could have fit in a castle. The indentation in the cushions of one of the chairs indicated someone had been sitting there not too long ago. I shifted, and the weight I hadn't realized lay across my feet disappeared.

"Where am I?" I croaked.

A toilet flushed, and Kestrel emerged from behind the wall to my left. Dark shadows smudged the spaces under her eyes, and she looked thinner than when we had left Faerie. "Of course the second I go to the bathroom, you wake up. How are you feeling?"

"Like I've been beaten up by a Fae army." The final moments in the throne room flashed through my memory. "How are you?"

She turned her face to the window, and the light illuminated the irritation on her cheeks from copious tears. "I'm...not okay." Then she returned her gaze to me with a too-bright smile. "But I'm glad you're doing better. I'll get the doctor. He wanted me to let him know the second you woke up."

She left before I could ask any of my other questions, like where was Reine? Had she survived the encounter with her mother? All I could remember was piercing cold, lots of noise, and a big electric shock that zapped me into the dark place of unconsciousness. I had no idea where I was, when it was, and what had happened, and I wanted answers, dammit. I also wanted to hug my goddaughter. If I felt disoriented, she must have felt like the world had gone topsy-turvy. Although her real father was a Fae, for the purposes of the Earth authorities, she was an orphan.

Then guilt and grief pierced me. I'd held my best friend's hand as he died after I'd been unable to stop him from attacking Ellerin. If I'd tried harder...

A tall, blond man with eyes the color of the deep ocean and wearing a lab coat entered the room, followed by Kestrel and a man with curly, dark hair, dressed in slacks and a dress shirt under a leather jacket.

The doctor introduced himself, and his Caribbean accent gave his words a lilting cadence. "Good morning, Doctor Gordon. I'm Doctor Maximilian Fortuna—you may call me

Max—and this is my colleague, Gabriel McCord. How are you feeling?"

"Like crap."

He picked up the chart from the foot of the bed, then set it back down. "Sorry, habit. It's not like there's anything new in there. You've had a series of shocks, one apparently electrical. Do you remember how you got here?"

"No. I don't remember anything after the electrical shock. Please tell me where I am and why your names sound so familiar."

Gabriel McCord stepped forward. "We were supposed to come to the CPDC and conduct the investigation, but we got held up here. We sent Doctors River and Rial instead." He seemed to still be making up his mind whether that was a good idea. I couldn't blame him.

Max took over the explanation. "As for where we are, this is the Institute for Lycanthropic Reversal. Doctor River brought you to us after your electrocution incident. She didn't trust a human-oriented hospital to care for you. She said you're...a gargoyle?"

He looked at me with skepticism.

Kestrel sighed. "I told them that it's true. Apparently, they've never seen one of you before."

Gabriel's mouth quirked, making him appear more amused than skeptical. "I've heard we had gargoyles here, that they escaped to the Highlands and other remote mountainous areas after some persecution, but I've never met one. It's a pleasure."

"Likewise." All right, so that solved where I was and how I'd gotten there, but... "Can you tell me what's wrong with me?"

Max picked the chart up and flipped it open. "As for that, we're not so sure. You have persistent hypoxemia, although there's nothing obvious wrong with your respiratory system. Now that you're awake, we can do some more tests. If you feel weak, that's normal considering you've been in bed for a week.

Physically, you resemble someone who's gotten close to dying of starvation and exposure."

"I think I may have. And I'm hungry."

Max nodded. "I'll have a nurse come in and remove the feeding apparatus and catheter. I'd like you eating and moving around as much as possible. Also, if you can tell us what happened..."

"I got caught in the middle of a Fae battle between two crown princesses."

Both of them winced, and Gabriel asked, "Do you know who won?"

"I'm here, so I suspect Reine did. Did she say when she would be coming back?" Or *if* she would, my heart added.

Kestrel answered this time. "No, but Sir Raleigh's been popping in and checking on you." She kept her tone carefully neutral, but I sensed an undercurrent of bitterness. Right, Reine had kept her from resurrecting her father. I understood why, and I also felt for Kestrel. I probably would have done the same, given the opportunity when my father had been murdered by a Fae.

I took her hand and squeezed it. "Thank you for staying with me."

She tilted her head down again, but not before the tears in her eyes made her eyes sparkle. "I don't have anyone else who needs me right now."

39

REINE

I traced the border of the Gray Zone on the map spread out over the table in my grandmother's—no, my—"war room," as she'd liked to call it. She'd held meetings of her closest advisers in the circular space off the throne room, and I followed her tradition.

Today the room held four of us. We'd come there after the funeral for my grandmother, and the cold from the catacombs still clung to me. I rubbed the chill bumps along my arms left bare by my navy-blue mourning gown and stopped when I caught Troubadour, also known as Prince Basil Emerald Gloriag the Fourth, watching me. If anything, he'd made less of a secret of his attraction to me, and he'd never been subtle about it to begin with.

One of the castle servants appeared with a delicate white shawl, which proved to have been heated, and I nodded thanks and wrapped it around me. The maid disappeared, and I shivered again, not from the cold, but from the sense of the castle always watching me and responding to, sometimes anticipating, every need or desire.

There was one thing it couldn't do—bring Lawrence back.

"So, we're set, then?" I asked the Council of Three, the temporary ruling body of Faerie. "Troubadour, you'll continue to search the archives for clues as to the Great Rising and where the majority of it is prophesied to happen and convince your contacts in Cruaidh to send you their records. Ellerin, you'll travel through the land and gather tales. And Rhys, you'll watch things here and take reports of those who have seen and experienced the gwynhwyfvar and phantoms."

"Yes, Your Highness," they chorused. The title still felt weird, like it didn't fit somehow. I'd been crowned Queen of the Light Fae the day after my grandmother's death, as leaving part of Faerie without a queen for too long would cause destabilization of its balance, and gods knew we didn't need more chaotic energy. Then we'd had a celebration, including Aoine and her crew of potentially treasonous Fae, whom I hoped would be allies. And then it was back to work.

I suspected the Great Rising would come from the Gray Zone, as it had appeared as a blemish on the land after the Great War. Since its boundaries shifted where it wasn't contained by rivers, I wanted to know what had been there before and how it had changed. Consequently, I'd granted the Winter Gnome King his wish in exchange for his oath to provide us with information from within the Gray Zone.

Now that I'd become queen, I felt a connection to Faerie, particularly the light lands, and I could tell it would be quiet for a while. Reports of phantoms and revenants were rare, and the ones that had attacked us had been captured and were being held in the catacombs in magical coffins, where their flesh could grow and their spirits settle.

I looked at each of my council members in turn. I still found seeing Rhys without his scar to be disorienting. Sometimes his skin still didn't look quite right around where it had been, and I suspected his muscles were having to learn to function again in the scar's absence.

"I understand that I'm leaving you with a big task, and I will try not to be gone too long. I do appreciate all your hard work."

They bowed, and I left. I walked to my old rooms in the East turret, where I still slept. It didn't feel right to take the queen's suite, not yet. Not until I returned to Faerie permanently.

Rhys caught up with me. "You're really going back to the gargoyle?" He didn't sound disapproving, just curious.

"Yes, he helped us out a lot, and we owe him. I owe him. And I owe John to make sure Kestrel is settled."

"Oh, yes, the trickster. Poor kid must be devastated."

When we reached my rooms, I turned to him. "What do you really want, Rhys?"

He looked at the floor. "Are you sure you trust me, even after all that?"

I'd asked myself the same question a hundred times, and I always came to the answer. "Yes, you've made your mistakes. You also redeemed yourself by telling me and Ellerin what Maeve was up to, even if it was a little late. Consider this your chance to prove yourself."

"I will. Thank you." Then he did something surprising—he hugged me. "Be careful. I'll miss you."

My eyes stung, and I let the tears flow. Fae princesses might not have been allowed to show emotion, but I was going to make it so that Fae queens—and everyone else —could.

"I'll miss you, too, little brother."

I STEPPED through the portal to the standing stones where I'd defeated my mother the week before. They sparkled with a thin layer of dew that turned to steam as I watched. I suspected they still held some residual energy from the battle. A question from the largest of them vibrated through the air. It's not like I heard it. Rather, I felt it, one of the perks of being a Fae queen, I supposed.

"I don't know," I answered. "As far as I'm aware, he's still unconscious and at the Institute."

Sir Raleigh popped into the clearing beside me and twined around my ankles. He'd continued to speak to me occasionally, and this time he had good news.

"Oh, I stand corrected. He's awake but weak. I'm going to see him now."

I pulled my motorcycle out of the nearby cave. The dwarves had done a beautiful job repairing her, and although I hadn't thought it possible, they'd made her even faster so Sir Raleigh and I reached the ILR in record time without me having to add any Fae magic. Although my powers were still attenuated here, I had more than previously.

Max met me at the door. "I suppose the cat told you?"

"Yes. Can I see him?"

"Of course. You'll be good for him. Are things wrapped up in Faerie?"

"As much as they will be for now."

With Sir Raleigh trotting behind, we walked through the empty lobby and up the stairs to the third floor, the patient ward. Only a few of the beds were occupied, and I peripherally made a note of it, but I had more important things on my mind.

Kestrel jumped up from the chair where she'd been dozing. Lawrence sat in the bed reading a book, and he smiled when I walked in. Lawrence's color was still pale under his olive skin, and his eyes too bright. The oxygen tube gave a disturbing reminder of his frail state. Sir Raleigh jumped on the bed and nudged Lawrence's hand, requesting a caress. Lucky cat.

"How are you feeling?" I asked.

He shrugged. "Not great. How are you? What happened in Faerie?"

Kestrel stood and rubbed her eyes. "Now that you're here, I'm going to go back to the cottage and get some sleep."

"Go on. The wards will recognize you. Thanks for staying with him."

She nodded and left. She'd been polite to me since we'd returned, but there was definitely a coolness, and I'd felt too guilty to confront her. She never would have gone to Faerie had it not been for me, even though she'd been the one to ask. John would still be alive, and I knew she resented me for not allowing her to resurrect him. His body had been transported to the States and to a funeral home, and Corey was using his connections to have John prepared for burial and skip the autopsy the human authorities would want. Our cover story was that he'd been in a mugging that had gone wrong. Kestrel insisted on staying with Lawrence until he could go home, too, and no one blamed her. Although not blood-related, he was the only family she had left.

I pulled off my gloves and set them down on the table by the window. Max ushered out the nurse who had followed us in with, "We'll give you some privacy."

Once the door closed, Lawrence said, "I look like hell, don't I? I know you won't lie to me."

"You've looked better." Like when he'd been a naked gargoyle, but I stifled that thought. "You're definitely more handsome awake and with only the one IV and the oxygen tube." That was keeping his oxygen levels barely in the normal range, according to the monitor.

He followed my gaze. "Yeah, it's adequate, but that's all. What happened?"

"I talked to Doctor Caduceus about it. Apparently being in Faerie as long as you were damaged your lungs. He didn't have data as to what would happen if you came back here. No gargoyle has lived long enough after being poisoned in Faerie to try to recover, and the last time it happened was before, well, all this." I gestured to the setup.

"So, I may be on oxygen forever?" He shrank back into the pillows. "That's not a comforting thought."

I sat on the bed and took his hand. "I don't know. This is all new territory."

"Can you heal me?" He gave me a look of such hope it stabbed through my heart.

"Unfortunately, no. I already tried. I failed you...again."

He squeezed my hand. "You saved my stony gargoyle ass more than once, and I won't forget that. If not for you, I wouldn't even be here. Your mother had it out for me."

"Yes, but because of me." I sighed. "I am truly sorry."

"Don't be. I'll figure out how to live with this. And what about you? Shouldn't you be ruling Faerie or something?"

I didn't argue with his assertion that he'd figure it out. That's what he did. "Just before my grandmother died, she approved my plan for a slightly different ruling structure. I'm still queen, but the Council of Three is acting under my authority until I can get back."

"Who's the Council of Three?"

"Would you believe Ellerin, Rhys, and Troubadour? They represent the three Fae territories, and they're working on bringing the realm together in preparation for the next Great Rising. It's already starting."

"That sounds complicated. Why aren't you there?"

Did he really have to ask? "Because I have to take care of things here. I'm still on my Shadowed Path, which doesn't allow for loose ends...like you. And Kestrel."

And I couldn't go back until I knew they'd be okay.

A knock on the door heralded the arrival of Max with a man and a woman, both of whom had Lawrence's coloring—dark hair, and stone-gray eyes. More gargoyles?

"We're here for Doctor Gordon," the woman said in a tone that meant she would not be argued with easily.

We'd see about that. I stood and gave her my best Fae queen look. "Under what authority?"

The man showed us a fancy-looking badge that emanated magical authority, so it had some legitimacy. "We represent the Aerie, the governing body of the gargoyles. As you can tell, madame, Doctor Gordon is ill and needs medicine that you can't provide. Gargoyle medicine."

He had a point, but I couldn't back down that easily. "Yes, I gathered. Lawrence, what do you want to do?"

"Oh, no, madame, he doesn't have a choice." The woman's expression softened slightly, and she spoke slowly, as if explaining to a child, "We need to bring him home soon, or he's going to only get worse and die."

"Well, that's compelling," I muttered.

The male gargoyle's gaze ping-ponged between me and Lawrence. "Agent Minerva, this gargoyle and this Fae are bonded. That wasn't in our orders."

"Well, Agent Micah, that means they'll both need to come with us."

I laughed. "I'm afraid that's not possible. I have obligations here."

Minerva, who appeared to be the one in charge, asked, "Are any of them more important than the life of this gargoyle? Or your own?"

"Or my... What do you mean?"

"According to legend, when one member of a bonded Fae/gargoyle pair dies, the other one does, too. That's why Fae stopped the practice—they couldn't stand another race having such power over them."

"That's not what our legends say. They talk about gargoyle betrayal being what ended the tradition."

"Are you willing to take the chance? Plus, you being with

him will help him to heal more quickly, as you can strengthen him through your bond." She sounded like she found the idea disgusting.

I looked down at Lawrence, who blinked slowly, trying to follow the conversation. Then his head drooped, and adrenaline shot through my body. According to the monitor, his oxygen level was on a slow slide down, and the beeps that reflected his heart rate grew farther and farther apart.

Minerva swallowed, but she didn't flinch. "Your call, Fae."

"That's Doctor River. Do what you need to do."

Minerva took Lawrence's other hand, and Micah took mine. Just before they joined hands, he grumbled, "Our mother's going to love this."

Then, with a flash of cold lightning that descended like a stage curtain, the room at the ILR disappeared.

AUTHOR'S NOTE

If you'd like to be added to a special list just for Fae Files updates, please go to https://www.subscribepage.com/faefilesnews

HERE'S something you're probably seeing at the end of a lot of books: a plea for reviews. That's because they help our books to be found and helps other readers know they're good. Did you know that some major vendors only start showing books to potential readers when they have a certain number of reviews? I would be so grateful if you'd leave a few words at the site where you bought the book, and, if you're feeling frisky like Sir Raleigh on catnip, other places, too. Thanks so much!

I thought I'd reached the end of my Path... As it turns out, my challenges have just begun.

. . .

I WANT to see Lawrence healthy and whole after his ordeal in Faerie, but I can't escape the tug of my responsibilities to my kingdom. Plus, almost losing him means I can't ignore my feelings for him anymore.

Lawrence has his own issues. Now that he knows who killed his father, he's searching for a new meaning in life. When he looks at me, I see him fantasizing about domestic bliss, but I have to be loyal to my kind.

Oh, and his mom hates me.

We soon discover that the gargoyle enclave of The Aerie isn't the idyllic mountain village its inhabitants want others to believe. Loose ends multiply as I search for the source of the spell sucking the life out of the town. Can Lawrence and I work together to unmask the villain and free The Aerie? Or will our conflicting desires and responsibilities tear us apart...and spell the doom of gargoyle-kind?

IF YOU LIKE SNARKY HEROINES, complicated slow-burn romances, thrilling mysteries, and hot heroes with heart, you'll love Shadows of the Sky. *Buy the book and escape into the vivid world of Cecilia Dominic's spellbinding Fae Files series today!*

SHADOWS of the Heart can be ordered from your favorite online retailer or from your local bookstore via Ingram. You can ask them to look it up with the ISBN 978-1-945074-68-4

ABOUT THE AUTHOR

By day, clinical psychologist Cecilia Dominic helps people cure their insomnia. By night, this USA Today bestselling urban fantasy and steampunk author writes fiction that keeps her readers turning pages past bedtime. She prefers the term "versatile" to "conflicted" and has published both short story and novel-length fiction. She lives in Atlanta, Georgia, with her husband and the world's cutest cat, who may or may not have been the inspiration for Sir Raleigh.

Read More from Author Cecilia Dominic:
ceciliadominic.com

Sign up for Cecilia's newsletter and get a free story – or even two – at the following link:

https://www.subscribepage.com/CeciliaDominicbackofbook

If you'd like to be added to a special list just for Fae Files updates, please go to

https://www.subscribepage.com/faefilesnews

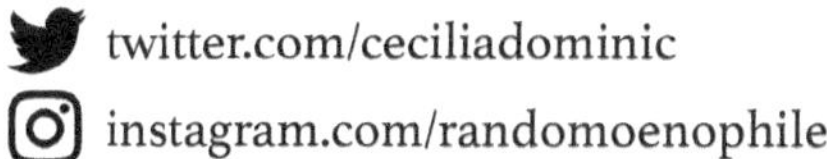

twitter.com/ceciliadominic

instagram.com/randomoenophile